NOAH'S KISS

"Tell me," he said, his hands covering Annie's so that even if she wanted to she couldn't let go of his jacket. "Does the minister kiss you like this?" He let his lips brush her temples, his breath against her checks as he spoke.

She stiffened and tried to back away from him, but the tree was behind her. "The minister doesn't kiss me," she said with her chin held high. "He respects me."

"And is that what you want?" he asked, his hand brushing back the hair that blew across her face, capturing a strand, and tucking it behind her ear. "Just to be respected? Or do you want to be loved?"

Books by Stephanie Mittman

Bridge to Yesterday
A Taste of Honey

Published by HarperPaperbacks

Harper
Monogram

A Taste of Honey

STEPHANIE MITTMAN

HarperPaperbacks
A Division of HarperCollinsPublishers

HarperPaperbacks   *A Division of* HarperCollins*Publishers*
10 East 53rd Street, New York, N.Y. 10022

Copyright © 1995 by Stephanie Mittman
All rights reserved. No part of this book may be used or reproduced in any manner whatsoever without written permission of the publisher, except in the case of brief quotations embodied in critical articles and reviews. For information address HarperCollins*Publishers,*
10 East 53rd Street, New York, N.Y. 10022.

Cover illustration by Aleta Jenks

First printing: November 1995

Printed in the United States of America

HarperPaperbacks, HarperMonogram, and colophon are trademarks of HarperCollins*Publishers*

❖ 10 9 8 7 6 5 4 3 2 1

*This book is dedicated to all the men who, like Noah,
wear their hearts on their sleeves and don't care who
knows how much they adore their wives.*

Thank you, Alan, for being one of them.

*Special thanks to the following people for their help with
the researching of A Taste of Honey.*

*Helen Prill, secretary of the Van Wert Historical Society;
Pete Emerick, wheelwright; Dr. Steven Bourla;
Dr. Steven Tremaroli.*

*And more thanks to my agent, Laura Cifelli,
and to my friend, Patty Murdock, for all their help
and encouragement.*

1

They could all hear the train whistle plainly. It howled from the west, raising gooseflesh on Annie's arms despite the warm late September afternoon. Swirling dust preceded the engine, covering them all with a film of gray that invaded their nostrils and coated their tongues as though this day were no different from all the others that had gone before.

In truth, the drought that had plagued most of Ohio throughout the summer of 1890 was still hard upon them. But this morning it could have been raining shucked ears of corn and fresh yellow rutabagas, and Annie Morrow wouldn't have noticed. For today was the day.

New York College for the Training of Teachers! A Morrow was actually going to college. Annie could hardly believe it, despite all the scrimping and saving she'd done to make it happen.

"Here it comes," Bart said, as though the storm of dust, the clatter of metal wheels on rails, and the shrill note of the engine whistle weren't signal enough. "Right on time."

Both she and Bart looked at Francie. Her face was pale, her hands gripping the new canvas travel satchel Annie had bought at Hanson's Mercantile. Francie gave them both a weak smile and looked around at the rest of the family.

The whole brood was there, all six siblings, from Annie on down to Francie, as far through the alphabet as their mother had made it before passing on and leaving Annie to raise them all. And now, after all the years of babies and toddlers, wild boys and willful girls, here they stood to send the youngest one off to college. Annie could hardly keep her feet on the platform. She bounced on her toes like an impatient child at the sight of the train and was gathering up the luggage before the metal wheels had even begun to squeal.

"He didn't come to say good-bye," Francie said to her oldest sister.

"Who?" Annie said in return.

"Noah Eastman. Even knowing how he feels about New York, I still thought he might bring the girls."

How could she be thinking of Mr. Eastman and his children at a time like this? Annie wondered. How could anything matter but getting on that train and starting in on a whole new life that didn't revolve around dirt and rain and crops?

"Here's something to eat on the train," Charlie said. He was the third oldest, but he'd beaten both Bart and Annie to the altar. No doubt his wife had packed the lunch. Charlie was lucky. He had married Risa Hanson and got both a wonderful wife and a job in the mercantile with her and her father.

"I'll miss you, Sissy," Francie said to Annie, her lip beginning to tremble. "I'm not so sure—"

"You'll do fine," Annie said reassuringly. "We've worked very hard for this day, Francie Morrow, and I ain't havin' tears marring it. Is that clear?"

"Yes, Sissy," Francie said, amid the din that rose around the pair as her brothers and sisters began to close in with their good wishes and sage advice.

"Eat plenty of vegetables," someone said.

"Write us everything that happens," said someone else.

"Pay attention to the teachers."

"Get plenty of rest."

"Don't talk to strangers."

"Keep your satchel on your lap."

"Do you have money to buy a cold drink?"

"All aboard!" a man in a blue uniform shouted, and the family stepped back so that the first Morrow ever to get beyond the eighth grade could board the train that would take her to her future.

Annie and Francie, oldest and youngest, walked together to the steps of the train. Bart followed behind, lugging a beat-up leather gladstone bag that appeared to be packed with the heaviest rocks in Van Wert County, Ohio. The sisters hugged each other tightly, Francie clinging just a little longer to the woman who had raised her from the day she was born.

"You'll do fine," Annie assured the last of her brood. "You'll do us all proud, like always."

"I wish I didn't have to go," Francie said.

Annie just had to look at the girl for Francie to nod her head with determination.

"You're right, as usual. I might not ever get what I want if I don't go now."

"That's my girl," Annie said. She took a step back and let the conductor help her sister board the train. Then he took Francie's bag and nodded at Annie, standing on the platform, her eyes misting over as she smiled and waved.

Bart took Annie's arm and led her away from the train before the whistle sounded once again. The whole Morrow family put their hands over their ears and watched the steam pour out of the engine as the wheels began to turn slowly and Francie headed for New York City.

"Guess you wish it was you," Bart said as he handed her up into the old buckboard. He stood staring up at her, a grimace on his face.

Annie shrugged. What good did wishing do, anyway? What did it matter what she wished? Did wishing keep her mother from dying? Did it raise the children she'd left behind or put food on the table when the crops got flooded out and the chickens up and died? Did it put dresses on Della or Francie's backs or shoes on any of the boys' feet? Of course she wished she were the one going off to school back east. But being able to send Francie was almost as wonderful.

"Waste of good money sendin' Francie to some fancy school when she'd be just as happy marryin' some handsome man and raisin' up a dozen or so little ones." Bart was still standing by the wagon as though he might change Annie's mind in time to yank Francie off the train and undo all Annie's hard work.

"Francie ain't gonna have to settle for that kind of life, Bart. All the work and the money was worth it if she can be an independent woman who'll be able to live where and how she likes."

Bart scowled, so Annie was relieved when a wagon coming down the street fast enough to raise a cloud of dust captured her brother's attention. The driver slowed only a little to avoid being caught up in the new electric wires they were laying across the road, then barreled straight in the direction of the Chicago & Atlantic Railroad station.

"Too late!" shouted Ethan, the youngest of the Morrow boys, over the clanking of the harness and the thudding of the buckboard as the man pulled his horse to a stop. "Just missed her, Noah. Train's gone."

So this was the famous Noah Eastman that Francie had mooned over as she packed her bags for her future. After Mrs. Jorgensen, the last housekeeper, had moved west, Francie had taken over caring for Mr. Eastman's girls, and after just three months she'd been ready to give up her scholarship and stay on as a hired girl—at least until Mr. Eastman thought she was old enough to marry him. Annie had straightened her out on that quick enough. If Francie thought love could make up for all the hard work of being a farmer's wife, she was just being childish.

In the end, Francie had done a turnabout and seemed finally to accept what Annie had been telling her all along—that New York City held the answers to her dreams. Finally Francie had agreed. Her fear was still with her, but Annie sensed an eagerness, too, as if Francie knew that the key to her future lay at the end of her journey.

Now, seeing Noah, Annie wondered what had turned Francie's head. He was painfully thin, nearly gaunt, and he looked like life had taught him a thing or two and left the lessons printed on his brow.

"Damn," he muttered and then looked guiltily at the two little girls who sat next to him, their bonnets askew, their faces dirty.

"Where's Francie?" the littler one said, bright eyes looking around her as though she'd never been to town. She was even more pathetic looking than her older sister. They both needed a good scrubbing and a brush run through their deep-brown locks.

"*Damn* means we missed her," the older girl said patiently. "It's Pa's way of sayin' things didn't work out like they was s'posed to."

A wide grin broke out on Noah's face. It seemed to erase the creases in his forehead, and it changed the lines that ran from the corners of his eyes into sparks that lit his face. Gooseflesh once again danced up Annie's arms and she hugged herself, always surprised to feel fall in the air in September.

Ethan did the introductions. He'd been working with Noah for over a year, since the summer of '89, when Noah had moved to Ohio to work the farm his uncle left him. Despite a ten-year age difference, the men seemed to be good friends. Bart mentioned meeting Noah once or twice at some Farmers' Institute meetings. Charlie added that he had seen him often in the mercantile. Della, when it was her turn to be introduced, smiled one of those warm smiles that had melted every man's heart from the time she was a toddler.

And then it was Annie's turn. "This here's Sissy," Ethan said, using the name Annie had been stuck with since Bart had learned to talk. "Sissy, this here's Noah Eastman and his girls, Hannah and Julia."

Noah stared at Annie until it was clearly impolite. And he kept on staring, his mouth open and his eyebrows coming down close over his eyes.

Annie knew that both Della and Francie were prettier than she was. Della had those beautiful blond curls, fiery green eyes that beckoned men to seek their depths, and peaches that resided permanently in her cheeks. Francie was a paler version of her sister, her blond hair only wavy, her green eyes more mosslike than emerald, her complexion fair and delicate.

Annie was stuck with brown hair. It was on the light side, especially after the summer she'd just spent in the fields, but not light enough to pass for blond. And it was thin and limp, and despite all her trying a strand or two always escaped her bun. Her eyes, too, were light brown. This time of year her skin turned the same light brown as her hair and eyes.

Still, she thought, even if the man was shocked to find

she didn't have her sisters' beauty, the least he could do was have the decency not to show it.

"I'm Sissy Morrow," Annie said, an edge to her voice she couldn't hide. "Francie's sister."

"You're Sissy?" Noah asked, fighting for control of his voice, which came out an octave higher than usual. "Francie's Sissy?"

He pulled his buckboard closer to her own. Words fought his thick tongue and he stammered, unable to complete a thought.

"But I thought . . . that is, Francie said . . . I mean, the way she spoke of you, it seemed—" He shook his head as if that might unscramble the thoughts and make the words come out straight. She was so young. So pretty. So slim and graceful sitting there with that ramrod-straight back. Before he could stop them, more words poured out of his mouth. "I thought you'd be a lot older. The way Francie talked about you, even the way Ethan did—they made you sound like their mother!"

He had expected her to be fat. That was the first thing. Anyone who could cook the way Ethan described one of his sister's meals ought to weigh a couple hundred pounds, at least. He'd tasted one of her incredible strawberry pies this summer. Francie had brought it, and Ethan had been quick to give the credit to his oldest sister.

Oldest. That was it. He sat staring at the woman who faced him in the rickety wagon. Why, she couldn't be more than twenty-four or -five! Her skin was unfashionably tanned and it glowed with a healthy outdoorsiness he admired. She wasn't lardydardy like Francie's other sister, who guarded her looks like they were the queen's jewels. Her hair was the color of melted taffy; and he had a ridiculous urge to taste it.

This simply couldn't be Francie and Ethan's Sissy. Their Sissy was so strict that Ethan washed his shirts out Saturday nights if he knew he'd be going home on Sunday. She was full of wisdom that she doled out like castor oil and Francie spouted half a dozen times a day. "Sissy says this. Sissy says that." Sissy was someone who was always canning fruit. This woman sitting just out of his reach couldn't be her. This woman didn't make him think of apples and pears and plums. The only fruit that came to his mind when he thought of this woman was the forbidden kind.

He hadn't had thoughts like these in years. After Wylene, he'd tried not to think of women at all. He'd resigned himself to raising their two daughters alone. Now, looking at the woman he had spent all summer hearing about, new blood pumped through his veins, bringing wild thoughts to his head and crazy feelings to his heart.

"Mr. Eastman," she said, extending her hand and letting him take it in his own. It was rough from work, good hard honest work, and he wished he was the kind of man who could put it to his lips gallantly and inhale the soap smell he knew he would find. "It's nice to finally meet you. Francie spoke real highly of you and your children."

"And you as well," he stuttered, sounding like an idiot. She didn't have any children. He tried to recover. "I'm honored to meet you, Miss Morrow. You're kind of a legend around here."

"Aw, don't go swelling Sissy's head any bigger than it already is," Ethan said with a laugh. "Want me to take Hannah on Buckshot with me? I'm goin' out your way."

Noah asked the little girl if she'd like to ride with Ethan and her eyes lit with excitement. Ethan took her out of the buckboard and put her on his shoulders, then sauntered toward his horse. Once there he set her in the saddle and climbed up behind her, handing her the reins.

Annie Morrow's eyes were on her brother, but Noah

knew she was well aware that he was still looking at *her*. He tried to pull his gaze away, but he was still trying to comprehend that this, this beautiful woman with caramel eyes was Sissy Morrow. Sissy the spinster, who had stayed to raise her siblings and given up any life of her own. Sissy, who had managed to keep five brothers and sisters safe from harm from the time she was—how old had Francie said? Nine?

Even after Ethan had turned Buckshot for his farm and Noah could hear the horse's hooves fade into the distance, he still stared like a fool at the honey-colored angel before him, her stiff back the only sign that she was aware of his attention.

Bart, whom Noah knew only casually, climbed up into the seat and picked up the reins. There was a chorus of good-byes among the various brothers and sisters and in-laws, which he watched unabashedly. What a family she had raised! What an amazing job such a little bit of a thing had managed to do!

"Well, good-bye, Mr. Eastman," she said, as her brother released the brake. Even her voice was like penuche, smooth and silky with no hard edges.

"Good-bye, Miss Morrow," he said, tipping his hat and trying to seem as though meeting an angel were an everyday occurrence.

"Sissy will do fine," she said. "Everyone calls me that."

"I don't think so," he said. "A woman like you deserves a name of her own."

Bart huffed and snickered at the horses, telling them it was time to head back to the farm. There was field work to be done and, with Ethan working at Noah's, just Bart and Annie to do it. She smoothed the printed lawn of her skirt, fingering the delicate fabric. She'd gussied herself up, as

Bart would say, to send Francie off in style. But she'd be back in her patched cotton wrapper before lunchtime rolled around, and as dirty and tired tonight as she was last night, before the sun met the earth.

The ride home was a quiet one, her brother shifting often on the leather seat he'd pulled from Pa's old buggy, Annie dreaming about the life that awaited her baby sister.

"Well, they're all gone now," Bart said, breaking the silence and pulling Annie back from lessons she would never learn in a school she would never attend. "'Cepting Ethan, and it won't be long for him."

"I sure envy him," Annie admitted. "Bein' a man and all, he can just up and go west with no never mind about it." Last year he'd missed the first wave of open land in Oklahoma, but there were rumors that in less than a year there'd be more, ceded by some Indians Annie had never even heard of. And Ethan had a hunger for adventure, a need for excitement that Annie knew would never be satisfied in Van Wert. She'd managed to keep him in Ohio this long, but now that he was nineteen she knew it was only a matter of time.

"I never did see a woman as green with envy as you been lately. What's eatin' at you anyways?" Bart threw an eye in her direction and must have caught the hurt on her face that she couldn't hide. She knew it was petty and wrong to be jealous of her own brothers and sisters, and she certainly knew better than to let Bart know even if she was. Always wishing he'd been the eldest, he liked to point out to her as often as he could just how imperfect she really was.

"Nothing's eating at me. I just meant that a man's got more choices than a woman, that's all."

"But it ain't all. You think it wasn't written all over your face that you wished it was you, not Francie, goin' to that fancy college?"

He shifted again.

"Those pants need lettin' out?" she asked. Since he'd started courting Willa Leeman, he was eating two dinners every Sunday and a few extra helpings of pie during the week.

"And ya sure envy Della. Always have," he said. He hadn't responded to her question with words, but she noticed he sucked in his stomach and sat a little taller on the seat.

"Della's the most beautiful woman in all of Ohio, probably," Annie said. "Ain't a woman who ever met her didn't turn green at the sight of those pretty blond ringlets framin' that handsome face."

"And she's livin' in town and got precious darlin' twin boys of her own," Bart added. "Not to mention that Peter'll probably be vice president of the Van Wert National Bank someday."

"I don't envy no one for their children, Bart," she said, picking at a small pull on her dress. "Much as I love 'em, raisin' five children was enough for me."

Enough for a lifetime. If she never washed another diaper or braided another head of hair, if she never had to explain why the sky was blue or why there wasn't enough food on the table . . . oh, she loved every one of her brothers and sisters, but she was grateful that time was behind her. She was grateful that now she could look forward to being the lady of the house instead of the family's mother hen.

Bart stopped the wagon and turned to her. "Don't you think you'll be havin' any children of your own when you marry Reverend Winestock?" he asked, and waited for her to answer as if it mattered a great deal to him.

"Well," Annie said, her eyes on the tips of her worn Sunday button shoes, "he and Elvira were never blessed. And he's nearly forty and not likely to—"

"Is that what's been troubling you, Sissy? You know Elvira Winestock was a sickly woman all her life and the fault probably laid with her. And bein' forty don't hardly stop a man from wantin' to be with a woman in that way. Hell, look at Pa, makin' all those trips to town after supper."

"He liked a good walk after dinner, and he was always runnin' outa tobacco," Annie said, but the minute the words were out of her mouth she realized she'd been naive to take her father at his word. Her cheeks grew hot. Bart, her younger brother, had apparently known the truth and while she had been foolishly doling out nickels for tobacco money, her father had been enjoying a very different vice indeed.

"Miller Winestock is a man, Sissy," Bart said, returning to the subject. "And a man has needs."

"I know that," Annie said. "But he doesn't seem . . . that is, he's not like Pa. He's more like you—serious, hard-working, devout."

Bart looked at her strangely. "Men are pretty much the same," he said. "We all got needs. And sometimes they make us lose our heads."

Now what did that mean?

"And that brings me to somethin' I want to discuss with you," he continued, but now he was the one looking at his boots. "Comes a time in a man's life when work ain't enough. Especially workin' alone."

"Alone?" she asked. Where had she been if not next to him, in the fields and in the barn?

He squirmed yet again and Annie wanted to scream at him. What was he getting at? Did he want her behind the plow too?

"Well, not alone now. But once you're married . . . when *are* you gettin' married, Sissy?"

She shrugged. Elvira Winestock had been dead about eight months. She supposed Miller would want to wait at least a year out of respect for his first wife.

"Do ya think it'll be soon?"

She shrugged again. The tone of his voice surprised her. Clearly he was eager to have her marry the minister. But that didn't make sense at all. Then she'd be out of the house and he'd be truly alone. Unless— In an instant she was no longer in the dark about where the conversation was going. She just didn't want it to get there.

"Like maybe in a few weeks?" he said hopefully.

"No," she said, with all the finality she could muster. "I don't think it'll be in a few weeks. Why?"

"Well, me and Willa," he started, but she didn't need to hear any more. Her brother was going to get married. And once he did, he'd bring Willa Leeman home to Annie's house. And they'd take her parents' bedroom, the one Annie had moved into after her father had died. And it would be Willa's house, Willa's and Bart's.

Now he was saying something about how he and Willa would be happy to let her stay as long as she liked. She'd always be welcome in her own home. But she knew it wouldn't be her home anymore.

Of course, it wouldn't matter. After all, she'd be moving into town, getting married, taking over the duties of a minister's wife real soon. She'd be putting on a clean dress in the morning, serving tea to the ladies, checking on the welfare of the congregation, seeing to her husband's supper. And at the end of the day that dress would still be clean. What more could a woman want?

Annie studied the dirt under her fingernails that, no matter how hard she tried, never seemed to go away completely. "That's wonderful for you," she said to Bart, whose relief was spread across his face. "For you and Willa both. I'm sure you'll be very happy."

"We'd like to be married soon," he said. "Real soon."

There was a sense of urgency that was unmistakable. "Of course," she said. "I'll talk to Miller after services tomorrow." And tell him what? That Willa and Bart had to get married, and that meant that Annie would lose her home and she wanted his?

It was the God's honest truth. She did. Miller's home had rugs in every room. Annie had taken care of his wife often, during her last years, and had seen them all. He had a genuine Sterling range in the kitchen and a heater in the bedroom. Best of all, he had a separate room for bathing that had running water, a porcelain-lined tub, a toilet, and a steel sink. And as if all that wasn't enough, in a few months he'd even have electricity.

Why, if there was anything more a woman could want, Annie Morrow just didn't know what it could be.

Noah found Ethan and Hannah waiting for him in the barn when he got home. Crouched down to her size, Ethan was wiping tears from the child's face with his handkerchief when Noah entered the barn.

"What's this?" he asked. Hannah rarely cried, and it was a good thing, too, because it tore at Noah's guts to see the little girls unhappy. "Are you hurt?"

Hannah shook her head solemnly. Noah looked at Ethan, who shrugged his confusion.

"You want to tell me what's wrong?" Noah asked.

Hannah shook her head again.

"Well, then, how about we wash up and have some supper? Mrs. Abernathy left us some stew going that ought to be ready right about now." He hated stew, but he tried to make it sound inviting for Hannah's sake.

"I miss Francie," Hannah said. So did Noah. She'd been a ray of sunshine in their lives, always smiling, eager to be helpful, kind to the children. She was as sweet a child as he hoped his own would grow into. And the fact that she was not much more than a child herself hadn't prevented her from being a real help to him during the hot summer when he'd had to replant so much of his crop because of the drought. And she'd somehow managed to keep the children cool and fed and out of his hair.

Now that he'd met her sister he wasn't surprised. Anyone raised by Annie Morrow couldn't help but be special. With the exception of Della, who seemed to be consumed with herself to the exclusion of most everything else, he liked the whole family, spouses included.

"Me too, cutie," he admitted, reaching for his daughter's hand. "If I were Ethan, I'd hightail it home so fast the dust wouldn't get there till Tuesday."

"Francie ain't home, Noah," Ethan said, as he took Hannah's other hand. "There's just Sissy and Bart, and he ain't there but to plow and reap and then he's off to Willa Leeman's house in town."

They stopped by the buckboard and Noah lifted out a sleeping Julia. "That'd be enough for me," Noah said. It had been a long time since a woman had been waiting for him. Until now he hadn't given any thought to its ever happening again. He planted a kiss on his daughter's sweaty forehead and swore at Ethan. "Hell, you could have told me she was beautiful. That way I wouldn'ta just stared like a dimwit and tripped over my tongue."

"Who?" Ethan asked.

Noah just shook his head. He supposed with Della and Francie in the house the boys had never noticed Annie's special brand of beauty. *Annie.* Maybe that was it. They were only seeing Sissy, good old reliable Sissy. How on God's green earth had they missed *Annie?*

Mrs. Abernathy's stew filled the small farmhouse with a heavy odor, making the air feel hot and the walls close. Her meals and her presence both had that effect on him. The children didn't seem overly fond of her either. Of course, it could just be the stark comparison of Francie's chipper voice, her small frame, and her easy way, with

Mrs. Abernathy's sharp commands, her bulk, and her discontent.

It seemed to Noah that in the few weeks she'd been with them, Ruth Abernathy's nose had been out of joint more often than Julia could wet a diaper. Desperation had made him hire her, and desperation was keeping her there. Desperation and his conscience. He thought of how Francie had begged him to let her stay on, pleaded with him to think of his children and how attached they'd grown to her, even flirted with him to consider her for a wife. Of course, that was out of the question.

How she'd smarted when he'd admitted he thought of her only as a little sister, or even another of his children some of the time. She accused him of simply being noble and not wanting to stand between her and her education. She refused to believe the truth—that while his children loved her, he did not. At least not in the way she wished.

There was so much ahead of her in life that he couldn't rob her of, not even for his little girls' sake. Not many things were as important as a good education. Even if in the end you didn't put it to use. Even if you gave it all up and spent the rest of your life battling with nature for a few acres of corn and a grove of apple trees. For Francie there was college and a big wide world where someone would love and treasure her the way she deserved. The way every woman deserved. And every man, for that matter.

Wylene had had the same dark hair that surrounded his little girls' faces. But rightly or wrongly, it was a woman with honey hair and skin and eyes who was dancing through his mind.

2

The Morrows had been attending the Pleasant Township Methodist Church since long before Annie's mother had passed away. Zena Morrow had taught her oldest child the importance of worship, and Annie, without much help from her father, had raised her siblings to be faithful churchgoers. Every Sunday found them in their regular pew, third from the back on the left, and this Sunday was no exception.

Miller was well into his sermon, and Annie's thoughts were drifting, when the door opened at the rear of the church and Noah Eastman walked in. One of his girls was high on his arm, the other was clutching his trouser leg. He dipped his head to the minister and took the last available seat in the back pew.

"Welcome, welcome," Winestock said, giving Noah a chance to settle down with his children before continuing with his sermon. "You picked an excellent day to join us. We speak now, in this time of harvesting, to remind the farmer what the Lord has told us of the harvest.

"'Thou shalt not wholly reap the corners of thy field, neither shalt thou gather the gleanings of thy harvest. And thou shalt not glean thy vineyard, neither shalt thou gather every grape of thy vineyard; thou shalt leave them for the poor and stranger.'"

Miller always rose to a fuller stature when he had a new parishioner. His voice deepened to a full baritone, his gestures became more meaningful. He was good looking enough when he was leading his congregation in prayer: trim, distinguished, his gray hair full and wavy. When he was caught up in his sermon, he was masterful, commanding, wondrous.

Annie's view of the pulpit was blocked by Jane Lutefoot's blue bonnet. She leaned closer to Risa, her sister-in-law, in order to get a clearer view of Miller at his best.

"Isn't he handsome?" Risa whispered near Annie's ear.

Annie nodded. Miller was thinner than Bart, his hair even thicker than Charlie's, his dimples deeper than Ethan's.

"I think that little bit of silver in his hair is very appealing," Risa said.

"Mmm," Annie agreed. It was more than a bit gray. And while Risa was a couple of years older than her husband, Miller was as old as Charlie and Ethan combined.

"He's staring at you," Risa said, nudging Annie slightly.

Now Jane's hat was out of the way and Mr. Witherspoon's head, two sizes too big for his body, blocked her view. She leaned in the other direction.

"We should," the minister said, "take our neighbor to our bosom, take his troubles as our own, and delight in his joys as our own."

"I think he'd like to take this neighbor to his bosom," Risa said, poking Annie, who felt her cheeks color.

"Risa!" she said under her breath.

"And those children of his," Risa continued. "Did you ever see such little darlings?"

Children?

"What?" Annie asked, sure she'd heard wrong.

"The Eastman girls. Aren't they the dearest?"

"The Eastmans?"

"Ssh," Charlie admonished.

Annie resisted the urge to look over her shoulder. She sat straight in her seat and stared at the back of Mrs. Lutefoot's hat. Who was staring at her? Mr. Eastman? But that was ridiculous. She didn't even know the man. They'd met only yesterday.

But he had stared at her then. Gaped at her, his mouth falling open. Something about her had taken him by surprise. She couldn't imagine what it could be. She surely wasn't so ugly that he had come to the Pleasant Township Methodist Church to get another look. What in the world had Francie told him that had gotten the man to church?

"He doesn't go," Francie had said when Annie asked why she hadn't ever seen Noah Eastman in church. "Since his wife passed on, his faith's been wavering." Their own father had been much the same. When Zena was alive he had somehow made it to services every Sunday, but after her death there was always something—the planting, the harvest, his rheumatism—that made it impossible to attend.

Was he watching her now? She refused to turn her head to check but held herself straight and kept her eyes toward the pulpit, though all she could see was the flash of Miller's hand every now and then as he gestured toward the Lord.

Once she and Miller were married she would sit in the front pew and be able to watch the fire in his eyes when he called out to the Lord, see the dimples in his cheeks when he smiled at the smallest member of his congregation. Never again would a button pop from his shirt as it had last week in the middle of "Nearer my God to Thee." She would test them all on Saturdays while he perfected his sermon and rehearsed it before her.

"The Women's Missionary Society asks that I remind you all of their booth at the County Fair. Miss Orliss asks that those of you who have promised pies and cakes get them to her place before eight o'clock next Saturday, and she and Mrs. Wilkins will see that they get to the fair.

"The Sabbath school picnic is scheduled for two weeks from today." The minister paused, and behind her Annie heard the rustling of movement. No doubt Noah Eastman, a stranger to the ways of the P.T.M.C. and its minister, was rising to leave.

"One more thing," Miller said. "It has been eight months now, to the day, since Mrs. Winestock was called to the Kingdom of God. It has been a hard time for me. While all of you have endeavored to make my grief lighter, one or two of you have crossed my bridge of sorrow and reached out your hands to me in the spirit of love and friendship." A murmur of sympathy swept through the congregation, and several eyes, including those of her family, strayed in Annie's direction. "You have been there to help me, to soothe me, to comfort me, and without your support I could never have served this congregation or the Lord. And now I have an announcement to make."

Annie was as surprised as the rest of the crowd, and as expectant. While she and Miller had an understanding, nothing had been said, no vows pledged, no public declarations made. Her heart raced as he continued.

"Our first Harvest Social since Elvira died is upon us, and we will have to plan without her help." Risa's hand patted her thigh in sympathy. No doubt Risa had known what she expected Miller to say. She was never any good at hiding her feelings. "In all the many things both great and small, we miss her. But the Lord directs us that life goes on, and someone must take her place. Should any of you wish to fulfill Mrs. Winestock's responsibilities regarding the Social"—he paused—"please see me after the service and I will—"

"Sissy'll take care of it," Bart said loudly. "She did all the arrangin' last year, what with Mrs. Winestock feelin' so poorly."

"Miss Morrow is one of those people who take their obligations as seriously as I do. We owe to the Lord, we owe to each other, and we all owe a debt of gratitude to Miss Morrow. Would you help us out again?"

A subdued Annie nodded her assent, and the people who were sitting nearby clapped in her honor. It was obvious to her what Bart was trying to do. With his plans linked to her own, he was hoping to give the minister a gentle push. He probably hoped that with the town's acceptance of her as a helpmate, Miller might marry her and get her out of her house all the sooner.

She looked at the oldest of her brothers, seated just beyond Charlie, but Bart's gaze went over her left shoulder and she turned her head to follow it. Willa Leeman was returning his smile with one of her own. And just beyond her, Noah Eastman sat with his eyes unabashedly glued to Annie Morrow.

The blessing said, the service was concluded and Annie hurriedly made her way to the door. Miller was shaking hands with parishioners and Annie failed to catch his eye. She stood slightly off to the side, waiting for him to seek her out.

"You look real pretty in that dress," a voice said behind her. It was a low, mellow voice, and though the words were perfectly respectable, the tone was warm, intimate. They had only had one conversation, but she knew to whom that voice belonged.

"What do you say?" Risa prompted.

She swung around, expecting to find Noah Eastman staring at her. Instead, her niece, Cara, stood clinging to her mother and Noah was crouching beside her, his hands holding on to his own girls.

"Thank you," Cara said shyly, before tucking her face into her mother's skirt.

Noah laughed and rose to his full height. He was tall and lanky and looked like he could use a good meal.

"Sissy," Risa said, "have you met Mr. Eastman?"

He reached for her hand and Annie had no choice but to give it to him. She noticed that the child who had been attached to it now wrapped her arms around his leg, and he spread his stance just slightly to accommodate her.

"We met yesterday," Annie said to Risa, trying to keep her eyes from his. They seemed to be magnetic; once she looked in them she found it very hard to pull her glance away. "And, of course, I've heard plenty about him from Francie and Ethan." Now it was she who knelt down. "And you must be Hannah. And you, Julia."

Noah was still holding on to her hand, reluctant to let it go, and he pulled her gently until she was upright again. She was a vision in a pale yellow dress that set her skin aglow with its goldenness. Her eyes were even with his Adam's apple, and she kept them there while he spoke. "But we haven't been properly introduced."

Risa was watching her almost as intently as he was. While Annie's eyes strayed to the minister, who was still busy greeting people and seemed to take no notice, Noah couldn't take his gaze from her face.

"Noah Eastman," Risa said formally. "May I present my sister-in-law, Annie Morrow. Sissy, this is—"

"I know who he is," she snapped at Risa, then raised her eyes to him and said more gently, "What brings you suddenly to our church, Mr. Eastman?"

"Noah, please," he corrected.

To his disappointment, she stood waiting for his answer without repeating his name. If she sensed his discomfort, she didn't show it. In fact, she seemed embarrassed herself.

"Francie thought the girls," he stammered, indicating Hannah and Julia, "that is, she said you—"

Annie stiffened and thrust her jaw forward in a gesture that, despite her size, seemed formidable. After a big sigh that seemed to restore some calm, she said with exaggerated patience, "Mr. Eastman, Francie has gone east to school. If you think for one moment that I'd let her throw away this opportunity in order to get mixed up with a farmer and live the same life I already lived when she could have so much more, do so much better, you can just forget it. Comin' to church is not going to change my mind about the kind of life I want for Francie."

He supposed he looked like an idiot, standing there blinking at her. "Francie?" he said when he found his voice. "What does this have to do with Francie?"

"Ain't that why you're here?" she asked. "Why else would it matter what *I* thought about church?"

Risa picked up little Cara in her arms and hid behind the child's head. Only her wide eyes watched him, then Annie, and then him again.

"You did a fine job raising Francie and Ethan," Noah explained. "I'd like to do as right by my girls."

"And you couldn't find a better example to follow, young man," Miller Winestock said, coming up behind Annie and startling a gasp out of her. She grabbed the minister's left arm to steady herself and then, surprisingly, left it there.

Mr. Winestock patted her hand patronizingly and then extended his hand to Noah. "It was a pleasure seeing you join us today. I understand better than most how the loss of a loved one can test your faith. But it is only through God's mercy that we can find the will to go on and forge new lives for ourselves in the absence of those we hold so dear."

"I didn't come for me, Mr. Winestock," he said bluntly. His eyes ran over Annie, from the tip of her bonnet down to her button shoes. "I came for my girls."

"Ah, but if you open yourself to the Lord, He will heal your pain." He patted Hannah's head, ruffling her dark hair. "I understand you're from back east—Pennsylvania somewhere?"

"Johnstown," he said. It always evoked the same reaction.

"Oh, my Lord!"

"Johnstown!"

"Then your wife . . . ?" the minister said.

Noah hung his head. So many people had been lost in the flood—family, friends, the people he did business with. It had been a miracle that he and the girls had been spared. If something was going to bring him back to God, the fact that he and his children were thirty miles west of their home at the time the water hit might just do it.

"It's something I don't like to talk about," Noah said honestly.

"Well, you're here now," the minister said. "You are among friends who will help put the tragedy behind you."

Noah nodded and said again it was something he didn't like to discuss. He looked up at the blue sky and the trees. "Nice day," he said, despite the fact that the minister had ended the service with a prayer for rain.

Winestock took the watch from his pocket and flicked it open. "Getting late," he said to Annie.

Before him the honey-eyed angel took a possessive step forward. "Will you be comin' to supper?" she asked the minister.

"Mmm," Winestock answered distractedly. "Could any-one resist one of your meals? And we can discuss the social and some other church business as well."

Annie nodded. The look on her face gave her away. It seemed to Noah that she was trying to show him she was spoken for, as Francie had told him, but the good Reverend Miller Winestock wasn't so willing to do the speaking. A piece of him went out to her in sympathy. But the rest of his feelings were doing an all-out jig at Winestock's reticence.

"I'm making your favorite," Annie said, as if she had him to supper every night of the week and twice on Sundays. "Roasted chicken, sweet potatoes, and a plum pie for dessert." If the fact that she cooked for Mr. Winestock on a regular basis wasn't painful enough, the menu nearly did Noah in. He fairly drooled on his freshly washed Sunday shirt.

"That'll be nice, Sissy," the minister said, and then caught himself. "Miss Morrow. I'll be happy to take supper with you and Bart." *Sissy?* He was calling her *Sissy?*

"Bart ain't joinin' us," Annie said quietly. "I believe he'll be down to the Leemans' tonight." She gestured with her head toward Bart, standing next to Willa, his arm possessively resting on her waist.

"Oh, I see," Winestock said. "And Ethan?"

Annie looked at Noah Eastman. Like Risa, he'd stayed there listening to every word she and Miller had exchanged. She raised her eyebrows at him as if to ask whether he knew Ethan's plans. Ever since her brother had started working there, he took most of his meals with the Eastmans. Money was tight in Van Wert County, and Ethan's room and board was part of his pay. It was ridiculous, really. There was plenty of room for him at the farm, and if she was cooking for herself and Bart, what was one more mouth? But Ethan valued his independence and he did make some money, all of which he was able to put by for the moment he could strike out on his own.

"I'm sorry," Noah Eastman said, "but I'm afraid I did give Mrs. Abernathy the day off to go visiting her family in Grand Lake. I expect Ethan will be showing up at your place for supper."

Miller looked visibly relieved. "Well, then," he said, waving to a congregant and taking a step away from the group, "I'll see you at four-thirty."

"That'll be fine," Annie said.

Charlie came over to where they were standing and took his daughter from Risa's arms. "You shouldn't be picking her up anymore," he chided.

Risa's face flushed and Annie knew in an instant that her sister-in-law was once again pregnant. If there was one thing a Morrow man could do, it was propagate. Sometimes it seemed the Lord was talking just to the Morrows when He said to be fruitful and multiply.

"Risa!" Annie said knowingly. "You lettin' out your waistbands again?"

Charlie's smile was like new shucked corn, wide, white, and even. Of course he was happy. Planting the seed was the easy part. It was Risa who'd have to bring forth the fruit of their union, Risa who'd have to devote the next seventeen years or so to rearing the child, Risa who'd stay up nights with him when he was sick, Risa whose heart would ache when the child suffered even the slightest pain.

"That's wonderful!" Noah Eastman said, pumping Charlie's arm. "Nothing like children. Nothing!"

Nothing for a man but pride and vanity. Nothing for a woman but work and worry. "I hope it all goes well," Annie said to Risa, stroking her arm gently. "If you need anything, anything at all, you just send Charlie for me, you hear?"

"I'm fine," Risa assured Annie. "This is when they give you the least trouble. You'll see."

Annie smiled politely. No, she would not see. Not if she

could help it. She'd paid attention to the whispers of the older
women in town and knew all about how the calendar worked
and when and when not to encourage a husband's affection.
She'd raised all the children she was going to. This was no
time to start a new family. She was too old, too used up. All
her children were gone, and she intended to keep it that way.

"Sissy?" It was Charlie talking, but she hadn't heard
what he said.

"What?"

"I asked if you was gettin' your own life in order now
that Francie's outa your hair and all your chickens have
flown the coop."

"My life is always in order," she snapped. What was the
matter with everyone lately? Bart trying to marry her off in
a matter of weeks, Risa suggesting she have babies at her
age, Charlie telling her to get her life in order. And hadn't
Della brought her out two positively ridiculous dresses last
week and told her it was time for her to repackage the
merchandise before it went stale? At least Francie and
Ethan weren't trying to tell her what to do.

"There's Ethan," little Hannah cried out and broke
away from her father to run to him. Ethan scooped her up
and came toward the group, a big smile on his face. Annie
had a soft spot in her heart for Ethan as big as would fit in
her chest.

"Hear you're comin' for supper," Annie said. "Got fresh
plum pie coolin' on the windowsill right now."

Ethan's eyebrows came down and he looked at
Eastman, who was quick to speak. "Gave Mrs. Abernathy
the day off. Went to Grand Lake."

"But I thought—" Ethan started.

Eastman interrupted him. "Guess she left after you did.
Mr. Winestock'll be there, too."

"But I was the last one to leave," Ethan said.

Eastman busied himself with Julia, who was beginning

to rub her eyes. "You tired?" he asked the little girl and lifted her against him, letting her head drop onto his shoulder.

Francie had been like that, Annie thought. She could always tell the child was tired when she began to rub her eyes. So Mr. Eastman knew his youngest well. Francie had said he was a good father. That was a rare quality in a man, and she had to admire it, however begrudgingly.

"Bart's going courtin'," Eastman explained to Ethan, as if that meant something.

Apparently it did, for Ethan's head began to bob like it was on a spring. "Oh, yes. Courtin'," he said. "What time's supper, Sissy?"

If there was a style to the decor of the Morrow farmhouse, it would have to be called "old." If there was a theme, it would be "used." And if there was a look Annie was trying desperately to achieve, it would be "clean." The farm succeeded on the first two counts. The last was hopeless, though Annie never stopped trying.

But what the house lacked in beauty, Annie tried to make up for in warmth and hospitality. There was always an extra plate for company, and her cooking was designed to make everyone forget that farming meant dirt, dust, and despair. It was hard to remember the drought with Annie's meal on the table.

At least she hoped that was so as she watched Miller Winestock push back his chair. It grated on the old wooden floor and stuck in a rut. "That was some good meal there, Sissy," he said. "You're sure to make a fine wife someday."

Annie froze, the forkful of pie halfway to her mouth. This was the closest he had ever come to a proposal. Still, he hadn't said she'd make *him* a fine wife.

"Ethan," she said, "the gate on the coop's been catchin'

my apron all week and I can't get Bart to fix it. Do you think you might have a look at it?"

"Sure, Sissy," he agreed easily. He made no move, though, to do it.

"Maybe you best have a look before it gets dark," she suggested. *Shoo!* her eyes said. *Go. Go.*

Ethan looked outside as if to judge the darkness. There was at least an hour more of light, maybe more.

"Tell you what," he said. "You give me another piece of pie and I'll not only look at the gate, I'll fix it." He smiled at the minister.

"You can eat pie in the dark," Annie said. "Which is more than I can say for fixin' the fence. Now go."

Ethan looked surprised, but he didn't argue with his sister. For that, Annie was grateful.

"What did you mean," Annie asked once Ethan was out of the house, "about my making a good wife?"

Miller looked up. Annie's hand rested on the table between their plates. The table was as scrubbed as Annie could get it, but there were burn marks and pot charrings that couldn't be cleaned away. And a new layer of dust had already settled around them, as though she hadn't spent the hours between church and supper dusting the very room they sat in.

Not surprisingly, Miller's hands remained in his lap. He sighed heavily. "You are a fine woman, Sissy Morrow. Not to mention a good cook. You've kept a fine house from a young age. And when poor Elvira was suffering so, you were a comfort to her beyond measure."

"And?"

"And I owe you a good deal. And I hope someday to repay it. After all, you surely have the makings of a very fine wife. A man would be lucky to call you his own."

She waited, but he seemed to have nothing further to say on the subject. He made it sound as though it was his duty to marry her and that he felt he wasn't getting too bad a bargain. She was a good cook, a good housekeeper, and an honest woman. If he was looking for more than that, she didn't know what it could be.

His fingers played with the rim of her dishes. At least she knew they had started out clean, tucked away carefully in the cupboard with the cheesecloth spread over them. She wondered what would happen to her precious dishes if Willa had china of her own that she wanted to use.

Annie had taken such care of their china. It had been her mother's treasure, brought all the way from England by Annie's great-grandmother. The children had never been allowed to do anything but eat off it. No setting the table, no clearing the plates. It was Annie's responsibility, and she had taken it so seriously that even now, seventeen years after her mother's death, all that the set lacked was the one bowl her father had smashed the day her mother died.

He had been spooning broth into her, trying to build up her strength, when she had pushed his hand away and shook her head. "Sissy," she had said, calling the little girl to her side. "Love them for me, Sissy. Love them all like they was your own." Then she'd smiled at the nine-year-old and her father and sighed. It was her last smile and her last sigh. Her eyelids hadn't even fluttered when Jack Morrow had thrown the bowl across the room, to shatter into a million pieces.

Less than an hour later she was gone and Annie was diapering the week-old Francie and giving her a sugar teat.

"Bart is plannin' to ask Willa to marry him," Annie told Miller. "Maybe right now he might be talkin' to her pa."

"Well," Miller said with a nod, "that'll be one wedding I'll be happy to perform. Bart and Willa are both good people. I'm sure they'll do honor unto the Lord."

"Yes," she agreed. "But you see, Bart has managed the farm since well before Pa died, and—"

"And done a good job too," Miller said, wiping his mouth with a napkin and looking around the room. Annie saw his gaze linger on the dusty floor.

"Drought's been real hard on the house. Soon as I sweep, a new layer settles. Anyway, the farm is really Bart's, and when he marries Willa, they plan on settlin' here. Not surprisin', really. But it kinda leaves me in a pickle."

"Oh, I see." He shifted uncomfortably in his chair, then took her hand in his. "Sissy, if you're asking me to accelerate our proposed nuptials—"

"Ain't nothin' wrong with that gate that I can see," Ethan said as he barged into the house, the door slamming behind him.

Annie felt her cheeks pinken slightly as Miller quickly took his hand away. "I can't," he said quietly. "Give me a few more months, for Elvira's sake and Van Wert's."

Van Wert, she thought. The whole town had them as good as married already. Was there anyone who would raise an eyebrow if she were to marry Miller tomorrow? Yes, she thought. Miller would.

Ethan plopped down in his seat at the table and reached for a slice of pie. He was still young, so it was hard for Miller to fault him for his impatience, his constant champing at the bit to be off to his next adventure. Still, sitting across from a young man who seemed to be perched on hot cockles was not his idea of a relaxing evening. The truth was, his sister had done the best she could with him, as she had with the rest of her family.

And there seemed to be so many of them. Miller wondered what it would be like to have so many relatives coming out of the woodwork all the time. He didn't think he'd care for it overly.

"So," he said to Ethan in an attempt to make polite conversation with the young man, who was quickly making his third piece of pie disappear. "You like working for Mr. Eastman?"

"That I do," Ethan answered, his mouth full of pie. "He's a gentleman and a gentle man, fair, honest, hardworking, and real good to his girls."

"They even remember their mama?" Sissy wondered.

"Oh, surely they must. The flood was only last year, and the little girl is what, two or three?" Miller asked Ethan.

"This many," Ethan said with a laugh, holding up two fingers and bending a third at the knuckle. "That's what Julia says, this many!"

"He seems to be a good father," Sissy went on.

"Yes, but he don't know much about farming. Don't know what he done before. Lucky for him he's got me to show him the ropes."

"Shame about his wife," Miller said.

He expected Sissy to agree, but she was oddly silent. Perhaps she was busy with thoughts of her own. Who knew what women were thinking about when they went all quiet and seemed to withdraw? His Elvira would sometimes be silent for hours. But those were peaceful, contented times for him. Now the silences of being alone were somehow not as welcome.

"He don't talk about her at all," Ethan said.

"That's not good for a man, keeping everything bottled up inside," Miller said. "I surely know that."

"Maybe," Sissy said, "it's best to put the past behind you and go on from there."

He knew she was referring to Elvira, not Mrs. Eastman, but he pretended not to notice. It was his job to do the mourning, not hers.

"Sissy," he said, "I think it would be a kindness to the man and his family to find a way to help him honor his wife. It must have been a terrible thing, leaving her behind in Johnstown. Why, we don't even know if there was a body. We have a duty to help him." He kissed the cross around his neck.

"Maybe he just wants to be left alone about it," she counseled. "If he wanted to share his grief—"

"But that's just it," he said. "We have to help him share his grief whether he wants to or not. Didn't you hear my sermon today? If you and the others hadn't helped me, I don't know what might have happened to me. Now I must pass on that help, reach out my hand to someone else crossing that bridge of despair."

When he'd finally gotten them both to agree, he assigned to Ethan the task of finding out more about Mrs. Eastman. With reluctance, because of both her poor penmanship and her grammar, he asked Sissy to write to the Johnstown Methodist Church and find out what might be an appropriate memorial for Wylene Eastman. The task of soliciting contributions he reserved for himself, knowing his discretion was far better than any of the Morrows, who were incapable of keeping secrets. He had always admired Sissy's candor, but the thought of a wife with that quality did unnerve him just a little.

In fact, everything about Sissy Morrow unnerved him: her strength, her directness, her spirit. The women in his life—his mother, his wife—had been quiet, demure beings who saw to his needs and rarely voiced an opinion of their own. When they were alive, they depended on him for everything, both physically and intellectually.

His status conferred on them a respectability and a place in the community that was a minister's stock in trade. He elevated them to a level neither could have achieved without him, a thought that made his chest swell with pride. Sissy Morrow, on the other hand, needed none of his importance, for she was already one of the most beloved and respected members of his congregation. She had managed so well, from such a tender age, that he felt almost superfluous around her.

Perhaps she didn't know the finer points of upper class society. He was sure she'd never read Thomas Hill's *Manual of Social and Business Forms,* which suggested that a husband be "strong, brave, and wise" while a wife need only be "confident in his bravery, strength, and wisdom." He didn't know if she'd read any book on etiquette or, for that matter, any book at all.

He'd get used to Sissy, he supposed. She had many fine qualities he would no doubt come to treasure as he got older still. There was so much he admired about her already. She cooked and cleaned better than any hired help and had a good head on her shoulders despite her lack of education. She was already performing most of the duties a minister's wife was expected to see to. Their marriage would be almost a formality.

Except, of course, for the one thing which only marriage provided. Elvira had been sick for years. Remembering back to their earlier years he was forced to admit that their time together in the marriage bed hadn't been one of God's miracles, even when she'd been well. Elvira had been a frightened, shy woman who was deathly afraid of pain. There had never been any question about children.

But Sissy was a young woman. Who knew what she would expect from him? It was something that, as a man of the cloth and as Elvira's husband, he had never had to give much thought to before. Now, sitting across from his bride-to-be, he found the idea daunting.

But he had an obligation he wouldn't shirk. Sissy had been there in his wife's hour of need—which, in all honesty, was many, many hours of many days, weeks, months, and even years—and he would do what was expected of him. When the time was right, of course.

*   *   *

"I'll walk you out, Miller," Annie offered, when it seemed like the discussion was over. Ethan appeared to be nailed to his seat and ready to start a fourth slice of pie.

Out in the dusk she stood by his fine carriage. It wasn't fancy, but it was more elegant than anything her family had ever owned. The horse, too, was a beauty, one of the finest driving horses in all Van Wert County.

He stood with his hat still in his hands, fingering the brim as though he were a schoolboy with a bad case of nerves.

"What's bothering you, Miller?" she asked. With three brothers, she'd seen enough nervous men to recognize the signs.

He swallowed hard. "You're a lot younger than I," he said.

"So?"

He put the hat on his head, searched for a place to put his hands, and then stuffed them in his armpits. "Folks might talk about how I could nearly be your father."

Well, at least he was thinking about marrying her, even if he didn't sound exactly eager. If it wasn't for Willa Leeman taking over her house, Annie wouldn't be all that anxious herself. But their age difference? That hadn't even occurred to her.

"Do you really think so?" she asked, a little flattered. No one ever thought of Annie as young, least of all Annie herself. After all, she'd been mother to five siblings who were now all grown.

"I suppose not most," he admitted, "but some might."

"Oh." And, she thought, it wouldn't just be Willa taking over her house. Unless Annie was mistaken, there was a bun in Willa's oven that would be popping before they all knew it.

"A man of God has to be careful about these things. If I can marry a woman fourteen or fifteen years my junior, what's to stop someone else? Think of your brothers."

She could hardly think of anything else. Bart had already announced his intention to marry Willa, who was roughly the same age as he was, twenty-tree. Charlie was married to Risa, two years his senior. That left only Ethan. And Annie didn't really think there was much danger of him marrying a five-year-old.

"And, of course, there is Elvira's memory. A year of mourning is the least I can do to show my love and respect for the woman who was my wife for eighteen years."

"That's longer than Francie's been alive," Annie said, moved by his argument. Eighteen years was even longer than she'd been raising her sisters and brothers, and that seemed like a lifetime. A cool breeze swept over them, and she rubbed her arms to keep herself warm. Autumn always showed itself first at night, and it was promising to be a cool September. "I can see how you feel. I surely didn't mean to make it sound like I was asking you to set a date."

"It's not that," he said, shifting his weight and checking his horse's bridle. "Elvira shared my house and my bed for my whole adult life. Now you're asking me to brush her memory aside, and it's not easy. You're young. Maybe you can't understand about a lifelong commitment to one person."

Who was he to tell her about lifelong commitment? Wasn't she still worrying about each and every sibling? Wasn't Francie always on her mind even though she was so far away? And Risa with child again? Risa wasn't even her own.

"I ain't asked you for anything, Reverend Winestock," Annie said, backing away from him and looking out over the horizon. It was too dark to see much past the barn. And there was nothing to see but flat, dry land.

"No, no," he said, sensing his mistake. "I didn't mean to make it sound like you were being unreasonable. I'm just saying that I have to close one chapter before I open another. Elvira was my Bible, so to speak."

"And me? Am I some dime novel?"

"That came out wrong too. It's just that while you have no obligations, no duties, I have responsibilities to my congregation, to the memory of my wife, and to my Lord, as well as to you."

"I don't really like bein' thought of as some sort of duty. No one's forcing you, Miller." Her voice snapped more than she intended.

"And I don't need to be forced," Miller said. He tipped her chin up and held her eyes with his own. "I do think marrying you is a fine idea, Sissy Morrow. As soon as the time is right."

Right for you, Miller, or for me?

His hand was warm against her chin and it lingered there, his thumb stroking her skin. It felt odd to have a man touch her face, not unpleasant, really, just odd. There was no magic like in the tales Della or Risa told of their courting days. She stood patiently waiting for him to release her, feeling nothing. As suddenly as he had touched her, he backed away, as though he'd just remembered where he was and what he was doing.

"You're cold," he said. "You should go inside."

She nodded but didn't move.

"Do you want me to give you my coat?"

She shook her head, her thoughts on Risa and Della's stories and on something Bart had said earlier in the day. Here she was trying to push Miller into an early marriage without even being sure what she could expect in the bargain. There were, she reminded herself, worse things than living with Willa Leeman under her roof.

Especially if Bart was right about Miller being like other

men. Was she fooling herself about what he would want from her in marriage? Della's diary had been full of men trying to raise her skirts. And Bart had claimed all men had needs. But Miller was a minister. Bart had to be wrong about him. He just had to be.

Well, better to find out now than after they were married. Her breath was coming in short little gasps at the thought of what she had to do, but her mind was set on finding out. She smiled at Miller as seductively as she knew how. She doubted she was any good at it, but with Miller being a minister and all, he wasn't likely to be an expert or have much to compare her with. Not sure he could see her half-closed eyes or pouty lips in the dark, she softly asked, "Would you like to kiss me?"

His body rocked slightly as if she had hit him with her words. "What?"

"To seal the promise," she said. She closed her eyes and tipped her head back slightly, waiting to see what kind of kiss he would give her. Della, when she'd been dating, had explained all the different types. A kiss on the cheek meant he wasn't really interested. Lips closed signified inexperience. Open meant eager but not pushy. If his tongue found its way into her mouth, a good girl knew the man had too much passion or too much experience for her to handle. That was Della's favorite type. Annie didn't know what she'd do if he tried anything like that.

But he didn't.

He didn't try anything at all. She opened her eyes to find Miller standing stiffly a few feet from her, a look of surprise on his face.

"I don't think a kiss would be s-such a good idea," he stuttered. The hat slipped from his fingers and he bent to retrieve it. Looking up at her from near the ground, he added, "I wouldn't want to tarnish your reputation."

Clearly no one would see them. If the Reverend Miller

Winestock had "needs," as her brother called them, they were well under control. That was all Annie wanted to know.

"Thank you, Miller," she said softly. *And thank you, Lord!* "I think it's very kind of you to think about that."

"Oh, not at all. I respect you, Sissy, and I'm sure you feel the same about me." He sighed heavily. "It's been many, many years since anyone but Elvira found me attractive."

"You're a very handsome man, Miller. I'll be proud to be your wife someday."

"Yes," he said, "someday. But for now you have the letter to Johnstown to write and the church social to plan. Elvira always took care of that."

Elvira hadn't taken care of anything in years. If Annie had felt any guilt over not being in love with Miller, it faded when she realized that neither one of them was foolish enough to let something like love cloud their judgment.

The good minister wanted someone to take care of his elegant house in town and see to the concerns of the church. Annie Morrow wanted to live in that house and invite all the ladies of the church to tea. He wanted someone waiting in a clean dress at the end of the day, anxious to serve him a hardy supper and nothing more. How many stars had she wished on, praying for just such a life? If ever there was one, this was a marriage made in heaven.

If only Bart and Willa could wait just a little while longer.

3

This time only two blankets signified the Morrows' place at the Sabbath school picnic. For years Annie had marked the changes in her family by the number of blankets at the annual affair. At the first one she could remember, there was just one old patchwork quilt, the remnants of which she now sat on. Once Charlie was born the family graduated to two blankets, one for her parents and one for the three children. By the time her mother died, there were three blankets: the one her father brooded on alone, one for Charlie and Bart, too old to share with the babies, and one for Della, Ethan and Francie. And Annie had gone from one to another, seeing to each of them.

They went on like that for years, until suddenly Peter Gibbs entered Della's life and they were a four-blanket family. A year later Risa joined them, and they went to five. And then the tide changed. Pa had died. This year the edge of Charlie and Risa's blanket was lined up next to his in-laws. Bart shared Willa's blanket where the Leemans were set up. Ethan, always the one to fall through the cracks, couldn't be counted on to show up anywhere, and Francie was off in New York.

So Annie got herself comfortable on the old quilt and waited for Della and Peter and the twins. Above her, the blue sky was cloudless. Only the hint of a breeze stirred the poplar trees that surrounded the meadow. Families were clustered under their shade while children ran free in the middle of the field, ringed by the safety of community members who watched out for all the children as if each was their own.

As always, the children were playing tag in the meadow. Alone on her blanket, Annie watched them and tried to remember if she had ever played the game herself. Even when her mother was alive there were always the babies to look after, too many for Zena to care for herself. And in the middle of nearly every picnic, Pa had always spirited her mother away for a short while, leaving Annie in charge.

She had wondered what they had been doing, her parents, alone in the far meadow. She remembered them returning with flushed faces, her father picking grass out of her mother's hair. How young her mother always seemed! Of course, she *was* young. The last picnic of Zena's life, she'd been six months along with Francie. So the one that stood out so clearly in Annie's mind had to have been the previous year, September 1872. Zena would have been twenty-four years old.

Two years younger than Annie, and in love. Ethan was still an infant that fall. Annie had been rocking him in her arms when her parents had come, laughing, over the ridge, their arms around each other's waists. She didn't know then what they had been about, but she knew now, and her cheeks flushed hot at the thought. . . .

"Lotta blanket for one little woman," a man's voice

said, startling her. She looked up and saw three silhouettes against the sunlight. She shielded her eyes to make them out, but she knew who they were without looking.

"Mr. Eastman," she said with a nod, "Hannah, Julia. Hello." The two girls smiled shyly at her, neither coming out from behind their pa's legs. "Would you like a cookie? I made some special just for today."

"We saw your wagon," Hannah said as Annie reached for the basket and rooted around until she found two perfect cookies, each decorated to look like little girls, and held them out. Their eyes lit up, but their hands remained locked around their father's legs.

"It's all right," she assured them. "I've made these for Francie every year since I can remember. I was halfway through decoratin' 'em this time before I realized I'd have no one to give 'em to. You'd be doin' me a big favor if you ate 'em right up."

She held them out again, and this time Noah Eastman's hands met hers. For a second, she froze. His fingers had merely grazed her own, yet she felt like her forefingers were stuck in one of those Chinese finger traps they sold at the fair. No matter what her brain said, and to tell the truth it wasn't saying much, her hands refused to let the cookies go.

"Got a letter from Francie a couple of days ago," he said, his eyes taking her measure as if he wondered if she too had heard from her sister. "Don't know when a letter has ever meant so much to me. Your sister is one special girl there, Miss Annie. I can't say just how much. But then, just look at who raised her." He eased the cookies from her grasp and handed them to his daughters. His voice was like warm water washing up her body, easing aching bones and soothing calloused skin.

"I miss Francie," Hannah said, eyeing the cookie longingly.

"Me too," Julia chimed in.

The children's voices brought Annie back to reality.

"Go ahead and eat them," Annie said. "Or are you savin' them for later?"

Their father still stood on the grass, but the girls had edged their way onto the blanket, giving Annie a good look at them. The braids in Hannah's hair had obviously been slept in. Julia's cheek revealed her breakfast. Still, they were in clean clothes, and this was the third Sunday Noah had taken them to church.

"She saves things she thinks are pretty," Noah Eastman said with a nod in Hannah's direction. "She's got a collection of pink rocks by her bed. She's got flowers pressed between the pages of every book I own. I don't know what we'll do when she sees the leaves change color. No doubt there'll be more in my house than on my trees."

Every book I own. Was he a reader? Lord, how she had tried to master that skill. Oh, she knew her letters and she could follow a recipe, understand a message, sing from a hymnal. But reading for pleasure, that was something she just couldn't seem to get the hang of. Each word seemed to stand there on its own, not connected to the ones that came before or after. When she wrote letters for Miller she often needed Risa's help, or Charlie's.

If only she hadn't had to quit school to raise the children. If only that law about sending children to school for at least twelve weeks a year until they were fourteen had been passed sooner. She remembered clearly her father's irritation when he was forced to allow her to attend school. She'd already been taking care of the children for four years when they came knocking on his door, Miss Orliss and the schoolmaster, Mr. Harmon.

"But Sissy ain't a child," her father had whined. "Who'll watch the little ones?"

"It's the law, Mr. Morrow," Miss Orliss had said.

"When'll she do the washin' and ironin'?"

He'd have argued all day if Annie hadn't turned to him

and said, "Please." Later he'd admitted that was what had swayed him. He said he couldn't remember her ever asking for anything before, and since the law was on her side anyway, he couldn't deny her this one time. And so he'd given in.

It had been the most wonderful weeks of her life, even though she was so far behind the other children she was forced to take her lessons with the ten-year-olds. Even though they'd had to swallow their pride and accept the money Perrin DePuy had left the Union School for poor kids to buy books and eyeglasses and things. And even if all her chores were waiting when she got home, with Bart fuming at her for leaving him to watch the little ones, it was still heaven. She'd wished it could go on forever.

"You can't save a cookie," Hannah's father told her. "It just won't last, honey. Some things just aren't meant to last."

Annie snapped back to the present and reached in the basket again, this time taking out a broken cookie she had passed over on her first foray. "Eat this one, sweetheart," she said, offering it to Hannah. "And you can still save the other."

Tears glistened at the corners of Hannah's bright blue eyes, as if she was touched by the gesture. Annie knew how ridiculous that idea was. After all, the child was no more than a baby. And yet when Hannah reached out and touched Annie, her little finger trembling as it approached Annie's cheek, Annie read something in her eyes. A kindred spirit, the look said. Just the look set Annie's heart pounding.

Where was Della, anyway? Annie had been conspicuously alone for over an hour while family after family poured into the meadow. Even Noah Eastman, who hadn't made it to church on time yet, had arrived before her sister. Alarms went off in Annie's head. Della, loving mother though she was, was so easily distracted. What if something had happened to one of the twins?

Her fear must have been written across her face, just as every emotion she'd ever experienced had been, because he knelt down at the edge of the blanket, his face too, revealing worry.

"What's wrong?" he asked. "What is it?"

She shook her head and brushed away his concern as if it were a fly buzzing around her head. "Della's late. I just thought something might be amiss."

"From what Francie says," he said, settling himself on the quilt uninvited and accepting a bite of cookie that Julia pushed into his mouth, "Della is always late. Francie says she likes to make an entrance."

According to Francie, Noah Eastman spent his days in the field while she minded his children. Annie wondered when it was the two had so much time to discuss her family's habits. The thought of them deep in conversation didn't sit any better with her than the fact that he seemed to be quite at home on her blanket, his children climbing over the two of them as if they belonged there. Of course, the children couldn't be blamed. No one had taught them any better.

"Francie seems to have told you a whole lot."

He shrugged in response, lifting one shoulder and one eyebrow almost apologetically. "Heard anything from her?" he asked. He seemed genuinely interested in her response.

"She seems kind of lonely, but that's to be expected, I'm sure," Annie said. "She ain't never been away from home before, and I guess I didn't do too good a job gettin' her ready to be on her own."

"I'm sure that's not true," he replied. "Why, from what she writes, she's already been all over that city, from Morningside Heights all the way down to—"

"Oh! There's Della now," Annie interrupted, pointing toward the Gibbses' wagon with her sister and her nephews in it. Peter, Della's handsome husband, eased the boys to the ground.

Having spent more than their fair share of time with their Aunt Sissy, the boys made a beeline for Annie, almost knocking her over with their enthusiasm. At nearly three, the two boys had all the force of a tornado. Between kissing and hugging and diving into the picnic basket, which they were sure contained goodies baked especially for them, Samuel and James Gibbs managed to push their aunt right into Noah Eastman's lap.

He was hard. His thigh was like the stones that bordered the stream. Each rib felt like the railing of the headboard on her bed. The hand that grabbed one arm to steady her was like the pliers Bart used to fix the chicken coop. But he didn't smell like the chicken coop, or even like one of her brothers. He smelled warm, and slightly pungent, and faintly like bay rum. His cheeks were clean-shaven. And his heart was pumping every bit as fast as hers.

She tried to right herself by putting her weight onto her elbows. A low groan warned her that the point of one elbow rested squarely on his most private parts. "Oh, my!" she gasped.

"No," he said in a rather strained voice. "Definitely mine!"

Embarrassed, she tried to roll off him, but that put her breast in contact with his knee. She jerked back, taking him by surprise. In his effort to help her, he had begun to reach toward her, so when she rolled back, and he leaned forward—

"Sissy?" Della said, staring down at what must have appeared to be a man and a woman engaging in some rather heavy sparking amid four children, two of whom had begun to cry about broken cookies.

"What is going on here?" Peter asked, looking down at

the flurry of activity and reaching out to stop James—or
was it Sam?—from grabbing what was left of Julia's
cookie from her hand.

Annie's cheeks went from merely warm to searing hot as
Peter's loud question attracted the attention of families on
the neighboring blankets. Noah Eastman got a hand under
her back and pushed her to a sitting position. She tried to
straighten her hair and clothes, but Della kept staring at her
as though she had disgraced the family. When she looked at
Noah Eastman he was staring at her chest, his own rising
and falling much too visibly for Annie's own good.

Annie looked down at her blouse and saw the gaping
opening where a button should be, smack where her
breasts were the fullest. Her hand went up to cover herself
at the same moment that Samuel began to choke and flail
his arms. His little face became mottled and he got on all
fours like a dog, coughing and coughing before anyone
realized what had happened.

"The button!" Annie yelped.

Noah Eastman's eyes widened and he grabbed the boy
and raised him by one foot, pounding him on the back
until the little white pearl came flying from his throat and
three children and four adults all dove for it at once.

It was Hannah who landed on it, and she turned it duti-
fully over to her father while nearly the whole Pleasant
Township Methodist Church stood staring down at
Annie's blankets and the chaos that was occurring on
them. Annie was too mortified to look up. Shocked out of
their tears by all the commotion, Julia and Hannah sat
staring first at their father and then at Annie.

"Oh, thank heavens," Della finally said, swooping down
to pick up a rather shaken Samuel.

"What happened?" someone asked.

By the time the story got to the Reverend Miller
Winestock, and he'd made his way to the front of the

crowd, the two principals were laughing so hard they could hardly sit upright. Della, having been told the circumstances, was smiling indulgently, and Peter was scolding the twins.

"Miss Morrow," the minister said, and the crowd seemed to part as though Moses had come to the Red Sea. "Is everyone quite all right?"

Annie was still clutching her blouse closed, but her shame had melted. That was, until she heard Miller's voice. The future wife of a minister didn't sit around on a blanket with some man with whom she was barely acquainted, her clothing askew, and laugh about it. In fact, she didn't laugh about anything. That was why Annie thought herself perfect for the role. Until this afternoon, she couldn't remember laughing since she was a small child.

She took a deep breath. So many faces seemed to hang on her words. She opened her mouth, but nothing came out.

"This was really all my fault," Noah Eastman said. "You see, I just stopped by Annie's—Miss Morrow's—blanket to tell her—" He halted and turned to Annie. "I have a message from Ethan. That was why I came over." He turned back to the minister. "I was just going to tell her that Ethan asked that she save some dinner for him, but then she"—he turned back to Annie—"very generously, I might add"—he again raised his face to the minister—"of course, you know how generous Annie—*Miss Morrow*—can be."

If it was possible, Annie felt her face turn redder still.

"We're fine, Mi—Reverend Winestock. Somehow one of the boys knocked a button lose from my shirtwaist, and then Samuel decided it was more appealin' than my cookies and choked on it."

"Good Lord!"

Annie nodded. "Mr. Eastman got it out. Everything's over except for the starin'."

And staring there was. Miller stood there looking at her until she realized that her knee was touching Noah Eastman's thigh. She scooted back, but that took her hand from her blouse, and the gasp that rose when she did made her wish she had never come to the picnic in the first place.

Noah Eastman stood to take his leave. With the show apparently over, the crowd broke up.

"I'll make you girls some new cookies," Annie promised. "I'm sorry the boys crushed them." She looked sternly at her nephews.

"Sorry," James mumbled. Samuel just shrugged. Well, he'd been through enough, she supposed.

"Miller, I've cooked enough for all of Ohio, it seems. Would you like to sit and have some roasted chicken with me and my family?" She gestured toward her blankets, but this time she kept one hand firmly on the front of her shirt-waist.

Miller looked at Noah Eastman, who was still standing by the blanket, his two girls in his arms. Without saying anything he nodded and pulled up slightly on the front of his pant legs as he lowered himself to the ground.

"I'll be seeing you," Noah Eastman said, his sparkling eyes trained on her chest as though he had made a private joke.

Annie merely nodded at him; the words stuck in her throat. She wiggled her fingers at the girls, who waved back.

"He's a strange one," Peter said, once he had settled Della and the twins. From their picnic basket he pulled a green bottle that Annie suspected was one of those new fine wines Peter had taken to buying lately in Cincinnati. As he worked at the cork he kept up a steady conversation. "Friday he came into the bank and opened an account. Imagine, lived here for over a year and suddenly he says he needs to establish credit. Can't imagine what for."

"Peter," Annie began. "You know how I feel about the drinking of alcohol. Why, even Della's been coming to the Temperance Society meetings."

"Sissy," Peter said, with an impish grin that no doubt worked on Della a lot better than it worked on her, "if it's good enough for George H. Marsh to peddle, it's good enough for me to drink."

"I can't be responsible for Mr. Marsh," Annie said sternly. "But—"

"If you don't complain to him—" Peter began.

"Well, when you build a park and put a fountain in it, I'll stop trying to reform you. Maybe."

"Samuel has something in his mouth again, dear," Della said, and Peter calmly reached over, fished out a rock, and threw it toward the trees.

"Didn't swallowing that button teach you anything?" Peter said with an exasperated sigh.

"Aren't we going to eat?" Della asked. Peter poured a glass of wine for himself and gestured to Della, who looked at Annie and declined. "What did you bring, Sissy?"

"That's another thing," Peter said, looking at Annie. "Why does he call you Annie? Everyone knows your name is Sissy."

Annie couldn't serve up lunch with her button missing. And Della didn't seem of a mind to do it. Miller, Peter and the boys all looked at her expectantly. On the next blanket, Jane Lutefoot sat primly, her umbrella shading her from the sun. In the center of the spread was a vase of flowers the likes of which Annie had never seen before and which had no doubt been grown in that new glass house Mrs. Lutefoot was so proud of. Imagine, Annie thought, a house just for flowers! Annie wondered if she might have a needle and thread with her.

"Her real name is Annie," Della said when no one else answered Peter. "But she's always been Sissy."

Annie hardly heard them. "I'm going to see if I can borrow a needle and thread," she said absentmindedly.

Mrs. Lutefoot, after giving Annie a flower she called an orchid, proudly showed her the chatelaine that had been her mother's. The sterling clasp held her house key, a small pair of scissors, and a little silver case containing several needles wound with thread.

Annie made her way over the rise and walked slowly to the far meadow, her mind sifting memories the way a prospector pans for gold. Here, in the meadow, away from the children's shouts and the neighbors' prying eyes, her parents had come. Ethan had been a June baby. Had they conceived him here, in the copse of trees where she now hid to mend her dress?

Her hands worked the needle between her breasts, and she imagined a man's hands there. Her father would no doubt have accompanied her mother if she'd lost a button. If they were married, would Miller have come to help her? Would his hands stray and forget the task they had come to do?

Foolish thoughts, all of them. Miller Winestock was a minister, a man of God. He wouldn't have the same lustful thoughts her father must have harbored about her mother. The two men had nothing in common whatsoever.

She was standing with her back to the hill when he spotted her, the pale green of her dress hiding her within the grove of young oaks. From her motions it appeared she was repairing the damage done to her dress by her exuberant nephews.

His reaction to her touch had surprised him. True, he was no ladies' man. He'd only sown a handful of wild oats before settling down with Wylene and starting a family. Still, he'd touched a woman's arm, held a woman against him, and been able to breathe at the same time.

But not so with Annie Morrow. She wasn't soft like other women, but firm. Her skin was smooth and she smelled of vanilla and soap. He'd felt the silky strands of hair that had escaped her efforts at looking fancy, and it took all his control not to pull the pins from her hair and bury his face in it.

"Miss Morrow?"

Her hands were on her breasts and she dropped them to her sides and stood perfectly still.

"I saw you go over the hill and I . . . I just, that is . . ." He expelled a powerful breath, full of frustration. "Damn it, I can't seem to get two words out in a row when I talk to you."

"Why's that?" Her head was down and she kept her back to him, unaware of how the sunlight lit a spot on her neck as though directing him just where to place his lips.

"Awe," he admitted, as much to himself as to her. "Awe, plain and simple."

Her head snapped around and she looked at him with disbelief written all over her delicately bronzed features. "Awe?"

"The way Francie talks about you, how you raised all your brothers and sisters when you were just a baby yourself. And Ethan, the way he talks about your cooking, and the way you made the house a home. I just couldn't wait to meet you. I knew just what I was going to say."

But then he'd seen her and it had taken his words away. Admiration had given way to awe. And affection was giving way to something he was afraid he wouldn't be able to control.

"I meant to tell you how much I admired you, and how I sure would like your help and advice from time to time, and when they talked about you I got this picture in my head of this angel . . ."

"And then you saw me," she said flatly, as if she expected that he would have been disappointed. Her eyes searched his and seemed to be surprised by what they found.

"And then I saw you," he said finally, his smile broadening as though just seeing her had made him happy. "And you were . . . you are—"

"Mr. Eastman? You down there, Mr. Eastman?" a voice called out from the top of the ridge.

"Damn." He turned from her and shouted back up toward the hill, "I'm here!"

"Hannah with you?" the voice yelled back.

Annie looked around them. There was no sign of his little girl.

4

Annie followed Noah up the steep parched slope, taking two steps for each one of his, the breeze whipping her skirts around her and impeding her progress. He looked back for a moment as if he thought perhaps he should wait for her, but she waved him on with her hand. By the time she caught up to him he was surrounded by several people all talking at once.

Peter Gibbs seemed to be in charge. Noah had left the girls with him and Della when he'd gone looking for Annie. Now Della, blond and beautiful in her apricot-colored shirtwaist, stood with Julia in her arms, the little girl's face streaked with tears.

"One minute Hannah was here," Peter said, running his fingers through his well-kept brown hair, "and the next she was gone. Mrs. Lutefoot said she saw her go off toward the ridge, so I checked there. No one over there has seen her."

Noah was listening to Peter without looking at him. Chin raised, he was searching over the tops of everyone's heads, scanning the field for traces of a little girl dressed in pink. Annie knew well the fear he felt, the knot in his stomach that tightened with every breath as he thought of Hannah alone.

The sky was a deep clear blue. At least they didn't have to worry about the weather. She went over possibilities in her mind. Devil's Lake was at least a mile away, too far for Hannah to walk, by Annie's reckoning. While her heartbeat grew faster and faster she thought of one awful possibility after another. Snakes? She couldn't remember the last time anyone was bitten. Wild animals? An occasional fox, a small coyote, nothing that would threaten an adult. But Hannah was just a child. How far could she have gotten on those two chubby little legs in just a few minutes?

"Where could she be?"

"Whatever would possess a child to simply walk off like that?"

"What if she gets lost?"

From the crowd's tone it was easy enough for Julia to sense that her sister might be in danger, and the poor baby sobbed and stretched her arms out to her father. For a moment she commanded all his attention. "Shh, now," he told her. "Everything's all right, honey. Daddy'll find Hannah."

It reminded Annie of the time Ethan had been missing. He couldn't have been more than four or five. He'd scared the daylights out of the whole family, but no one as much as Annie, who had a gift for imagining the worst. Despite that, or because of it, she fought now to stay calm.

"Mr. Eastman," she said. "What was Hannah talking about before you left?"

"What?" He was organizing searchers, sending some in one direction, some in another, all the men fanning out from the meadow while the women minded the children with more than the usual care.

"Before you came down to the trees, what was the last thing Hannah said to you?"

His eyebrows came down close to his eyes, leaving several wrinkles in their wake. He wasn't following her thoughts, but Charlie, who along with Risa had made his way to the front of the crowd, nodded at her.

"Ethan," he said, a smile on his face at the memory.

"Exactly," Annie said.

"Would someone mind explaining to me what you're talking about?" Noah said tightly. If there was something that could help him find Hannah, he wanted to know *now*.

"When Ethan was a young boy," Annie explained, "about Hannah's age, he got it into his head that he wanted to be a cowboy."

At the surprise on Noah's face, she shrugged. "Don't ask me. It's a stage little boys go through. Charlie did too. Anyway, he wanted to be a cowboy and nothing we said would change his mind. Then one day Charlie and Bart were arguing about whether the sun rose in the east or set in it, and Pa settled the argument by announcin' that the sun set in the west and would be doin' it in an hour or two, and they'd best be finishin' their chores before dark. Well, just before dark we noticed Ethan was missing. We looked everywhere: the barn, the pasture, everywhere."

"Then Annie put two and two together," Charlie said. "As usual. Ethan wanted to go west, and now he knew which way that was. We followed the sun and found him about a mile from the house, sittin' by the side of the road eating one of Annie's cookies from a sack he'd taken with him."

"The point is," Annie said, "Hannah must have been going somewheres. All you gotta do is figure out where she wanted to go."

Noah looked impressed, but to Annie it was a simple matter of experience. If seventeen years of watching little ones didn't make you some kind of expert, she didn't know what would.

Noah, his breathing a little more regular, his shoulders slightly more relaxed, looked at the little girl in his arms. "Julie honey, did Hannah say where she was going? Did she say what she wanted?"

Julia's deep blue eyes got big and round and her chubby finger came out of her mouth and pointed at Annie. Well, that wasn't much help. Here Annie was and there was no sign of Hannah. And she hadn't been down by the oak grove, either.

"Della," Annie said, turning to her sister, whose attention was focused on her own children. "What was she doing before you noticed she was gone?"

Della answered without looking up, busy with the twins. Apparently, Samuel had just put something in James's mouth and Della demanded that he spit it out. When an earthworm landed in her palm, she swayed slightly. With a sigh, she said, "I really didn't notice. She was going on and on about cookies, but the boys were—Samuel!" Her hand was below her son's chin. "Spit yours out. Now!"

"Well," Charlie surmised. "Sounds like Hannah's got a crush on our Annie."

"Or her cookies," someone in the crowd said, laughing. "I know I'd walk clear to Columbus for one of her pies!"

"You don't think she'd try to walk all the way to the Morrows' farm, do you?" someone else asked.

Charlie was scanning the horizon looking due south toward his sister's home. "I wouldn't think she'd even know the way."

Risa, one finger in the air as if she was pointing at an idea, said something about being right back. While Annie tried to soothe a very frightened Julia and keep Noah calm at the same time, she watched her sister-in-law make a beeline for Annie's wagon.

"No," she said, shaking her head. "How would she know which one was mine?"

But Risa was already there, pulling back a blanket that was tucked under the seat. Soon it was clear she was talking to someone, but the words were lost in the distance. A small head emerged over the wooden slats of the buckboard and there was a flash of pink in the sunshine.

"Hannah!" Noah yelled, as much in relief as anger. "Well, I'll be damned!" Without asking, he deposited Julia in Annie's arms and in just a few strides he was at her wagon and lifting Hannah over the side. Annie rushed after him, along with most of the crowd that was left.

Noah was clutching his daughter to him, his features relaxing. Gently, without any of the anger Annie expected, he asked the girl, "What in the world were you doing in this wagon?"

Hannah looked around, frightened eyes wide, as she took in all the people gathered about her. Most of Annie's family, the Lutefoots, Miller Winestock: they were all waiting for her to answer. She trembled and her lower lip quivered so badly Annie wasn't even sure she could talk. Her heart went out to the child.

"Were you looking for more cookies?" she asked, keeping her voice low, tenderly cupping Hannah's chin in her hand. The tiny chin didn't belong to one of her own brood, but it had an awfully familiar feel in Annie's palm.

The girl shook her head. A tear was knocked loose from her eye and crawled down her cheek.

"Good children don't worry their parents," the minister told her. "I know you are a good little girl, and you must never do something so thoughtless again."

Noah stiffened beside Annie, shifting slightly so that Hannah's back was to the minister. "I don't think Hannah was trying to worry me. I think she had something else in mind altogether." His arms wound protectively around his daughter while he glared at Miller Winestock.

Somehow, and not just because she stood between the two men, Annie felt as though she were a part of a dance they seemed to be doing, as though Hannah's actions and the proper response to them had something to do with her. She took a step backward, as if that would take her out of the line of fire, but Hannah reached two shaky arms out for her and she couldn't move away.

Noah tried hard to keep the smile off his face. Had anything ever fit together as perfectly as this? Annie, so smart to know that a child, his child, would be seeking a dream. Hannah, picking Annie out like that, hiding in her wagon, stretching out her arms to her. And all just a day after that remarkable letter from Francie. It was as if he'd planted trees in his fields, gone to sleep and, after an evening of rain and a morning of sunshine found a harvest of apples just ready to be picked.

He might not be much of a farmer, not yet, but he knew this was the time to pluck the fruit God had offered him.

"I think Hannah was hoping Miss Annie might just take her home if she hid out in her wagon. Can't say I blame her. I only wish I thought of it first."

"Me too," little Julia chimed from within Annie's arms.

The color rose in Annie's cheeks. My, how that woman could blush! And the pink of those cheeks against that golden complexion would be enough to warm a man's heart in January.

The minister wasn't satisfied. "Well, yes," he said. "I'm sure the little girl misses her mother, as I know you do. Still, it's a parent's duty to raise a child with a firm hand."

If Miller Winestock was waiting for Noah to take that firm hand and lay it on his daughter's bottom, he'd be old and gray and toothless before it happened. The child missed a mother, all right. Who could blame her? She'd never really had one, and now that she'd laid eyes on Annie she didn't seem about to let her go. There was something about the woman that was so natural, so nurturing, so warm, even a child could feel it. Without any effort at all she could make a person feel safe.

"Sweetie," Annie said to Hannah in the softest voice he'd ever heard, a voice that flowed like golden honey from lips Noah wanted like the dickens to touch, "I don't have any more cookies with me."

The sun was hitting her hair, turning it into burnt sugar strands, and Noah could hardly pay attention to the words she was saying. He'd like to see that hair tumbling down her back, her naked back, taffy strands teasing tanned skin. But of course, her back would be paler, untouched by the sun. . . .

"Mr. Eastman?" Annie was staring at him as she lowered Julia to the ground. So, for that matter, was Charlie Morrow's wife, Risa. There was a funny smile on the other woman's face, a smile that implied she had been reading his thoughts. He shifted Hannah in his arms, hoping that if his Sunday pants were revealing any of the desire he was feeling, Hannah's squirming body would both hide it and make it go away. It had been so long since physical feelings had been any part of his life he'd almost forgotten how to handle them.

"Mr. Eastman? Are you all right?" It was Annie once again, her eyes searching his face, the tip of her tongue touching her upper lip. It reminded him of a butterscotch-colored kitten, that sudden flash of pink between her lips— lips he knew he was going to taste sooner or later.

"I . . . It's just . . . with Hannah running off . . ." Damn and damn again! He was absolutely incapable of uttering a complete sentence in her presence. Like some eight-year-old caught with his hand in the candy jar, he could only stammer and look guilty. Not that he didn't have good reason to feel guilty with the thoughts that were barreling into his head unbidden. In his mind he saw her fine straight hair like a curtain against the skin of her back. She was close enough for him to smell the vanilla scent that surrounded her. His mouth watered.

"You did scare your daddy," she said to the child in his arms. "Can you tell him that you're sorry?"

"Sissy, I don't think a simple apology—" Winestock began. The good minister had slipped again and called her Sissy instead of Miss Morrow. He'd heard that she was spoken for, that there was an understanding between her and Winestock. Though he would have preferred that they weren't, it seemed that the rumors about their impending marriage were true. For now. But you couldn't be expected to honor another man's claim if he hadn't actually staked it. And whatever his reasons were, Miller Winestock had not made any announcement regarding his affection for the lovely Miss Morrow, nor had there been any formal word of his intentions.

"Samuel! Put it down! Now!" The horrid boy held a wriggling centipede not more than two inches from little Julia's face. Her eyes were wide, but to her credit she wasn't flinching. Peter grabbed his son's hand and the bug went flying. It sailed through the air and landed on the puffed sleeve of Annie's starched white blouse.

"Here, I'll—" the minister began, pushing himself between Annie and Noah and reaching for her arm with pasty-white fingers.

Before Winestock had finished his sentence she had formed an O with her thumb and forefinger and flicked the bug from her dress. "Hmm?" she asked, looking up in surprise.

"I was only offering to help you," the minister said. He seemed mildly disappointed, perhaps even appalled. "But you seem not to require assistance."

She was no hothouse pansy, this Annie Morrow. If a hundred crawling legs on her didn't lift one of those lovely eyebrows, nothing would shake her, Noah figured. It didn't seem to him that Winestock had the proper appreciation for a woman who could hold her own on a farm where any moment might demand a cool head and a steady hand. He didn't think the minister had the proper appreciation for much about Annie Morrow besides her undisputed cooking skills. If he had, he'd have told the world she was his a long time ago. *Well, he who hesitates is lost, as the old saying goes. Sorry Winestock, but you lose.*

"So bugs don't bother you?" he asked, trying to keep up a normal conversation while his whole being was rocking to the core at just being within three feet of her. It was his first full sentence, and it was about insects. He could have kicked himself.

"Mr. Eastman," she said with a laugh that made his heart dance inside his chest, "I'm a farm girl. Bein' afraid of bugs, likin' to stay clean, swoonin' at the thought of wringin' a chicken's neck, and wearin' little strap sandals—those are all privileges reserved for city women. I ain't had such luck yet." Her eyes flew to Winestock with such longing that she might just as well have run Noah's heart through a cider press and squeezed it dry.

5

The first note was in the flour Bart brought home with him from Hanson's Mercantile. Annie was halfway through making the cookies she had promised Hannah and Julia when she reached into the sack for some flour to dust her cutting board and hit something that crackled. She looked into the bag. The corner of a piece of paper stood sticking up from the white flour like a flag planted atop a mountain by some brave explorer. Her hands were covered in flour and she hesitated, realized that the paper was already coated, and reached in, pulling it out gently so it didn't rip.

It was a small slip of paper, folded carefully in two. On the outside was her name, written in the neatest Spencerian hand she had ever seen. She tried to remember whether she had ever received a note addressed to her before. Of course, she'd gotten one whenever one or another of the children had misbehaved in school, or when Mrs. Winestock needed something done for the church, even a thank-you here or there. Annie looked at the note again. This was different. Besides the fact that it was coated in Hanson's best all-purpose flour, it was addressed to *Annie Morrow*. Not Sissy. *Annie*.

Only one person called her by her given name. Only one person would have put her given name on a piece of paper and slipped it into her grocery order: Noah Eastman. She put the note, still folded, on the edge of the table and returned to her baking. Anything concerning Mr. Eastman could certainly wait. There was a sheet of little girl cookies in the oven almost ready to come out, one waiting to go in, and enough dough left to make her nephews some cowboys and Indians.

Cooking for seven people over the years had left her unable to make small batches of anything. Her math was good enough to cut down a recipe, should she ever actually use one, but somehow her brain could never tell her hands that all her babies had flown the coop and she wasn't cooking for an army anymore. Well, with Risa expecting again and Willa, though Bart had never actually said as much, likely to be carrying, there'd be five little ones come a year from now to be watching over and cooking for.

Not on this old cookstove, though. Oh, the pies she could turn out with Miller's new Sterling range! Elvira had hardly used it before she'd passed on, and since her death Miller took his meals out. The town, especially the spinsters in it, took pity on the widower and invited him over or brought food in. His range was practically brand new.

At Miller's place the pie safe wouldn't have to be draped with cheesecloth to keep out the dust. And she'd be just a few blocks from Charlie and Risa and not far at all from Della and the boys. If she married Miller in six months or so, and that was giving him a little extra time to break the news to the congregation slowly, she'd be close enough to Risa to help with the birth of the new baby.

Willa, of course, would be farther away, but, it being her first, Annie could still get out to the farm with plenty of time to sit around and wait for nature to run its course.

The kitchen was stifling. She'd kept the windows closed in an effort to keep the dirt off her cookies, but she could feel sweat dripping out of every pore and turning the flour on her hands to glue.

Trying to pull herself together, she rinsed them in a basin of water that sat by the sink, getting cloudier and cloudier as the morning wore on. Her mind might be on a hundred other things, but her nose told her, as it always did, that her cookies were done. The sweet warm smell of butter and sugar melting filled the kitchen and softened her fears, as baking had always done from the time she was little.

Waves of heat blasted out of the oven and she backed away from the stove. She was going to have to open a window after all, she thought, as she removed eight perfect little girls from the oven and placed the new sheet gingerly inside. How Francie had loved these cookies! Annie had already received two letters from her. In them Francie had thanked Annie over and over again for making her go to New York, but both of them had ended with a veiled plea to let her return home and make a life for herself in Van Wert now that she had seen what the rest of the world had to offer.

As if there was a life to be had in Van Wert. And she always asked about Noah Eastman and his girls.

The note still sat on the edge of the counter, the heat in the kitchen wilting its edges. Maybe it was an apology for embarrassing her at the picnic on Sunday. He certainly owed her one. Miller had been sour the rest of the afternoon. He'd gone on and on about how Hannah should have been punished for running away and he didn't know what was wrong with young people these days. Annie hadn't been able to tell if he was referring to Mr. Eastman or his daughter, since Miller always held himself so much older than everyone around him.

He kept bringing up the age difference between himself and Annie as if it were some huge barrier between the two of them, a hurdle to be approached cautiously and measured carefully to make sure it was surmountable. That was the word he'd used: surmountable. She'd had to ask him what it meant and he'd given her the same look he always did, as if he was disappointed with her lack of education. He knew as well as everyone else in Van Wert that she had left school to raise her siblings. So why did he seem surprised when she hadn't heard some word before? Who'd he think she was likely to hear it from? Bart? Ethan?

The screen door creaked and slapped.

"Bakin'?" Bart said when he came in from the fields for lunch. "Hell of a hot day to be bakin'. It's hotter'n Hades in here, Sissy. Why ya got all the windows closed?"

With him came a heavenly breeze and Annie realized he'd left the door open. She threw a towel over the cookie rack and sighed. Dirt. Dirt everywhere. Dirt all the time. She wished she was already married to Miller and living in town. At least there the wind didn't sail through your house and bring all the dust of the prairie along with it.

"Shut the door," she told her brother. "Does all of Ohio have to be on that table for every meal?"

"I never seen it as dry as this," Bart said. "Washed up at the pump and before my hands were dry they were fulla dirt again. Guess I'll try again in here."

When he finished he pulled the towel off her cooling cookies and dried his hands. He noticed something on the floor, and as he bent to pick it up Annie realized it was the note from Mr. Eastman. It must have blown off the table when Bart opened the door.

"That's for me," she said, going to take it from his hand.

"'Annie Morrow,'" he read. "What is this, anyway?" He opened it before she could pull it away from him. "What is this supposed to mean?"

She should have read it the moment she found it. Read it or destroyed it. Anything but left it for Bart to find. What if it was about Francie? Francie would never forgive her for letting Bart see something personal. "What does it say?"

"It says, 'Your skin is the color of baked bread.'"

"What?"

Bart looked at the note again and then handed it over to his sister. Sure enough, that was what he had written. Even Annie could read those words. *Her skin? Noah Eastman was talking about her skin?*

"Where'd that come from? Who sent it?" Bart asked.

There was no signature, thank goodness. "Risa must be feeling playful with the new baby coming," Annie said, trying to sound unruffled while her blood raced and her heart pounded against her apron so hard it was a wonder Bart couldn't see it. What in the world could he be talking about? *Your skin is the color of baked bread?* "It was in the flour sack. Sit down and I'll get your dinner."

She shooed him out of the kitchen and went directly to the new sack of sugar waiting to be opened on the counter. She ripped it open and stuck her hand in. Sure enough, *crackle, crackle.* This one said her hair was like burnt sugar swirled atop a beautiful cake.

She jammed the note in her pocket and spooned up a plate of sausages, sweet potatoes, and greens for Bart, her hands working automatically while her mind danced around the two notes that now rested in her pocket.

She'd ordered beans from Hanson's, too. She didn't even want to think about what *that* note might say.

Re-covering the cookies with the towel Bart had used, she heard him say something from the table in the dining room, but couldn't make it out. Her head was spinning with a hundred thoughts. Why, those notes sounded like he was trying to court her! But that was ridiculous. She was marrying Miller Winestock. Everyone knew that, even if the minister hadn't said it in so many words. And if Noah Eastman was interested in any Morrow, it was Francie. Weren't they exchanging letters? And weren't all Francie's letters to her full of questions about Mr. Eastman and his girls?

Bart called for an answer, and Annie, trying to hide her confusion, came into the dining room, Bart's glass of lemonade in her hand.

"What?" she asked, taking a seat across from him. She looked around her. "Isn't it getting dark in here?"

Bart looked toward the window and sighed. "Saw some clouds this morning. Sure hope we get some rain."

"Reverend Winestock's is gonna be one of those houses with electricity, you know," Annie told Bart. "He'll just be able to press a button and lights'll come on all over his place."

"Mmm," Bart responded. He seemed overly interested in his meal, and Annie went on.

"Imagine! Electricity. I wonder how long it'll be before the whole world has it. Probably years and years. They'll be livin' in one century in town and it'll be another century on the farm." She knew clearly which century she longed to be in. It might not make any difference to her brother, but it sure did to her. "Bart?"

He pushed a large piece of sausage into his mouth and followed it with some potato. There was a long pause; then, without looking up, he said, "We're gettin' married on Saturday."

Annie swallowed hard. It wasn't as if the news was a surprise, though he could have told her a little sooner. He'd spent the morning in the fields, so the arrangements must have been made well before this moment. And without so much as a by-your-leave to her, either. Well, Bart had pretty much taken things for granted all his life, and while Annie felt she did the lion's share of running the household, Bart fancied himself the head of the house.

"Saturday," she said, nodding. "That ain't much notice. You gonna be able to spare me with the harvesting? There'll be an awful lot of bakin' and cookin' to do to prepare. Not to mention the cleanin'."

Bart kept his eyes on his plate, a habit he'd developed as a little boy when he knew his words weren't going to please whoever it was he was talking to. "Wedding party's at the Leemans. Willa's ma will take care of it all." He finally met her gaze and smiled halfheartedly. "You won't have to do nothin', Sissy. Just be a guest for a change."

"That's nice, Bart," she said, swallowing her hurt. Already things were out of her control. "Real nice. Martha Leeman is a good woman, and I'm sure she'll put out a fine spread. You tell her I'll be happy to help."

Bart stuffed more sausage in his mouth before speaking. "No need," he said.

There was only the sound of Bart eating, his fork scraping the plate, the gulp of food going down his throat, the clink of the glass of lemonade against his teeth. With just the three of them in the house, Annie would hear everything that went on between Willa and Bart.

"You smell somethin'?" Bart asked.

Annie lifted her head and sniffed. The last batch of cookies was burning.

"Oh, no!" she said, rushing from the table and into the kitchen. A thin stream of smoke rose from the oven. Grabbing a towel she eased the door open. A half dozen cowboys and three Indians had been reduced to charred scraps. The remaining three Indians had survived with mild burns that could be hidden with icing if she got them out of the oven soon enough. She reached for the cookie sheet and pulled it out, hitting the side of the oven with her hand.

The tray clattered to the floor as she yelped and put the heel of her hand in her mouth.

"What the devil?" Bart said from the doorway and crossed the room in two strides. "Let me see it," he ordered, pulling her hand out of her mouth to see the reddened patch of skin.

"I'm all right," Annie said, despite the tears coursing down her cheeks. The burn wasn't serious. She could always make more cookies.

"It don't look too bad. Put some petroleum jelly on it and I'll wrap a hankie around it for you." He looked at her face and was clearly surprised by her tears. "Does it hurt so much?"

Unsure how her voice would come out, she just shook her head, opened the cabinet door, and reached in for the jar of ointment. Gingerly she dabbed it against the burn as the tears came faster and faster, now punctuated with sobs.

"Sissy, it ain't that bad. You ain't even got a blister." Bart pulled his hanky out of his back pocket and tied it around her hand. He sighed heavily and shook his head. "Two women in the same house. How am I gonna stand that?"

Annie tried to smile as Bart bent over and picked up the dead cowboys and Indians.

"Sissy," he asked while he was still reaching down, "could me and Willa have your room?"

The Reverend Miller Winestock was going through his mail when he heard a knock at the door. If there was one thing he disliked, it was the order of his day being disrupted. But being a minister meant seeing to the needs of his congregation at any hour, and—looking at his watch—

two in the afternoon didn't seem unreasonable. In fact, as he knew from Elvira's etiquette books, calling hours were from two to five where lunch was served at one and dinner at six or seven. Still, he imagined whoever it was at his door must be in great need of him. The wind had picked up considerably over the course of the morning, so that now a veritable sandstorm raged outside.

At the second knock he called out that he was coming and hurried to the door. On his steps stood Sissy Morrow, her hands protecting her face from the blowing clouds of dust, her skirts buffeted around her. Blackie and the wagon were outside. In all the months, the years, that she had seen to Elvira, she had never once let the weather stop her from making the journey into town. Like the old Greek writer said about messengers, "Not snow, nor rain, nor heat, nor night," nothing ever stopped Sissy Morrow.

A gust of wind tore at her dress as if to prove it, and he reached out his hand and pulled her quickly into the house, shutting the door behind her. Her arm was muscular, as he knew it would be. Despite her small size she was nearly as strong as he, having proved it over and over when she'd aided, sometimes even carried, his wife.

"What a day!" she said as she untied her bonnet and tried to fan the dust from her face. The loose hairs that surrounded her face lifted and then settled back down and she pushed them back toward her bun. "I must be a sight," she added, looking uncomfortable.

"Yes," he agreed. "The wind has surely picked up." Powdery dirt fell from her clothes onto his rug, leaving a small pile of light brown dust around her as she shook herself off.

"Oh, Miller! I'm sorry," she said when she followed the line of his eyes to the floor. "I'll clean it up, of course."

"Don't concern yourself," he said politely. One thing he had always appreciated about Sissy was that she, too, seemed to treasure cleanliness and place it right up there by godliness, as he did. A tidy house, he firmly believed, was the sign of a civilized man. "Whatever brings you out on such a dreadful day? Is something wrong?"

More than the dry earth had put a pallor over her countenance. Her eyes were sad, her usually smiling mouth turned down. His first thought was that she was ill, a natural reflex, he supposed, spending so many years with Elvira. But she didn't look unwell, merely unhappy. Whatever was bothering her, he hoped he could rectify it simply. Having done it so often for his wife, it was something he'd come to enjoy, solving the little problems women thought so grave.

"I need to get married right away," the woman before him said. No preamble, no easing into it. Well, every woman couldn't be his dear wife, and Sissy had charms of her own, though they lay closer to the kitchen than the parlor. Before he could find his voice, she continued. "It's because Bart and Willa, as I'm sure you know, are gettin' married on Saturday."

"And?"

"And they're going to live at the farm. Bart wants my room, the one that Papa lived in before he died, and Willa will want to put her dishes in my kitchen and it won't be my kitchen anymore and I can't stand the dirt and I want to be in town for Risa's baby and—"

Thank the good Lord, she took a breath. "Sit down," he instructed gently. He supposed there was something to be said for Sissy's directness. Coming right to the point might not be the genteel way of approaching a distressing situation, but it did save the aggravation of imagining even more serious problems than were actually at hand.

"Risa has been blessed again?" he asked. Was this at the heart of her unhappiness? Did she wish for a child of her own? It certainly wasn't out of the question. In fact, the idea pleased him somewhat. "How wonderful. But surely you don't need to be there so far in advance, unless . . . is something wrong with Mrs. Morrow?"

"Oh, no," she said, as if he had missed the point. "Risa's fine and the baby ain't due until spring. It's Bart and Willa that's the problem."

"Yes," he said solemnly. Bart had made it clear that the rush to marry Willa Leeman was not frivolous. All the Morrows were ingenuous people, with the possible exception of Della. Bart had been ready to spell it out for him when Miller had put up his hand and nodded. "I know about Bart and Willa's problem, and Saturday that will all be taken care of. A blessing is a blessing whenever God sees fit to—"

"No," she said again, this time impatiently. Her shoulders fell in what looked to him like desperation. "It's not their problem, it's mine."

Miller tried to keep his face devoid of emotion. In his mind he backtracked over the conversation, and it seemed to him that all she'd mentioned was babies. What in the world was she trying to tell him? That she wanted a child? But why was that a problem? And what was her sudden rush? Unless . . .

"Miller?" Despite her words she was the one looking oddly at him. "Are you all right?"

"What is it you're trying to tell me?" he asked. "Don't be coy. It doesn't suit you."

"Coy?"

He sighed. She didn't know what it meant. Well, he had years to work on her education. Or he thought he did before this ridiculous conversation had started.

"Out with it, Sissy. If you've a 'problem,' it's best I know it now." He couldn't believe what he was saying. Sissy Morrow? No one was interested in Sissy Morrow but him. The whole town knew she would someday be his wife.

"Willa will be the woman of the house, Miller. Don't you see? It will be her house now, not mine. I'll be the old maid aunt and she'll move Mama's dishes; or worse, she might break them, and—"

"That's your problem?" he asked, amazed that he could have imagined anything else. "You're upset because you will have to share your household with another person? Sissy Morrow, you've had five children with you in that house and two parents, God rest their souls. Now there isn't room for three of you?"

She mumbled something he couldn't make out about her bedroom. Tears were collecting in her eyes and he chided himself for making light of her problem, despite the overwhelming relief.

"What?"

"They want my bedroom."

"I'm so sorry, dear." He was trying to sound sympathetic, as he had always done with Elvira. "But surely there are other rooms you could use, with Francie away at school and Della married."

That should have solved it, but Sissy didn't let go as easily as his wife.

"Miller," she said, so sadly and quietly that he had to kneel beside the chair in which she sat in order to hear her, "I don't want to wait. Can't you marry me now?"

He should have seen that this was the direction in which she was headed. He should have steered the conversation toward something else. She was a good woman and telling her *no* was something he could not do easily or without remorse. But tell her he must, and ask her to understand.

"How long has Elvira been gone?" he asked her, his eyes searching hers.

"But Miller—"

"Eight months, Sissy. Eight months." He hadn't realized

how big her eyes were before. Big sad eyes that begged him to change his mind. He tried another tack. "If your father had remarried only eight months after your mother died, what would you have thought? How would you have felt?"

"But my mother was—" She stopped herself, much to Miller's relief. He would not tolerate criticisms of Elvira, just as he would never tolerate criticisms of her. Not that he had ever heard any, but he might. And he would say to her critics, "Sissy Morrow is a fine upstanding woman, beyond reproach, beyond correction." Though in Sissy's case, unlike Elvira's, a few refinements wouldn't be totally out of order. Like her insensitivity, so obvious now.

"Is it asking so much of a husband of eighteen years that he honor his wife's memory with a year of mourning?"

"No," she said. Her mouth opened and closed again. She'd thought better of arguing with him, thank the Lord.

"Is it asking too much that we wait just a few more months before anouncing our intentions to the people who look to me for guidance and leadership?" He made the question sound genuine, as if her answer mattered, when in fact on this one point he would not be moved. Then he waited, the wind against his windows the only sound in the room.

"I'm sorry," she said finally, blinking rapidly but not allowing a tear to fall. "Of course you feel that this is too soon. I don't suppose I'd care for you so much if you hadn't been so good to Elvira and if you didn't feel the loyalty to her memory that you do. I admire you for that, and I shouldn'ta let my own needs and bad feelings make me ask you to do somethin' you don't want to do."

Her eyes were on her hands, wringing the skirt of her dress like a small child awaiting a scolding. "It's not something I don't want to do," he admitted for the first time, both to himself and to her. Seeing Noah Eastman still so bitter about his wife after all this time had touched a responsive chord within his own soul. It was time to move on, or nearly time, anyway.

"Then you'll . . .?" she asked, her eyes raised to him like a supplicant begging forgiveness.

"No," he said, shaking his head sadly. He wished, truly wished, he could do as she asked, but Elvira's memory was too fresh, his conscience too strong, his obligations too clear. "We cannot always do what we wish, Sissy. I must wait the year as much for my own peace of mind as for Elvira's dignity. Can you understand that?"

She nodded, sad eyes locked on his.

"Can you accept that?"

She nodded again, without hesitation.

"And we'll not discuss it again? I will not, cannot, change my mind, and I so do not wish to disappoint you again."

She shook her head. "I won't ask you again."

Taking her in his arms and comforting her would have been easy, but Miller prided himself on never taking the easy way out. His hands stayed behind his back and he rocked gently on his heels.

"Well, then," he said, trying to inject some lightness into his voice. "Is there anything else I can do for you today?"

He was anxious for her to leave now that the argument had been settled to his satisfaction. The mail still awaited him, and among the other correspondence he had noticed a letter from the Minister of the Johnstown Methodist Church in Pennsylvania. He had already collected a tidy sum on behalf of Wylene Eastman, much to his surprise, since Noah Eastman was still rather new to Van Wert and not a particularly friendly individual. Of course, people gave because Miller had appealed to their better nature and as always they responded to him.

"I'd better go," she said, rising and heading for the door when she sensed that the conversation was over.

"Looks like rain," he said, as he opened the door for her. "Better take care."

"Oh, I'm a hearty soul," she said over her shoulder as she headed out into the wind.

After Elvira, he hoped it was so.

The first drop of rain, fat, cold, and hard, hit Annie just as she and Blackie arrived at the Eastman farm with the cookies she had baked for the girls. She grabbed her basket, scrambled out of the wagon, and ran under the porch roof like a protective mother hen anxious to keep her chicks dry. As if her day hadn't gone badly enough, now she would have to return home drenched and cold and with little to comfort her.

At the far end of the field, Ethan and Noah were mere silhouettes barely visible against the horizon. Annie couldn't imagine how they had managed to work through the dust storm. Surely, though, the rain would stop them.

Her firm knock was answered by Mrs. Abernathy, a heavy woman with a perpetual frown on her face. Annie and she had no more than a nodding acquaintance from town, and she waited patiently for Mrs. Abernathy to invite her in.

"Yes?"

"Hello, Mrs. Abernathy," Annie began politely. "I've come to see the girls."

Hannah had followed Ruth Abernathy to the door and, with a finger twirling her curls, had her eyes glued on the basket Annie was holding. Julia was nowhere to be seen.

"Raining?" Ruth asked, ignoring Annie's request and looking around her. "Felt it in my bones since last night."

With bones buried as deeply in fat as hers were, Annie marveled that Ruth could feel anything. "I guess the wind brought it. Looks like it's about ready to pour. Felt the first few drops already. And nothing could be more welcome than rain, huh? May I come in? I've got something for the girls." She waggled her fingers at Hannah, whose eyes shone brightly in answer.

Shouts from the field drowned out Ruth's answer.

"Rain!"

"Hallelujah! Rain!"

As if the sky was waiting for the two men's announcement, it opened up to their cheers and applause while they grabbed each other around and danced toward the house.

"Sissy!" Ethan yelled. "Hey! It's Sissy!" He was like a drunken man, sliding toward the house, the rain pelting him and flattening his hair against his head. He pretended to wash with it, rubbing his armpits, scrubbing his face, slapping his shirt.

"'Down went McGinty,'" he sang, "'to the bottom of the sea. He must be very wet, for they haven't found him yet. . . .'"

Annie licked her lips and imagined the rain falling on her, washing her hair and her clothes and rinsing away the dirt of three months of drought. Before she knew what he was doing, Ethan grabbed the basket from her hand, shoved it at Ruth Abernathy, and dragged her off the porch and out into the storm.

"Ethan!" she yelled. "My dress!" But he was swinging her around, kissing her cheek and singing about the bubble where McGinty ought to be.

Hannah inched her way toward the edge of the porch in time for her father to scoop her up in his arms, despite Mrs. Abernathy's protests, and twirl the little girl about while the rain drenched them. He too was singing, and Annie couldn't stop herself from joining in. Eyes closed shut against the rain, she tipped her head back and opened her mouth, letting the drops pound her tongue and pool in her mouth.

Ethan released her and she tottered until she almost lost her balance. Then arms were around her again, and she was hugged until her feet came up off the ground. Only a few minutes ago it seemed like nothing would ever change. The drought would last forever and she would be stuck on her dirty farm with her brother and his wife for what might as well be eternity. Now the wind had shifted and rain was soaking her to her very soul and anything was possible.

When she opened her eyes, it was Noah Eastman's smiling face that she found just inches from her own.

Rain! Glorious rain! Rain that would water the crops and save the harvest and fill the barrels and make the front of Annie Morrow's light-brown dress stick to her body, revealing two ripe breasts with stiffened peaks. He hugged her to him again and felt the strength in her, the firmness of her body.

Her face, her hair, her neck, everything was dripping with clean fresh water and he wanted to lick her skin and see if she was as sweet as the honey she always brought to mind. He settled for kissing the top of her head.

Her eyes were wide with surprise, but before she could object, he was swinging her around and pretending it was the rain that had him so heady he was like a drunken man. God, but her skin glistened in the rain like gold. A strand of her hair was pressed against his lips, and he caught it with his tongue and sucked the rainwater from it. Oh, she made him crazy! Crazy enough to pull the pins from her hair and spread the silken strands out with his fingers to let the rain get at all of it.

And all the while he saw the wonder in her eyes and shrugged it aside. "Rain!" he shouted again. "Isn't it marvelous?" He lifted the tail of his shirt to her face and wiped her eyes. He was touching her face! A finger brushed her cheek, as soft as his daughter's. "There. Can you see now?"

"Mr. Eastman," she began, and he could feel the reserve in her body, "I think you'd better let me loose."

Ethan chose just that moment to close in on them with Hannah in his arms. The little girl was laughing and waving her arms, but the moment Annie saw her, she sobered.

"She's cold," she said, extricating herself from his embrace and taking his child from Ethan's arms. "Come on, sweetie. Let's get you out of these wet things."

She headed for the house, her body clearly outlined in her wet dress. He followed at enough of a distance to watch the sway of her hips beneath several layers of fabric. On the porch Annie wrung out Hannah's dress, first just the skirts, then, seeing the futility of it, slipping it over her head and throwing it across the railing. The little girl shivered and Annie hurried her toward the door.

"You'd better dry her off," she said to Mrs. Abernathy, when the older woman opened the door and shook her head in disgust.

"Don't you come in here dripping all over the place," she scolded the adults on the porch. "All that water's gonna turn to mud in here."

With that she slammed the door and left the three drowned rats making puddles on the porch.

6

Noah and Ethan, being men, had both taken
their shirts off and wrung them out. But of course, Annie
couldn't do the same. Noah could see her shaking with
cold while he and Ethan tried to wring out her skirts without getting overly personal. Finally he decided it was his
house and Mrs. Abernathy worked for him and he'd be
damned if he'd let the woman he planned to marry freeze
to death on his own front porch. Planned to marry? He
nodded his head as if in answer to his own question.

With a firm grip that seemed to say it was decided, he
threw open the front door, grasped Annie's hand, and pulled
her into the house. "Mrs. Abernathy," he said as if he'd just
inherited a title, "get some towels and bring them into my
bedroom. Miss Annie, you go in there with Mrs. Abernathy,
get out of your wet things, and find something decent
enough to come out here in when you're done. I'll get a fire
going in the stove and you can warm yourself and dry your
honey—I mean your hair—when you come back out."

The women stared at him without moving.

"Go ahead," he said, like a schoolmaster sending an errant child from his classroom. He headed for the stove but stopped when he realized that no one was doing as they had been told. "What's the matter with all of you?"

Ethan whistled under his breath and picked up Hannah, who was snuggled deep in a threadbare towel. "Well, who anointed your daddy the pope?" he asked the little girl.

Before Noah had a chance to answer that criticism, Mrs. Abernathy voiced one of her own. "I don't take to bein' ordered about," she huffed, but she headed for the linens all the same.

As for Annie, he guessed she was just too cold to be thinking straight. She remained in the middle of the room, her teeth chattering, a pool forming by her feet. Her jaw hung open slightly as her eyes scanned the rows of books he had lined up on every surface around the room.

"And you'll get those boots off, too," he told her. He noticed his command of the English language had miraculously returned, and when she remained glued to the floor he decided to test his limits. "Madam," he said with great authority, "you may either divest yourself of your sodden garments or I will—"

"Divest?" she asked in a small voice that made him feel like a pompous fool.

"I think you'd better get out of your wet things," he said, chuckling at himself. He surely didn't want to make her feel any more ill at ease than she undoubtedly already was. "I've clean shirts and overalls in my bureau," he added.

He gestured toward his room and she'd already started for it when it dawned on him what he had suggested. He'd actually told her to go through his drawers. What that woman did to his mind!

"Wait! I'll get them for you," he said, racing her to his room and pulling things out like some animal foraging through a refuse pile. Everything he owned would be too big for her, but he supposed she would manage to make do. "I'm sorry I don't have anything more—" he started.

"I really should go home," she said before he finished. He eyed her soggy garments and tried to send her a look that said she was being foolish. It seemed to work as well as his tongue, since she took the pile of clothing from him in his doorway and went obediently into his room. Mrs. Abernathy followed her and put two towels that looked like he'd used them to clean a pig's trough on his bed.

"You ain't gonna put them men's pants on, are you?" she asked Annie, who by now was shivering so badly that he wasn't sure she'd be able to undo her own buttons.

"She will, if she knows what's good for her," Noah said. "And you will help her." He closed the door firmly, without slamming it, and turned to find Ethan and Hannah gaping at him, both wide-mouthed and big-eyed. "What are you two staring at?"

"Why, Noah, I just ain't never seen you so . . . so . . ."

"Overbearing?" He could see Ethan had never heard the word before. "Bossy? Loud-mouthed? Biggety?"

Ethan laughed at the last description of his employer. "Yeah," he said. "Biggety. I ain't never seen anyone tell Sissy what to do."

"Well, she was cold and wet and uncomfortable." Noah defended himself. Even a woman as capable as Annie needed someone to tell her what to do every now and then. Some women were so busy taking care of others they neglected to take care of themselves.

Ethan laughed and rubbed his cold arms. "And I'm damn sure I never seen Sissy do what anyone ever told her, leastwise till now."

A few pieces of coal got the stove going, and Noah rubbed his hands over it, then signaled for Ethan and Hannah to join him. The three stood trying to warm themselves as they waited for Annie to join them. It wouldn't be long before he'd have to lay in a supply of coal and get the furnace fired up for the winter. He made a mental note to check it out before the weather really turned cold.

Mrs. Abernathy came into the room with Julia trailing behind her. "Don't you follow me, you bad little girl," she was saying. "You ain't gettin' none of those cookies after what you did in that bed of yours."

Naturally, Julia began to cry, and just as he was about to get her, Annie came into view. She had a towel wrapped around her hair, framing a face that glowed from the cold rainwater, his plaid shirt, the sleeves rolled several times over so that her hands showed beyond their edge, and his overalls. The denim straps came down over her breasts, the top edge of the bib nestled somewhere beneath them. The waist fell across her hips, the crotch nearly between her knees.

She shuffled into the room in bare feet and stood waiting.

"Come by the fire," he said. "And Julia, come say hello to Miss Annie."

Annie came toward the stove, looking like an angel God had dropped in a hayloft, her smile soft and warm and directed at little Julia's tear-streaked face. "What's this?" she asked the child, touching her cheek. "Are you raining, too?" She knelt down beside the girl and searched her eyes, her eyebrows, her forehead.

"What are you doing?" Hannah asked. She moved closer to Annie and watched the woman examine her sister's face.

"I'm looking for clouds," Annie said matter-of-factly.

"Clouds?" Hannah asked.

"Mmm," Annie said, as if looking for clouds on a child's face was a serious business. "Clouds."

"What will you do if you find them?"

"Why, blow them away, of course," Annie said. "Oh! I found one!" She blew and blew against Julia's forehead until the child began to giggle. Then Hannah started laughing and Ethan joined in. "Where's that basket I brought, Mrs. Abernathy? I've got something for the girls in there, something I promised them yesterday."

Both his daughters began to bounce on the balls of their feet, their faces lit with the kind of excitement usually reserved for Christmas or their birthdays.

Mrs. Abernathy stood like a stone wall, her hands crossed over her pendulous breasts. "Julia ain't allowed to have any treats, Miss Morrow. She's bein' punished for soilin' her sheets again."

Julia's face fell, crushing Noah's heart. The child was only two, but Mrs. Abernathy was sure that Julia was willfully refusing to use the child-sized chamber pot with which Hannah had been so successful, and that the only way to get her into the right habit was to be strict with her. He had forbidden the woman from spanking the child over the matter, but he had agreed to the punishment as a compromise. Now he wasn't sure he had done the right thing. It was one of the problems he had planned to ask Annie about before he met her. He was ashamed to admit that, once he had seen her, the question had simply vanished from his mind.

Now she was looking up at him questioningly. When he was silent, she said, "I made the girls a promise. Are you asking me to break it?"

"No," he stammered. "Of course not." Then to Mrs. Abernathy he said, "Please get Miss Morrow's basket. I believe she's won her point."

The smile on Annie's face was as bright as the ones lighting Hannah's and Julia's. And all three got even brighter when she opened the basket and the girls saw the treats that waited for them inside.

As for Noah, his treat was sitting a few feet away from him on his kitchen floor clad in his overalls, two small red feet close to the stove.

*   *   *

The house was dark when Annie returned home. Bart was no doubt still at the Leemans'. She tied the wagon out front and headed for the house. Bart would unhitch Blackie and put him down for the night.

After all the noise and commotion at the Eastman farm, the quiet house was lonely and bereft. The parlor suite sat forlornly in the living room, its worn seats calling out for the children who once sat there. "Keep your feet off the divan," she'd told them often enough, her words echoing the ones her mother had used until she died. Now her mother was gone and all the children had moved on. But the divan still stood in the parlor in readiness.

If she had it to do over, she wondered whether she would care about the children's shoes dirtying the sofa. All her standards seemed to be knocked out of kilter lately. Everything she'd believed all her life was somehow topsy-turvy. And if all her beliefs were at sixes and sevens, she didn't even want to think about her feelings.

The house smelled stale and stuffy, and Annie went around opening the windows an inch or two despite the rain that was still coming down hard outside, all the while thinking about the day. She was still smarting from Miller's rejection, even while she consoled herself with the knowledge that he did care for her. She had no doubt after today that he did want to marry her and would do so when the time was right.

Upstairs she went from room to room with a lamp in her hand, seeing to the windows. In Francie's room she discovered a pile of her belongings at the foot of her old bed. Anger welled up in her and then subsided as quickly as it had flared. Bart had only meant to be helpful, she supposed. In a way it was kind of nice that he was so eager to be married and get on with his new life. People in love should be impatient to be together. Of course, it was his lack of patience that made this hasty marriage necessary in the first place.

If only he and Willa could have waited until spring. Then she and Miller would already be married, and everything would have worked out the way she planned.

Through the window she saw Bart come riding up on Paint. His collar up against the wind and rain, he rode the horse straight into the barn, only to come out a few moments later to unhitch Blackie and lead him in as well. For just an instant she wondered what it would be like to be Willa, waiting upstairs for Bart to come home to her. Not that she had any great affection for her brother. There were times she could hardly stand him, but to be someone's wife, to have someone to depend on and turn to and share burdens with—now that was something she envied.

And the fact was, she would have it herself, and soon. What was a few months when she would be able to spend the rest of her life not just as someone's wife, but the *Reverend Miller Winstock's* wife. A chill ran through her and she hugged herself, running her hands up and down her arms to warm them. Always before she had been eager at the prospect of marrying Miller and moving to town. Now suddenly she looked out over the dark quiet farm, moved by the years she had spent toiling there, raising her brothers and sisters and tending her garden. Life in town would be a big change.

Her brother ran toward the house, his feet splashing in the puddles of water the dry earth couldn't absorb fast enough. The door smacked open below her and then slammed shut.

"Shit!" he shouted.

At his voice, her common sense returned to her. She would love living in town with Miller, she thought with a smile. Good-bye Bart, good-bye mud, good-bye cussing.

His heavy boots thudded on each step as he climbed to

the second floor, muttering to himself about the goddam rain and how was a man expected to make a living from God's earth when God seemed hell-bent against giving him the right conditions to do it.

"You in here?" he asked, poking his head in the door of Francie's room.

"Yes, Bart," Annie said with a sigh. "I'm in here. I see you brought in some of my stuff for me."

"Well?" he asked, obviously waiting for something. When she didn't answer, he said, "You set a date then?"

"What?"

"You and Miller. You were there long enough. I didn't leave till close to seven. Went over to Willa's for dinner when I seen I wasn't gonna get none here. So when is it?"

"When is what?"

"When are you gettin' married? Ain't that what took so long?" He stepped into the room and tried to get a better look at her. Annie shrank closer to the wall.

"No."

"Well, you mind tellin' me what kept you at the reverend's house so long? He and you didn't—I mean, you two weren't all alone? At his house? Just you and Miller?"

Annie didn't like his tone or his implication. Did he really suppose that she and Miller would succumb to their baser instincts just because he and Willa had? "Bart!" she said with a huff. "What are you thinking?"

He shook his head as if to clear it. Annie could feel raindrops that flew from his hair hitting her face. "I don't know." He laughed. "You and the reverend." He laughed again.

"What's so funny?" It wasn't as if they were too old or .decrepit to share some passion eventually. They were just mature enough to keep it reined in until the appropriate time.

"It just hit me, this picture of you and Miller." He was laughing so hard he plopped down on her bed in his wet clothes.

"Well, get them dirty pictures out of your mind. I wasn't even *at* Miller's most of the time."

Bart stopped laughing and leaned closer toward her. He squinted at her in the dim light and cocked his head. "Turn the light up, Sissy. It's damn dark in here."

"What do you want anyway, Bart?" she asked. She left the lantern as it was.

He reached out and pulled her arm so she stood only a foot or so from him. "What the devil? What you got on, Sissy Morrow? Are you wearin' a man's pants?" He grabbed the lantern and turned it up.

Annie stuck her chin out and glared at her brother defiantly. Who did he think he was, bellowing at her and demanding to know things that were none of his business?

"Where did you get them clothes?"

She shrank away from the light and the disappointed look in her brother's eyes. "They're Mr. Eastman's."

"You want to tell me how you come to be in Mr. Eastman's overalls?" His voice was tight, and she knew it was taking all the control he had not to bellow at her.

"I took some cookies over to the Eastman girls, if you must know. I got caught in the rain, and Mr. Eastman lent these to me to come home in." Outside a screech owl celebrated his find, but in the stuffy little room where Annie and her brother stood staring at each other there was only the sounds of Bart trying to get his breath under control.

Finally he asked, "You don't want to marry Miller, is that it?" There was genuine concern in his voice. "You just want to stay on here with me and Willa?"

"No! I don't want to stay here at all. You know what I want, Bart, as well as I do. I want to move into that fancy house of Miller's with his plumbin' and his 'lectricity and take care of him and—"

"Listen to me then, Sissy. You ain't pretty enough to be messin' around with what ya got in your pocket. Miller wants to marry you. He ain't lookin' for beauty or smarts or nothin' but goodness and faithfulness. Well, you sure got that in abundance. Or ya did . . ."

The words stung and Annie bit her upper lip to keep her emotions under control. It wasn't enough to tell her that she wasn't beautiful or smart. He had to imply that she was untrustworthy simply because she had been at Noah Eastman's farm in a rainstorm.

"Well, I guess it's no wonder I ain't married yet then, is it?"

His tone softened. "Aw, Sissy. I didn't mean you wasn't a good catch or nothin'. I just don't think you ought to be nowheres near that Eastman fellow. Don't you see the way that man looks at you? He drools like a hound dog who's smelled a bitch in heat."

"Ugly as a dog but the man still wants me? He must be pretty desperate there, Bart."

He grumbled some words she couldn't make out and then recovered himself somewhat. "God in heaven, Sissy, don't ya know nothin'? A man's got needs and a woman has ways of satisfyin' them. He ain't lookin' at a woman's face when he's tryin' to bury himself inside her. And he ain't worried about the rest of her life neither. He's thinkin' on one part of his body and hers and the rest of it be damned until he's done. And when he'd be done with his needs, he'd be done with you." He shook his head as if she were hopeless.

"I wouldn't be throwin' too many stones, mister, if I was you. Were you thinkin' about Willa when you gave in to your lust and planted your seed? Were you worryin' about *her* future?"

He ran his hands through his hair and looked around on the bed for something to dry it with. He looked to Annie as if he expected, after all he'd said, for her to provide him with a towel. He could freeze to death before she'd give him a handkerchief.

He shook the water off like a dog and sat on her bed as if pondering something of great importance. Finally his face brightened a little.

"Maybe it ain't as bad as all that. Maybe he's hopin' to marry you. After all, you could raise up his girls for him. Lord knows you're good at that. And Ethan says he don't know shit about farmin', so you could help him with that too."

"So now you got him wantin' to marry me? Did you forget how ugly I am?" Was there a grain of truth in what Bart said? Did she look good to Noah as someone to look after Hannah and Julia? Hadn't he said something about how he admired the way she'd raised Francie and Ethan? And what about his interest in Francie? Was one Morrow just as good as another when it came to raising his girls? And who cared how Noah Eastman thought she looked anyway? She wasn't marrying him, she was marrying Miller, who was surely above looking for beauty and certainly wasn't in need of someone to watch his children.

"Now, Sissy," Bart said, the wheels of his mind spinning so fast Annie thought she could see them. "Nobody said you was ugly. In fact, you're kinda pretty in a different sort of way. Sort of like a boy who ain't come into his manhood yet."

"Oh, thank you," Annie said, tears blurring her vision. "What a lovely thing to say to the woman who has cooked for you and cleaned for you and taken care of you for seventeen years. I always wanted to hear that I looked like a boy!"

"I didn't mean it like that," Bart said, assessing her openly. "You got nice eyes and a pretty smile, and you ain't got an ounce of fat on you, without you bein' scrawny either."

It was sad to think these were probably the nicest things Bart had ever said about her. She stood still, bearing his scrutiny in the hope that he'd come to the conclusion she was not as awful as he had first imagined.

"The truth is, with a little lace and ruffles you wouldn't be half bad. If you dressed like Della or Willa, and curled your hair, and—"

Holding her up to Della and finding her lacking was one thing, but she'd be damned if he was going to put her up against Willa and find fault.

"Willa has a horrible nose," Annie said. She hadn't actually meant for it to come out, but she was never good at hiding her thoughts.

Instead of being angry, Bart laughed. "Don't she though? But she's got other charms—the way she laughs, the way she moves her head in that girly way, her walk— you know what I mean. She's all woman, Sissy. I bet she ain't never had dirt on her hands."

"Fine lot of good she'll do ya on this farm, then," Annie said. The truth was she had no idea what Bart meant. *Movin' her head in a girly way.* What way was that? Did men move their heads different from women? And was she moving hers like a man?

"I wasn't lookin' for a helpmate, Sissy," Bart admitted. "I wasn't really lookin' for a wife, if ya wanna know the truth. But now that I'm gonna have one, and a baby too, I sure am glad it's Willa. I won't mind doin' all the work myself, knowin' what's waitin' for me at the end of the day."

"Are you telling me you love Willa?" Annie asked. *Need* was something she could understand. Even lust, while she couldn't condone it, she could accept. Contentment, what she felt with Miller and the prospect of spending her life serving him, she could agree to. But love? Love was something, especially with regard to Bart, she just couldn't fathom.

His face broke out in a surprised smile. "Yes," he said. "Between me and you, now, yes."

"Bart! That's wonderful," she said, pretending to be glad for him, when all she really felt was confused.

"What about you? You love Miller?"

"Of course," she said, smiling at him as brightly as she could. Surely she loved Miller—as much as he loved her, anyway. Maybe some people weren't meant to love. Maybe some relationships were based on other, higher things.

"Then if I was you, I'd stay away from Noah Eastman. Just the way he looks at you don't seem decent. I don't know what Miller might think if he saw Eastman sniffin' your skirts." He looked her over, smiling at the overalls she wore and pointing. "Or his own trousers coverin' your legs."

"Miller has nothing to worry about," Annie assured him. "I'm not interested in Noah Eastman. I spent my whole life on a dirt farm raisin' kids that weren't mine. I'd have to be crazy to do it again, don't ya think?"

Bart looked over his sister again, taking one of her hands and measuring it against his. He folded the tops of his fingers over hers, making her feel small and almost delicate. "I don't know," he said. "Maybe this life suits you, after all. I don't know."

But half an hour later, Annie knew, as she pulled the covers up under her chin and tried to fall asleep. The air smelled wonderfully fresh and new from the rain. A cool breeze ruffled her hair and tickled her nose. She knew for a certainty that farm life didn't suit her at all. She was meant to rise above it. Inside her was an elegant lady just bursting to come out and meet society.

But each time she closed her eyes she saw herself dancing in the rain with Noah Eastman, his smile squinting his very blue eyes and his laughter filling her ears. And she felt the hug that Hannah had given her when it was time to leave, and Julia's sweaty brow which she'd kissed goodbye as the child slept on the sofa, unwilling to be sent to bed before the party was over.

Oh, no, she thought, her train was finally coming in, and she wasn't about to let it get derailed by some sweet-talking widower who needed someone to take care of his girls and make him a decent meal. No matter how desirable he might make her feel.

"Mrs. Miller Winestock," she whispered aloud. "In a few months I will be Mrs. Miller Winestock."

Cold damp air washed over her and made her shiver. Nestling deeper into the covers, she found it impossible to find any warmth.

7

By Saturday Annie had moved all her things out of the bedroom that for the last two years she had called her own. Her dresses hung once again in the closet she had shared with Francie and Della. Her underthings lay folded in the drawers that she had used as steps to get to the top of the dresser before she was tall enough to reach there on her own. Her shoes, one pair of oil-grain buttons so worn down at the heels they were only suitable for working in the garden or helping Bart, and her dress boots, India kid with more polish than leather left on them, sat by the foot of the bed.

Francie had taken almost everything she owned to New York. Della, over the years since her marriage to Peter, had stripped the room of every trace of herself as well. Now, as Annie looked around, the room that had held her two beautiful sisters, their clothes always strewn about, their laughter and their squabbles regularly exploding through the walls, their lavender and rose water forever scenting the air, seemed empty and lifeless.

Bart was humming in the room he was to share with his bride. Annie heard him so clearly she might as well have been in the room with him. For the hundredth time she thought about what that would mean for her this evening, and all the evenings to come, until she would take her own vows and join Miller in his bed at the beautiful house on Summit Street.

She concentrated on his bedroom as she remembered it. Elvira had been a great one for gewgaws and lace, and every piece of furniture, each the choicest quarter-sawn oak, was covered with a handmade lace doily. Because she had been confined to her bed for much of the last year of her life, her sheets had been ordered specially from a store in New York called Bloomingdale's, and they were fine linen rather than the muslin Annie was used to. The headboard, against which she had propped Elvira nearly every day for months on end, stood taller than even Miller or Noah Eastman.

Noah Eastman. Now what would make her think of him? Especially now when she was imagining herself in the beautiful bedroom with the fancy French bevel plate mirror and the rose carpet. She pushed the thought of Mr. Eastman aside with more difficulty than she wanted to admit. It was hard enough thinking about sharing a bedroom, and a bed, with Miller. Letting Noah Eastman into the same imaginings was downright indecent.

Bart had generously taken over her chores for the morning, milking Edwina and Harry—named by Ethan when he was too young to be argued out of a man's name for a cow—and feeding the chickens, which Annie had always refused to name on the grounds that if they named them, how could they eat them? In return for doing her chores, Bart expected her to remove the last vestiges of her belongings from his soon-to-be bridal chamber.

Of course, he was right. There shouldn't be any traces of another woman in the room he shared with his wife, even if the other woman was only his sister.

Which brought her mind right back to the bedroom on Summit Street and all Elvira's belongings scattered about it: her hairpins resting on the small table beside the bed, her robe thrown over the footboard, her dainty slippers tucked beneath the bed in case she was feeling up to a trip to the water closet.

Ah, the water closet. More than anything else Annie Morrow coveted in this life, despite the sin of it, she coveted her neighbor's bathroom. In all her twenty-six years she had never taken a bath anywhere but in the kitchen. Except for the coldest days in winter she had trekked to the privy out beyond the toolshed every day of her life. While she had a pump for water in the kitchen, if she wanted to wash in the privacy of her own room it had always meant hauling water up the eleven steps to the landing and carrying what hadn't spilled the rest of the way to her room.

Two families she knew had installed wind-wheel pumps, one with great success, the other with enough problems to convince Bart they'd be better off without one. When Orra Dow, who called the wind pump a blessing, showed her the water tank in the small room off her kitchen and explained how she was able to heat the water before it went into her tub, Annie thought she would just die from envy. It might not have been very Christian, but Annie was surely looking forward to inviting Orra over to the house on Summit Street and letting her use the fancy water closet once she and Miller were married.

Married. Once she and Miller were married.

If Bart hadn't stopped humming and begun banging drawers and cursing, Annie supposed she would have daydreamed the whole day away. Instead, she put away the last of her underthings and went to see what had Bart so riled.

"Ain't I got even one clean shirt?" he shouted when he saw her in the doorway. "I can't get married in an Electric lacing shirt! Everyone'll think I'm in a hurry to get undressed!" He held the navy-blue shirt with the button-on lacing placket out in his extended arm as though he didn't want it to touch his freshly washed body.

"No, I suppose you can't," Annie admitted, trying hard not to laugh at the sight of her freshly shaved brother, his face a mess of tiny rags that clung to the nicks on his cheeks like sugar dots on her best cakes. She'd never seen him so nervous and hadn't the heart to prolong his agony. "Top of the closet," she said, gesturing with her eyebrows at the brown paper package that rested there.

Yanking it off the shelf and ripping the paper with a zeal she'd only seen him exhibit at mealtimes, he looked over the fancy laundried shirt she'd bought him at Hanson's Mercantile. Charlie had given her a hard time about allowing her to pay, saying that Bart was, after all, his brother too. But Risa had understood and they'd compromised by letting her pay the wholesale price. The pleated bosom was all linen, the shirt double stitched with French placketed sleeves. It had cost her nearly a dollar of her egg money.

The look in Bart's eyes told her it had been worth every penny. With a single finger he touched the fabric as though his clumsy hands might ruin it.

"There's a new collar too," Annie told him. "I hope it fits you. I ain't bought you a new one in a long time. You might have grown some."

He found the collar beneath the shirt and wrapped it temporarily around his neck, checking the fit. Bending his knees slightly so he could see himself in the bureau mirror, he tilted his head this way and that, admiring himself. When he turned to Annie he was so proud she was afraid he'd never get his swelled chest into his new shirt. "What I said last night, Sissy," he said quietly, "about your not bein' pretty? Well, you sure look beautiful to me right now." He looked at his face again in the mirror and pulled gently at one of the rags. "Thanks," he added. "Don't I look the dandy?"

Annie nodded enthusiastically, stunned by this new man that had suddenly come to live in her brother's body. When had Bart ever cared how he looked? Was that love's doing? And was she really learning about love from the big ox who had tormented her most of their lives?

It was too much to believe, she thought, as she went back to her own bedroom and opened her closet. The same old dresses hung there waiting for her: the green printed lawn with the barely noticeable patch; the yellow seersucker with the tear near the hem that seemed to compliment her skin; the old rose dotted Swiss that had developed a sheen from so much wearing.

Well, she supposed the dotted Swiss would do. After all, it wasn't *her* wedding. She pulled it out and laid it on the bed, then returned to the closet for the chemise she would need to wear beneath it. Once it was out of the way and she saw the dress behind it, her hand hesitated. Della had brought the rust-colored sateen dress over a few weeks ago, along with an even fancier silk foulard.

She pulled the sateen dress out and held it beneath her chin. It shimmered in the late morning sun and just running her hand over it sent a shiver through her body. Never in her life had she worn anything so fine. She sashayed over to the mirror and glanced at her reflection.

Looking back at her was her plain face, still tanned from her summer of work in the fields, her flat hair hanging close to her head in limp strands, and a dress that belonged on a fairy princess. Not only would she look ridiculous, Miller would be shocked. Why, she didn't believe in all the time she'd known Elvira Winestock, she'd ever seen her in something that actually shined. No, she'd always worn the most tasteful of clothes, befitting her station in life as the minister's wife.

She did remember some talk in her mama's kitchen before the minister and Elvira married, but she was a child at the time and all the talk about Elvira being Elmer Wells's daughter and overreaching herself hadn't meant much. Elmer had been some sort of inventor or plumber, as Annie recalled. His money, what there was of it, was earned installing furnaces in people's cellars. Looking back on it now, she supposed Elvira had spent the rest of her life making up for her father. She was unfailingly polite, soft-spoken, and never at a loss for the right thing to say.

Annie sighed. The dress in her arms sagged to the floor, and she let it drag there on her way back to the closet. Elvira had worn a great deal of black. Annie looked through her meager pickings again. Her only black dresses were her mourning clothes, worn after her father's death. They were both heavy woolen dresses, her father having died in the dead of winter at the end of 1887. If she wore either of those, she'd probably pass out from the heat.

Besides, her brother's wedding was a festive occasion and she certainly didn't want to give anyone the impression that just because he'd had the misfortune of falling for Willa Leeman that Annie saw any cause for mourning the marriage.

"Aren't you ready?" Bart asked, standing in her doorway as gussied up as ever she'd seen him. His mustache was waxed to a point that she thought just might draw blood if he wasn't careful kissing Willa after the ceremony. He smelled of Oakley's Violet Water, Willa having expressed a strong dislike for bay rum. His hair, parted in the center and slicked down on his forehead, made him look quite dashing, and Annie was quick to tell him so. More surprising than his appearance was his reaction to her compliment. He blushed.

"Why, Bart," Annie started, then caught herself. He was surely self-conscious enough. There was no call for her to add to his discomfort.

He checked his watch, pulling it from his waistcoat pocket like a banker or businessman instead of the farmer he was. In his fancy clothes he looked more like Charlie than ever, and she marveled at how her brothers and sisters looked so alike and she was doomed to be the ugly duckling. Hadn't Della even told her as much when she'd read her the fairy tale?

"Sissy? Aren't you comin'? I gotta leave here in eight more minutes." He looked at his watch again as if to check his figuring.

"They ain't gonna hold that wedding without you, Bart," Annie reminded him. "Besides, I got one more thing to give you before you go off and get yourself married." She opened the small jewel box on her dresser and reached in for her mother's brooch. To Charlie she had given Zena's ring, with which he had married Risa. To Della she had given Zena's emerald pin on her wedding day. After the brooch for Bart there was still a pair of earrings for Ethan to give to his bride, whoever she might turn out to be. For Francie's future husband she had saved their father's watch.

Bart looked at the brooch she placed in his hand. It had a cluster of little pearls and one longer pearl hung down from the gold and moved in his palm.

"For Willa," Annie said softly. "From Mama."

Bart's eyes glistened as he smiled at his sister. "I think Reverend Winestock is a real lucky man, Sissy." His voice choked and he stood silently looking his sister over as if he'd never seen her before. It made her decidedly uncomfortable.

"Go hitch up Blackie. I'll be down in a minute." She shooed him out of her room and shut the door behind him. The old rose dress still lay across her bed, looking more fanciful than ever against the patched old quilt it rested on.

"The yellow," she said aloud, her shoulders sagging with

disappointment. "And I'd better think about making some new dresses before I become Mrs. Miller Winestock." Sometimes she felt like an embarrassment to him. There was little enough she could do about her poor education and her looks. She didn't have to make it worse by wearing clothing he would be ashamed of.

The Leemans, no doubt anxious to make everyone in Van Wert County aware that their daughter was to be a married woman, had invited many more guests than even their large house could contain. Men sat on the porch railings, cigars in hand, while children played on the lawn, their mothers perched on lawn chairs watching over them like hens with chicks. Jane Lutefoot's oldest son rode in circles around the house on one of those tricycles that were suddenly becoming the rage. At the completion of each circle he took another girl and carefully helped her balance on the handle bars for a spin around the house.

Bart jumped from the carriage and headed for the house without a thought to Annie, who, being used to brothers rather than suitors, helped herself down from the carriage and scanned the yard for Risa. As she figured, Risa sat on a wicker chair amid several toddlers, her laughter carrying on the wind toward Annie.

"Well, now that the groom's here, I guess the ceremony is about to start," Risa said, rising with effort from the low chair. Annie reached over to give her a hand, but Risa waved it away. "Too soon to start accepting help." She laughed. "You'll be sick of lending a hand by the time I really need one."

Annie laughed back with the woman who had become as close to her as her sisters, maybe even closer. Annie would do anything for Risa, and Risa knew it. It was probably why she was so careful not to take advantage of her sister-in-law. Before Risa could protest, Annie scooped up Cara and settled her niece onto her hip. The child wrapped her arms around Annie's neck and planted a wet kiss on her cheek.

The little girl smelled of store-bought soap and talcum powder. It was a smell that made Annie remember bed-time, with Francie nestled up against her, warm and soft, listening to Annie weave stories of gingerbread boys and girls. She hoped Mrs. Leeman had thought to make cook-ies for the children.

"You hear from Francie?" Risa asked. "She can really write a nice letter, can't she?"

"Mmm," Annie agreed. "New York sure sounds like a fascinating place. I just wish she was out doing more instead of sitting around and writing everyone in Van Wert letters."

Risa stopped walking and turned to look at Annie. If she was waiting for an explanation, she wasn't going to get one. Risa knew who she meant, and she didn't see any need to use his name any more than she had to around her sister-in-law. Someone at Hanson's had to have helped Mr. Eastman put those notes in her groceries, and Risa wasn't fooling Annie any with those wide innocent eyes.

"The reverend here yet?" Annie asked casually as they made their way toward the sprawling house on the edge of town. Miller's house, its whimsical gingerbread facade belying its serious occupant, was just down the road. Since he was still officially in mourning, it was possible that he would only come to perform the ceremony.

"Mm-hm," Risa answered. "He's inside with Willa. I think he's counseling her about her duty to Bart. A little late, if I don't miss my guess. She's so stuffed in that silly white dress I think Bart's gonna need a cooper's adze to get her out of it."

Annie felt herself blush, but Risa paid her no mind.

"I haven't seen that handsome Noah Eastman and those adorable girls of his yet," she went on. "I wonder if they were invited."

"From the looks of things," Annie said, "there ain't a person in Ohio who wasn't invited."

"Well, maybe he's inside," Risa suggested as she climbed up the stairs, leaning somewhat heavily on the railing. "Nothing like carrying to make you feel older than your years." She smiled at Annie, a shared smile that seemed to say, Wait and see!

Annie purposely ignored her and squinted her eyes in search of Miller. When she saw him, she lowered Cara to the ground and smoothed the front of her dress, a move apparently not lost on her sister-in-law.

"Why didn't you wear one of those dresses Della gave you, Sissy? That rust one would be so good with your coloring." She pushed a lock of Annie's hair behind her ear and patted it in place. Annie felt it come loose to tickle her chin immediately.

"Not appropriate," Annie said, her eyes trying to connect with Miller's without success. He was standing with Mrs. Leeman, his head nodding solemnly as he fought to swallow her cake. He coughed, his hand over his mouth, and reached for some punch a young girl was passing around on a silver tray.

"For what?" Risa asked, still bothered about the dress. "Maybe not appropriate for a funeral, but this is a wedding. It's all right to look happy."

There was a commotion out on the back lawn that drew several people to the window. "Oh, mys" were followed by tsks and sighs.

"Don't tell me," Annie said, trying to see over Risa's head. "Samuel again."

Risa nodded her head and sighed so hard that the hair against her forehead rose in a wave before landing back exactly where it belonged. Why was everyone's hair so agreeable but Annie's? "Peter's got his hand halfway down Sammy's throat," Risa explained. "I wonder what he's got in there now."

"Probably Thomas Lutefoot's tricycle tire," someone suggested.

"Or the whole darn bike," Charlie said, as he joined his wife and sister.

Annie gave him a quick peck on the cheek and made her way into the parlor. "Miller," she said when she'd finally gotten through the crowd and found herself face to face with the minister at last. "It's nice to see you."

"About the other day," Miller said without introduction. "I'm sorry, Sissy. It's good of you to understand."

She nodded curtly. "I thought you might not be here until it was time for the ceremony." Not that she objected, of course. It was just that it seemed to her either he was in mourning or he wasn't.

"I thought about not coming," he admitted. "But Mrs. Leeman was quite pertinent."

"Oh," was all she could manage.

"It means she refused to give up," he explained, assuming she didn't know what he meant. Her cheeks reddened at his words and deepened when he patted her hand, as if to say it didn't matter that she was so uneducated.

"Actually, Reverend Winestock, I believe you meant to say persistent." The voice came from behind her, but she knew to whom it belonged without turning around. "Pertinent, of course, means relevant. We all mix up our words sometimes. The important thing is to speak so we are understood, don't you agree?"

Miller's face colored and he scratched his neck. "Mr. Eastman," he said, something apparently on the tip of his tongue. "I'm glad to see you. There is something—"

Annie felt a small hand slip into hers and looked down

to find Hannah next to her. She smiled at the little girl, but when her father patted her head, Annie gasped.

"What happened to your hand?" she asked him.

If he'd ever seen eyes that big before, he didn't remember them. Big, and the softest, smoothest brown imaginable. Prettier than he remembered, too.

"Darnedest thing," he admitted, shaking his head. "I was taking apart the furnace this morning, making sure the cold weather didn't catch us by surprise, when I found the pipe had rusted right through." He held up his hand to show the result.

"You cut your hand on a rusty pipe?" Her eyebrows drew together with a concern that touched him. She cared! Suddenly the throbbing in his hand was nothing compared to the pounding in his chest.

All he could do was nod.

"Did you clean it?" she asked, grabbing his hand and examining the bandage in which he'd wrapped it. "Did you wash it out with carbolic acid? Did you flush it with boiled water? Does it require stitching?"

"Yes, yes, yes, and no." He laughed, so delighted with her attention he could hardly remember the awful jagged cut that crossed his palm and the blood that spurted from it when he'd managed to remove what he hoped was the last of the metal.

"Perhaps you should see Dr. Morgan," the minister suggested as he removed Noah's hand from Annie's and made a pretense of examining it himself.

"It's nothing," Noah said, in an attempt to dismiss him. "Actually, I'm more concerned about the damage to the furnace. I admit I'm not an expert in the field, but according to the book I'm using as a guide, the furnace seems to have a design flaw which could surely have caused a fire."

"That's impossible," Winestock said, as though it were a personal affront. "Those furnaces have been around forever. If there was a problem it would surely have become apparent before now."

"Unless it took this long for the flaw to"—he almost said *manifest itself,* but he wanted to keep the conversation accessible to Annie, and he wasn't sure just how far her vocabulary stretched—"show up and cause a problem."

"Your reasoning is erroneous," Winestock countered, his volume rising.

"It isn't necessarily wrong," Noah said, making sure Annie understood without embarrassing her, "if the problem only occurs after years of use."

"Then it's not a design flaw, as you put it." The minister was nearly bellowing. He seemed to be taking the matter personally, and people were beginning to grow uneasy around them.

"Perhaps not," Noah said, hoping to put an end to the argument. "As I said, I'm no expert." Tomorrow would be soon enough to look into it. He'd have to order some new parts and perhaps he could find someone to help him. He'd see if Charlie might let him place the order after church and save him another trip to town.

"No, you're not," Winestock said, then recovered himself. "Nor, of course, am I. But there are matters at which I *am* considered an expert—"

"Like marrying folks!" someone shouted, breaking the tension in the room.

It didn't appear to be what Winestock was going to say, but he let the matter drop and agreed that it was time to get the wedding under way. Noah noticed how the whole Morrow family seemed to come together and, since Hannah still had hold of Annie, he stood with them, eliciting only a raised eyebrow from Annie and a wink from Risa, his ally.

Someone with an amazing lack of musical talent began

playing the organ and small children covered their ears in protest. Annie stood stoically as if the music was not some form of torture, but Noah couldn't hide the faces he was making without raising his hand and pretending to cough.

He leaned forward slightly and, with his bandaged hand covering his mouth, whispered into Annie's left ear, "The yellow in your dress brings out the gold in your hair."

Her eyes widened. She stood perfectly still, her gaze directed at the minister, who stood waiting for the bride to make her way down the aisle that was created by friends and relatives on either side of the room.

"And it makes your skin a honey color that turns a man's mind to mush and makes him spout gibberish like this while he's pretending to cough."

The corners of her mouth lifted before she could hide the smile with a hand. Little lines radiated from her eyes like sunbeams through the clouds. She cleared her throat, tried to lower her hand, and then raised it up again when she couldn't wipe the smile from her face.

Bart's bride looked like the side of a barn wrapped up in white bows. She seemed to be trussed like a turkey, her corset so tight she was turning blue, and the dress looked like it might start shooting buttons in every direction if she so much as breathed. Noah threw a quick glance around for the little boy with the penchant for swallowing small objects. If Willa took a breath he'd no doubt have several buttons down his throat before the crowd stopped gawking.

Now Annie, on the other hand, would make a beautiful bride, her deep coloring against a soft white dress, her slim body with those straight shoulders standing so proudly before God and man. He itched to pull the pins from her hair again but contented himself with blowing at the loose strands and watching them tease her cheek.

Beyond her stood Ethan, acting as best man. Ethan gave him a friendly nod, and Noah responded with a wink, anxious to show that there were no hard feelings after their conversation this morning. Ethan had asked about Wylene, and Noah had been evasive enough for Ethan's nose to get out of joint. In the end, Ethan had supposed it was none of his business, and Noah hadn't told him otherwise.

Miller Winestock rambled on and on about the sanctity of marriage, and all the while Willa was swaying slightly and Bart's arm was steadying her. Noah paid the man no mind. His attention was focused on Julia, who was beginning to rub her eyes, on Hannah, who seemed to be squeezing the lifeblood out of Annie's hand, and on Annie herself, who stood mesmerized by the good man's uninspired monologue.

She seemed captivated by the insipid minister, enthralled by Winestock's banal speech on the joys and responsibilities of marriage. Well, what did he expect? She'd probably never heard any of Shakespeare's sonnets, never experienced the purity of Elizabeth Barrett Browning's vows of love. But she would, he promised himself. She would hear them all.

It was finally over. Miller didn't think he would be able to give it his best, but he had risen to the occasion. Elvira would have been proud of him, carrying on despite his loss, uniting others and wishing them all the things he and Elvira had never been granted—children, old age, peace.

And all of it with a thorn in his side: Noah Eastman. Maybe the others didn't remember who had installed the furnace at the Eastman farm, but Miller certainly did. Stuart Eastman had thought nothing was too good for his family, not even the latest heating advances, and that kind of thinking had put him so deeply in debt that even after he was dead and buried and had left the farm to his nephew Noah, there were still two payments due the bank.

He supposed it wasn't entirely Stuart's fault. Miller's father-in-law, Elmer Wells, had made it seem as though his new furnaces were the answer to both Ohio's cold winters and the scrofula everyone knew was caused by the lack of ventilation. He'd gotten the school board to purchase one for the new schoolhouse and the Andersen Hotel had taken two. Stuart Eastman wasn't the only farmer intent on safeguarding his family from the vitiated air that led to disease. Somewhere among Elvira's papers Miller guessed there were probably original bills of sale for all the New Wells Furnaces that Elmer had installed.

His wife had saved everything that had to do with her family, though she never had much to say about any of them except her mother, whom she credited with training her to be a lady. In fact, when Elmer finally passed on, Miller could have sworn that his wife actually seemed relieved of a burden she had carried all her life.

"Reverend Winestock?" He looked up to see Bart Morrow standing before him, a grin splitting his face wide. "Or should I be calling you Miller? Come on over and have some punch with the family."

Miller's eyes followed the jerk of Bart's head and took in the Morrow clan, laughing and smiling as always, in a tight circle at the edge of the parlor. Among them was Noah Eastman, discussing something with Charlie and Ethan that had the two men guffawing and nodding at the same time. Miller's chest tightened. He had to warn the Morrows, warn the whole town, about Noah Eastman. He was a man who couldn't be trusted. Miller had the proof in his pocket, if necessary.

He followed Bart over to the group and was pleased when, at his arrival, Sissy gave him her brightest smile and hurried to his side.

"It was a beautiful service, Miller," she said. She was wearing the same yellow dress he'd seen her in nearly every Sunday at church. Della, of course, was in the latest style, her puffed sleeves hiding half the people on either side of her. Risa was in a pretty dress too, as were nearly all the ladies at the party. His eyes drifted down to Sissy's feet. As he knew they would be, they bore her old black boots, while the toe of her sister's fine kid slipper rested inches from her own.

As if she sensed his censure, she tucked her feet beneath her skirt as gracefully as she could. Well, no one could accuse her of vanity or wastefulness. Those were admirable qualities and he wished, for a fleeting moment, he could tell her so. In fact, there were, of late, so many things he wanted to tell her, but their meetings never seemed to be appropriate times to speak of his approval or his respect.

"Oh, I do love weddings," Della said, her blond ringlets bouncing around her head as she spoke. "There is so little to celebrate in Van Wert, after all. And I do love to wear my best."

"You look quite lovely," Miller said. He had come to learn when a woman was fishing for a compliment and was quick to comply. "Fetching, I would say. You should always wear green, Mrs. Gibbs. It so favors your eyes."

It was a chore to flatter the women in his congregation, but the effort was rewarded handsomely when the collection plate was passed or the church needed a new supply of coal or more volunteers to take care of the myriad things that kept a community close to God. He was grateful that Sissy Morrow wasn't one of those women who needed to be patted and praised at every turn. At this stage in his life, a sensible woman would be a godsend.

Miss Orliss from the school board worked her way into the crowd, offering congratulations to the Morrow family in general and Bart more specifically. Then she turned to Sissy.

"What do you hear from your darling Francie?" she asked. "She's such a sweet girl, and so bright too."

Sissy smiled and agreed. "She seems to be doing well at college," she said without a hint of boasting.

"Well, you know she could be a teacher right here without wasting all that time and money in New York," Miss Orliss went on. "We surely could use her, with Mr. Jackson retiring. You tell her if she doesn't want to stay in the big city, we sure want her home on the farm!"

"I'll tell her," Sissy said. Her eyes followed Ethan as he made his way across the room to that Willis woman, about whom Miller had heard a rumor or two. Miller saw the corners of her mouth turn down with disgust, but she remained politely where she was and allowed Miss Orliss to continue pumping her for more information on Francie's progress.

An altercation between two of the children broke out and Miller stood by trying to sort out the various small ones and determine who had insulted whom. One of the Gibbs twins, Miller couldn't tell them apart, had his finger pressed to the chest of the younger of the Eastman girls. The older one—Hannah, he thought her name was—was seething. Hands on her hips, she was yelling at the twin while her sister broke down in tears.

"Well, you don't have a mama," the boy said. "So mine's prettier than yours."

"James!" Peter Gibbs said, gasping. "What kind of thing is that to say? Apologize at once!"

"No, wait a minute," Noah Eastman said, and knelt down to the children.

Miller patted the letter in his pocket. He was relieved that the truth would come from the man himself. It never reflected well on the tale-teller, even if the tale was true. Better that Noah Eastman tell them all about his wife. Surely his children must know.

"James is right in a way and wrong in a way." He took

the finger out of his younger daughter's mouth and wiped her tears with his unbandaged hand. "You know your mama's gone, honey. Someone else saying it doesn't make any difference. But James, just look at these two girls. You know they didn't get their good looks from me!"

"James, I'm still waiting for an apology," Peter repeated, his hand clenching his son's shoulder.

"Mama was beautiful," Hannah said quietly, her hand tenderly touching her younger sister's cheek. "And she loved us both more than anything in the world. Right, Pa?" She looked at her father and he nodded, the pain on his face so evident that Miller had no choice but to hold his tongue.

"Any mama would love you two more than life, sweet babies, and as long as she's *here*"—he touched first Hannah and then Julia on their chests with just one finger—"you will always have a mama. You remember that."

Miller patted the letter inside his breast pocket once again, as if to make sure it was really there. A faint crackle of stiff paper answered him. Noah Eastman's big lie seemed to shrink in the presence of his two motherless girls.

"Don't know how many times I've had to tell them," Noah said, rising to his full height, his knees cracking loudly as he did. "Nothing is more important to a child than knowing they were loved."

Ethan grabbed Sissy's hand and squeezed it hard. "Guess I was about as old as Julia when Mama died. Did I ever thank you, Sissy? I don't remember."

Sissy's eyes were filled with tears. Miller supposed that was understandable under the circumstances, but he hadn't taken Sissy for one of those women who cried easily. He was glad when she managed a smile.

"Of course you thanked me, Eth," she said, squeezing his hand in return. "You thanked me by turning out just fine and making me proud of you. Mama would have loved you so."

"Please," Della said. "This talk is just too mawkish for a wedding. I hear music out back, I think."

"Not the organist, I hope," Charlie said, to a round of laughter and wholehearted agreement.

The group moved toward the door and away from Miller. He watched as Noah lifted his littler one easily onto his arm and took the other one by the hand. Her father leaned over and listened to something the older girl said, then nodded, touching her cheek gently without letting go of her hand.

Miller pulled the letter from his pocket and let the light from the window fall across the words.

Dear Reverend Winestock,

We received your letter today and must admit confusion. We do get many requests for memorial suggestions for victims of our tragic flood, but yours took us by surprise.

Our church records indicate that Wylene Eastman left Johnstown over two years ago, shortly after her second daughter was born. A letter addressed to her mother bore a New York City return address but was returned due to the death of both of her parents.

In addition to his in-laws, Mr. Eastman, who left Johnstown two days before the South Fork Dam broke, lost his father, a sister, and several cousins.

Do you wish to place a plaque in their honor?

Miller folded the letter and put it back into his jacket. He'd already collected almost twenty dollars for Mrs. Eastman's memorial. He was going to have to do something about that. Elvira would have known just what was required. He considered asking Sissy but realized how foolish that would be. This was, after all, a matter of some delicacy.

8

Thwack. *The headboard hit the wall,* again and again and again. Annie heard it clearly despite the pillow she clutched around her head to deaden the sound. *Thwack. Thwack. Thwack.*

"Oh, God!" Bart groaned. "Oh, God!"

Thwack. Thwack. Thwack.

"Oh! Oh!" Willa chimed in.

Silence. Then, "Did I hurt you? Are you all right?" The voices grew muffled, then turned to moans.

Thwack. Thwack.

"Uuuhhh!" So loud Annie wondered why the builder had bothered to put up walls in the house at all.

"You're so beautiful," Bart whispered, and still Annie heard him. "Look how you glow in the moonlight."

Look how you glow in the moonlight? Who did Willa have in there with her? That Walt Whitman Francie was always quoting? Or the other one, Sidney Lanier?

Mumbled words followed, and Annie released her grip on the pillow. She knew, vaguely, what had transpired between

Bart and his new wife. Anyone who lived on a farm had the basics down before they were five or six. But there was more, of course, to it when people did it. Animals couldn't really touch or talk. They couldn't look into each other's eyes, or kiss, or do whatever she imagined put a cocky smile on a man's face or the blush in a woman's cheek.

Thwack. Thwack.

Not again! Annie threw her feet over the edge of the bed and grabbed up her pillow and quilt. Without bothering to find her slippers she opened the door to her room and stepped out into the hall.

"Ssh." It was Willa's voice.

"It's only Sissy. Take the damn thing off! I want to see you. All of you."

She slipped quickly through the hall and hurried down the stairs. She'd try the divan first. If that didn't work, there was always the barn.

In the nearly total darkness she made herself a bed on the sofa and snuggled down into it, wrapping her arms around her middle. Well, Bart was in love. It occurred to her that it was somehow different from being married. He didn't just have a partner now. He had someone whose skin glowed in the moonlight.

Well, she thought wickedly, your skin may glow in the moonlight, Willa Leeman, but mine is the color of honey in the sun and makes a man's mind turn to mush.

She nearly choked on the thought, coughing and sputtering and sitting up on the divan in the dark. Noah Eastman. She pulled the covers up to her chin. Everyone had silly thoughts in the dark. Minds turning to mush, indeed!

Noah's hand hurt. After he'd put the girls in their beds, unhooked the wagon, bedded down the horses, and sat on the edge of his bed, he was sorry he hadn't asked Ethan to leave along with him, but it was the boy's brother's wedding, after all. In the quiet of the house he thought about the wedding. Lord, his hand hurt.

He wondered where in hell he'd hidden the whiskey. After Wylene left him he'd learned the hard way that you could either be a good father or a good drunk but not both. An ache in the heart couldn't be cured with anything that came in a bottle, but his palm was surely calling for help now.

Clutching his left wrist within the crook of his right arm, he headed for the kitchen. A drink, maybe two, and he'd rest easier for the night. By morning, no doubt, his hand would be nearly as good as new.

It didn't take him long to find the hard stuff or to down it. He'd forgotten just how much liquor could burn. It charred his tongue before searing a path down his throat, across his chest, and down into his belly. Damned if it didn't feel awful and wonderful at the same time.

By the time he'd gotten off his Sunday clothes and climbed into his bed his hand no longer ached; in fact, he was hardly aware of it. The only sensation that was clear to him was a blaze in his stomach that was still heading lower.

It had been a good day, he thought. A fine day. He'd seen Annie. Talked to her. And any day in which he had seen her and talked to her and not made an ass of himself was a fine day, indeed.

Yellow suited her, though she deserved a finer dress. When he'd noticed the tear near the hem, so carefully stitched, he wanted to rip the garment off and present her with the best dress in Hanson's Mercantile. And her boots! She was ashamed of them, he could tell. Such dainty little feet should be clad in satin slippers or nothing at all.

His eyelids grew heavy. Must be powerful stuff, that whiskey, to make him think he could give Annie Morrow what she wanted, what she needed. She also needed a good, thorough kissing, he was sure.

The thought brought a smile to his face. In just moments he would be dreaming about her, about her soft skin and her firm body and about what those honey lips would taste like when he pressed his own against them.

"Sweet dreams," he whispered in the dark, but whether it was a wish for her or a promise to himself, he wasn't sure.

The patter of rain smacking at the windows woke Annie just before dawn. Every muscle complained as she stretched out to her full height on the sofa, the heels of her feet reaching over the padded couch arm. It had been a terrible night, and not just physically. Twice she'd woken up in a cold sweat, unable to remember what had happened in her dreams.

The one dream she did remember turned her cheeks red with embarrassment. In it, she was seated in her regular pew in church and Miller was well into his sermon. She hadn't been paying attention because she could feel Noah Eastman's gaze resting on her back, undressing her with his eyes, until she sat there in her chemise and Miller pointed his finger at her. As she went to rise, even the chemise disappeared and she stood naked before the congregation. Amid the gasps and cries, a familiar voice said that her skin was the color of baked bread and could sustain him for life.

Annie's head fell into her hands. As if it wasn't bad enough that thoughts of him were invading her days, now he had found his way into her nights. No wonder Francie fancied herself in love with him. He was a man who got right under a woman's skin, the kind of man Annie should have warned Francie about, not sent her to work for.

Well, Francie was in New York, safe from Noah Eastman's charm. And that was just where she was going to stay. If Miss Orliss and the school board thought Annie would seriously consider passing on their offer of a position to Francie, they ought to be tied to their beds and locked away for a good long time. Her letters were just beginning to reveal a new Francie, one that was looking to the future. What had her last one said?

Annie rose and went to the old combination bookcase. Opening the drop leaf, she pulled out the packet of letters from Francie and chose the last one.

Dear Sissy,

Last night I went to an exhibit of photographs by a reporter from the "Evening Sun" named Jacob Riis. He is going to put them together to make a book that documents the terrible conditions in which some people in New York City live. It truly made me angry to see children and old people so without hope.

Poverty in Van Wert is nothing compared to poverty in this city, where no one knows or cares who you are. I hope someone will take their cause up and help them. I would if I were to stay in this city, which I don't intend to.

I still miss home a great deal and wish I could sit at our table and feast on the apple pies I know you must be baking by the dozen.

Noah wrote that he sees you at church (that was a surprise!) and that Hannah and Julia are getting very attached to you. Knowing you, the attraction must be mutual. Does he ever ask about me? I write him nearly every day, except in the last week or two as I have been very busy.

Tomorrow I have an exam and after that I am going to a rally at City Hall. New York is full of interesting people and things to do, but no one and nothing compares to what I left in Van Wert.

Give my love to everyone,
Francie

Annie clutched the letter to her chest. Francie was making the adjustment, just as Annie had known she would. How proud their parents would be if they could only see how well all the Morrows had turned out. In just a few more years Francie would be a certified teacher, Ethan would be settled down somewhere with a wife, no doubt, and Annie would be married to Miller Winestock.

Soft feet padded down the stairwell, and Annie looked up to see Willa coming down the steps in her white muslin bridal nightgown. Her feet were bare and she took each step carefully, the hem of her gown raised so that she could see her feet hit each stair tread.

At the bottom of the steps she looked up and her mouth formed a small O at the sight of Annie sitting on the couch. She clutched the neckline of her nightdress closed and looked embarrassed.

"I didn't realize—" she started. "Good morning, Sissy. I was just going to get some water. What are you doing down here?" She looked at Annie oddly and then, when she realized what must have driven her sister-in-law from her bed, her eyes widened and she gasped. "Did we . . . that is, could you . . . I mean . . ."

"I had a little trouble sleeping," Annie said evenly. "It must have been all the excitement of the wedding, combined with the new bed. I thought I'd come down here and look at Francie's letters, and before I knew it I'd fallen asleep on the divan." She smiled at Willa and stood up, wrapping the woolen blanket around her shoulders. "Can I make you some coffee? You could take a cup up to Bart."

"He's still asleep," Willa said in a whisper, as though suddenly their talking might wake him up. Hastily she added, "I don't know why he's so tired."

Annie fought to keep her expression under control. From what she'd heard last night, it would be a miracle if they could get Bart up before noon. "Well, tired or not, we've got church in a little while. I suppose it's not my business anymore, but I expect he'll want to be going, so you best get him up soon."

"Do you think he'd like it if I brought him up some coffee?" she asked.

"Well, yes, I do," Annie answered. "You wanna make it, or should I?"

Willa stood looking at her feet for a moment, then mumbled, "I'm not really sure how to do it."

Oh, she would be a great help to Bart, all right. Maybe it wasn't such a bad thing that Miller hadn't agreed to move up their wedding. This way Annie would have some time to teach Willa how to be a good wife. At least she could learn to make coffee

"Bart usually does the milking for me on Sundays," Annie said. "I don't suppose you know how to milk a cow, do you?"

Willa stared at her with big, frightened eyes. Annie could imagine a man wanting to take care of and protect such a woman. Good thing, too, because there wasn't much doubt he'd have to.

"I guess this is as good a time as any to learn," Annie said with a sigh as she headed for the door. "When we're done I'll show you where the feed is for the chickens, and then we can make some coffee. How's that?" She turned around and found Willa standing just where she had left her. "Willa? You comin'?"

The girl looked bewildered. She clutched at her nightgown and stared down at her bare feet again. "Are you going out like that?" she asked, pointing at Annie's sleepwear with surprise.

"There ain't no one to see us for miles," Annie said, in what she hoped was a reassuring voice. "'Cept Edwina and Harry, and they don't care what we've got on long as we give 'em some relief. You might want some boots, though."

"Yes," Willa agreed and hurried up the stairs, Annie watching the dainty way she held up her hem. Only the toes of her feet hit the steps. Instead of the clodding Annie was used to from the boys, there was hardly a sound. Was that one of those feminine things Bart was talking about when he said that Willa moved in a *girly* way?

Noah Eastman liked his seat in the Pleasant Township Methodist Church. He had a perfect view of Annie Morrow and couldn't see the good Reverend Winestock at all. Charlie had refused to open the store on a Sunday, but Risa had invited him over after church so he and Charlie could look over the catalogs and decide which fittings should be ordered first thing Monday morning. Since no money would change hands, Charlie decided it was not improper, and Risa seemed tickled at the prospect of talking to Noah without a crowd around.

The service was the same uninspired patter that Winestock had preached the previous week, it seemed to Noah. Of course, that wasn't peculiar to this minister but to religion. Every Sunday the congregation begged forgiveness of a God who spent the rest of the week dashing to bits their dreams and hopes with too little rain or too much, too little sun or too much, too little—

"As it tells us in the Good Book," Winestock bellowed, his voice reaching the back of the church and echoing there, " 'If we say that we have no sin, we deceive ourselves, and the truth is not in us.' For we know that 'great is the truth and mighty above all things.' "

The truth. He looked over at Annie for the millionth time that morning and saw the scarlet color creep up her neck. She dropped her head and covered it with her hands, but out of the corner of her eye she stole a glance at Noah. When she saw that he was staring back she turned her head away so quickly that her whole body jerked and her prayer book fell off her lap with a clatter that turned several heads.

How curious. Unless, of course, Francie had written to her, and she knew the lie he was living. Would Francie have confided in her oldest sister? He didn't for a minute think otherwise. And Winestock? Did he know as well? He studied Annie's back, the curve of her still pinkened cheek, the grace of her neck, and decided that if Annie knew the truth and its power she had kept it to herself. That would account for her discomfort, wouldn't it?

The woman was too honest not to be affected by his lie but too kind to do anything about it. A grimace caught his lips as he cursed the position he had put her in. It was only natural that Francie, still little more than a child, would have told Annie what she knew.

"We all know by heart the words of the Lord in John 8:32. Let us say them together, all of us."

The congregation answered him as one: "The truth shall make you free."

Annie pulled her shawl around her as if she were stark naked underneath, adjusting every edge just so, fidgeting in a way he had never seen her do before. The woolen shawl hid the pink dotted dress completely. It was just as well. Pink didn't suit his Annie. It was too cute and girly for so ripe a woman. With her coloring she should wear russets and golds and mosses. And she should lie in the falling leaves with him and . . .

"Pa?" Hannah pulled on his sleeve. "Everyone's leaving."

"So they are," he said, chucking her under her chin with his good hand. "Shall we leave, too?"

When he looked up Annie was already gone.

9

Sunday had dragged on, giving Annie ample opportunity to go over and over the conversation she had heard between Miller and her sister Della. After assuring his congregation that he would indeed be at the Harvest Social the following night, he had remarked to Della that he was looking forward to seeing what the latest fashion was and depended on her to keep him up to date now that Elvira was gone. Annie had felt the sting as surely as if he had slapped her face.

Now she stood in the girls' old room frowning at herself in the mirror. She had imagined the silk foulard, with its dark paisley print and black velvet trim, would look better on her than it did. She hadn't realized that Della's breasts were so much bigger than hers that the dress would gap badly at the low neckline. She supposed Della had worn the dress when she was still nursing the twins, and that accounted for the oversized bodice.

Had Annie only thought to try it on in advance, she supposed she could have taken it in. Instead she had spent

Sunday putting a hem in Willa's skirt. Willa had meant to do it, but the suddenness of the wedding had thrown off her plans and Bart had wanted to take her for a ride, despite the weather, so Annie had been stuck with the job.

There was nothing to be done about it now except hope that the rust-colored sateen dress fit her better. She pulled the foulard off and pulled the russet one over her head. Tiny covered buttons ran down the back of the dress, so Willa's knock on her door proved to be perfect timing.

As Willa fastened each button, the dress came to hug her bodice in what even Annie had to admit was a flattering way. When Willa finished with the buttons, Annie ran her hands down the satiny skirt to make sure it lay right and then set about fixing her hair in the no-nonsense bun she had been wearing for as long as she could remember. It kept the long strands out of her way while she cooked and cleaned and tended the garden. The wisps near her face never cooperated, but she had long ago ceased concerning herself with them.

"Why don't you try leaving it down?" Willa asked. She looked quite beautiful in a pink china-silk dress trimmed in silver gray. Her own hair was loose around her shoulders, a mass of curls controlled by a single ribbon that made her look younger than her years.

"Oh, I don't think—" Annie began, then turned to look in the mirror. "What would Miller—that is, Mister Winestock—think?"

Willa came into the room and stood behind Annie. She took her new sister-in-law's hair in her hands and began to play with it, watching in the mirror as she tried this style and that. "What if we just pull back the sides?" she suggested, holding two wings at the back of Annie's head while the rest of her hair hung loose, nearly to her waist. "I have a ribbon that would go very well with your dress," she offered.

Annie looked at herself in the mirror, but what she saw were Willa's hopeful eyes. The girl was anxious to do something nice for the woman who, in the course of just a day, had taught her more than her mother had in all the years she'd been at home. "That would be very nice, Willa." Annie smiled. After all, she wasn't a minister's wife yet. If she was ever going to kick up her heels a little, she supposed it had better be now.

Bart knocked on her door, despite the fact that it was wide open. Annie's startled eyes made him smile with embarrassment.

"Willa said it was more polite," he explained. He stared at Annie as if she were a stranger. "You look real nice, Sissy," he said, his voice rough.

"Willa's training you awfully good," Annie said with a smile. So what if he didn't mean it? It was still wonderful to hear.

He seemed ill at ease, standing there in her doorway looking her over from head to toe. The paper-wrapped package in his hands crackled, and he seemed to suddenly realize he was holding something. "I was on my way to hitch up Blackie. Found this on the porch. Got your name on it." He handed it to her and stood waiting for her to open it.

In Risa's neat handwriting were the words *To Annie Morrow. See you tonight.* Annie looked up at Bart, who shrugged in return, then scooted aside to make room for Willa's return.

"What's that?" she asked, reaching for Annie's hair and brushing up the sides.

"Are you sure about this hairdo?" Annie asked. She looked to Bart, rather than the mirror, and saw him nod. Standing still, she let Willa tie the hair back with the ribbon and make a fancy bow. She felt foolish wearing it like a young girl, but not only was Willa trying to do something nice for her, it was the way Willa often wore her own hair, so if she complained about how young she looked, she'd be insulting Willa in the bargain.

"Aren't you going to open your package?" Willa asked. "What could it be?"

Annie didn't remember ordering anything from the mercantile. She didn't think she'd asked Risa to loan her anything, either. And the fact that it was left on the porch certainly made her wonder. But nothing prepared her for the contents of the package.

Light brown-kid strap slippers with an opera toe, brand new, and in her size, rested in the palms of her hands. Her jaw went slack, her arms dropped to her sides, and her heart pounded against the confines of her fancy sateen bodice.

"Risa sent you shoes?" Bart asked, his face screwed up in disbelief. They both knew with another baby coming, a gift for no occasion was quite an extravagance.

"Oh," Willa said. "Did Risa and Charlie stop by today? I'm sorry we missed them."

If Risa had sent her the slippers, she'd have certainly bothered to say hello. But if she hadn't, who had?

Annie remembered the look of pity on Miller's face when he'd looked down at her boots at Bart's wedding. She'd been ashamed of the old shoes, not for her own sake but for his. The smile that lit her face didn't escape Willa's notice.

"Why, Sissy Morrow! Have you got a beau?"

Bart looked at her questioningly. She knew what he was thinking but she dismissed it. Noah Eastman had no reason to send her a pair of genuine-kid-opera-toed-one-strapped-light-brown-ladies'-sandals.

Her brother shrugged in a gesture of defeat and headed for the door. "Well, I'll hook up Blackie. You ladies wait at the door. I'll carry you to the wagon." He looked at the shoes in his sister's hands. "Don't want you messin' up those new shoes, now," he said, finally giving in to a smile.

"Carry us?" Annie said to Willa over the noise of her brother bounding down the steps.

"Oh, Bart always carries me in the rain. I thought you must have taught him that." Willa looked at her with big innocent eyes.

Bart—big, burly, brains-o'-barley Bart—always carried her in the rain? Maybe there were a few things Willa might be able to teach Annie instead of just the other way around.

Miller had had a headache all Sunday afternoon, and Monday had brought him no relief. He wondered if perhaps he had been too heavy handed with his sermon on the value of truth, but he'd had Noah Eastman on his mind when he wrote the piece, and the fact that Mr. Eastman was deceiving the community, and involving Miller in that deception, weighed greatly on him.

The warmth and friendliness that the whole Morrow family had shown Eastman at Bart and Willa's wedding hadn't been lost on Miller either. Of course, the Morrow family welcomed everyone with a joy that set them apart from the rest of the community. But Miller felt some responsibility toward the Morrows, not just because they seemed vulnerable but because someday they would be his relations. It was a relief to him that Francie had gone off to school back east. According to the rumors he heard, she had become too attached to Mr. Eastman and his girls for her own good.

The music was in full swing even before most of the town had shown up, and Miller felt every beat in his head. A cold compress would feel so good, but the cup of punch in his hand would have to suffice. He held it to his head for a moment and felt the coolness relieve the ache.

A swell of applause returned the throbbing, and he swung around to see the cause of the commotion. The newlyweds had arrived, Willa dressed to the nines, Bart holding out his arm so proudly to his new wife. Behind them a woman in a reddish-brown dress stood waiting. It took him a moment to realize it was Sissy. Something about her—no, everything—looked different. For one thing her hair was not in its usual bun but flew willy-nilly all about her as the wind from the door blew her deeper into the Grange Hall.

She seemed self-conscious in the dress, not surprisingly. It was twice the fullness of anything he'd ever seen her wear and it shined in the light as though lit from within. Had he not been so familiar with her, known the strength in the arms hidden by the full sleeves, the sensible brain beneath the silly bow, the permanent stain of canning berries on the hands that escaped the lacy cuffs, he might have thought she looked as attractive as any woman in the room. Instead, he saw her looking as foolish as she no doubt felt, dolled up in her sister's dress, no doubt, trying to be someone she most certainly was not.

She caught his eye and smiled at him. He smiled politely back. And then she did the queerest thing he could imagine. She raised the hem of her dress ever so slightly and gestured toward her feet. They were tapping to the rhythm of a waltz, and he thought she might be asking him to dance. He shook his head slightly as if to indicate that he would not be dancing, as he was still in official mourning. It took him a moment to realize that she was actually showing him her shoes. His head shake turned to a nod. They were lovely. Still, he thought it very odd for her to be pointing them out to him from across the room.

Her skirts billowed around her as the door swung open once again. Several people entered the hall, laughing, straightening themselves out from the wind that blew them in, smiling and talking all at once. Among the crowd was Noah Eastman. His two little girls were nowhere in sight.

Mrs. Abernathy hadn't been happy about it. Despite the fact that she spent her nights at the farm during the week, she still felt that her duties ended when the dinner dishes were done and the children were bathed. Noah was content with this arrangement. It allowed him to read to his girls, cuddle them and give them the love he felt they craved (which was only a small portion of the love he had for them), and put them to bed himself.

But this night he wanted to be at the Harvest Social without the children clinging to his legs. He hoped to dance unencumbered and, if his brain could manage to control his tongue, maybe even have a normal conversation with Annie. He wanted to concentrate solely on the woman who had begun to invade his days and nights, without having to keep one eye on each of his girls.

The first thing he saw when he entered the Grange Hall was the spun-sugar hair flying in the wind and whipping people within two feet of her. He had forgotten it was so long. The silky strands looked lighter against the russet fabric that hugged her back and nipped her waist. When the door was shut and her hair settled down he fought the urge to rush up to her, prostrate himself before her, and beg her to let him kiss her feet.

Instead he shook the hands of several neighbors, each of whom said something vague about his loss and seemed uncomfortable about bringing up the flood, as if somehow he didn't or shouldn't know about it. Risa saw him and smiled so brightly that he couldn't help but smile back. She had been so encouraging over lunch that he almost believed Annie would be happy to see him tonight.

Just looking at Annie's back was driving him wild. He was almost afraid to see her face. Before he was fully prepared she had turned to see who it was Risa was smiling at, and he got a view that stopped his heart. He couldn't breathe. He couldn't swallow. He couldn't talk. He stood absolutely motionless, unless one counted the dropping of his jaw.

He expected, if he expected anything at all, for her to speak to him in her usual way. She would ask about the girls, comment on the weather, ask if he'd heard from Francie, and then, when he was unable to answer, she would call his name using that honey voice of hers and ask if anything was wrong.

Instead, she stared back at him as openly as he was staring at her. But in her face he read a hundred questions he wanted to spend the rest of his life answering. *Yes, you look so beautiful it takes my breath away. Yes, you are the loveliest woman in the room—in the world. No, you should never put your hair up again. I don't know if I can keep my fingers out of it.*

He found his tongue with great difficulty. "You look lovely," he said. "The color of your dress suits you well." It wasn't what he wanted to say, but it seemed to please her.

She shifted her weight shyly, like a schoolgirl, and fussed with her hair. "I feel a bit silly, to tell you the truth," she admitted, then blushed furiously at the word *truth*.

"If we must be truthful," Noah said, "then you are surely the finest woman in the hall." It wasn't her dress or her hair he was confining himself to now. It was the very essence of the person before him.

"It's no wonder Francie is so fond of you," Annie said, biting her lower lip self-consciously. "You do have a way with words."

"I'm grateful to be able finally to get them out." He laughed and she did too, and he relished the feeling of sharing a joke with her. She smoothed her dress and lifted the skirt slightly as if getting ready to move away. He saw the toe of her slipper and the slight bit of stocking that covered the top of her foot. A bolt shot through him as strong as any pain he had ever felt.

"Well," she said, unaware of her effect on him, "I'd better go say hello to Risa and Charlie and the others."

Don't go! he wanted to shout, like some kind of fool. "Of course," he said, bowing slightly at the waist. "I do hope you'll save me a dance."

She smiled at him but didn't commit herself, and he watched her cross the room and be hugged to her sister-in-law's bosom, then passed to her brother for an equally strong embrace. His arms ached to hold her himself. His heart ached even more when he saw her approach the minister.

Winestock stood near the punch bowl. Noah supposed he was making sure that no hotheaded young man dared spike it with applejack instead of cider. When Winestock saw Annie coming toward him he smiled a benevolent smile that spoke of tolerance more than appreciation, affection more than love.

She raised her skirts with one hand and held out one foot slightly, wiggling it at the ankle and holding his arm for support. Noah imagined the conversation from the questioning look on the minister's face and the slight shake of his head, followed by the crushing sadness of Annie's face as the smile faded away.

He watched her return to Risa and point at the shoes. He watched as Risa shrugged her shoulders, true to her word as he knew she would be. He watched as Annie put her hands to her hips, demanding the truth, and turned to her brother, who shrugged in genuine bewilderment.

She glanced in his direction, then looked away, embarrassed. Her eyes scanned the room and settled on Ethan with a frown turning down the corners of her mouth. She walked over to him and gave the woman he was standing

with a polite nod. The woman looked a lot older than
Ethan, even from across the Grange Hall, and there was
something about the way Annie held herself that made
Noah think the woman was trouble. What was her name?
Tessie? It was clear that Annie didn't think very highly of
her as she turned her back to her and questioned Ethan.

And then he saw her turn in his direction, seek him out,
as he knew she would, and he nodded. *So, it occurred to
you that it could be me. Does that mean you're thinking
about me, too?*

He crossed the floor and offered his hand. The band
was striking up and she hesitated, but he wasn't taking no
for an answer. Gently, wordlessly, he escorted her to the
floor while her head turned toward Miller as if begging
him to put a stop to her movements. The minister smiled
the same patronizing smile and lifted his cup in salute as if
to say, 'Have a good time.'

And then she was in his arms, every muscle in her back
tense beneath the hand he splayed against her. He cursed
his bandage, wishing he could feel the hand it barely held
and feel the strength there.

"You're beautiful in the candlelight," he said, watching
the light flicker against her hair.

"They'll be getting electricity here before the new year,"
she said, as if to take away the compliment he had paid her.

"Pity," he replied.

They danced in silence for a turn or two, while he got
used to the feel of her in his arms, the smell of her just
inches from him, the taste of her name on his lips.

"Ah, Annie." He sighed.

"The notes, the gifts," she said, so quietly he had to
bend his head to hear her, "they will have to stop."

"They will," he agreed amiably. "After we've been married fifty years. Then it will be your turn to shower attention on *me.*"

She stopped dancing, and he nearly tripped over her frozen feet. "What?"

He felt people's eyes on them and bowed, loudly announcing his oafishness. "Forgive me. I have never been accused of being graceful. But then, 'Two stars keep not their motion in one sphere.'" She stared at him, unmoving. "They are all watching," he whispered. "Just follow my lead."

He danced with her in his arms as if she had wings on her shoes, her feet flying over his, barely landing before he lifted her and swung her around gently to land again.

"What did you mean," she asked when she could catch her breath, "about two stars?"

"It's Shakespeare. *Henry the Fourth.* Do you know any Shakespeare? He wrote the most wonderful sonnets of love. Have you heard them?" His lips brushed against her ear and he couldn't help himself. "'If I could write the beauty of your eyes / And in fresh numbers number all your graces, / The age to come would say, 'This poet lies; / Such heavenly touches ne'er touch'd earthly faces.'"

She moved in his arms as though she were in a trance, letting him take her in one direction and then another with no resistance and no will of her own. Finally the band stopped and he was forced to release her.

"Thank you," he said, watching the top of her hair move with his breath. "I enjoyed that very much."

Her head nodded slightly at his words, but her eyes were glued to the ground. Finally she raised a face to him that was a mask of confusion. "I enjoyed the Shakespeare," she admitted shyly. "I saw *Romeo and Juliet* once at the recital hall when I was very young."

"Did you?" he asked, anxious to simply prolong the conversation. "When was that?"

She started to reply but the band began to play again, and just as he was reaching for her waist, Bart appeared and took her hand.

"You're a real picture tonight, Sissy," he said. "I bet Mr. Winestock just wishes he could be in my shoes." With that he whisked her to the dance floor with more grace than Noah would have thought him capable of.

He considered it only polite to ask Willa to dance but found her dancing with Peter. That left Della, who was dancing with Charlie. Risa stood by herself, her foot tapping to the music. He approached her and held out his hands.

"Oh, I don't really think I'm up to it." She sighed. Her face brightened. "I saw you dancing with Sissy. Did she tell you how much the slippers pleased her?"

"I think she likes the gift much more than the giver," he admitted. "She told me the notes and gifts should stop."

Tapping her pursed lips, Risa was silent for a few moments. When she spoke it was with a determination Noah knew was born of love. "I hope you won't listen to her," she said. "In all the years I've known that woman, she has always put everyone else first and done what was expected of her. There is nothing I'd like to see more than Sissy Morrow happy." Her eyes searched the floor for her sister-in-law with a sadness Noah could almost taste.

"Don't you think the minister will make her happy?" he asked. He held his breath, waiting for her response. He had a lot of respect for Risa and she knew Annie so very well.

A grimace was his answer. "I don't think that man knows or cares about happiness. If the Lord didn't say specifically that we should be happy, then no, I don't think it would be a concern of his. Oh, he'd keep Sissy fed and dressed and taken care of, he'd see that she wanted for nothing, but happiness? Love? What that woman deserves after waiting so long for everyone else to find what they wanted? No, Noah. I don't think Miller Winestock will make her happy." Her answer should have stopped there. He'd have been very happy himself if she hadn't added, "No matter what *she* may think. And that's where your problem lies."

The song ended and the dancers came wheezing from the floor, laughing and trying to catch their breaths. Bart escorted Annie to the minister, who smiled and handed them each a cup of punch. Annie touched the cool cup to her chest and then raised it to her lips, her eyes darting to Noah's and then returning to Winestock's. She put down the cup and fanned herself with her hand, saying something to her companion about the heat, no doubt. He nodded and she crossed the floor and joined several others who were headed for the door to get some fresh air.

When the minister didn't follow her, Noah made his apologies to Risa and Charlie and headed for the door himself, complaining that the hall had become so stuffy he thought a bit of fresh air was in order. Risa touched his arm and squeezed gently. "I doubt," she said wisely, "that you'll find it much cooler outside."

She was leaning against a tree when he spotted her. The band had started up again and only one or two men, their cigars fouling the night, remained outside in the cool evening air. He strolled up to her and put his good hand on the tree trunk. With his bandaged one, he tapped her lightly on the shoulder.

"Oh!" she said in surprise. "Mr. Eastman. What are you doing out here?"

He was tired of the chase. The dreams and the desires were already overwhelming, but the moonlight on that angelic face pushed him over the edge.

"I think you know," he said. The tips of his fingers extended beyond the gauze of his bandage and he touched her cheek with them, only to find it was softer even than in his dreams. He tipped her chin back and let his lips graze her own. He had meant to do only that. He had meant to stop right there. He had meant only to show her his intentions.

He had certainly not planned to let the kiss deepen, to let his lips press hard against her own and open them to let his tongue play against the softness. He'd never planned on taking that full bottom lip between his teeth for even a moment, never planned to capture the sides of her face in his hands and stroke her cheeks until neither one of them could draw a breath.

And it took every ounce of will he had to finally release her, especially when he realized her small hands were actually clinging to his lapels, pulling him closer still to her trembling body.

"We can't do this," she said, shaking her head as if arguing with herself. "I'm marrying Miller Winestock. Surely you must know that. I don't know why I let you . . . how I could have—"

"Tell me," he said, his hands covering hers so that even if she wanted to, she couldn't let go of his jacket. "Does the minister kiss you like this?" He let his lips brush her temples, his breath against her cheeks as he spoke.

She stiffened and tried to back away from him, but the tree was behind her. It only took her tightness to make him back away enough to give her the room she wanted. "The minister doesn't kiss me," she said with her chin held high. "He respects me."

"And is that what you want?" he asked, his hand brushing back the hair that blew across her face, capturing a strand, and tucking it behind her ear. "Just to be respected? Or do you want to be loved?"

A crowd of people moved outside, signaling the end of another set of music. Noah backed up for propriety's sake, though he would have liked more than anything to pull Annie to his side and tell the throngs of people he was madly, wildly in love with her. He thrust his good hand deeply into his pocket and watched the emotions that crossed her face as she tried to compose herself. He saw the confusion he'd caused, and he saw the strong chin set determinedly.

"Sissy?" They both heard the minister call plainly. "Sissy Morrow, are you out here?"

"And I wouldn't call you Sissy," he said, in nearly a hiss. "You're not merely several people's sister, dear though they all are to you. You are a woman in your own right. If you would only allow it, you would be Annie, my Annie. You will always be my Annie."

He turned and walked away, his hand still in his pocket.

"Over here, Miller," he heard her say.

"Can you come inside and help with the punch?" he asked.

The last thing Noah heard, as he made his way to his buggy and climbed in, was Annie agreeing to go inside and serve everyone else. But despite what his ears might be telling him, he could still taste her on his tongue, still feel the tingle where his lips had touched hers. He had the satisfaction of knowing that she surely must be feeling it too. In the darkness he began to whistle.

She liked Shakespeare.

10

Annie fed the chickens, with Willa tagging along behind her and asking questions that Annie answered by rote. She gathered up the eggs, counting as she did, but in the end had no idea how many she had put into her basket. She milked Harry and couldn't tell Willa how the cow came to have a man's name. Harry was fairly old—she just didn't remember.

But the feel of Noah Eastman's lips against her own, *that* she remembered as if he were still pressed against her, the old oak tree supporting her when her knees began to buckle. Her mouth still tingled with the memory of his warm tongue and his foreign taste. And more strange than the tang of his mouth was her reaction to it. Even now she felt a clutch of excitement deep in her stomach, a rush of warmth that coursed lower and lower until she was aware of her femininity in a way she had never been before.

For a moment she considered the possibility that she might be in love.

"Sissy, watch where you're walking!"

Annie felt the squish of manure beneath her well-worn boots and hoped the leather would hold up to yet another hard scrubbing. Coming down from the clouds of last night's Harvest Social, she took a good look around her. Edwina was eyeing her angrily, impatient for her turn to be milked. The barn smelled rancid from the damp weather and the fact that Bart hadn't raked it out over the weekend. She was up to her ankle in cow dung, which clung to the edge of her skirts like a frilly brown ribbon of muck.

The egg basket, which Willa had been swinging as they did the chores, contained as many broken eggs as whole ones by now. That would cost her, because her egg money, along with her butter money, was nearly as important to the farm's income as their crop. This year, with the drought, it was the egg and butter money that would probably see them through the winter.

Two chickens ran into the barn, chased by a rooster who hollered at them in his randiest voice. What was he telling those chickens? That their feathers looked liked baked bread? That they turned a rooster's brains to mush?

Her laughter rang out in the barn like a madwoman's. She laughed and laughed until her sides ached. She clutched at them and laughed some more. Willa stared at her wide-eyed, her eyebrows lifting higher and higher, until she finally dropped the egg basket and ran from the barn with a shriek.

By the time Bart, with Willa trailing skittishly behind him, found Annie, she was at the pump scrubbing the hem of her dress, her shoes off, the laughter gone from her lips.

"You all right?" Bart asked. Her nod didn't satisfy him. He lifted her chin and searched her face.

"I'm fine, Bart. Something just struck me funny, that's all." She saw Willa peering around the bulk of her brother and smiled. "Sorry if I scared you. Sometimes I think sixteen years of farming has left me with manure for brains."

"Don't look like you'll be marryin' the reverend a minute too soon," Bart said. Willa whispered something in his ear and he patted her gently and nodded. "Willa's real sorry about them eggs."

Annie figured the broken eggs would have brought her about two dollars down at Hanson's. In her mind she had already settled on the fabric she was going to buy with the money, as well as the pattern she would use to make an elegant black dress that would make Miller proud. She shrugged at Bart as if to say there was nothing to be done about the eggs.

"Maybe they ain't all broken," Bart said softly. He nudged Willa toward the barn and she carefully picked her way there, skirts raised to avoid puddles, while he watched her every move.

"Don't let her worry about it," Annie said. "It ain't important."

Bart sat down on the stump near the trough and shook his head. "We got a baby comin'," he said, "or I'd give you the money myself, Sissy, I swear I would."

"The hens'll lay more eggs, Bart. Don't go worryin' yourself. And don't go worrying Willa, neither. The poor girl's got enough to learn about living on a farm without her lessons including the wolf at the door."

"You know, Sissy," Bart said, laying a hand gently on his sister's shoulder, "you're gonna make a fine minister's wife. Better than old Elvira Winestock ever was. Miller's lucky to be gettin' you."

Annie looked down at the muddy bottom of her skirts. The brown water had crept upward and soaked her petticoat as well. Her hands were wet and smelly and she knew she'd have to soak them in vinegar to get rid of the odor and get the manure out from under her nails. When she raised her head she saw clouds on the horizon. "Not half so lucky as I am to be gettin' *him*," she told her brother. "Not by half."

* * *

"Look," Noah told Ethan as the men stooped by the furnace in the low-ceilinged basement of Noah's farmhouse. He held out the worn piece of furnace pipe for Ethan to examine. "The pipe's worn through at the back side. The metal's thick enough, but it's soft. That made it easier to bend so it would fit, but it made the metal weak right where the strongest heat would be." He turned the pipe over and over in his hand, holding it up to the pale light that came through the small window near the ceiling.

"I don't know much about furnaces," Ethan admitted. "Are you saying that the fire burned through the metal? That don't make sense. Furnaces are made of metal. It can't burn."

"There's all different kinds of metal," Noah explained. "And each metal has a different melting point. You can burn right through a tin pan on an iron stove. And some metals are softer than others. The man who installed this furnace used a pipe metal soft enough to hammer into shape." He let the light fall on the dents he had found and traced them with his finger so that Ethan could see them.

"Well, don't they do that with horseshoes?"

What were they teaching the kids in Van Wert? This kind of stuff was basic science. There wasn't a child in Johnstown who couldn't have explained it to Ethan, Noah thought. "Heat," he said with a sigh. "Bending a hard metal takes heat. This was done with a hammer. The man who installed it must have thought the thimble would cover the weakened area and protect the ceiling from catching fire."

"So?"

"So the thimble wasn't long enough to do the job. So if I hadn't happened to be checking the furnace and getting it ready for the winter, the first time I fired it up the heat would have broken through the pipe and the wall would have caught on fire. That's *so*." And my girls could be dead before I'd have even been able to react, he thought.

"Furnaces are dangerous things," Ethan agreed. "That's why we ain't got one. At least, that's what Bart says, though I think he's just too cheap to put one in. You know, last year the Kellys were burned outa house and home when their coal pile caught fire and burned. Smelled that fire clear over to our place." The sound of a child crying carried down the stairs. "Lost their littlest one, Beth Ann, in it too."

The thought of a dead child sent shivers up Noah's arms. "Sounds like Julia again," he said, as he looked up toward the ceiling. "Guess I better see what the trouble is."

Ethan put a restraining hand on Noah's thigh, urging him to keep his seat. "Kids cry, Noah," he assured him. "It's part of growin' up and learnin' that the world ain't always the perfect place their daddies tell them it is."

"I hate it when they cry," Noah admitted. "If their mother were here—"

He stopped himself. Their last fight had been over letting Julia cry. The baby had been only a month old. Noah had come home and heard the baby crying and gone to see what was wrong. She lay in a wet diaper in the crib his father had made for their first child, Hannah.

"Wylene?" He'd run to their bedroom and found her reading a dime novel on their bed, still in her nightgown though it was late afternoon.

"Hm?" she said without lifting her eyes. "You home already?"

"Wylene," he said as patiently as he could, "the baby needs changing and nursing. Couldn't you hear her crying?"

"I'm not deaf," she answered. "I knew you'd be home before too long to see to her."

"And am I supposed to nurse her too?" he asked. "Wylene?" Still she didn't look up. "Where's Hannah?"

"Hm?" she said again.

The dam inside him burst then. He grabbed the book from his wife's hands and threw it across the room. Like an old cow she blinked at him without comprehending. Beneath her pendulous breasts were two wet spots, as though Mother Nature had responded to their daughter's cries without Wylene's knowledge. In the four weeks since Julia's birth Wylene had gone from Lydia Pinkham's Compound through everything on the druggist shelves and had wound up taking so many doses of Hostetter's Bitters she could hardly walk straight. At forty-four percent alcohol it was no wonder she didn't care about the girls she had brought into the world.

"Where's Hannah?" he asked again, raising his voice to be heard over the shouts of the infant in the next room.

"Your mother took her this morning," Wylene answered, lazily stretching on the bed. "I thought you'd pick her up on your way home."

The baby was shrieking and he turned to go get her. "How could I pick her up if I didn't even know she was there?" he asked, not expecting an answer.

"Just make it a habit," Wylene said. "In case."

"In case what?" he'd been foolish enough to ask as he changed the diaper on the tiny writhing being he was responsible for.

She hadn't answered him, but a week later he knew. In case she decided to pick up and leave. And he'd been foolish enough to be grateful that she had at least left the girls in his mother's hands and not just run out and left them to fend for themselves until he returned home.

For weeks he had lived as though it were only a temporary state, ignoring the comments of all the wiser neighbors who had warned him of Wylene's true nature, dragging the girls back and forth to his mother's house and trying the various combinations of milk and water and Mellin's Food Additives for Healthy Babies she gave him to feed Julia during the night. . . .

"But," he said to Ethan as he snapped out of the past and back into the present, "their mother's not here and I am, so I'll just go see what's got Julia going now." He pushed off against his knees to rise when the cries intensified.

"That there sounds like anger to me," Ethan said. "It's best you let the girls work it out for themselves."

He felt foolish asking if that was what Annie would do, so he simply nodded and sat down again and continued inspecting the parts of his furnace and comparing them to those in the book.

"I'll be leavin' early this afternoon," Ethan said after a short silence, "if that's all right."

Noah appreciated every hour Ethan gave him. Though the young man thought himself naive and inexperienced about everything but plowing a row and putting in an acre of corn, he was actually an encyclopedia of knowledge about everything that concerned a farm, and a lot more than that. He had an easy way about him that calmed the animals and at times even worked magic on the girls.

"Of course it's all right. Where are you off to, Tessie Willis's?" He'd seen Ethan joking with her at the social and hoped he wasn't seriously interested. Tessy reminded him too much of Wylene, with her sexy smile and her throaty laugh. Or maybe it was having seen her stagger down the street in the middle of one Thursday afternoon, so close to falling down drunk that in a flash all those moments with Wylene came flooding back and he found himself staring after her with such disgust it embarrassed him to remember it.

"Nah," he said. "Sissy's having the whole family out for a special dessert for the newlyweds." He lowered his voice as if he didn't want to be overheard by the pile of coal or the stack of old *Harper's Weekly* magazines in the corner. "I think she doesn't like bein' alone with the two of them all that much. It'll be nice for her when she finally marries ol' Winestock and gets off that farm for once in her life."

"Annie isn't marrying Miller Winestock," he said, as quietly as Ethan had spoken to him. "She's marrying me."

"What?" Ethan shrieked, jumping into the air and banging his head on the ceiling. "Ouch! Noah, that's great, better than great! When did you ask her? Was it the shoes that did it? When are you—"

Noah motioned with his hands to calm down and keep quiet. He knew he ought to be embarrassed, but he wasn't. "I said she was marrying me. I didn't say she knows it yet."

Ethan shook his head at his friend. "You had me going there, really you did. Does she know you're even thinking about it?"

Noah thought about the kiss they had shared by the oak tree last night. She had been as moved by it as he, of that he had no doubt. "Yes." He smiled. "I'd say she knows at least that much."

"You want to come with me to the farm?" Ethan offered. "I know Sissy'll have enough pie to feed half of Van Wert, and there'll be Soldiers on the Mountain for the little ones and half a dozen other desserts, what with Risa expecting and Sissy wantin' to start her showing."

"Soldiers on the Mountain?" he asked, having never heard of it and trying to keep the hunger out of his voice. As good as all the food sounded, the thought of seeing Annie again was so tempting he wasn't sure he could let good manners keep him from accepting Ethan's offer.

Laughing, Ethan explained that it was a dessert the whole family had a hand in inventing. "Sissy used to decorate her custard with leftover cookies. When Della was little they were Girls on the Meadow. When I was small they were Cowboys on the Range. By the time Francie was old enough to name them, Pa was in and out of the hospital so much she called them Nurses on the Ward."

"Don't tell me Annie made different cookies for each of you?"

Ethan nodded. "Samuel and James like soldiers, so that's what there will probably be tonight."

"And Risa and Charlie's little one?"

"Cara? Princesses on the Moor or some such thing."

While every sensible bone in his body told him he should decline Ethan's offer, and all the good manners and breeding his mother had instilled in him insisted that he refuse graciously, just the thought of seeing Annie tied knots in his stomach and sent shivers up his flesh.

"Well," Ethan asked, "you gonna miss a chance like that?"

"I *should* say no," Noah hedged, trying to be strong in the face of temptation.

"Miller might be there too," Ethan added. "Acting like he's already family when he ain't even made his intentions known yet."

"Does he go out to the farm a lot?"

"Depends who's countin'," Ethan said with a sly smile. "Don't it?"

The wagon pulled into the front yard, stopping near the watering trough so the horse could get a drink. From the kitchen window Annie saw that Ethan wasn't alone. As if the day hadn't gone badly enough!

Annie had spent the whole afternoon baking while Willa rested with her feet up at Bart's insistence. Then after all that resting, Willa had stirred herself to all but burn supper. Annie had been all set to shield her from Bart's temper when he'd claimed he liked his meat well done and took the portion she was sure even Blue, the setter they'd had as children, would have turned up his nose at.

She'd never seen him drink as much water in one sitting, but her admiration for his patience with his new wife grew with each mouthful he managed to swallow. He even seemed to be enjoying it, or perhaps it was just that he took pleasure in Willa's pride at having managed to turn out a meal on their stove.

Then, after Annie had done the dishes, Della, Peter, and the boys had shown up and Samuel had managed to catch the corner of the tablecloth, and before anyone knew what had happened two of her mother's plates had crashed to the floor and broken. Annie had bitten back tears when she'd picked up the pieces, and then again when Della had referred to the china as "those old plates," suggesting it was time to replace them anyway.

Just as Risa and Charlie had pulled up, Miller had come and been rather unnerved by what greeted him. It seemed as though the baby Risa was carrying had gotten its days and nights mixed up and Risa was in the throes of morning sickness when she arrived, despite the fact that it was nearly six o'clock in the evening. Seeing her mother sick had thrown Cara into hysterics, and Annie's bodice was still wet with her tears.

And now, here, waltzing up to the door as if he'd received an engraved invitation, was Noah Eastman, stealer of kisses, quoter of sonnets, buyer of shoes. He had Hannah by his good hand, and Ethan carried Julia in his arms. The foursome was laughing, but she saw Noah sober up as he approached the door.

"What's *he* doing here?" Bart asked, as he looked over Annie's shoulder and took in the crowd.

Annie's heart was pounding so hard in her chest she didn't trust herself to answer.

"Well, I guess we got plenty," Bart said, in an attempt to be gracious. "I ain't all that hungry anyway."

"There's plenty," she assured him, stifling a laugh. It was no wonder he couldn't think about dessert after all that charred meat he'd downed.

Willa opened the door and welcomed the newcomers.

Annie could hear Noah explaining that Ethan had invited him. The crowd moved amiably into the dining room, but no one took seats at the table.

Pale-faced, Risa returned to the kitchen and offered to help Annie get things onto the table.

"Now, Risa, since when do I need help?" Annie replied. "Don't you think you might like to lie down awhile? You look pretty done in."

Her sister-in-law broke a small piece of crust off one of the pies and popped it in her mouth. She closed her eyes and let the sweetness replace the sour mouth she must have had from her retching.

"I'll be fine in a minute," she assured Annie. "What happened to your blouse?"

Annie looked down at the tearstains and reached for an apron, gesturing with her free hand that it was nothing. Of course to Risa that was the same as saying that Cara had messed her aunt's dress, and Risa was quick to apologize. A moment later she quieted and her posture straightened as if she was straining to hear something in the other room.

"Is that Mr. Eastman I hear?"

"Ethan asked him along," Annie said, hoping she wouldn't get any ideas. "Which reminds me. If you're feeling well enough, I've a bone to pick with you."

Risa was breaking off her third chunk of crumb topping, but her hand stilled and she feigned a bit of dizziness that didn't fool Annie for a moment.

"Risa," Annie started, "what you're doing ain't fair. Not to him"—she jerked her head toward the dining room—"nor to me."

"He's not complaining," Risa said, giving up the act.

"It's wrong of you to be taking sides. Here you are helping Noah by slipping his notes in my foodstuffs, and I don't even want to think about what those shoes must have set him back."

Risa studied Annie so closely she was uncomfortable. What her sister-in-law was looking for, Annie couldn't imagine, but when she spoke it seemed like Risa was out of patience. "Taking sides? Is that how you see it? Do you think Reverend Winestock has come to my store and asked me to send you a message? Do you think he's tried to buy you presents and I've refused to sell him something? Don't you know I'd walk to San Francisco for a ribbon to match your hair if you wanted one? Don't you know how much I want to see you happy?"

"But I *am* happy," Annie replied, when she'd recovered herself. Though she and Risa were as close as sisters, closer certainly than she was with Della and probably just as close as she was with Francie, they had never said as much, had never put into words the lengths they would go to for each other. Risa was truly Annie's best friend. "And marrying Miller will make me the happiest woman in the world."

Risa shook her head sadly, but all she said was, "If you say so."

"So no more helping Mr. Eastman with whatever it is he is trying to do?"

"Don't you know what he's trying to do, Sissy?" she asked. When Annie offered no response, Risa continued. "He's courting you, honey, plain and simple. He's in love with you."

"No," Annie said simply and adamantly. "No. Maybe he is courting me, I don't know. Lord knows, I've never been courted before. But he is most definitely not in love with me. Why, just a month ago he was in love with Francie. The man is in love with the idea of gettin' a mother for his girls, that's all. He ain't in love with me. And he ain't gonna get Francie back from New York, either."

"That man never loved Francie," Risa argued. "She's

just a baby herself. What went on between them was all in her head."

Maybe Risa was right. If anything *had* gone on between them, Annie thought Francie would have confided in her. It had certainly seemed to her at the time that all the dreaming was on Francie's side, but now, with Noah actually courting *her,* she wondered if he hadn't encouraged the young woman's fantasies in the hope of getting her to stay and watch his girls.

Willa came into the kitchen, followed by Della and an assortment of children, all drawn by the sweet smelling desserts and having trouble waiting.

"Sorry," Annie apologized. "I was just waiting for Risa to recover her health. Seems her little stowaway isn't much for buggy rides."

"Oh," Della said, "you should only know what it's like with two! Having twins every pain is doubled, every ache is twice as bad."

"Mm," Risa said, pretending to agree. "I remember you certainly were twice as big." She smirked at Annie, who scratched at her nose to hide her smile.

"Yes, I was," she told Willa, finding a new listener for her old stories. "And my labor was twice as long, but it was worth it. Nothing, nothing," she repeated, looking pointedly at the stomachs of both Willa and Risa, "is as special as having twins. People look at you differently, speak to you differently; why, they act as if I'm an authority on bringing up children."

"Isn't it amazing how some people can act?" Risa said. "If someone needed an authority on bringing up children, I can't think of anyone better suited than Sissy. She knows everything about—"

"Are we havin' dessert tonight?" Ethan said, poking his head through the door. He looked around and saw four women and blushed to his blond roots. "This a womanly thing? I didn't mean to interrupt nothin'. I just thought—heck, Sissy, them pies smell so good. Couldn't we eat first and then you ladies could compare waistlines?"

"Seems you brought a few extra guests," Annie said, her eyes boring into her brother's.

"Mrs. Abernathy has to be the worst cook in all of Ohio. She burns the meat, salts the greens till you can't hardly taste 'em, and she thinks dessert's a sin, though you couldn't tell by the size of her corset. I just thought, you always make so much extra—"

"Bring out some extra plates," Annie told him. "You'll have to use the wooden ones," she added, surprising Risa, who knew how much pride she took in her good dishes.

"But Sissy," she started, "this is a special occasion."

"I ain't got enough," Annie said and bit her lower lip. "Not anymore."

When she came through the doorway, a pie in each hand, Noah wasn't the only man to cheer. He suspected the others were cheering her baking, but he was delighted to be able to express his joy and not be taken to task for it. Of course, the sweet scent of melted sugar and butter, the spicy aroma of cinnamon, and the autumn warmth of crisp fresh apples was nothing to ignore either.

"Apple," she announced, setting down the pie in her right hand. It was heaped way out of the crust in the shape of a craggy mountain with a crumb topping that was just the way he liked it, chunky so that when you bit on a piece it exploded in your mouth. "And pear," she said, setting down the one in her left.

"Square Dancers at the Grange Hall," Risa announced as she carried the big bowl of custard with dough dancers swirling atop it. It was obvious to him that two extra dancers had been added for his daughters.

"Rhubarb pie," Willa said, holding the one pie with two hands as though she was afraid of dropping it. Annie was so quick to take it from her, Noah guessed it wouldn't have been the first thing she had dropped that day.

Della came out, with Samuel holding one of her hands and James holding the other. "Well, I've got the guests of honor," she said, holding up their hands as if they had gone ten rounds and won. After the few encounters he'd had with the boys, he thought the image surprisingly accurate despite their age.

"All my guests are guests of honor," Annie said over the din created by the pulling back of chairs and the settling of children. "But tonight's very special guests of honor are both guests and hosts."

"Wait," Peter said. He ran toward the living room and returned with two bottles of wine. He made a ceremony of opening the wine, smelling the cork and twirling a bit of the dark red liquid in his glass.

"Peter, I thought we understood each other with regard to alcohol in my house," Annie said, a frown marring the perfection of her face.

"Bart doesn't mind," Peter said, as if the house and the rules in it were now her brother's province. "He and Charlie are joining me. Anyone else?" He lifted his bottle in invitation.

"'Look not thou upon the wine,'" Winestock began, "'when it is red, when it giveth its color in the cup, when it moveth itself aright. At the last it biteth like a serpent, and stingeth like an adder.' I shall pass, thank you, Mr. Gibbs."

Remarkably, having known first-hand the effects of too much drinking, Noah had to agree and passed on the wine as well. Besides, if there were going to be points scored with Annie, Noah wasn't about to let the scales tip in the minister's favor.

They all waited while Annie's pompous brother-in-law finished pouring wine for those who wanted it, and then she let him take over her announcement. "To Willa and Bart," Peter said, raising his glass and gesturing for everyone else to follow. "May they share great joy, and may they always have a clean shirt, a clean conscience, and a dollar in their pockets."

"To Willa and Bart," everyone agreed and raised their glasses, both empty and full, in their honor.

"No!" Annie yelled and started chasing one of the twins. "He's got the cork!"

If it hadn't been so serious, Noah thought it would have been comical, a line of five or six adults all running after one small boy who whooshed under tables and between chairs with the agility that only a three-year-old possesses.

But Noah prided himself on being smarter than even the most precocious three-year-old, which he didn't credit Samuel with being in the first place, and being rather experienced with children in general, he knew that if he sat still until the boy, intent only on the adults chasing after him, ran right past his chair, Noah could simply whip out an arm and catch the boy by the scruff of his neck. Sure enough, Samuel flew by his right side and Noah grabbed hold of his jacket with one hand and, with the tips of the fingers of his injured hand, plucked the cork from the boy's hand just as it was on its way to his mouth.

"Not this time, Sammy my boy," he said, handing the cork over to Annie and the boy to Peter. "Better luck next time."

"I am done in," Della declared. "Could someone else serve the pie?"

"Oh, Della," Risa cooed. "And for the first time ever you were actually going to help?"

"First the custard," Annie said, in an effort to defuse the situation. "Samuel, I'm tempted not to let you have any. I want a promise from you that only my good cooking is going into that mouth of yours tonight. Understand?"

Samuel made a face that Noah couldn't decide was agreement or not. Annie seemed to feel it was not.

"No custard. And I was going to let you dish it out, too." She looked very sad and disappointed, her lower lip protruding so that Samuel would change his mind. It had a very different effect on Noah, who remembered pulling on that same soft lip with his teeth.

"I will," Samuel said, reaching for the spoon, but Annie held it out of his reach.

"You will not until you promise me that nothing but my cookies and custard will cross your lips." She wiped the edge of the custard bowl with her finger and stuck it in her mouth. "Mmm," she said. "This might be the best I ever made."

Lord, he was undone! Right there at her dinner table he was going to embarrass himself. He pulled a napkin onto his lap and shifted uncomfortably in his seat.

"Can I sit on your lap?" Julia asked him. He reached for her and settled her on his leg for the time being. This was, in its own way, rapidly becoming the longest evening of his life.

"He won't do it again," Della assured her sister. "Let him dish it out."

Annie clearly disapproved of Della's methods of disciplining, but she didn't seem to feel it was her place to raise someone else's child.

"Remember," she told the boy as she handed him the spoon. "You get to dish out the portion for you and your brother, but he gets to chose which one is his."

Noah didn't quite understand her rules until he saw how carefully Samuel tried to make the portions exactly equal, since James would get to choose his dish first. How many times had he heard Hannah complain that Julia was given more cake than she was? And how many times had Julia cried that Hannah's plate held more?

The woman should be canonized. Her methods of child rearing should be turned into law and her name engraved in Washington, D.C., next to President Washington's: ANNIE MORROW, THE MOTHER OF HER COUNTRY!

The pie deserved another plaque, and the custard, which he finished for Julia after she fell asleep in his arms, merited an award as well.

"So what do you hear from Francie?" Peter asked. "The letters she writes to Della are all about the latest fashions and the controversy over women's underclothes. I can't believe that's all that interests her in New York City."

"The last letter we got," Charlie said, "was all about the department stores on Fifth Avenue. She said that in some of them all the goods are spread around on several different floors and the customers simply help themselves if they want to, instead of the way we do it."

"It sounds like such an exciting place," Ethan said. "She sent me a clipping from the newspaper about a march that turned so ugly the police had to use their billy clubs, and she said I ought to come to New York and become a policeman if I really wanted adventure!"

"What about you, Sissy?" Risa asked. "What does she write to you?"

Annie looked at Noah accusingly. He wondered if perhaps Francie had told her about Wylene. It was just as well if she knew. He didn't want any secrets between them.

"She writes that she misses home," Annie said. "I think with the slightest encouragement she'd pack her bags and be back in Van Wert." She stared at Noah until he felt he ought to duck. Her looks alone were lethal. "It would be a shame if she gave up everything now, only to come home and marry up and have babies and never do anything important with her life. Don't you think?"

"I don't know," Noah mused aloud. "I don't see marrying up and having babies as not doing anything important. After all, if our parents had felt that way, where would we all be?"

Annie opened her mouth and then closed it. Her jaw was very, very tight.

11

On Monday night Annie had tried to teach Willa how to prepare the sponge for the bread they would bake on Tuesday. In the morning Annie's combination of yeast, sugar, water, and flour had been ready to be formed into bread, while Willa's lay flat in the bottom of the bowl. Assuring her that they would try again toward the end of the week, she had helped Willa make some fairly successful loaves of brown bread and turned out two pies for the party while Willa rested. When she pulled the bread out of the oven she noticed the color of the crust and compared it to her forearm. She was a good two shades lighter, but she knew that Noah had been right. No doubt at the end of the summer her skin had been the color of baked bread.

Wednesday was taken up with the wash. Willa was surprisingly well taught in this area, but because of her condition, she restricted her help to telling Annie what she should do, as if Annie wasn't well aware that delicates and whites weren't to be thrown in with woolens or calicos and ginghams. Willa timed the boiling of the washtub while Annie did the manual work of scrubbing all the clothes in hot soapy water, attacking them with the tin wash plunger as though they had purposely gotten themselves dirty, and finally lifting the soaking garments and depositing them in a second tub, where they were boiled with soap for half an hour.

While one load boiled, Annie scrubbed another, then drained the first load, rinsed the clothes with clear water and bluing, and put them through the ringer. Willa chatted away affably, assuring Annie how much more pleasant it was to do the wash with another woman for company rather than all alone. Annie nodded in agreement much of the time, afraid that if she let herself speak she'd tell Willa that help would be appreciated a great deal more than company. She'd made her sisters help when they were still at home, just as her mother had pressed her into service when she was a little girl. They were usually more bother than aid, but their laughter and their questions had made the job go faster.

By Thursday Willa was only breaking half a dozen eggs at each gathering and had given up going into the barn with Annie for milking, claiming that the smell gave her the collywobbles. Annie thought that any work at all seemed to make Willa sick, but the times when she milked Edwina and Harry while Willa went up for her nap were rapidly becoming her favorites.

They were far better than the hours spent with Mrs. Leeman when she came to visit her daughter. Willa's mother, apparently unable or simply unwilling to believe that her daughter would have allowed Bart any liberties before marriage, felt a sudden need to warn her daughter that once she was with child she would have to turn her husband from her bed or risk the loss of the baby. After Mrs. Leeman left, Annie had to spend a good part of the day reassuring Willa that no harm had been done and she was sure many couples did not abstain for all that time no matter what her mother had said.

Though Annie wouldn't have minded if Bart and Willa stopped banging the headboard for a while. By the middle of the week she was sorry she hadn't told Willa that her mother was probably right.

Between ironing and mending on Thursday, Annie took down the summer curtains and dusted the windows. The weather had turned much colder as the week wore on, and Saturday she hoped to get Bart to help her put up the heavy drapes and bring the warmer blankets down from the attic.

Friday she pickled tomatoes and canned plums. Willa ate.

Saturday Ethan brought home his dirty laundry and, since he was there, decided to stay for dinner. After dinner he asked Annie to mend some trousers and sew on a couple of buttons and wound up spending the night.

For the most part, the days were the same as always, filled with enough work to tire her body but never enough to turn off her mind. And so while she cooked and cleaned and milked and minded the chickens, she dreamed. She dreamed of the fancy house on Summit Street with the hot water heater in the kitchen and the sparkling Sterling range. She dreamed of buying her milk and butter instead of coaxing it out of Edwina and Harry. She dreamed of lights that came on with the touch of a button. She dreamed of setting the table for a man who would say to her the things that Bart said to Willa. Well, a girl could dream.

The daydreams were a comfort to her, but those that came at night, they were different. She'd lie in the dark listening to the sounds of Willa and Bart, who, while they'd quieted down some had decided for reasons of their own that Annie knew more about safe childbearing than Willa's mother.

They'd moan softly, or cry out, or just simply whisper and giggle while she tossed and turned in the big bed that had once held Francie and Della and her all together. And in her throat she would feel that soft moan rising up as Noah had pressed his lips to her, and she would taste the cider that lingered on his tongue, and she would pull the pillow tighter and tighter against her chest as the peaks of her breasts stiffened until she would finally fall asleep.

But sleep gave her no relief. In her dreams there was always Noah Eastman, Noah with his soft lips and his easy smile and his strong hands. Hands that he used to pull her to him, hands that held her tight against his body, so tight she could hardly breathe, and she'd wake up gasping for breath and hoping she hadn't been heard by Willa or Bart.

By Sunday she was at the end of her rope. Without even giving Ethan an argument when he refused to get up, she dragged herself to church. She was reluctant to face Miller after the dreams she couldn't control, afraid to let Noah see her for fear that her emotions, as always, were written on her face. Bart, sensing her hesitation, extended one hand to her and one to his wife as they entered the Pleasant Township Methodist Church.

Miller watched the various congregants enter his church. He raised his head and smiled at one or another, lowered his head to put the finishing touches on his sermon, raised it again in time to see Bart Morrow coming in with his wife on one arm and his sister on the other. Sissy looked tired and pale and her eyes remained downcast as she made her way to her usual row and then slid into the pew to join the rest of her family.

He hoped she wasn't ill. He couldn't go down that path again. It was one of the things he liked best about Sissy Morrow: she was never ill. And she was so much younger than he. Surely she would outlive him and he would never have to nurse her the way he had done with his dear Elvira.

Elvira. A smile touched his lips. He turned it toward some incoming parishioners, but the smile was for her, for the good, proud woman he had married with never a moment's regret.

Though they had never bothered him, her humble beginnings had embarrassed Elvira for long after they were married, but he remembered the moment it all changed for her. They had been having dinner with Dr. Hamilton at the Xenia Seminary in Bellefontaine.

Jokingly, or perhaps only half so, he had said that the best way to get people to services in the winter was to be sure the church was warmer than their homes. "Perhaps then the new furnace, rather than your wonderful sermons, is responsible for your great success," Elvira had teased.

"A new furnace?" Hamilton had exclaimed. "But how fortunate you are! I've been pleading for one for two years, but I cannot get the school to pay for it! How ever did you manage?"

It had come out then that Elvira was Elmer Wells's daughter.

To her surprise, Hamilton had said, "Oh, but you're a lucky one, Winestock. Imagine! Not only is your wife beautiful and smart, but your father-in-law is in the most important business we have in our country today. Not counting the railroads and the mines, of course."

He still had his loyal congregation and his lovely home and his memories. And soon enough, for the days just rushed through his fingers, he would have a new wife to keep him fed and see to his needs.

"We will start today on page—" he began, only to be interrupted by the Eastman family, late as usual. He waited with exaggerated patience for them to take their seats. "Page twenty-two of the Plymouth Hymnal. All rise."

It was amazing, when he thought about it, that he could conduct a whole service while his mind was on a hundred other things, some mundane, some as important as his ordination or his wedding.

Today, though, his thoughts were on Noah Eastman. The man troubled him greatly, though he couldn't really say why. Was it the fact that he had lied about his wife? Miller had to admit that in all honesty the man had never said his wife had perished in that awful flood. He had said he couldn't talk about it. And since he had lost his parents and relatives, that was certainly understandable.

"In the hymnal. . ."

Damnation, why did he have to be so fair? Was it because he was a minister that he always gave everyone the benefit of the doubt? Couldn't the man simply irritate him without making him feel guilty about that very irritation?

And why did Eastman insist on calling Sissy "Annie" when everyone in the county had called her Sissy since she was barely able to walk? The man came to Van Wert, and suddenly Sissy Morrow wasn't Sissy anymore.

His sermon was all about respect. Respect for each other, respect for one's parents, one's elders, one's memories. Respect in the end for the Lord, though "God is no respecter of persons" (Acts 10:34), and so on. He spoke of respect for the dead and wondered whether his congregants took his words at face value or looked deeper into his meaning, surmising that he meant Elvira or, with the funds he had collected, Wylene Eastman. He supposed each listener attached his own meaning, remembered his own dead, and this morning he didn't care.

He couldn't see Sissy. He wished he had the nerve to ask the women in his parish not to wear those ridiculous oversized hats to his services. Jane Lutefoot blocked his view of three of the Morrows and two of the Montgomerys behind them.

"May God in his infinite wisdom be merciful."

It was over.

"Excuse me," cried a voice from the back. "Before you all leave—"

"Mr. Eastman?" He had felt it in his bones, and bones simply didn't lie. "Do you have an announcement?"

"It's about my furnace," he began.

Miller groaned loudly enough to be heard all the way in the back of the church.

"I've gone over the whole installation and found a serious defect."

"In *your* furnace," Miller reminded him.

"Yes," the man replied, "in *my* furnace. But there may be the same defect in yours"—he pointed to Samuel Dow—"or yours." This time he pointed straight at Miller himself.

"The pipe that connects the furnace to the rest of the house rotted through, due to the heat, even though there was an adjustable thimble to guard against just such an event. I am convinced that the metal used for the conduits was too soft and too easily melted and I believe that had I not found the weak spot in the pipe I would have had a fire in my house and perhaps lost it—and my family along with it."

His family. The comment only served to remind Miller that he had lied about that very family. "If, as you claim, the connecting pipe would have caused a fire, why haven't there been any fires? Many of us have furnaces in our cellars. There have been no fires."

"I lost my house last year," Brian Kelly said, rising with his hat clutched in his hand. "Lost our darling Bethy, too."

"What kind of furnace did you have?" Eastman asked, but Miller refused to let Kelly answer.

"This is ridiculous!" he exclaimed. "I cannot believe

that a furnace pipe installed fifteen years ago, problem-free until now, could cause a fire. If it were going to do so, it would have done its damage a long time ago."

"Not if it took all these years to weaken the metal to the point of breaking through," Eastman explained.

"Mr. Eastman, I fear you are an alarmist, and I must ask that you not use my church to frighten the good people of Van Wert. You are a stranger here, and you must be forgiven for not understanding this, but we in Van Wert are a community. We watch out for each other. We care about each other. And the men who built those furnaces and installed them were our own people. They would never have done anything to endanger the lives of their neighbors."

Everyone turned to look at Eastman. Miller saw the backs of their heads and couldn't read their faces. He only knew that Eastman's claim was ridiculous and he couldn't let him tarnish a man's reputation with scurrilous claims.

"I'm only suggesting that people check their furnaces. Make sure there is no danger. What can be the harm in that? If you have a Wells furnace, you should make sure that the pipes are sound. Have you never heard that it's better to be safe than sorry?"

The congregation turned back to him as one, questioning eyes looking to him for guidance. "There's a Wells furnace in this very building, Mr. Eastman. Why don't you and I and some of the others go down right now and check it out?"

"Excellent," Eastman said, as if he'd won his point.

"And if we find it to be sound, I want no more talk of this matter in my church. Agreed?"

"But lives could be at stake," he said.

Miller had no doubt that the man was in earnest, no matter how misguided he was. "No more, Mr. Eastman. Agreed?"

"I can't agree to risking people's lives when I know that there is a problem in that flue system."

"Let's go take a look, Mr. Winestock," Bart Morrow suggested. "If there's no problem here, I won't bother lookin' at home."

"We don't have a—" Sissy began, but Bart hushed her. He was a good man, Miller thought. The rest of the community respected him and he'd be a powerful ally, should he ever need one.

Bart, Mr. Eastman, Mr. Kelly, and several other men accompanied the minister to the bowels of the church where a Wells furnace, its emblem of shiny red letters affixed to the front, stood waiting for cold weather to set in.

Eastman, in the lead, ran his hand up the back of the pipe that protruded from the top of the furnace. "It's sound," he said, surprise in his voice. "Of course, it should be taken apart, checked from the inside, but it feels all right." He knocked against it with his fist, and the sound, deep and resonant, echoed in the high-ceilinged room.

'Well then," the minister said.

"Who else has these furnaces?" Eastman asked. "We should check them all."

"I'm sure I don't know," Miller said. He didn't add that it would not be a very difficult matter for him to find out.

Noah had no doubt that his furnace and any others installed in the same way would cause a fire.

"Anything left of your house?" he asked the man who had said he'd lost his house and daughter the year before.

The man shook his head.

"Was it a Wells furnace?"

Again the man shook his head. "I don't recall. It didn't look like this one, that's for sure."

Noah looked at the big church furnace. "Neither does mine," he admitted.

"Well," Bart said, looking around the room at Kelly and the other men, "I guess that settles it. Eastman's furnace ain't any kinda trend or nothin'."

"Would it hurt to look at other furnaces?" Noah asked, hoping his exasperation didn't show. "Closing your eyes to the problem won't make it go away." Though everyone in Van Wert seemed to think it would. And hadn't he, many times, been guilty of the same thing? But not when it could mean lives. Never when it could mean lives.

"Look all you want," one of the men said. "You got time to waste this time of year, go ahead. I got corn shocks to cut, a field of clover seed waiting to be hulled, cattle cars to bed, hogs to ship. With the weather gettin' colder so fast, I ain't got time to go pokin' around in other people's cellars."

Winestock clearly wasn't pleased with the man's less than charitable concern for his fellow man. With a withering look he said, "Time for neighbors is time well spent, Mr. Webb. And if I believed for moment that there was even the threat of a problem, I would lead the charge into every cellar in Van Wert to make sure my people were safe. As I am sure you would."

He raised his eyebrows and waited for a nod from Mr. Webb.

"But," the minister continued, "I am convinced that this is an isolated incident. Perhaps your furnace was somehow modified by your uncle before he left the farm to you, Mr. Eastman? While you were still in Johnstown, with your family?"

There was something about the way he emphasized *family* that caused Noah to lose track of the conversation momentarily. It was almost as if Winestock were sending a message meant just for him. His tone seemed to hold a note of warning.

"There is always that chance," Noah conceded, backing down only slightly. He might be making something out of nothing, but he couldn't see that it was worth the risk to ignore the possibility.

"I got hogs to ship," Mr. Webb said. His face turned scarlet and he looked at the ground. "Not today, of course. But I best be gettin' on home."

"I'm sure we all have better things to do than stand around this cellar," Winestock said.

"I got Sissy's dinner waitin'," Bart said, his mouth almost watering. "Not that Willa ain't a great cook, mind you. But Sissy insists on makin' Sunday dinner. She sure is one for tradition." He put his arm on the minister's back and asked if he was joining them, adding that Sissy had promised them a ham, which meant sweet potato pie and pickled beets as well.

The pickled beets seemed to do the trick, but it didn't escape Noah's attention that the man needed to be bribed.

12

"*A man of God takes the flock* that is given him,"
Miller said between bites of ham. "And we leave the judg-
ing to the Lord. Still, a man is a man, and he can't help but
feel more compassion for one member of his congregation
than for another." He looked around the table. Annie supposed he was searching for someone to agree with him.

"That's true," she said, trying to spear a piece of bright-
orange sweet potato with her fork. Willa had helped with
the potatoes, making them the way her mother had taught
her. Apparently, the Leemans liked their potatoes on the
hard side. Afraid that Miller would think she had lost her
ability to cook, she said, "Have you tried the potatoes?
Willa made them."

"These here are potatoes?" Ethan said. "I thought they
was rocks. I was gonna excuse myself and go look for a
chisel."

"Eth!" Annie scolded when she saw the defeated look
on Willa's face. "I brought you up with better manners
than that. Apologize to Willa, please."

"I was just funnin'." Ethan defended himself. "You're one of the family now, Willa. You shoulda heard some of the things I've said about Sissy's cookin' over the years. You remember them disks you made that Blue kept buryin'?"

Annie nodded. They were her first attempt at a new kind of biscuit, and she had thought they were pretty good. But the dog had gone wild, ripping them off Ethan's plate and running with them to the yard, only to dig a hole and drop the biscuit in and run back for another. "I guess they were pretty awful."

"You were learnin', that's all," Ethan said kindly. "No one comes out perfect to start, Sissy. You came a damn sight closer than the rest of us, that's for sure."

"I think, Ethan, that we can do without the profanity, don't you?" Miller said, responding only to Ethan's use of the word *damn* and not to his praise.

"Pardon, reverend," Ethan said. "But a curse ain't as bad as a lie, right?"

Miller put the tips of his fingers together as though in deep thought. He looked at Annie, opened his mouth as if to say something, and then closed it. She wished she could read him better, know what he was thinking, what he was about to say. Risa and Charlie did it all the time, finishing each other's sentences, having whole conversations and coming to decisions without more than half a dozen words exchanged, and those were usually, "But don't you?" and "It's all right."

"A lie is a terrible thing," Miller said at last, as though coming to an important conclusion. "But it is not our place to call out the liar. It says in Timothy that when, in the latter times, some shall depart from the faith, they may speak lies in hypocrisy, but their conscience shall be seared with a hot iron."

As always, he warmed to his subject, but this time as he spoke he seemed to burn rather than simply warm. He

struck the table with his fist and raised his voice until Annie
was afraid the dishes in her cabinets might crack. With the
shaking of his head, his hair flew out of its neat fashion
and stood away from his scalp, giving him the appearance
of someone who had just awakened from a bad dream.

Annie and her brothers sat staring at him, stunned. His
face was a mottled red and his hands were shaking. His
voice still echoed in the room.

"Boy," Ethan said finally, "I sure won't be profane
around here anymore!"

They waited for Miller's reaction, each of them uneasy.
Annie had never seen him so agitated, even during the
course of Elvira's illness. Bart was looking between her
and Miller as if something were wrong between them.
Ethan seemed to feel the outburst was all his fault, and
Willa was attacking her potato with a knife, sticking the
point in, pulling it out, and sticking it in again.

"My potato is excellent," Miller finally said, as though
his outburst had never taken place, although the natural
color was only now returning to his face and his breathing
becoming even. "One can't expect to cook like Sissy
Morrow overnight, or someone else might win a ribbon
every now and then."

"Let me get you some more," Annie said quickly, rising
from her seat and grabbing up the serving platter. "There's
plenty in the kitchen."

"You feelin' all right now?" Annie heard Bart ask Miller
as she pushed through the kitchen door. "You been upset
since church, seems to me."

Annie stood by the door and listened.

"It's Eastman," Miller admitted. "Imagine the nerve of
that man trying to impugn the reputation of an honest
hard-working man like Elmer Wells."

Annie snorted. Elmer Wells was no more honest and
hard-working than Wilber Gebney, the town drunk. In

fact, before he was put into the furnace business by his father-in-law, Elmer Wells *was* the town drunk.

"Noah's just worried about the people in this town," Ethan said, jumping to his defense. "He don't stand to make a penny, nor too many friends, goin' around checkin' people's furnaces, but he's willin' to do it because that's the kind of man he is."

"You don't know what kind of man he is," Miller said. "You—we all know very little about him, really. And what I know, I don't like."

"Neither do I," Bart agreed.

Annie knew full well why Bart didn't like Noah. She just hoped he didn't mention anything to Miller about the way Noah looked at her.

"More ham," she sung out, pushing her way through the door, "and no more unpleasant talk."

"Mama says that disagreeable words make for a disagreeable stomach," Willa said.

"Your mama never ate a meal with five Morrows around the table," Ethan said.

"Well, you're all grown up now, and it's time we had a meal without an argument," Annie insisted. Her whole dinner was being ruined, and just when she was hoping to show Miller the benefits of marrying her. If only once Miller would look at her the way Bart was gazing at Willa.

"I could use some more water," Bart said, rising from the table. "Anyone else?"

"Oh, I'll get it," Willa said, rising as well, the pitcher in her hand.

"Then let me help you," Bart offered, taking the pitcher from her and extending his arm.

Now everyone knew it didn't take two grown people to get a bit of water from the kitchen to the table, but no one said a word or even smirked or smiled as the two left the room.

"They sure do seem happy," Ethan said when they just sat staring at the closed kitchen door. "Is it as bad living with them as you thought?"

Annie thought of the extra work Willa made for her. She thought of how little Bart was able to get done when he had to stop his work several times a day to check on his new wife. She thought of how her nights were spent, the pillow clutched around her ears, trying not to hear what they were doing. Her cheeks felt heated as she thought about the dreams she'd been having ever since Willa had moved in.

"No," she lied. "It ain't all that bad."

"Why would it be bad?" Miller asked. "Willa's a good woman. I'm sure she's a great help to your sister."

"Yeah," Ethan agreed with a laugh. "Much more help, and Sissy'll need a maid and a cook."

"Eth," Annie warned, "Be nice."

"I'm always nice, to you," he said and blew her a kiss.

"You should be nice to everyone," Annie said, then caught herself. Ethan was too old for her to still be mothering. He was a grown man and deserved to be treated like one.

"I'm nice to everyone who deserves it." Ethan defended himself. "But there are those that don't. Like ol' Ruth Abernathy. That's one mean—"

Miller's head picked up, and Annie kicked Ethan under the table, effectively shutting him up.

"It's hard to know which folks deserve your kindness, son, and which ones don't. It might seem that Mrs. Abernathy is less worthy of your consideration than Mr. Eastman, when in fact—"

"Bart!" Willa cried as they came through the door. "Stop that!" Her face turned three shades of red as she looked at the minister's fallen jaw. "Oh, my!"

"They were just—" Annie began, but stopped when she saw the shocked look on Miller's face.

"Sorry, Mr. Winestock. My fault," Bart mumbled, escorting Willa back to her seat and pulling out the chair for her. When she was seated he squeezed her shoulder lightly despite Miller's stern gaze.

"Yes," Miller said, clearing his throat. "Well."

"Tea or coffee anyone?" Annie offered, rising from the table. "I've apple brown Betty."

"I'll help you," Ethan said, jumping up and nearly upsetting everything on the table so that everyone reached out to steady glasses and pitchers and the like.

Annie was tempted to say that his kind of help was the kind she could do without, but she didn't. Nor did she ask why suddenly, after all these years, he thought she needed help at all. Instead she just nodded and let him follow her into the kitchen.

"He's an old fart, Sissy," Ethan said, once they had come through the kitchen door and closed it. "You'd be much better off with Noah."

Annie turned to study her youngest brother's face. There was no bitterness or anger there, just earnest caring. "I think I know by now what's best for me, Ethan," she said, touching his cheek and surprised to find such coarse stubble there. "I've lived long enough to know that no one and nothing is perfect. Miller can be stuffy at times, but he has a good heart and he is a good man."

"And he's got a nice house, Sissy, but no matter how good his heater is, it ain't gonna keep you warm at night. It takes a man to do that. A man who loves you."

"Loves me? Miller loves me. He loves us all. And what do you know about love anyway, little brother? In all your experience, you think you know what it is?"

"Sissy, I just want you to be happy." He tried to wrap his arms around her, but she fought him.

"I will be happy! I'll be happy just as soon as Miller and I are married and I can leave this farm and all of you behind me." Her hands went up to cover her disobedient mouth. "I'm tired, Ethan. I'm tired of pumping water, of gardening, of taking care of everyone. I'm entitled to some rest, aren't I? Do you know that Miller's house has a toilet in it? That his'll be one of the first to have those electric lights? That there is a bathroom upstairs where I can take a bath and then climb into bed?"

"But *he'll* be there," Ethan said, pointing toward the door. "He'll be in that bed waiting for you."

She thought of Miller's white body lying between the sheets waiting for her to come to him and let him use her. Well, she had liked kissing with Noah, all right, so there was every reason to believe that she would like kissing Miller just as much. More, even, since she respected Miller so much.

"That's the best part," she said to Ethan with a smile pasted on her face.

"You're still the worst liar I know," Ethan said as he turned on his heel and walked toward the door. "I ain't hungry, Sissy. I'll be goin' on home now."

After living all his nineteen years under the Morrows' roof, how could he think of Noah Eastman's farm as home?

Ethan's boots clunked heavily on the porch, startling Noah. He hadn't expected him back for quite a while. He put down the letter from Francie that he had been reading and went to the door.

"What are you doing back so early?" he asked. Ethan's shrug spoke volumes. "What's wrong? Is it Annie?" His heart began to pound irrationally in his chest. He yanked Ethan into the house and thrust him toward the table.

The boy more or less shuffled his way and sat heavily in the chair, his eyes scanning the letter that lay before him. Noah scooped it up and folded it. "I'll tell you about

Francie in a moment. First tell me what's got you acting like a dying duck in a thunderstorm."

"She means to marry him, Noah," he said shaking his head, "She really does."

"I know," he said quietly. She was not a woman who gave her word lightly, of that he was sure.

"But he's not right for her."

"No, he isn't."

"I told her, Noah. Told her straight out that he was a coot and she ought to be marryin' up with you." The boy's eyes were wide and moist.

"You did? And what did she say to that?"

"She said he had a bathroom. Imagine that! Didn't argue none about him bein' old and crabby. She just said he was a good man and she was tired. And he had a bathroom." Ethan sat shaking his head.

"You did real well, Ethan," Noah said, a genuine smile on his face. "Real well."

"I did?" Ethan asked, clearly confused. "But she says she's gonna marry him, not you."

Noah nodded. "But that was before. You ever hear of fighting fire with fire?"

"Oh, not them damn furnaces again."

Noah laughed, a hardy guffaw that clearly meant he had control of the situation. "No, not the furnaces. But if you can fight fire with fire, why not fight water with water?"

13

After Ethan had made his sudden exit from Annie's table, a hush had fallen over the group. Bart had taken to staring at Willa, sending her some sort of signals that made her blush. Miller had seemed tense and irritated, and after two helpings of her apple brown Betty, both with freshly whipped cream, he'd taken his leave. When she'd offered to see him to his buggy he had declined, claiming it was too cold a night for her to be outside on his account.

He hadn't fooled her. Not for the first time, he had been uncomfortable with her family. They were ill-mannered, uneducated, and high-spirited, but she loved each and every one of them, even Willa now that she was family, and it hurt her to see the disapproval in Miller's eyes. For one thing, they were no worse than most of his parishioners. Van Wert had more farms than businesses, and farmers just didn't have time to cultivate the niceties of life along with the soil. For another, much as Elvira had managed to rise above them, her family was certainly no better than Annie's, and for a good part of his life, Elmer Wells was a darn sight worse.

Her hand covered her mouth even though she hadn't uttered the word. If she hoped to be a minister's wife, she had better learn to speak like one. And that meant no cussing, and better grammar. Most of the women she knew spoke better than she did. It was easier for farmers to spare their daughters for schooling than their sons. And then there was the chance that their daughters, well educated, might snare husbands that were better off than their families were.

Well, there was too much for her to do on a brisk Monday afternoon than think about her speech. The ground was getting harder every day, and she had to fight to get the beets and turnips out of the soil. It was already proving a good year for beets and she had been able to put by several dozen jars of pickled ones for the winter and spring.

The crop she pulled today she planned to can without pickling so the various children could enjoy them in the months to come. Now only three little ones, there would soon be five, and Annie was planning for all of them, despite the fact that the two infants wouldn't be born for quite a while and would exist on their mothers' milk for a good time after that.

Cara hadn't been weaned until long after the doctor had said it was all right to start her on solid food. Annie could tell it was because Risa hated to give up the closeness of nurturing the child herself. Sometimes Risa would wince in pain, but for the most part Annie had never seen a more contented look on anyone's face than Risa had when she was nursing Cara. The painting of the Madonna that hung in the church must have been made at such a time.

What must it be like? she wondered. She was so deep

in thought she didn't even hear a wagon approaching until it was nearly on top of her. Startled, she dropped the basket of beets and looked up to find Noah Eastman sitting there. One girl stood on each side of him, tucked safely in the bend of his arms—the same arms that had held her firmly yet gently against him only nights before. He said something quietly to his daughters, then alighted and gently plucked each one down, setting one and then the other firmly on the ground.

"Wait here," he said to them and started toward Annie, who was busy picking up rolling beets and hoping her face wasn't the same color as her vegetables. His feet stood in her vegetable patch, two brown boots, caked with soil, inches from her hands.

"Mr. Eastman," she said, looking up and pushing the hair out of her face with her forearm. She was a mess, her hair falling down, her dress dirty, her shawl only half on her shoulders, one toe peeking through her left boot. "I wasn't expecting visitors."

"I haven't come to visit," he said. His voice shook and she took note of him for the first time. Something close to terror was written on his face.

"Are the girls all right?" she asked.

He nodded curtly. It seemed he could hardly speak.

"What is it then? What's wrong?"

He looked at the children and then back at her, as if wishing he could bridge the distance between them. The girls were shivering, and so was he. "Can we go inside?"

"Of course," she said, feeling like a fool, although he was the one to have come out in the brisk October air with no jacket for himself or coats for his girls. She walked past him toward the girls and smiled in welcome. One set of eyes were bigger and more solemn than the other as they stared at her approach. "Do you two like apple brown Betty?" she asked. There was still an awful lot left over after she and Ethan had both lost their appetites the night before.

"Oh, God, Annie!" he said from behind her, his words catching in his throat. She spun around and stared at him, but he seemed to recover himself. "Come on, girls. Miss Annie'll give you something to eat while we talk." The girls didn't move. "It's all right," he told them. "Come on."

In the kitchen she pulled the brown Betty from the pie safe and dished out two servings. When she gestured with a plate toward Noah, he shook his head. "Milk?" she asked the girls. Without waiting for an answer, she reached into the icebox and removed the pitcher, poured two glasses, and set one in front of each of them. "Your papa and I will be in the parlor," she told them, and led the way.

"Annie," he began, pulling a chair close to the couch, its legs scraping noisily on the wooden floor.

"Shh!" Annie said, her finger to her lips. "Willa's takin' a nap." She sat, just close enough to hear him but far enough to be proper. It took him a moment to collect himself, and her mind raced to guess at the problem. Suddenly she felt all the starch seep from her backbone. "Oh, my God! It's Ethan! What's happened to Ethan?"

"No, no," he assured her, his hand reaching out and rubbing her arm in just the same way her mother had when she was a little girl and frightened of something. But instead of soothing her, his touch only made her breath harder to catch, her fear harder to control. "Ethan's fine. He's taking Mrs. Abernathy to the train." His face hardened at the woman's name.

"How come you're here then?" she asked, still trying to keep calm when just his nearness was enough to rattle her nerves. It seemed that the children were fine, he was fine, Ethan was fine. So what did he want in the middle of a Monday afternoon? And what would be Bart's reaction when he came upon first Noah's rig and then Noah himself in their parlor, alone with his sister? "I don't think you should—"

"I need you to watch after my girls."

"What?"

"Hannah and Julia. To take care of them."

"To what? You mean you want to leave them here while you go take care of something? I suppose I could, just this once, but you can't go makin' a habit of it. I got enough work to do without surprise company in the middle of my day."

Noah studied his hands, tracing the scar that still looked red and sore. Then he reached out and took one of Annie's hands in both of his. He traced her calluses with the tip of his finger and examined the blister that was forming on the inside of her thumb. "You should wear gloves when you work. This must hurt."

She pulled her hand away from his, but his warmth still surrounded every finger. "I'm used to it. What are you doin' here, Mr. Eastman? What do you really want?"

"I want you to come work for me. Like Francie did. I want you to look after the girls while I get the harvesting done."

She jumped away from him as though he were the serpent himself come to her door with the apple. "That's out of the question. I can't do that."

"It would only be temporary," he added. "Just until I find someone else."

That he would even suggest such a thing! "I got my own home, Mr. Eastman. I ain't sitting here in my parlor, day after day, reading dime novels and whiling away my hours."

A look of pain crossed his face that was so raw she was immediately sorry, although she didn't know what for.

"I know that." His Adam's apple bobbed furiously in his throat. "I wouldn't have asked you otherwise. Believe me."

"Well, it's no matter. Why don't I keep the girls here with me and you can go stop Mrs. Abernathy from leaving? How come she's goin', anyways? She got some problem with her family? Or was her problem with you?"

"Me?" he yelled. "Me? A problem with me? What would make you think—"

"Sissy? What's going on down there?" Willa called from the top of the stairs. "Is everything all right?"

"Yes, Willa," Annie began, but Noah interrupted.

"No. Nothing is all right. Don't you see I have no choice? Do you think I'd put you in such a position? I'm willing to meet any of your terms, do whatever you like, but you've got to help me."

There was desperation in his voice, in his body, his eyes. It was more than just wanting her, for she was sure he did, fat lot of good it would do him. It was more than just needing someone to watch his girls. Something had gone horribly, terribly wrong, and he was turning to her to fix it.

The door to the kitchen creaked and opened slightly. "Daddy!" Julia cried and threw herself toward him. Hannah followed soberly, her eyes on Annie all the while. And any doubt Annie had evaporated at the sight of the girls.

Heavy steps on the porch warned Annie that there was still more trouble to come.

"What in the world is goin' on in here?" Bart shouted. "Eastman, what are you doin' here?"

Over Julia's howls, Annie could hardly make out Noah's plea. "Will you help me?" he asked.

"I ain't hired help," Annie explained. "I can't drop everything here and just—" She stopped when she saw the tears gather in his eyes. Had he really thought he could just ask her and she'd drop her own life and take up his? "You shouldn't have let Ruth Abernathy leave."

He stood Julia on the couch and gently undid the buttons to her dress, all the while cooing at her and telling her it would be all right. When he slipped the dress down her arms and turned her back to Annie, the first thing she noticed was the raw red marks on the child's pale skin.

The second thing she saw was the tear that landed there from Noah's eye.

"'Spare the rod,' she said to me," he said as his voice cracked. "That was her explanation. 'Spare the rod'—"

"Oh, my God!" It was all she could get out before her throat seemed to close. She turned and walked toward Hannah as if in a trance. Beside the girl, she knelt and opened the top two buttons on the back of her dress. It was enough to tell her what she wanted to know.

"Willa, get the Kickapoo Indian Salve from the kitchen," she directed. "Bart, pack up the laundry and put it into Mr. Eastman's wagon. I can do it over there along with theirs." She turned to Noah. "Get her dress off, and we'll put some ointment on to make her more comfortable." She unbuttoned the rest of Hannah's dress and helped the little girl step out of it.

"Sissy, you can't go over to Mr. Eastman's place. What will the reverend think?" Bart asked.

"You ever seen a more clear example of Christian duty? Because I sure ain't," Annie shot back. "Besides, Ethan's there if I need him."

Willa stood by, looking rather faint, while Annie saw to the girls' backs. Even Bart seemed moved by the stoic acceptance of the two babies and, though grumbling all the way, he carried the laundry out to the wagon.

"There's a book in the kitchen that'll tell you how to boil up them beets, Willa," Annie said as she helped the girls get dressed. "If you have any trouble, just ask Bart. I know he'll be glad to help ya."

Noah threw Annie's shawl over her shoulders as she made her way out of the house. She draped it around herself and Hannah, whom she held in her arms. When they got to the wagon, Bart took Hannah from Annie and gave his sister a reluctant hand up to the seat, steadying her as she climbed the wheel and finally handing the child back once she was safely aboard. Noah handed her Julia and she cuddled both girls to her gently, wrapping her shawl around the three of them as Noah leaped into the wagon and gave a salute to Bart.

"I'll take good care of her," he said.

"You damn sure better," Bart said gruffly, "or you'll regret it."

They rode in a silence that was neither companionable nor angry, but seemed to be forced by the presence of two very shaken little girls.

"I wasn't sure you'd agree to come," Noah said after a while, as they headed toward his farm.

"Oh, I believe that and next you'll be sellin' me fresh roses in winter," she said with some annoyance. "You were as certain as dollars to doughnuts, and don't pretend otherwise."

"I suppose," he said, with the hint of a smile touching his mouth. "Still, I don't know how to thank you."

"You said, back there in the house, any terms I wanted. Did you mean it?"

He threw a curious look her way but nodded. "Of course I meant it."

"Well, here are my terms." She put up her fingers to number them. "First, you ain't to come in the house while I'm there. You want me, you come knock at the door and I'll come out, but I ain't gonna be alone in your house with you."

"Done," he agreed.

"This is, like you said, temporary. You gotta be trying your hardest to find someone else to take over this job. I'm getting married in a few months and I can't be watching your little ones when I got a husband to take care of."

"No," he agreed. "I can see how that would be a problem. I'll look—in fact, you could look for me—and the minute you find someone to replace you I'll be happy to hire her."

"I'll have to be making your dinner early so I can get home to my own family. If Bart has to eat much more of Willa's cooking I might have to learn leeching or something."

"We can eat whenever you say, right, girls?" He chucked Hannah under the chin, but the child only stared at Annie.

"And fourth, or is it fifth?" she asked. When he didn't respond, she continued. "One thing I gotta know: have you read all those books in your house?"

"I have," he said.

"Then I expect you could teach me?"

"You can't read?" he asked. He couldn't keep the surprise out of his voice.

"I'm all right with words," she said, swallowing her pride, "but whole books are another thing. I didn't get much in the way of schooling, as you probably know, and they didn't start a school library till after I was out of the Union School. And being as how I'm gonna be a minister's wife"— she didn't want to miss the opportunity of reminding him of that—"I need to read and write better than I do."

"I would be honored to teach you," he said. Why, he even seemed to mean it. "But to be honest, you know, the ladies have formed a Library Association. Wouldn't you rather join the library?"

She knew all about the Library Association. Hattie Brotherton and Clara Cavett themselves had come to her house and invited her to belong for what they called the small sum of three dollars a year. Even if she'd had three dollars to spare, and that was a laugh, it would probably take her a whole year to read just one of the books. She didn't need the good ladies of Van Wert knowing that the minister's wife could barely read. "You don't want to do it, then?"

"Oh, no," he assured her. "It would be an honor. I can't think of anything that would give me more pleasure."

She'd seen the way he looked at her, and she thought that Bart was probably right about him, so she doubted this last statement was true. Still he seemed so genuine about it that she pressed her luck.

"My speech ain't great either," she admitted. "Do you think you could help with that?"

"*Isn't* great," he corrected. "And though I'd rather hear you speak than do almost anything, I'd be happy to help you speak in a way that pleases *you*. Though anyone who isn't pleased with you the way you are now is a fool. Still, I'd be happy to help."

She was telling him her faults, and somehow he was turning them all around and praising her. She couldn't remember the last time anyone had praised her for anything besides her cooking. He made her feel that even if she never roasted another chicken or baked another pie, he would still think she was a worthwhile person just by virtue of being Miss Annie Morrow.

"Well," she said, cuddling the girls closer to her and sharing her warmth. "I think we got a deal."

"*Have* a deal," he corrected. "I think we do."

And he began to whistle.

The girls always liked it when he whistled. He'd started it when they were babies, afraid that his singing voice was more likely to make them cry than put them to sleep, and they'd taken to it, calming almost immediately as soon as he began. Today was no different for Julia, whose little body began to relax against his.

Hannah remained stiff against Annie's side, listing first one way and then the other, mumbling something he couldn't quite make out.

"What's she saying?" he asked.

"I can't hear her. I asked, but she's too upset yet to tell me. Let's give it a little time."

He went back to his whistling, but it wavered as he thought about the marks on her back.

"You want to sit with me?" he asked his older daughter.

She shook her head and clung more tightly to the woman next to her.

"What? You don't want to sit on the ol' hot water bottle?" he joked, patting his lap. "Miss Annie must be mighty warm to pass snuggling up to your pa."

"I ain't warm at all," Annie admitted. "I wish I'd thought to bring some blankets."

"We'll be home soon enough," he said, trying to move closer to them and share his warmth, little as it was.

"Was it right, then?" she asked.

"Huh?"

"Ain't. I said I ain't warm and you didn't correct me. Was it right?"

"There's no such word as *ain't*. It doesn't matter how you use it, it won't be right. The word you want most of the time is *isn't*, although sometimes it's *am not*. It depends."

"Keep talking," she said under her breath. "About anything."

He looked past her at Hannah's closed eyes and nodded. It wasn't like her to ask about her grammar at a time like this, so he should have known she was doing it for his children's sake. But even for their sakes he could think of nothing to say.

"It looks like a cold day for laundry," Annie said. "'Course the cold is welcome when you're working over the boiling pots."

"What?"

Annie jerked her head in Hannah's direction. "But when you're hanging out those wet things in the cold wind." Her voice faded out.

"I can see that the cold would be a problem," he agreed, feeling like a total fool. His children had been hit by the woman he had expected to care for them, protect them from harm. They had been betrayed, and he had put them in that position.

"Quite a squaw winter we're having," Annie said, startling him.

"What?"

"Guess it means we'll have a nice Indian summer. That's what they say, you know."

She kept up the banter for the better part of three miles before finally going silent.

"Sure is cold," he said, to fill the sudden quiet.

"You can stop," Annie said with a sigh. "She's asleep."

"Why the hell were we talking about the weather and the laundry?" he demanded, now that he was free to talk.

"Because the best thing to do when a child is scared is to make things seem as regular as you can. The more upset you get, the more upset she'll get."

"How did you get so smart?" he asked.

"Smart? I ain't—I'm not smart at all. Anyone can tell that just by listening to me. But I know children. That ain't—oh, it's *not* smarts. It's experience."

"Do you think I'm smart?" he asked her, holding her eyes with his.

"If you really read all those books, I'd say yes, you surely must be."

"Well, then, if I'm smart then I must be right about how smart you are, don't you think?"

"No. Just because you're smart doesn't mean you can't be mistaken."

He laughed and shook his head. "Not only are you smart," he said to her before redirecting his attention back to the road, "you just outsmarted me."

And, he decided, when he thought about her conditions,

you also outsmarted yourself. You gave yourself away with your terms. I know what you treasure, and I can give it to you. But more than that, despite her first condition, that he wasn't to come into the house when she was there, her other conditions demanded that he do just that. How else could he teach her to read and speak better if he stayed away from her?

As for finding someone to take her place, he was convinced no one could do that. If she wanted to waste her time looking, he had no objection, but as far as he was concerned she would not be leaving him to marry Miller Winestock or any other man. After what his girls had suffered, he just couldn't believe they were about to be hurt again. Even if God could be that cruel, he couldn't believe Annie Morrow would be.

"We're here," he whispered, pulling the horse to a stop and easing down from the wagon as carefully as he could so as not to wake the sleeping children. He rounded the cart and reached up for Hannah. Annie's strong arms held her out to him, and he shushed the child back to sleep and carried her inside.

When he came back out, he stood watching Annie from the doorway. She had moved Julia onto her lap and wrapped her in the shawl. With her forefinger she was smoothing the frown lines on Julia's little face and cooing to her quietly. If he'd seen a lovelier sight, he couldn't recall it.

She looked up and smiled at him, and he came forward to take his baby. "I'll be right back for you," he whispered as he turned toward the house, but she was out of the wagon and leading the way, opening the door for him as he bore his little girl.

Once inside, she let him take the lead, following him to the girls' bedroom and taking in the room as he laid the girl on the bed next to her sister.

"Let's let them sleep in their clothes," she whispered. "They need their rest."

He nodded and turned to leave but saw she wasn't following him.

"I could give you your first lesson before I head out to the fields," he offered. She looked at him suspiciously. "On the porch," he added.

She threw a last look at his daughters, then followed him out of the room. When he stopped at the bookcase she paused a few feet from him, and her eyes widened at the selection in front of her.

"What do you think you might like to start with?" he asked her, moving closer under the guise of searching for a particular book. If he just reached out his arm, he could touch her. Reaching for Shakespeare would put him in contact with her right arm. The *Almanac* would surely let him brush against her breast.

He put his hands behind his back and took a step away from her, cautioning himself that there was a world of difference between having her in his house and keeping her there. And no matter how much patience it took, he was determined to keep her in his house until it became her home, and forever after that.

He let her take her time, enjoying just being near her, watching her excitement as she studied the spines of his books. She looked at his bookcases the way he looked at her laden dining room table. They were a perfect match. "Go ahead," he encouraged her. "Choose one."

"Any one?" Her eyes were wide but, like him, she kept her hands neatly pinned behind her.

"Touch them," he said. "See how they feel. Heck, smell them if you want. There must be one that appeals to you."

"Oh, there is," she admitted somewhat shyly. "But it'll take me a long time to get through it, and I don't feel right about keeping a book from its rightful owner for so long."

"Which one is that?" he asked, purposely ignoring her comments about how long she would need the book. If things went as he planned, and he was going to see that they did, the book would be back in his house along with all her belongings.

"*Little Women,*" she said as her hand stroked a volume bound in red leather.

"That," he said with relief, "is a wonderful story of four sisters and their mother. They are a very close family, and I think you'll like all of the girls and even see some of yourself and your sisters in them. I know I've often thought that Della is more than a little like Amy."

"I know," she said softly. "I think so too."

"Then you've read it?" he asked. He was disappointed that he couldn't open a new world for her. It was a small thing, reading, but it was something he could give her that she had seemed willing, even eager to take.

"I started it when Della was in the eighth grade," she admitted. "She'd leave it at home when she went to school and I would read a page or two when I finished my chores. She took it back to school before I got too far."

"That was a long time ago," he said, noting the longing in her voice still after all these years.

"Well, Francie had it out of the school library too. I got a little farther with it then."

He pulled the book from the shelf and put it in her hands. "Take as long as you need. I don't want it returned until you're done."

"Oh, but that could take a long time," she argued.

"I can wait," he said. "As long as it takes." Even, he thought, without saying as much, if it took the rest of their lives.

14

The next morning she arrived with the red leather book tucked under her arm, blue smudges under her eyes, and a smile that made him warmer than the autumn sun.

"I got almost a chapter read last night," she said proudly, waiting on the porch for him to kiss the girls good-bye and head for the fields.

"I told you there was no rush," he reminded her. "Hannah won't be ready for Louisa May for years and years."

"Well, I didn't really want to put it down. She sure is a wonderful writer." She yawned, daintily covering her mouth with the back of her hand. "Sorry."

"The reading going slowly?" he asked.

She nodded.

"Any words in particular I can help you with?" He reached for the book, his knuckles touching the sleeve of her coat. He was pleased when she didn't back away.

"Oh," she said, "I've got a dictionary for that. It's just

that I have to read a page more than once to get the sense of it."

He took the book from under her arm and opened it randomly. "Read," he ordered and held the book in front of her.

She looked shyly at him and then again at the book.

He softened his tone and reminded her of their bargain. He could hardly hold up his end if she refused to be a pupil. She started at the top of the page, oddly enough in the middle of a sentence. But it didn't seem to matter, since she paid no mind to periods, commas, or preposi tional phrases. She was so intent on recognizing every word that she had trouble knowing where to put in the pauses, running word after word and sentence after sentence until nothing made any sense.

He was keeping Ethan waiting, he knew, on this dry warm day perfect for harvesting. He could teach her about reading some other time. He had corn to get in. She stopped reading and looked at him with her eyes full of embarrassment.

"I'm not a good reader, I know," she said.

"You didn't miss a word," he praised honestly. "But you did run them all together. Pause here." He made a mark with the pencil he was holding at the point of a comma to show her where to break the thought. "And here. And here."

She gasped. "What are you doing? Don't write in it!" She looked at the book he held out to her with horror. "Oh, but you've ruined it!"

"Ruined it? How have I done that? Books are for reading, Annie, for savoring, for enjoying. They're not for saving. Do you think when Miss Alcott wrote this book she meant for it to stay on some shelf untouched? Or did she wish, in her deepest self, that someone like you would do to it whatever it takes for you to understand her meaning?

I bet if she were here, she'd circle phrases and draw arrows and pictures and cross out words and make changes and say, 'I could have done this better, if only I'd known I was writing for Annie.'"

Annie stared at him with such astonishment he had to laugh.

"Hey, Noah," Ethan yelled as he neared the porch with the broadcast seeder. "Lesson one: a farmer works in the light and plays in the dark. Remember?"

It was endearing, the way her face turned red at the implications of Ethan's comment. Much as he wished he could sit all day and watch as each of her emotions marched across her face like placards revealing her inner thoughts, he knew that whether he got to play at night or not, Ethan was right about what a farmer had to do with his days.

He eased the girls from his lap and stood. Three beautiful faces looked up at him, and only with great effort he said, "I've got to go help Ethan now. You girls mind Miss Annie and do as you're told."

He'd used the same words to them about Ruth Abernathy, and he saw the fear on their faces. Kneeling in front of them, he looked at first one and then the other of his precious children. "This is Miss Annie we're talking about. There's nothing to be afraid of when Miss Annie's here."

She'd planned on doing the wash she hadn't gotten to yesterday, what with all the settling of children and finding her way around the Eastman farm. One look at those sad faces and she knew the wash would have to wait.

"I don't suppose anyone would like to help me make cookies?" she asked. If only she'd brought her cutters with her they could make cowboys or party belles or some such thing. Without them she'd have to think of something extraordinary. "Snowmen!" she exclaimed, figuring that glasses could make circles and the rest would be easy. "Would you like to make snowman cookies?"

The girls looked to their father first, caught his nod, and eagerly bobbed their heads up and down. Noah patted first Julia on the head, then Hannah, and then Annie, as well. His fingers tangled in her hair, which caught on the rough calluses.

"I'd better go," he said and hurried from the porch.

She stood looking after him for a while, until Hannah called her name and she realized how foolish she must look. "Well, ladies," she said, taking them by the hands. "Shall we?"

The morning went faster than it seemed to at home. Hannah was old enough to be of some help, and Annie put her in charge of the rolling and cutting with the edge of a cup, a drinking tumbler, and a small glass Annie thought might be used for whiskey.

As she went through the cabinets searching for flour, sugar, raisins, and the like, she kept a sharp eye out for any alcohol but found none. Whatever would Miller think if he found her helping out in a house where a man, a man alone at that, indulged in the very spirits the decent people of Van Wert were organized to oppose? She herself had attended many temperance meetings, and despite her brother-in-law's views on the subject, she was convinced the only alcohol that belonged in a home was that which the doctor prescribed.

Since Julia was allowed to do the decorating of the cookies, Annie made a mental note to tell Ethan and Noah what each one was intended to be. They made girl snowmen, and boy snowmen and cow snowmen and cat snowmen, and when they were down to just a little dough, they made melted snowmen too.

Noah's foodstuffs left a great deal to be desired. Most of the food on his shelves came canned from Hanson's. Annie wished she'd brought some ham from home or at least a couple of chickens to serve the family dinner. As it was, she had to make a hash that she was nearly ashamed to serve.

The men (Annie let Noah come into the house since Ethan was with him), didn't seem to think the meal was less than wonderful. Or, if they did, they didn't let on. And if clean plates were any sign, the food was well received.

"Ah, Sissy," Ethan said when he finally pushed himself away from the table, "you sure can cook."

"And you sure can hunt," she reminded him. "So why ain't—"

"Isn't," Noah interrupted, then wiped his mouth with his napkin and reminded his girls to do the same.

"*Isn't*," she corrected, "there any meat around here? Where are all them—"

"Those," he said very quietly, just to her.

It was like learning to speak all over again. Only this time each word he said seemed to give her chills, as if he was saying something meant only for her. "*Those* rabbits and quail and such?" She waited for another correction. When none came, she smiled and laughed at herself. "Phew! I didn't think I'd ever get that question out!"

"I'm sorry," he said. "If you'd prefer that I didn't—"

"Oh, no," she said shaking her head adamantly. "We've got a bargain. I watch after the girls, and you watch after my talking."

"And who watches after you?" Ethan asked of Noah.

Was it her imagination, or did Noah's cheeks turn just a little pink?

"We best get back to work," was all he said. He stood, stretched, and placed a kiss on Julia's head, one on Hannah's, and then came toward Annie.

She backed up quickly, too quickly, and upset her chair, lost her balance, and went crashing to the floor, smashing her elbow against it and letting out a howl.

In less than an instant, Noah and the girls had her surrounded, taking very seriously what had her brother holding his sides from laughter.

Her elbow tingled and pins and needles ran up and down her arm while her hand felt numb. Whoever named it a funny bone sure had a strange sense of humor. She gripped her elbow tightly and he insisted on examining it. Gentle hands ran down her arm from her shoulder to her wrist, squeezing here or there as if he knew where each bone should be right through her skin—skin that tingled and produced little bumps of goose flesh along the length of her arm. Cautiously he bent and unbent her elbow, taking pains to make sure it was not seriously hurt.

"Is she all right, Pa?" Hannah asked.

"Are you?" he asked her, still resting on his haunches and bending over her.

"Of course," she said, trying to get up despite the girls on her skirts and the closeness of a man who made it hard for her to breathe.

"What about her bum?" Hannah asked.

"My what?" Annie said swallowing hard. The child couldn't have said what she thought.

"Your bum. Pa could kiss it and make it better like he does for me and Julia." She stood there with wide innocent eyes while the adults around her seemed too shocked to say anything.

Then Ethan began to laugh. Not a polite, easy laugh but a guffaw born in the gutter that seemed to be at Annie's expense.

"I'd be happy to," Noah offered, trying to keep a straight face, "if Miss Annie would like it."

"Get away from me," Annie said, pushing at Noah and knocking him down so that he lay sprawled on the floor with her, while Ethan stood laughing and pointing, and the girls looked from one adult to another, growing wary as Annie huffed and snorted trying to get up, and Noah lay motionless except for his stomach, which bounced up and down as if he had swallowed a joke but wouldn't let it out.

Julia wagged her finger in Annie's face. "Cookies," she said with a deadly seriousness that struck Annie's funny bone like nothing else had.

She looked around her. Noah was sprawled on the floor, convulsed with laughter. Ethan was sliding down the wall, honking with amusement. Hannah and Julia were standing very still, confusion written across their innocent faces. Annie's giggles bubbled up and she reached out and pulled the girls against her chest, tickling them softly as she did.

Soon all five of them were laughing easily on the floor of the Eastman farmhouse. The smell of cookies filled the air along with the sounds of laughter and the warmth of five happy people. In an instant Annie realized how simple it would be to just give in. The thought flashed across her mind like a slap that sobered her. With a smile she didn't feel she lifted the girls and headed them for their father, then stood and ran, blinded by the tears that were flooding her vision, toward the kitchen.

She fumbled with the door and fought her way in, rushing to the sink and pumping water to cover the sounds of her sobs. She was not, not going to give up everything, now that she was so close to the life she had always dreamed about. She lifted the apron she wore, stained with Hannah's spilled juice, marred by Julia's chocolatey hands that had smeared her skirts when they hadn't found her apron.

She didn't hear him come into the kitchen, wasn't aware that he had snuck up behind her until she felt the strong hands on her shoulders and the pull that left her back resting against his chest.

"Don't cry," he said, as he stroked her hair and lifted the edge of her apron to wipe her tears. "Please don't cry. Tell me what you want, Annie my sweet. Tell me and I'll make it so."

"I want to marry Miller Winestock," she said, her voice cracking with the words.

"I know," he said, smoothing her hair out of her face. "I know."

"I don't want to like you, or your children, or care what happens to all of you."

"I know," he said again. "I know."

"I don't know what's wrong with me. I'm either laughing or crying or fretting all the time."

"I know," he said once again, wiping at still more tears.

"You have to find someone else, Noah," she said, letting the name she had used in her head finally pass her lips. "You have to let me go."

His breath fanned her hair and sent the loose ends across her face. His lips brushed the side of her head, and she turned her face so he could reach her temple.

He kissed it gently over and over again while he murmured words of sympathy.

"I'm sorry. I'm so sorry," he said over and over again, as if he really regretted barging into her life and confusing her. "I'll do whatever you want."

"Then stop," she said, even though her head tilted farther back and pressed against his chest. "Promise me you'll find someone else to take care of the girls. Promise me you'll do it right away."

"Don't ask me that, Annie," he begged. "Please, don't ask me that." He kissed the top of her head, took handfuls of her hair, and pressed them against his nose as if he could inhale the very essence of her, took gulps of air as if he could swallow her whole.

"There's no other way. You have to find someone else. It can't be me. Do you understand that it can't be me?"

From the other side of the door they clearly heard Ethan's voice. "I'm goin' back out to the fields, Noah. You comin'?"

"What should I tell him?" Noah asked, his hands running up and down her arms in time to her breathing.

Tell him you're staying with me. Tell him you're never letting go. "He's coming, Eth," she shouted through the door. She wrenched herself from Noah's arms. "Take a cookie and tell the girls how good they are," she said, wiping her cheeks with the back of her hands.

"Are you coming?" he asked, pausing at the doorway and turning back to look at her. Etched in his face were the new pain lines she had put there.

She shook her head without saying a word.

He nodded. Somehow the two gestures spoke volumes.

In the morning the stubborn woman he was in love with stood on the porch waiting for him to come out of the house. When he did, she nodded curtly in his general direction and gave him a wide berth as she went in and shut the door firmly behind her.

What had he ever done to merit the trials he was living through? Not that he was one to feel sorry for himself, but there were times when it seemed to him that life ought to owe him some compensation for what he'd been through, all he'd lost, all he'd suffered. And he really believed deep in his heart that Annie was that compensation.

As he harvested corn with Ethan he let his mind have free rein with what his eyes could see. A beautiful woman hanging out clean sheets, her honey hair blowing in the breeze, the bedding slap-slapping against the wind, his two little girls handing her up the clothespins. Their songs drifted to him on the currents of air. *If only* played in his head like a litany, over and over again.

The truth was, he had rushed her. Pushed himself on her when he should have held back until she wanted him as much as he wanted her. Of course, she would never want him as much as he wanted her, for there was no measurement for that. What was the word astronomers used, infinity? That was how much he wanted her, and more. Infinity to the infinite.

And Annie? What was it she wanted? A dull minister who would offer her a rest after all her toils and little else.

"I'm going to town, Ethan," he said suddenly, stopping the horse and jumping from the seeder.

"Noah," Ethan sighed, sensing that the sudden errand had nothing to do with farming and everything to do with his sister. "Farmers gotta farm, dammit. Are you a lover or a farmer?"

"I'm a farmer in love," Noah called over his shoulder as he unhooked the horse. "And unless you want Miller Winestock for a brother-in-law, you'll wish me luck and do what you can while I'm gone."

"You know," Ethan said, coming over to Noah and putting a hand on his arm to stop his motions, "Sissy raised me since I was a baby. If it turns out you hurt her, even without meanin' to, I won't never forgive or forget."

Noah thought one of the most wonderful things about the marriage he knew in his heart would take place between himself and Annie was that he would have the great good fortune of being able to call Ethan Morrow his brother.

"Ethan," he said, "if I do hurt your sister in any way, I won't need you to never forgive and forget. I will never forget or forgive myself."

"That won't change anything," the young man said, "except there will be two of us."

*   *   *

"A wind wheel?" Risa asked him, as though she wasn't sure she had heard correctly. "You want to order a wind wheel?"

She was beginning to look like she was carrying, just a little. There was a softness to her body, a roundness to her face he dared not mention. The glow, though; he thought it was all right to comment on that.

"You look especially pretty today," he said. "There's a—"

"Plumpness," she supplied with a smile. "I look like I swallowed a balloon from the fair, and I've hardly started. The doctor says this child isn't even as big as my thumb"— she held up her hand—"and look at me already."

"Really, Mrs. Morrow," a woman standing near the counter said with disgust. "This is certainly not an appropriate topic to be discussing with a gentleman, especially one you barely know."

"Oh, but—" Risa started, then stopped herself. "No, of course, Mrs. Webb, you're right. I guess I'm just feeling— that is, a wind wheel, you said?"

"Yes." He nodded. "I'm hoping to put a bathroom into the farmhouse."

"What a good idea!" Risa beamed. "A bathroom! Why, anyone would be happy about that!"

"I know I am," Noah said, smiling politely and biting the inside of his cheek.

"You know," Risa said, looking at Mrs. Webb and clearly thinking aloud, "sometimes people sell their old ones. Do you know anyone who might be selling a wind wheel, Mrs. Webb?"

"Why, I would think you'd want Mr. Eastman to order a new one," she answered, very surprised. Then she leaned over the counter and said in the lowest of voices, "You won't make any money, dear, if you tell people to buy used goods."

"That's true," Risa agreed, "but I know how much Mr.

Eastman must want this wheel, with the weather getting colder, and he'd surely be better off if he didn't have to wait for it to be delivered and then risk the ground being frozen and not be able to get it in until spring." She said the last several words pointedly as if she was trying to tell him that time was of the essence. As if he wasn't so aware of it that he'd left Ethan in the field without a horse just to rush into town to order the damn thing.

"Yes," he said as evenly as he could, "I am anxious to get it set up and running before the year is out. Would you know of one for sale, Mrs. Webb?"

"Well," she said, scratching her chin, "let me think."

"Of course. And may I say that I can't remember when I've seen such a lovely bonnet? The blue certainly compliments your eyes." What could be seen of them between the rolls of fat, anyway.

She preened as only fat ugly women can, and then her face brightened. "Why, I think that Warren Stevens out toward Bellefontaine just got a whole new system for bringing water into his place. You check with him. I'm sure he had at least one windmill. Maybe more. Yes," she said, nodding her head and quite satisfied with herself, "you check with him."

"Thank you," he said. "Thank you very much." He turned to leave and halfway across the store was struck by an attack of conscience so strong it nearly pulled him back to the counter.

"Mrs. Webb," he said, capturing her attention again, "you seem exceedingly well informed. Might you know of someone willing to watch two children and cook meals?"

"Then that *was* Ruth Abernathy I saw hustling onto the noon train yesterday," she said. "I thought it was her. Well, that must have put you in quite a bind, I'd say, her running out on you like that."

"Yes," he agreed and thought better of bringing up the

circumstances under which Mrs. Abernathy had left his employ. There were those who believed in her methods and would see him as some foolish man bent on spoiling his girls. "Quite a bind."

"Maybe Sissy—" Risa said, then stopped when she saw the look on Noah's face.

"Miss Morrow has other plans," Noah said diplomatically. *She doesn't know she's marrying me.*

"Of course she does," Mrs. Webb said. "She's marrying the reverend come the new year. Everyone knows that. Just as soon as his mourning's up, I expect they'll be tying the knot."

"Oh, do you think so?" Risa said.

"Yes," Mrs. Webb said definitely.

"No," Noah couldn't stop his mouth from saying.

Mrs. Webb turned to him in surprise. "No?"

"Mourning is a hard thing to measure," Noah said, suddenly pontificating. "And one must be allowed his full cycle of grief. It is not a thing to be tied to the calendar and put behind one as an obligation."

The older woman looked at him with sympathy. "But then, of course, you would know, poor dear. A woman's value is always underrated until she is gone, wouldn't you agree?" she asked Risa, who was taking his measure with her eyebrows low over her eyes and her hands on her hips.

As if Risa's stares weren't enough, he watched Mrs. Webb's eyes narrow as if she suddenly remembered something that had been evading her. "Aren't you the man with the furnace?"

"I suppose I am," he admitted with half a smile.

"The one from church?"

"That would be me."

"Well, my husband went down to the cellar after church and wouldn't you know it? We've a Wells furnace."

"Really?" he asked, not hiding his interest. "Have you had any trouble with it before?"

"We're not having any trouble with it now, young man. I just feel that, as you suggested, it is better to be safe than sorry. I still have two children at home, and a grandchild that spends more time with me than with his own mother, but that is another kettle of fish, isn't it?"

"Did your husband check the pipe?" he asked.

"Well, that's why I brought the whole matter up. Do you think you might drop by one day, before the weather really turns, and check it for us? My husband doesn't know his pipes from his cigars, and I'm afraid he's just made hash of it. He didn't know what he was looking for, so I thought maybe you could come by and have a look."

"I would be happy to," he said truthfully. "If only everyone would let me check, I would feel a whole lot better about the winter coming on."

"Friday would be good for me, Mr. Eastman," she said with a bat of her eyelashes.

"Friday it is," he agreed.

"Excellent." Mrs. Webb beamed. "And Mr. Eastman, I know just the girl for you."

15

Before dawn Annie got up and made her way down to the kitchen. Bleary-eyed and bone tired, she put up water for tea and formed loaves of bread for Willa to bake while Annie was at the Eastman farm. Then she pared the vegetables for the stew and headed for the cellar, where there was still some sacked beef on the bags of ice. If she got everything together in the pot, Willa ought to be able to cook it up with very little trouble.

The cellar was cold. Even in summer it rarely reached sixty degrees, and now, with the weather turning colder every day, it wasn't much above freezing even by the foot of the stairs. Lighting the lamp she kept there, Annie warmed her hands around it for a moment and then, pulling her robe tighter to her body, made for the far corner where the ice stood beneath the chute.

Despite the tray in which it rested there were puddles of half frozen water spread across the floor, and she shivered as the cold water seeped into her worn slippers and bit at her toes. The Acme icebox in the kitchen barely had room for a pitcher of milk and a dozen eggs, never mind chunks of meat. With all the room the ice took up, there was hardly any room for the butter she had hoped to take into town yesterday.

Soon, she promised herself. Soon she would have a dry air refrigerator and sideboard complete with water cooler attachment. Miller loved his water cold, with a little lemon, when it was available. And instead of selling her home-churned butter she would be buying someone else's. No more bartering under Mr. Hanson's distrustful eyes.

"Sissy? That you down there?" Bart's voice called from the top of the steps. He was up early, considering what she'd had to listen to the night before.

"It's me," she answered. "Somethin' wrong?"

She heard his heavy feet on the steps and watched as he crouched down and made his way toward her. Like many of the cellars in Van Wert, theirs was low-ceilinged and only the smallest women could stand erect in them.

"Need any help?" he offered.

Well, Willa might not know how to bake or cook or milk a cow, but she knew how to turn a man into a husband, all right.

"Just gettin' some beef," she answered.

"For breakfast?"

"No," she said as though he were a small child, "for supper."

He took the lantern from her and held it over the bags of ice, freeing up her hands to find the cut of meat she wanted. There was less to chose from than she would have hoped, but on the brighter side, it didn't take all that long to look.

"That mean you're goin' out *there* again?" He said *there* as if he didn't like the taste of the word in his mouth.

"You know I am." But that wouldn't stop him from starting another argument, she was sure.

"How does it look, you goin' and takin' care of his kids?"

"To who?"

"To everyone," he said, though he meant *to Miller*.

"If anyone's lookin', I suppose it looks like I'm doing the same thing Francie did all summer—with your blessing, as I recall."

Bart hit his head softly on the ceiling and grumbled. They were making their way back to the stairs, each step squishy and cold now that her feet were wet.

"That was different, Sissy, and you know it. Francie wasn't engaged or nothin'."

"Well, Bart, I ain't—I mean, I'm not engaged or nothing either. And if Miller don't like me helping out at Mr. Eastman's, he can say so."

"You're pigheaded," he said flatly. "You know that, don'tcha? Pigheaded." He clumped up the stairs behind her, keeping time to their steps with his words. Left—right. Pig—headed.

There were only eight stairs. That fact had never made Sissy so happy before.

"You get up just to call me names?" she asked him when he followed her to the kitchen. By rising early and preparing his supper before she left, Annie had hoped to avoid fighting with her brother. But since he was already up, she thought the best path might be just to make him his breakfast. If there was one thing that seventeen years of cooking had taught her, and taught her well, it was that a man's anger ebbed with his hunger. She put the meat on the counter with a thud and reached for the frying pan that hung over the old wood box stove.

"Fried this mornin'?" she asked him as she reached into the icebox for the eggs, "or scrambled?"

"Scrambled," he ordered. "With potatoes. But Sissy, feedin' me ain't gonna shut me up."

"*Isn't*," she said.

"Huh?"

"*Ain't* is not a word, Bart."

"Don't be ridiculous," Bart said with a laugh. "I just said it, so what is it if it ain't a word?"

She didn't know, but she couldn't wait to get to Noah's so she could ask him. The man knew everything! And he had a way of explaining it all that made her feel smart for asking instead of foolish for not knowing. He never sighed and seemed sad the way Miller did when she asked him to explain a word she'd never heard. And he never lost his place in what he was telling her, either. Miller always had to begin again, and sometimes he lost his patience along with his thought.

"It's not a proper word. Noah says—"

"Noah? You're callin' him Noah now? Jeez, Sissy, the next thing you know you'll be washin' his drawers."

She turned away quickly, stirring the eggs as if she were whipping up cream, and hoped Bart couldn't see her scarlet cheeks. She'd been washing men's drawers since she had taken over the role of mother to her siblings. It hadn't occurred to her when she started in on the Eastmans' laundry yesterday that it would be improper for her to wash his underthings.

It wasn't until she was hanging them on the line that she realized she was touching parts of his clothing that had been intimately touching parts of him. His form-fitting Derby ribbed underwear had bulges and bumps that, despite the boiling and wringing, still revealed the man whose body they had been keeping warm. When a leg teased her face in the breeze and then wrapped itself around her, she had been so unnerved that she swatted at it as if it were a swarm of bees and the girls had convulsed in giggles at her feet.

Without consciously doing it, she pulled down four plates from the shelves and began to dish out the eggs.

"We havin' company for breakfast?" Bart asked.

She looked down at what she had done. Two plates contained just enough eggs for small but growing girls. One plate held her usual amount, and one was a farmer's portion. Quickly she scraped the two smaller portions together into one.

"Is Willa up yet?" she asked. "Or should I cover these?"

"She ain't feelin' so good this mornin'," Bart said, his eyebrows knit together with worry. "That's just normal, ain't it?"

She could have corrected him, but she chose not to. Just knowing about using the right words gave her a confidence she'd never felt before. Why hadn't Francie corrected her? Or Charlie? Were they all afraid to hurt her feelings? And what about Miller? He must have just thought it was hopeless. But Noah took the time to correct her gently, and he never failed to praise her with a smile or a nod when she corrected herself. Soon, she thought, she wouldn't be making mistakes at all.

"She's not having any pain, is she?" Annie asked. "And no bleeding?"

Bart blanched at the question. He hadn't turned as white when he'd caught his hand in a thresher and the doctor said he might lose a finger.

"She seen Dr. Randall yet?" Annie asked when he refused to talk about so delicate a subject with her.

"A woman doctor!" he said. "Fat lot of good seein' Emma Randall ought to do. Why she—"

"How many of your men doctors have been in Willa's condition, Bart?"

"You don't gotta be a cow to treat a sore teat."

"No," Willa said as she came through the door, her hair a mess, her complexion a little green, her smile wan. "But I bet the cow would appreciate it if you were. Morning, Sissy."

The smell of breakfast cooking on the stove, the smoky bacon, the melted butter for the fried eggs, the onions sizzling with the chunks of potato, overwhelmed her all at once and she covered her mouth with her hand and ran from the room. Annie chased after her with a bowl and held it in front of her while she had the dry heaves.

"I bet you can't wait for this to all be over," Annie said in her most soothing voice, while she rubbed Willa's back.

The woman turned around and looked at Annie like she'd lost her mind. "Bart's baby is growing inside me, Sissy. A piece of him is with me all the time, getting bigger and bigger every day. Oh, I don't like the morning sickness much," she admitted, "but I wouldn't change my condition for anything in the world."

Well, Annie thought, she never did credit Willa Leeman with much in the way of brains.

Someone was stomping on his porch. He looked out his bedroom window and saw Annie, half blue with cold, rubbing her hands up and down her arms and stamping her feet. But was she knocking or coming in? No. And why? Because she knew he was still inside.

He hurried to the door, pulling his shirt on over his long johns as he went. "Get in here," he ordered. "It's colder than a witch's—uh—nose. Now come on in."

He stood with the door open and waited while she considered his invitation. She took in his open shirt, the overall straps which hung around his hips, and didn't take long to decide. "I'll wait here," she said.

"That's just ridiculous. You'll catch your death. I won't go anywhere near you. Just come in."

She crossed her arms over her chest. Even under her shawl he could tell it was a nice chest. Her breasts stood out proudly, the buttons straining slightly at the fullest point. "I'd rather wait," she said.

"Oh, for heaven's sake," he said, letting his irritation

show. He came out onto the porch and stood very close to her. "Now will you go in? I'll stay out here."

"Now who's being ridiculous?" she asked. "At least finish dressing and get your coat."

She smelled of yeast and something sweeter. Vanilla? It made his mouth water. "I'm not cold," he said honestly, warming at just being near her. "Now go on inside."

"Men," she huffed under her breath. "They're all happy to tell you what to do as long as it's what suits them!"

"So then I'm not the only one you're—" he was going to say *annoyed with,* but she shut the door in his face, so there was very little point.

With her gone, he was freezing. What ever happened to autumn? Used to be a nice long time between summer and winter, he remembered. Russet and orange days with mild temperatures just right for hiking or catching a frog or hooking a fish. Nowadays, he just blinked and summer had turned to winter.

And winter would mean that any day now people would be going down and turning on their furnaces. And maybe more than their coal money would go up in smoke.

He opened the door and glanced around for Annie. The banter of happy children came from the kitchen and so he called out, "I'm getting my coat. Anyone who wants to kiss me good-bye should come now."

Hannah came running through the doorway with Julia shouting after her to wait. He could hear Annie telling the littler one not to run. And then he heard a clunk and a cry.

"Oh, Julie!" Annie said. "Poor baby!"

He picked Hannah up on his way and entered the kitchen to find Annie kneeling down and checking a tearful Julia for bruises. She kissed the palms of both of Julia's hands, one of her knees when she could find it under all the layers of clothing, and an elbow right through her sleeve.

At that one Julia began to cry again, and Annie took a closer look at the arm of Julia's dress.

"I think it's bleeding a little," Annie told him.

"Bud!" Julia exclaimed. "I got bud!"

"Blood," Hannah corrected. "Let me see."

He lifted Julia from the floor and sat her on the counter, making room for Annie to help ease the child's arm out of her sleeve. As Annie turned Julia's arm slightly, he saw two small drops of blood hardly worthy of more than a kiss, and so he bent to kiss her elbow and somehow wound up kissing Annie's finger instead.

It was an honest mistake, but she reacted as if he'd tripped his own child and bloodied her just so that he could get the chance to graze her finger with his lips.

"You can't do that. I told you already." She shook her head. "This won't work. I can't stay here like this. I just can't."

A pin was slipping from her silky hair, but he didn't dare touch it. He watched, fascinated by its torturously slow trip, as the weight of her hair eased the fastener lower and lower until it slid out of her hair altogether and fell to the floor. One hand balancing Julia as if she couldn't trust him not to let his own daughter fall, eyes sending daggers as if he had caused her hair to come undone, she bent to pick up the pin.

The curve of her back was something to behold. Her white shirtwaist was well worn, and beneath it he could see the straps of her chemise. She was so very lovely, and he knew that his next words, while they cut him to the quick, would please her very much.

"I may have found someone to watch the girls."

Her head jerked up. Her hold on Julia tightened. For a fleeting moment pain crossed her face and he thought she might tell him it wasn't necessary to replace her after all.

Instead she raised her eyebrows and said, "Really? Who?"

Mrs. Webb hadn't mentioned her name, when he thought about it. "I'm meeting her tomorrow," he said. "Someone in town asked me to have a look at their furnace and I inquired as to whether they might know of anyone fond of children. Unlike yourself, of course."

She bristled at that but refused to bite. "Good," she said curtly.

"Fine," he replied, just as sharply.

"Well," she said.

"Yes, well," he returned.

She reached behind her and pulled her hair back into the tight knot she liked to keep it in and tried to stab the silky mound with her pin. His eyes fell to her chest, pushed forward by her arched back, and then climbed her slender throat, the chin that was tucked against it, and then rested on her bottom lip, caught between her teeth as she maneuvered the pin through the waves of hair.

If he could watch her twist that hair up every morning for the rest of his life, he would die a happy man. If he could watch her take it down every night, he would choose to never die.

"I'd better go," he said, easing Julia's arm back into her sleeve and taking her down from the counter. His arm brushed Annie's skirts, gently slipping over her hip, and steadied Julia on the floor.

"Has she got much experience with children?" Annie asked. "You'd best make sure she knows that Julia ain—isn't using the chamber pot just yet."

He nodded.

"Not that there's any rush, sweetheart," she assured the little girl who stood between them, studying her father's boots. "Make sure she isn't gonna go pushing her faster than she's ready to go. Do that and you just move your day problem into the night and spread it out over years instead of months."

He nodded again.

"And make sure she knows the value of vegetables and fresh air. A child can't have too much fresh air, so when she puts Julia in for her nap she should leave the window open."

He nodded again.

And then he smiled. Finding a housekeeper of which Annie would approve would be like trying to finish Aladdin's window—impossible.

Annie found the liquor in the back of the highest cabinet quite by accident. It gave her one more worry about leaving the girls in the care of someone else. She considered and dismissed the idea that the bottle might have belonged to Mrs. Abernathy. Besides her attendance at the temperance meetings, which Annie well knew could be all for show, just like her concern for the children, if the bottle had been hers, she'd have surely taken it with her when she left.

Her imagination ran wild all afternoon. What if in a drunken rage he hurt the girls? What if in a drunken stupor he slept through their cries of pain or fear? What if the new housekeeper found the liquor and walked out in anger, leaving the girls to fend for themselves? Worse, what if she drank the liquor instead?

She saw herself with two choices: she could mark the bottle and check it the next day to see if Noah was a regular drinker, risking God only knew what in the meantime, or she could pour the bottle out and save untold grief for everyone involved. The choice seemed clear, and the bottle was almost empty when a voice rang out behind her.

"If it was a problem for me, do you think there would have been three quarters of a bottle left?"

The sound so startled her she dropped the bottle, which clattered against the steel sink, making a racket.

"There's nothing to get so upset about," his smooth

voice said. "I don't mind. I don't expect to be cutting my hand again any too soon."

"Your hand?"

"That's why I opened it. To dull the pain a bit. It did too good a job," he added.

"There's other things you could've taken." She kept her eyes on the sink and her back to him. "I've some Humphreys' specifics that I keep in my cabinet for just those kinds of emergencies."

He took a few steps. She heard his boots on the floor, but she still hadn't turned around and had no idea how close to her he had come. She prayed she wouldn't feel his hands against her shoulders, spinning her around. She prayed and prayed and yet she was disappointed when after a while he still hadn't reached out to her.

"I'm still a good three feet away," he said, as if he could read her mind. Her cheeks warmed at the thought. "You're safe."

She looked at him over her shoulder, knowing his words were the farthest thing from the truth. She wasn't safe in the same room with him. Not in the same house. She wondered if even the whole town was big enough for the two of them. "I'm sorry. I guess I got carried away. I don't abide with drinking, but it ain't my place to go pouring yours down the drain."

"*Isn't.* And no, it's not. But I don't mind. You're all the intoxication I need, Miss Morrow. In fact, you're more than I can handle right now."

"Don't say stuff like that." There was a quiver in her voice that was new to her. She smoothed her hair back toward her bun and ran her fingers over the flare of her skirts. It didn't make her feel any more in control.

"I mean it." His hands just hung at his sides as he watched every move she made.

"I know." The words were dragged out of her against

her will. Another kind of woman would have enjoyed the power she held over Noah Eastman. Would have used it. She, so far removed from courting and mating, was scared half to death by it.

"I'm not a drinker, Annie," he said, looking past her at the sink. "Some here and there, maybe. I like to think I use whiskey wisely and well."

"Using it at all ain't—" she was frustrated by her own tongue and took a minute to tame it.

"You're flustered, that's all," he said. "I know how that feels, all right. Remember when I couldn't get out two words in your presence?"

She couldn't help but laugh. "I think I liked you better then," she said.

He shook his head. "No. You like me better now. You like me so much it frightens you. But you'll get over it."

"The liking you?"

Now it was his turn to laugh. "No, you'll never get over that."

The smell of whiskey was all around them. Julia's voice rose in the other room, and Annie knew she was awake and needed changing. Noah's muddy boots had left a trail from the front door to the middle of the kitchen. Supper needed to be served and she'd had to settle for potato pie since she hadn't found any meat to prepare. "I'll get over it," she said evenly. "See if I don't."

As if to convince herself, she brushed right by him, letting her arm touch his as she passed, and went to see to Julia.

If Annie thought that would help, she saw her mistake quickly when Julia reached out pudgy little hands to her and uttered something that sounded all too close to "mama." Her arms wrapped tightly around Annie's neck and she planted a wet kiss on her cheek.

A moment later a second pair of arms wrapped around

her knees. "Don't go away," Hannah said. "I love you, Miss Annie."

"Me too," Julia added.

"I'm all cleaned up," Ethan called from the parlor. "Supper ready?"

"I'm taking it off the stove now," Noah shouted.

He was taking it off the stove? She hurried to put Julia in a clean diaper and get out to the parlor. Noah had something up his sleeve, helping her like that, and she was anxious to see just what it was.

The table was set, rather haphazardly, and the potato pie sat on a trivet near the head. Ethan came in from the kitchen with a water pitcher just as Annie slipped Julia into her chair.

"He's hitchin' up Blackie." Ethan looked at her quizzically. "How come you're in such a hurry to leave?"

"All set," Noah said, wiping his hands on his overalls as he came in. "She's ready when you are."

"Don't go," Hannah said. She grabbed a piece of Annie's skirt and hung on tightly.

One minute he was asking her to take care of his children, and the next he was shooing her out of his house. Annie stood there trying to get her bearings in what felt like a shift in the wind.

In just a few strides he crossed the floor and knelt down beside Hannah, prying her little fist open to release Annie's dress. "She'll be back tomorrow," Noah said and looked up to make sure it was so. She nodded at him. Hadn't she agreed to take care of the children until he found a replacement? Did he think she would abandon the girls now?

"Of course," she said gently as she fondled the top of Hannah's dark head.

"If we behave ourselves," Noah added.

Annie wasn't sure just who he meant.

16

Noah had been standing on the porch for several minutes by the time Annie arrived the next morning. With just a nod he unhitched Blackie, led him to the trough, and tied him off there. Then he headed for the fields, leaving a very bewildered Annie at his front door.

Boy, he wished he'd had one of those new cameras he'd been reading so much about. *You push the button, we do the rest,* the advertisements read. He'd be willing to pay good money to save the look on Annie's face to show to their grandchildren someday. You know, he'd tell them, your grandmother didn't know at first that she was in love with me. Just caught her by surprise. See?

Ethan was standing close to the barn, ready to start the day's work when Noah approached. "Sissy don't look none too happy," he said.

"No," Noah agreed, unable to keep the smirk from his lips. "She doesn't, does she? Wonder why that is?" If she was so intent on his staying away from her, and on leaving his farm, why had the idea that he'd possibly found someone to take over watching the children rankled her so? She made it seem as though he'd thrown her out of the house last night, when all he'd done was hitch up her horse and let her leave early. Shouldn't she have been glad to go?

And this morning he'd done just as she wanted. Or said she did. He was out of the house when she got there and he hadn't said a word to her. So how come she was peering out the kitchen window at him with her brows drawn down and a pout that looked like disappointment touching her full lips?

Because, dammit, she wanted him every bit as much as he wanted her. She wanted him and his kids, bless their little conniving hearts. When Hannah threw her arms around Annie before supper and begged her not to go, Noah wanted to dance the child around the room in gratitude. She was getting to Annie in a place that was inaccessible to him, her need to mother a small one. The maternal instinct that Wylene had been born without flowed through Annie's veins like alcohol in a drunk. It was a self-perpetuating need, and the more she fed it the more it craved.

"Noah?" Ethan asked. "We gettin' to work today? Looks like we ain't got a lot of time before the rain starts." He gestured with his head toward the horizon, where dark clouds were gathering force and beginning to threaten.

"Yes, of course," Noah said, his mind on everything but the harvesting. "Eth, if it rains, do you have any plans for the afternoon?"

"Plans? I planned to spend the day harvestin', same as always. If it rains, I'm free as a bird." He looked at Noah. "Or ain't I?"

"Well," Noah explained, "I have some big plans, and I was thinking about putting them in motion this afternoon."

"Why do I think they got somethin' to do with my sister?"

"Because you are not only intelligent but perceptive. Plus, you know I can't keep her out of my mind."

"Noah," Ethan said as they made their way to the far end of the field, Ethan's eyes on the ground, Noah's on the sky, "you know I like you a lot. I like workin' for you, I like them two girls of yours. But before I take one step to help you with this plan you have that concerns Sissy, I gotta know what you have in mind."

Noah stopped in his tracks and stared at the younger man beside him, touched. "My intentions are completely honorable. I fully intend to marry your sister."

"Oh," Ethan drawled, "I know that. I can see that, and you told me more than once already. That ain't what's botherin' me."

Noah waited patiently for the boy to fish around for the right words. He hoped he found them soon, as Ethan was digging a good-size hole with his left boot.

"Look," he said finally. "My sister's had a rough life. I can't remember a day when she wasn't up before the rest of us with that damn smile plastered on her face to greet us when we came down to the kitchen, not a night when she wasn't the last one to go to sleep after makin' sure all of us were fed, healthy, and accounted for."

"And?"

"I keep thinkin' about how easy she'd have it with Mr. Winestock. I keep thinkin' she's earned it."

He was at it again, the foot of the boot covered with dirt and still headed for China.

"I know that," Noah said slowly. He also knew that he would do everything in his power, starting today, to make her life easier. And he knew one more thing that he thought made all the difference. "But I can make her happy. Can your Mr. Winestock do that?"

When Ethan raised his head his eyes were glistening. There was a magic Annie wrought, a loyalty that was planted deep and which flowered into love. Noah had seen it in Francie when she mentioned her sister's name. It was here in Ethan. Charlie and Risa were caught up in her spell, and even big old Bart showed a protective side when it came to his older sister.

"Come on," he said to Ethan, slapping him on the back and bending to the day's work. "We've got a lot of work to do before the rain starts."

"And what about once it does?"

"We're going to buy a wind wheel," he said in a whisper. He looked over his shoulder toward the house. "I want a bath room in that house before the first of the year."

"Does she know?" Ethan asked, his smile bright enough to light up the dark day.

"Hell, no! You think I want her marrying me for my bath room? Your Reverend Winestock might settle for that. But Annie's going to marry me for love."

"And the bathroom?" Ethan asked. "What's that for?"

"Just leveling the playing field, son," Noah said.

"Huh?"

"After the wind wheel we'll stop and take a look at Mrs. Webb's furnace," he added.

"Won't be long before people start firin' them things up," Ethan said.

Noah nodded and put his back into his work. He just hoped he was wrong about the furnaces.

And right about Annie.

"Tessie Willis?" Annie nearly shrieked. He had to be joking. He couldn't be thinking of leaving two helpless children in the care of that hussy. "Ethan, he isn't really considerin' hirin' her, is he?"

"I've always kinda liked Tessie myself, Sissy," Ethan said. He was grinning like a little boy.

The door swung open and a gust of cold rain entered

his house along with Noah. He was soaked to the bone, just like Ethan, and he shrugged out of his jacket and headed right for the parlor stove. "Did you tell her?" he asked.

"You're shiverin', both of you," she said to them with disgust. Would Tessie Willis even notice? Noah's clothes stuck to him like they'd been painted on, outlining every muscle and bulge of his body. She'd notice, all right; even falling down drunk, she'd notice that. "Get out of them wet things. Your dinner's on the stove. The girls are in bed."

Ethan and Noah exchanged looks. "So what do you think?" Noah asked Annie. "Tessie be all right with you? She can start on Monday."

Start what? Annie wondered. Surely it wouldn't be the girls she planned on watching. "Does she have any experience?" Annie asked. She didn't remember hearing of Tessie doing anything that involved children except risking creating them, though she wasn't one to go spreading rumors herself.

"Oh, she's got plenty of experience," Ethan said, then guffawed and nudged Noah with his elbow. "Don't ya think so, Noah? I mean, didn't it seem—"

The two of them were acting like schoolboys, and Annie wanted none of it. She crossed her arms over her chest and waited for them to settle down. Noah's eyes were on her, and it seemed to Annie that he was enjoying every moment of her discomfort.

He might not have been the most experienced ladies' man, but Noah Eastman had been studying Annie Morrow for over a month and by now he was able to read her every expression as easily as any book on his shelves. Clearly she disapproved of Tessie, as he and Ethan were sure she would. And that disapproval was just what he was counting on.

He fought to keep a straight face. It had been a perfect afternoon right down to the rain, which had let them leave putting up their shocks of corn and head off toward Bellefontaine. There they'd made a good deal with Warren Stevens for his old wind wheel, which he assured them had worked just fine before he replaced it with the latest thing on the market, which gave them running water in every room of the house. The wind wheel, he said, would supply two rooms if they ran the pipes the way he diagrammed. Wouldn't a warm bath feel good right now? He was freezing.

"Tessie's a warmhearted woman, that's for sure." Noah agreed with Ethan. "And she says she likes children all right."

"Humph!" Annie said, bristling around their feet with a mop. "Likes children *all right,*" she muttered. He raised his foot out of the way just in time to avoid being swabbed along with the floor.

"Think it'll take her long to learn to cook?" Ethan asked.

Noah choked and recovered himself. "Maybe Annie could leave her some recipes to follow." He turned to her with wide innocent eyes. "Could you? Maybe for those cookies the children like so much?"

It was a good thing the mop handle was kiln-fired birch. Anything softer might have broken under the iron hands of the woman who was taking her anger out on the floor.

"I ain't got a recipe for them. It's a handful of this and a pinch of that until it tastes right."

"*Don't have,*" he corrected. Let her remember she'd be losing his instruction too. "Haven't got, or don't have. But it's not really important anymore."

"It's as important as ever," she snapped. "Maybe more so."

"Really?" he asked as innocently as he could feign. "How so?"

"So she can't cook and she tolerates kids all right," Annie said stiffly. "What are her good points?"

"Well," Ethan said before he doubled over laughing, "I can think of two!"

Annie's face blushed scarlet, but she stood her ground. "Can she take care of these girls or not? Will she be able to keep them clean, fed, safe? Can you trust their very lives to her, after all they've been through?"

"I hadn't thought of that," he said, winking at Ethan while Annie bent to pick up the leaves that were finally drying and falling from their trouser legs. "After Mrs. Abernathy, I guess the girls do need an extra dose of reassurance."

"Of course they do." She sighed. "And not just reassurance. The woman who watches them has to be dependable. She has to be reliable. Why, I don't see how you could think that Tessie Willis—"

"You're right, naturally. I guess I'll have to spend more time with them while she's here."

"Well, I'd be happy to—" Ethan started, but Noah interrupted him.

"No, I couldn't let you, the girls are mine."

"Oh!" Annie said with a huff, obviously disgusted with them both.

"So what did you think about Mrs. Webb's furnace?" Noah asked, knowing it would frustrate Annie if he simply dismissed the subject of Tessie as if it were a fait accompli.

Ethan followed his lead and for a few minutes they discussed the differences as well as the similarities between the Webbs', the church's, and his own furnace. All the while Annie made little noises around them, groans and tsks, and mumbled to herself.

Finally, he acknowledged her presence and the fact that she had stayed late so that he and Ethan could run their errands. She had no way of knowing they were for her, that everything he did had come to revolve around her.

"I'm sorry we were gone so long," he began.

"Yes," Ethan chimed in. "But when Tessie starts going—"

He shot Ethan a look. He didn't want Annie to think he was interested in Tessie, just that he would let her watch his children. But it occurred to him that if she thought that not only was she risking Hannah's and Julia's well-being by allowing Tessie to take over the role of caretaker, but Ethan's as well, it might just push her over the edge here and now and he could stop the silly charade.

"Seems," he said to Annie as if Ethan wasn't in the room, "that your brother has taken a bit of a fancy to Miss Willis."

"Well," Annie said, "I always thought Ma's brains got used up on the first four of us and she saved Pa's brains for Francie. That left old Ethan here with only my cookin' between his ears. Made him sweet but not too much else."

It was the closest he had ever heard her come to criticizing her siblings, and he knew that though it was couched in jest, she had to be pretty upset to say something that might hurt her baby brother.

"Truth is, Sissy," Ethan said as though he meant it, "I always have liked Tessie Willis. I think people are damn unfair to her and I don't believe them rumors, either."

"Rumors don't hatch themselves," Annie snapped back, her hands on her rounded hips. "Scratch a rumor and you'll find a grain of truth somewheres inside."

Noah wasn't a fan of rumors, but he wished he'd believed the ones about Wylene. If he could save Ethan the pain he'd been through, at least it wouldn't have been for nothing. "I don't like casting aspersions." He caught himself and tried to explain. "That is, I think it's wrong to hint around and ruin a person's good name, but sometimes, just sometimes, you have to take those rumors as a kind of warning."

"Warning?" Ethan asked.

"You ever seen a mine, Ethan?" he asked.

Ethan shook his head. "I ain't never seen nothin' that ain't within thirty miles of Van Wert. Don't mean I won't, though."

"Well," Noah said slowly, searching for the right way to explain what he wanted to say. "At the front of a mine there'll be a sign. It'll say CAUTION, or BLASTING TODAY, or ENTER AT YOUR OWN RISK. Now there might be coal in the mine, or gold, or silver, or there might be nothing to gain and just plenty to lose. And there are those who will go in, damn the signs, and come out with their pockets full."

Annie huffed and he put his hand up.

"I'm not finished. There will be others, lots of others, who'll risk it all, go into that mine and never come out alive. And there are those who'll come out with nothing more than their lives, and they'll have to be grateful for that."

"Are you telling me that Tessie's got dynamite in her corset?" Ethan laughed.

"I'm telling you those rumors are danger signs that say KEEP OUT or, at the least, CAUTION, and if you go in anyway, there's no telling what you'll come away with." *Maybe, if you're lucky, you'll get two beautiful girls and a broken heart.*

The shock on Annie's face was something to see. When he realized what it must have sounded like he meant, comparing a woman to a mine and advising Ethan about going in, he felt the heat rise in his face.

"I didn't mean—" he began, but Annie had turned her back and was headed for her coat, which hung from a hook by the front door. She waved her hand to cut off his words and turned around with the iciest stare he had ever seen. And he'd seen some pretty cold ones.

"Tell the girls I'll see them in church on Sunday," she said as she wrapped herself in her two-cape covert-cloth macintosh and opened the door.

"Please," Noah said quietly, coming quickly behind her and shutting the door. "Give me a few minutes. I'll hitch up the buggy and take you home. I can't let you go in the wagon. You'll be soaked right through to your skin."

He stood too close to her, he knew. And he knew he shouldn't have brought up her skin, especially the image of her clothing wet and stuck to her. And he should have suggested that Ethan see her home. The plan was to give her enough distance from his attentions to make her miss them.

But it was dark. And cold. And rainy.

And she was soft. And small. And beautiful. Very beautiful.

And she was also too darn stubborn for her own good, he thought as he watched her pull away from the house in her wagon despite the many tragedies he warned her could befall a woman alone on a night like this.

Now he had Ethan and the images of Annie lying in a ditch, rain soaked and unconscious, to keep him company for the night.

And not a drop of liquor in the house, either.

Miller Winestock had heard the rumors before services began on Sunday. Mrs. Webb, a reliable source, had told him that Sissy Morrow had been watching the Eastman girls. It seemed Mr. Eastman had been out to check her furnace on Friday and admitted that Annie had been out at his place all week.

"We begin our readings on page eighteen," he said as people took their seats. He was not waiting for stragglers today.

Working at Mr. Eastman's was certainly a subject they would have to discuss over Sunday supper. Sissy was too full of the milk of human kindness for her own good. A man like Noah Eastman would suck that milk dry before

she knew what was happening. His allusion caught him off
guard.

"Uh . . ." He fumbled with his prayer book and knocked
it from its perch on the lectern. As he bent to retrieve it, he
heard the back door open and knew the Eastmans had
arrived. "Where was I?" he asked Dr. Morgan, who sat in
the front row.

"Are you quite all right?" Morgan asked.

It was extraordinary. He'd never lost his place before.

"Certainly," he replied and carried on as best he could.

Well, if she was out at the Eastman farm it explained
why she hadn't shown up on Tuesday, as she always did
with a little fresh butter and usually a pie. If he was totally
honest with himself, and he prided himself on being just
that, he had been disappointed when darkness fell and it
was clear that she would not be visiting that day.

It wasn't the butter or the pie, though both were of the
highest quality. It was the cheery countenance, the efficient
way she did a bit of straightening or mending "as long as
she was there," the pleasure of afternoon tea shared with
someone who hadn't come simply because he was the minister of the Pleasant Township Methodist Church.

The congregation sat waiting silently for instructions.
"A hymn," he suggested, then corrected himself. "That is,
let us all sing together, from page 462."

He knew the words by heart, and he let them come
forth from his lips without ever crossing his mind, which
was well occupied with other things. Mrs. Webb had told
him she had suggested that her niece Tessie, that unfortu-
nate young woman whose questionable habits and fre-
quent absences from Van Wert were the subject of more
than one sewing circle in town, work for Mr. Eastman. As
if the troubles the girl had encountered so far were not
enough for her to bear. He had suggested that if Tessie
were looking for work, he was in need of a secretary.

"Lovely," he said. "Let us read now from Genesis chapter four, verse nine 'And the Lord said unto Cain, Where is Abel thy brother? And he said, I know not: Am I my brother's keeper?'"

It wasn't his responsibility to see to it that every poor creature in Van Wert was kept away from trouble, but if he saw it coming, didn't he have some obligation to try to head it off? And wouldn't allowing Miss Willis to ensconce herself in Noah Eastman's house only lead to her own heartache? And if he could prevent that heartache?

The hiring of a secretary might be seen as an insult to Sissy, he conceded. But the fact was she simply couldn't fulfill that part of Elvira's duties adequately. Why waste her time on things she did so poorly when there were so many things she did so well?

The sermon went on by itself, the words leaping from the paper before him and coming out of Miller's mouth while he pondered the questions that haunted him. Mrs. Webb implied that Mr. Eastman might be looking for more in Tessie than a caretaker for his children. Was that wishful thinking on her part? Or was Noah Eastman looking for a woman despite his situation?

He didn't like the idea that Sissy Morrow was spending her days out there at his farm, even if, as Mrs. Webb pointed out fairly, her brother Ethan was there all the time too. Ethan, humph!

He made his way to the back of the church, shaking hands as he went. By the time he stood on the porch, Bart and Willa Morrow were already in their wagon and Ethan was helping Sissy into the back.

For the first time in months, it appeared he wasn't invited for supper.

17

After church on Sunday, Ethan got word from his sister that should Noah wish her to continue watching the children while he searched further for a suitable woman to take over her duties, she was not averse to the idea. Of course, the way Ethan put it when he told Noah was more like "She ain't gonna let Tessie Willis within ten feet of those precious girls of yours."

And then, surprise of surprises, Tessie told Ethan that she had taken a job with the Reverend Miller Winestock, putting her education to use. Both Noah and Ethan resisted any comments regarding Tessie using in the minister's service what she'd learned.

Things seemed even better than Noah had anticipated when Ethan added that Sissy had so much to do, being away from home all week the way she had been, that she was forgoing the Sunday dinner ritual in favor of getting some work done at her place. Ethan, not seeing what that implied, was naturally disappointed. But when Noah pointed out that she wouldn't be cooking for Winestock, Ethan agreed that missing one of Annie's meals was a high price to pay, but worth it to have her forgo cooking for the minister.

Things seemed to be going his way until Annie showed up Monday morning, the *Van Wert Bulletin* and *The Outlook* tucked under one arm, a basket on the other, and a determined look on her face.

"I'll be leaving in just a moment," he said when he opened the door. "Do you want to stand out there and wait?" She smelled wonderful, a sweet scent on the crisp autumn air. She looked wonderful, in a deep brown coat against a pale gray landscape.

"No," she said, trying to sound businesslike. "There's a matter I'd like to discuss with you."

"Of course," he said, holding the door for her and inviting her in. His shirt was open and he fiddled with the buttons. She watched him until she realized what she was doing and quickly looked away. He pulled up the straps to his overalls. "Can I take your coat?"

She worked the buttons, and this time it was his eyes that were glued to her hands. He didn't have the courtesy to look away, but waited until she was done and then helped slip the coat from her shoulders. "Thank you," she said. With her coat off, she looked like she belonged there, like she was home. His girls came running when they heard her voice, and she couldn't hide her smile. Why should she? Did she really think he didn't know she was crazy about his children?

"Were you good since I was here last?" she asked, and the girls both nodded.

"I didn't hear a peep out of either of you in church," she continued. "That made me very proud. I told my sister-in-law, Mrs. Morrow, 'My girls are being so good, they deserve a treat,' and she agreed."

My girls. Mine.

"What?" Hannah demanded, while Julia jumped up and down as best she could. "What did you bring us?"

"Well," Annie teased, "she thought a head of cabbage was just the thing, but I said, 'No, the girls don't want cabbage.'"

Hannah and Julia shook their heads solemnly.

"I didn't think so. My brother Charlie—do you know Mr. Charlie at the mercantile?"

The girls shook their heads again. Noah leaned against the wall and watched three pairs of eyes all dancing with joy at the game they were playing. *This is how it should be,* he thought. *Let it be like this forever.*

"Well, Charlie is my brother, just like Ethan is. And Charlie said—"

"We want a brother too, right, Julia?" Hannah said and turned to her sister for confirmation. Annie kept her eyes glued on the floor while Noah kept his chuckle to himself. *Slow down, Hannah. We don't want to scare her away.*

"Charlie said you would like a nice piece of pipe, like your papa ordered."

The girls made funny faces.

"You don't?" Annie asked. Her hair was only half up, just the front and sides. The back hung loose and free and nearly brushed the ground as she knelt beside his daughters. "I didn't think so. I asked Cara. I know you met her at church one day, 'cause I introduced you. Remember?"

The girls both nodded enthusiastically. Now that his parents were gone, they had no one in the world but him. No cousins, no aunts, no uncles, no one to get together with at Thanksgiving or Christmas or just on a Sunday afternoon. But once he married Annie, there would be family crawling over his house like bear cubs over a honey hive. And Annie would be the queen bee.

"And she said that there isn't anything she likes better than my cookies. What do you think of that?"

"Gookies!" Julia squealed. "Gookies!"

Annie smiled at the child's pleasure. "But not just any cookies," she told them. "These are Eastman cookies." She rose to her full height, which was a good head shorter than his, and reached for the small basket she had placed on the table. She reached in and carefully unwrapped two packages to reveal perfect duplicates of his daughters, down to their dark brown hair and bright blue eyes. Even their dresses were familiar. The cookie she handed Hannah had a pink dress just like the one Hannah wore on the day she hid in Annie's wagon, and Julia's was dressed in the wine dress she had worn to church last week.

"Think Tessie could have made those?" she asked, and rather snidely, at that, as the girls oohed and aahed and compared treats. She pulled out two more cookies, plain ones, and handed them to the girls, who rapidly put them in their mouths. "And would she know that Hannah wouldn't eat hers? And if she didn't, neither would Julia?"

"I never thought she'd be better with them than you," he said. "This is all your idea. I don't want to replace you." *I want to marry you, you silly little ninny. I want you to raise these two and a dozen more. I want to break my back in the fields every day to make sure you want for nothing, and then I want to come home and rest in your arms while you read to me and I help you with the words no one ever gave you the chance to learn.*

"We need to place an advertisement," she said, picking up one of the newspapers from the table and showing him the page she had folded open.

She stood close enough for him to read over her shoulder, so that her hair tickled his nostrils and swayed at his breath. Her shoulder nearly touched his chest, and he had to take shallow little breaths to avoid coming in contact with her.

"Look," she said, pointing to a small ad.

"Have you got piles?" he asked.

"Not that one. This one." Now she was touching him.

Her back pressed against his chest as she held the paper so close to his face he had to lean his head back to see it.

He read it aloud. "'Lady Agents. Make $18 a week easy. If you are in need of employment, send us your address and we will show you how to make $18 a week easy and sure. We guarantee it. You will be surprised how easily it can be done. Send us your address anyway. It will be to your interest to investigate. Royal Manufacturing Company, Box 44, Detroit, Michigan.' Are you thinking of getting another job? I thought you didn't have time for this one."

"How many people you think wrote to that company?" she asked.

"Do you want to place an ad for something?" he asked.

"I want *you* to place an ad," she said. "I'll tell you what to say and you'll write it down and send it in. OK?"

"For someone to watch the girls?"

"Yes."

"You'd let someone we don't even know come and stay with Hannah and Julia? We knew Mrs. Abernathy and look what happened."

"We'd make them tell us who else's children they watched and check with them."

"References," he said and nodded, pretending to go along. "That could take a very long time, Annie," he warned.

"But we'd be sure to get the right one," she said, looking up at him. "Not someone who falls off the sidewalk in bright daylight in downtown Van Wert."

"Did Tessie really do that?"

"I heard she did," Annie said, seriously enough for him to believe it happened.

"Ethan says—" he began, but she cut him off.

"And look at this advertisement in *The Outlook*." She shoved the paper at him, ending any discussion of Tessie Willis. "*The Outlook* is a good Christian paper, you know."

The ad read *Young lady as resident or visiting governess.*

Piano, singing, English branches and kindergarten. French for beginners. Highest references and urged the reader to contact the newspaper.

"I don't think a young lady," he said, "would agree to live here with a single man. After all, you'll hardly come into the house, much less—"

"Yes, but you could say all that in your advertisement. You could request an older woman, one who could teach the girls to cook and keep a garden and sew."

Someone like you, my Annie.

"Well, if you think we should," he agreed, trying to sound as reluctant as he could.

"Oh, yes, we definitely should," she said, picking up Julia and balancing her on her hip. "We can't let just anyone stay with them."

"No," he agreed. Not just anyone, at all.

The advertisement proved harder than Annie expected. Finally, after much crossing out and rewriting, it read:

> *Mature loving woman needed to tend two small girls. Must be excellent cook, good seamstress, clean. Also patient, kind, and friendly. Able to read and write. Write to Noah Eastman, c/o Post Office, Van Wert, Ohio.*

When they were finished Noah reminded her that he had hay to haul, a field to harvest, and Ethan waiting for him. As if on cue, there was a knock at the door.

"Must be Ethan wondering where I am," Noah guessed.

But it was Mr. Kelly who stood on the porch, his hat in his hand. He seemed surprised to see Annie at the door but only asked if he could speak to Noah.

"Come on in," Noah yelled from the table. He had just

added the fact that the job was located on a farm. Not that he really expected to place the ad, but if Annie insisted, it would at least buy him some time.

Mr. Kelly stood in the center of the room and fiddled with his hat.

"How is Mrs. Kelly?" Annie asked. "I haven't seen her except at church since—"

"Since we lost our Bethy," he finished for her. "She ain't the same, Mrs. Kelly, since the fire. That's why I'm here."

"I don't understand," Annie said, but it seemed like Noah did.

"Did you remember something about the furnace?" he asked. "Is that it?"

"The wife thought I should have a look at yours. Just thinkin' somebody else might have to go through what we did—it ain't somethin' ya get over, not never." Even now there were tears in his eyes.

"I'm sorry for your loss," Noah said, as he put a hand on Brian Kelly's shoulder.

"Well, you're no stranger to tragedy yourself, from what the reverend says," Kelly said, then looked sheepish.

"I lost a lot of people in the flood," Noah admitted. "Family, friends, neighbors. But to lose a child—"

"We was hopin' some good could come of it, but we didn't see none. Then you started this business about the furnaces, and we thought maybe there's a chance if we could save just one child, there'd be a reason Bethy died."

Noah bit the inside of his lip. Annie had seen him do it before, when he came to her about Ruth Abernathy. It was almost like he needed to feel the pain the others were feeling.

"Come on out and we'll go around and down to the cellar," he said to Brian. "Let's have a look."

"It's good to see you again, Miss Sissy," Brian said as the two men headed outside. "Yer lookin' right pretty these days."

"Thank you," she said, somewhat surprised. Lookin' pretty? What in the world had gotten into the men of Van Wert?

She supposed she would have stood there just staring at the closed door all day if Julia hadn't announced that she wanted to use the pot.

Miller Winestock did not like to see the worst in people. In fact, he took a certain amount of pride in the fact that, while he was rarely duped, he always found something about a person to like. And he understood how something could appear one way and actually be a wholly different situation than appearances would lead one to believe.

So even though four different parishioners, including Tessie Willis, who was almost directly involved, had implied that there was something going on between Sissy Morrow and Noah Eastman, he did not believe it. And the fact that he was on his way out to Eastman's farm had nothing whatever to do with the rumors.

He needed to clear up the matter of Eastman's not-dead wife. That was the way he thought of her. And he thought of her often. With over sixty dollars donated to her memorial, she weighed heavily on his mind.

He wasn't happy to see two rigs in front of Eastman's house when he got there. He recognized Annie's wagon, although Blackie was not attached to it. That meant she wasn't there for a quick visit but for the day. Which didn't, he reminded himself, prove anything untoward.

The other wagon could have belonged to anyone in the parish. So what if Eastman had company? Had he thought the man hadn't made any friends? Or had he hoped it?

Well, he would simply wait for the visitor to leave. Then he would confront Eastman about just what he thought he was doing. If it came to it, he would have to bring up his wife. The thought didn't disconcert him as much as he expected.

Sissy opened the door and stared at him. She had the smaller Eastman girl on her hip, and the bigger one was clinging to her skirts.

"On the pot!" the little one said. He had no idea what she meant, but Sissy shushed her.

"Miller," she said, her surprise, like everything else she thought, written across her face. He could swear he read guilt there too, but that was ridiculous. "What are you doing here?"

"May I come in?" he asked, looking beyond her into the house. It was neat as a pin, despite the two little girls and the lack of a woman in the household. Unless Noah Eastman was a very tidy man, and Miller doubted that, Sissy had certainly been spending a lot of time at the Eastman farm.

"Of course," she said, trying to act like a gracious hostess. "Please, come in."

"Thank you," he said and waited as she led the way.

He removed his hat. There were men's voices coming from somewhere, but he couldn't make them out. "Is Mr. Eastman home?"

"Miss Annie made cookies," the older girl announced. "Look." She pointed to the cookie on the table. "It's me."

He could see clearly that the cookie did indeed resemble the child standing before him. Next to the cookie he saw the *Van Wert Bulletin*. Circled in pencil was the address for advertisements, along with the fees.

"Can I get you anything?" Sissy asked. "I'm sure Noah and Brian will be up in just a moment."

"Brian?"

"Mr. Kelly. He came to see Mr. Eastman this morning about the furnace."

Everything that had to do with that man became an

irritation. First Sissy started watching his children and the next thing Miller knew he wasn't getting his weekly visit from her. It didn't escape his notice that she called him Noah when she referred to him, nor did he miss how right the child looked on the hip that was slung out slightly to accommodate her. The furnace business was the last straw.

"They're in the cellar?" Miller asked, barely in control of his rage.

"Would you like me to go get them?" she offered meekly. She could read him well, as Elvira had, and he had no wish to direct any of his anger at the sweet young woman who stood nervously before him.

"It can wait," he said. She tidied about him, busily straightening corners of already straight piles of books and magazines, the child on her hip twirling Sissy's hair around one chubby finger. "I missed your visit last week."

Her free hand flew to her cheek. "Oh, Miller! I forgot. I'm real sorry. I know how you count on that butter for your morning toast.

"It's quite all right," he said. "You must have been very busy."

"Well." She hedged. "I still shouldn't have forgotten. Let me get you a piece of pie, at least. There's a quince one in the kitchen."

She raced off before he could stop her. Unaccustomed to being left alone in someone else's house, he fiddled with the newspaper on the table and decided to see what they were saying this month in *The Outlook*. It surprised him to find the newspaper in Eastman's home. He hadn't pegged the man as a reader of a Christian family paper. When he picked up the paper he found beneath it the copy for an ad. He was reading it when Sissy came back into the room.

"Then this isn't a permanent arrangement?" he asked her, pointing toward the children who trailed her.

"Oh, no," she assured him. "I'm leaving just as soon as

I can." She sat down and confided to him in whispers the children wouldn't overhear that Mrs. Abernathy had hit the children with some sort of stick. He fought the urge to remind her that it was well known that to spare the rod was to spoil the child. Well known by everyone but the woman across from him, who was getting tears in her eyes just talking about it. He reached across the table and patted her hand gently.

The men's voices grew louder, accompanied by footsteps on the porch. He drew his hand back and rose so as not to be at a disadvantage.

"So then it's the same," Eastman said as they came through the door.

"Looks it," Kelly said.

The two men stopped at the sight of Miller, Kelly looking decidedly uncomfortable. Miller stared at the man, silently demanding an explanation.

"I heard he looked at the Webbs' furnace and said it wasn't nothin' like his," Kelly said.

"And?"

"And I figured if he was pullin' somethin' he'da claimed it was. So I come to look."

"And?"

"And I think it be the same as mine what blew up."

"Mr. Kelly, you don't even know yours did blow up," Miller said. This was just what he was afraid of, ignorant people jumping on some panic bandwagon.

"I know I got a little girl that's only a memory. I know I ain't never gonna see her grow up and marry and give me no grandbabies. I know what it's done to the wife, and I know there's gotta be a purpose to it. The Lord couldna taken my Bethy without there was some purpose." He wiped a runny nose on his sleeve.

"Of course there was a purpose," Miller agreed. "But it is not for us to know the Lord's design. I am not a stranger to loss, Mr. Kelly. You know that. But it's enough to know that while He works in mysterious ways, His is a master plan and we are accounted for, one and all."

"Well it ain't enough for me," Kelly said.

"If we can save others—" Noah began.

"This is ridiculous. Do you realize if you stop people from turning on their furnaces the influenza will run rampant in the county? Do you have any idea the numbers of children who will die without heat while you save them from an imaginary threat?"

"You don't have children of your own, Reverend Winestock, so beggin' your pardon, but you just don't know. A parent would do anything to save a child from harm: lie, cheat, steal. I can't see how checkin' a few furnaces is hurtin' anybody."

"He's ruining the reputation of a decent man," Miller said, pointing at Eastman. He wanted to tell them all about Wylene Eastman and that the man Kelly thought so decent was less than honest. But there was no point in bringing up Mrs. Eastman among these people. They would all side with a father trying simply to protect his children. He took up his hat and pulled it onto his head. Then he looked at the man he knew was trouble from the day he met him. "Remember, Eastman," he said as he pulled himself to his sermonizing height. "Let he who is without sin cast the first stone."

With that, he crossed the room and left the door open behind him.

"Miller?" Sissy said, running out behind him.

"It's cold out," he told her. "Go back inside."

"But Miller," she tried again.

This was not a good time to have a dialogue with her. He felt too emotional, nearly out of control. Such passion would be welcome from the pulpit, but it didn't belong between two people on a poorly tended farm in the middle of nowhere. "It's freezing, Sissy," he said, and got into his fine black buggy. "We'll talk another time."

She stood on the porch steps, her mouth slightly open as if she wanted to say something more to him. He flicked the reins in disgust.

Now the man was even coming between him and the woman he was going to marry.

18

Damn but it was cold. Noah had checked with Charlie and Risa on Sunday, and the bent piece of pipe he needed to fix the furnace still hadn't come in. He could understand the temptation to use the inferior metal just to get the thing up and running. It seemed like less of a crime, somehow, as he stood over the stove in the kitchen rubbing his hands together and worrying about keeping the girls warm with just a few stoves for heat. It was like being back in the Dark Ages and he didn't like it one bit.

A banging door and a friendly voice signaled Ethan's arrival. "You got any oatmeal?" he called out as he came into the house. To one of the girls he said, "Hi there, cutie," then continued into the kitchen.

"Oatmeal?" Noah asked.

"Got a hankerin' for it. Sissy used to make it for me on cold mornings like this. Then I'd get on Blackie and head on down to school before anyone else to get the stove goin'."

Noah dropped the spoon into the pot and it clanged throughout the kitchen. The school! "The furnace, Ethan.

Think, boy. What was the furnace like?" If only he could figure out why his and Kelly's furnaces were both death traps and the church's and the Webbs' weren't.

"Like all the rest of 'em." Ethan sighed. "It was a long time ago, before I did my growing. They always picked a small kid to do it 'cause the ceiling was so low down in that cellar."

"Watch the girls," Noah called over his shoulder as he headed for the door. What an idiot he'd been. The pipe only had to be bent if the ceiling was low. And only the *bent* pipes were the problem.

He didn't bother hitching up a wagon. He threw Ethan's saddle across Buckshot and hightailed it to town. If he wasn't in time, some poor child could pay for his stupidity.

She had intended to read last night. She would have, too, if Willa hadn't gone and picked those hickory nuts. And, of course, if it hadn't been Halloween. She'd gotten all the dishes done and put away and was getting ready to head up to bed when Willa suggested they do that silly prophesy game with the hickory nuts.

What a child Willa was, wanting to burn nuts and thinking it had any meaning at all. But Annie had gone along with it, naming in her head one nut for herself, one for Miller, and, just because the game called for three nuts, one for Noah Eastman. Willa had insisted it only would prove true if Annie put them on the stove grate herself, explaining that if a nut cracked or jumped the lover would be unfaithful, if it blazed and burned he loved the girl, and if two burned together, those two would marry.

It was a stupid little superstition, which Annie had never abided. It meant nothing to her that Miller's nut just lay there, turning browner and browner until it went black without ever catching fire, while the ones named for her and Noah rolled toward each other and, when they met, burst into flame. Silly, foolish game, she had told herself before bed.

But she'd been unable to concentrate on her book, despite the lessons, and she was tired and cranky this morning as a result. And cold.

She wished Bart would come into the nineteenth-century before the twentieth was upon them. Maybe when there was a baby in the house he'd see the value of putting in a furnace rather than relying on little stoves that couldn't hold enough coal to last through the night.

Well, this would be her last winter of trying to slip into her drawers without taking her nightgown off. The thought of dressing in the same room as Miller was sobering. She supposed, being a man, he'd have more interest in seeing her than she would in seeing him. Was there a measurement for none? She had only thought about undressing for bed and was counting on night to shield her. But when spring rolled around she'd have to get up pretty early to beat the light.

She sure would like a new pair of slippers for Christmas, she thought. The ones she had on were so worn she could feel the cold wooden floor right through them. She pulled up her woolen stockings and looked for her warmest dress. The first days of winter were always the worst. Soon her body would get used to it, and by December the window would be open a crack at night to let the fresh air in.

But those first few days were "oatmeal days." That's what the children had dubbed them because she always insisted they go off to school with something warm in their bellies that would stay there a good while. It had been a long time since she made oatmeal, she mused, as she slipped the dress over her head. Francie had rebelled against the hot cereal at an early age in favor of a seventeen-inch waist. She hadn't made oatmeal since Ethan was lighting the furnace at the school for a few extra pennies a week.

Well, she guessed, someone else must be doing it this morning.

"Oh, my God!" she said aloud and tore down the stairs and from the house like her tail was on fire.

His shouts must have awaked somebody, because he could hear the fire bell ringing loudly as he ran down the steps to the cellar of the Fourth Ward school. He'd seen the smoke from a block away and rode the rest of the way down Central Avenue screaming his fool head off.

"Is anybody in here?" he called when he pushed the door open and a cloud of smoke came billowing out at him. "Hello? Are you down there?"

A cough was his answer.

Shit. "I'm coming," he hollered through the haze. He lifted the collar of his jacket and covered his mouth with it. "Where are you?"

He couldn't see worth a damn. His eyes burned so much he could hardly keep them open, and it was barely worth the effort. The smoke was so thick he couldn't make out his hand in front of his face.

The fumes were racing for the open door and he got down on all fours and crawled along the floor, feeling for someone, listening for a cry, a cough, anything.

A wheezing sound came from his left. "I'm coming," he reassured whoever it was. "I'm gonna get you out of here. Can you see me?"

There was nothing, no sound except the whoosh of smoke rushing for the door, no motion except for the steady stream of haze that whirled around him and moved on. *Hold on,* he thought. *I'm coming.*

From behind him somewhere, a woman's voice screamed out in panic. "Paulie? Oh, my God! Paulie's in there!"

The child had a name. He added it to his litany. *Hold*

on, Paulie. I'm coming. He couldn't waste his breath on saying it aloud. His lungs seemed ready to burst and his nose and throat felt like he'd been down in the smoke for hours instead of minutes.

But he crept on, hoping he was going in the right direction. He felt a foot, so small it fit into his hand. "Paulie?" he asked. His voice was a rasp he didn't recognize.

There was no answer.

"Let me go! It's my baby down there. Paulie!"

He pulled the child closer to him and felt his chest. It rose and fell and he felt a lump in his throat that bore no relation to the smoke he was inhaling.

"I got him!" he yelled out to the woman, no doubt the child's mother. "He's alive." His voice was a whisper despite his effort.

He crawled back toward the door, half dragging, half carrying the child along with him, sheltering the boy's body with his own.

When he got to the steps he collapsed and two men grabbed the boy and passed him along, then reached in and hauled him out.

"Eastman?" someone said, as though he was the last person he expected to see. Over his shoulder the man told the crowd that was quickly gathering, "It's Eastman."

A moment later he felt the angelic touch of someone wiping his face with a cool cloth. It was hard for him to take in any air. "Annie?" he asked.

"I'm right here," she said. It was the last thing he heard before losing consciousness.

Risa was there, comforting Annie as she ministered to Noah. Charlie was there, seeing to Risa. There were others, Annie knew, a whole town's worth, but she wasn't aware of them. Oh, she heard the new Ahern steam engine rolling down Central Avenue from City Hall, four big horses pulling it. She heard Zack Hartman's dray following with the old hand pumper and all the men rushing for their assigned places at the long handles, heard Jake Fronfield, the fire chief, yelling directions and the whoop when the stream of water began to gush.

But Noah's head, his face still sooty despite her attempts to wipe it, rested in her lap, his even breathing a counterpoint to her own quick breaths. The lashes on his right eye were singed, as was his eyebrow and some of his hair, but his skin seemed untouched by the fire. Soot collected in every crease he had, making him look like a charcoal sketch of himself. With the missing hair it looked as though the artist had almost finished and then been called away.

His chest rose and fell steadily, but every now and then a cough seemed to erupt from his chest and his head would rise and fall heavily against her.

Her nostrils burned with the scent of singed wool and charred wood. Around them the air grew darker as gray smoke poured from the small basement door with the fury of a river overflowing its banks. It rolled out the door and spread itself wider and wider, washing over everyone in its path before rising toward the sky.

Noah coughed again, and Annie felt the clutch at the back of her own throat and tried to clear her windpipe.

"He doing all right?" Doc Woods called over to her as he saw to the small boy who lay motionless a few feet away.

"I don't know," Annie admitted. "He's alive, but he ain't—"

"*Isn't,*" a hoarse voice croaked from her lap. He opened one eye and gave her a half smile before closing it again. Ugly black spots appeared on his face like warts. When she touched them, they were wet. Charlie pulled out a hankie and bent down to wipe the tears from her face.

"Here comes Reverend Winestock," he whispered to

her. "Blow." He held the fine white cotton to her nose and she did as she was told. Then he hurried off to help the others fight the blaze.

She pulled her gaze reluctantly from Noah's gray face. Down the street, Miller was making his way toward the school, his face white, his hands shaking visibly as he raised them to his face, smoothing back his silver hair. From beneath his coat peeked a dressing gown and slippers. He stopped beside Paulie Mitchell's limp body first, laying a hand on the doctor's shoulder.

"Is he—?" He choked on the words.

"No," Doc Woods said. "He's got some bad burns on his hands and face, but I think he's gonna be all right. Fool kid probably tried to put the fire out himself."

"But he's not—"

"No. Just passed out from the smoke is my guess. A blessing, too. When he comes to, he's gonna be in an awful lot of pain."

Paulie's mother sat beside him on the ground, rocking back and forth, a sob escaping her now and again. Miller squeezed her shoulder, but when she raised her tear-streaked face to him, he looked off into the distance as though he couldn't bear to see her pain.

Maybe it was knowing that beneath his coat he still wore his nightclothes, but to Annie it appeared almost as if he were sleepwalking toward her. When he stood just a few feet away, he stopped and the head in her lap came into focus for him. What little color had returned to his face with the reassurance that Paulie would live seemed to drain at the sight of Noah Eastman lying with his head resting on Annie's lap.

"Is he all right?" Miller asked, keeping his distance as though he was somehow intruding where he didn't belong.

Annie nodded.

"He knew. He knew, and he warned us, and I wouldn't

listen," he said. There was no guilt in his voice, no emotion. It was as if he was trying to understand what had happened. "A boy could have died, and it would have been my fault."

"The floor's going," someone yelled from inside the building. "Get back!" Men scrambled out of the school-house, where they had been trying to keep the fire from spreading to the main floor.

Dazed, Miller stood there while men rushed around him. His coat flapped in the wind and he made no attempt to control it. He stared beyond Annie, beyond the towns-folk, beyond the town, his eyes on something Annie could never see.

"I'll take over now," Doc Woods said gently by her side. He slipped a folded blanket beneath Noah's head and encouraged Annie to slide out from under him. "Looks like the reverend needs you, Sissy," he said, jerking his head in Miller's direction.

She looked down. Noah appeared to be sleeping, but his hand searched for hers and she grasped it in her own. "Go ahead," he whispered and squeezed her hand gently. "I'll be fine."

"All right," she agreed. "But I'll be back, soon as the doc is finished seein' to you."

He nodded slightly. With a quick touch to his cheek, she pulled herself together and rose.

"Miller? Are you all right?"

He heard her, felt her presence next to him, but still he was all alone. What had he done? In the name of God and all that was holy, *what had he done?*

"Miller?" She took his arm and tried to usher him away from the bustle around him. "Come on."

"Sissy?" he said when he realized who was beside him. "What are you doing here?"

"It's all right, Miller. Come away from the men. We're in their way." She pulled at him and he let her lead him.

"Did he come for you, then? Or were you with him? Do you live there?"

"What?" she asked as though he was being incoherent. It was a perfectly sane question, he thought, under the circumstances.

"He knew. I understand that. But you? How did you know?"

She babbled about Ethan and the furnace and when he was a boy. It was hard for Miller to follow what she was saying. It would have been such a simple thing for him to have given the list of Elmer Wells's customers to Mr. Eastman. He had decided against it just to save Elvira's good name.

She had come to him with her father's reputation heavy in her heart, and he had lifted her above all that when he married her. Oh, how she delighted in being the minister's wife! He had little to offer a woman besides that: that elevation of status, instant acceptance by the community. It was his one prize possession to give a wife—respectability.

And Noah Eastman had wanted to take it away from her. To let people remember her as the daughter of a man who was responsible for fires and death and destruction. Had there been a Wells furnace in Brian Kelly's cellar? Elmer's papers said there was, but then there was one in the Webbs', the Taylors', the Gibbses'. There was one in his own home and one in the church. None of those had caught fire, so he'd had no reason to believe that any of them would.

And no one had been sure what had caused the fire at the Kellys'. If they had been sure—

"Miller, what's the matter with you?"

There was Sissy Morrow, good old Sissy Morrow, standing by him, trying to calm his overwrought nerves. She was a wonderful woman, a pillar of the community, loved by everyone who knew her. And soon she would be his. If she'd still have him after this.

"It's my fault," he admitted, raising his cold hands and touching her soft tear-streaked cheeks. "I could have prevented it with just a word, and I didn't."

"Don't be silly," she said, her own warm hand covering his as it stroked her cheek. "There was nothing you could have done. No way you could have known any better than the rest of us."

"But you, Sissy, you knew better. And so did that man. And I was so busy distrusting him that I refused to raise my hand to aid my own community. I was too busy preserving my wife's good name to worry about the welfare of a small boy and countless others."

"Elvira?" Sissy looked at him blankly. No one had more trust or belief in her fellowman than the woman who stood before him, he thought. "What does Elvira have to do with this?"

"I loved her, Sissy," he admitted, tears filling his eyes. "Out of love, look what I've done!"

"Ssh," she said. She wrapped her arm around his waist so gently it was like a feather touching his back. "I'll walk you home. Come, Miller. Let's go home."

If love made you do things too disgraceful to admit, perhaps it was just as well he didn't love Sissy Morrow.

"Yes," he agreed. He looked behind him and saw Doc Woods helping Noah Eastman to his feet. "Let's go home."

When they got to the house, Annie watched Miller fumble with the knob to the front door and then stand, foolishly lost, in his own front parlor.

"I'll make you some tea," she said after she finally got Miller out of his worsted overcoat and helped him to the silk brocatelle gent's easy chair in the parlor. Miller let his head rest against the doily that waited for him, and Annie hurried to the back of the house to get the water on.

She had never, not in all the years she had known Miller, seen him so stunned. Even when Elvira died he had seemed more in control, but of course her death had come as no surprise.

She unbuttoned her mackintosh, noting the black circle of soot that remained where only minutes before Noah's head had rested against her. She touched the spot gently as though stroking his hair. He was safe. For his children's sake she heaved a sigh of relief. For those two dear little ones to be left motherless *and* fatherless—well, she didn't even want to think about that.

When Elvira was dying, those last awful months, Annie had become very familiar with the Winestocks' kitchen. The tea was where she had last put it away. If Miller had ever fixed some for himself, he had returned the tea to where he had found it. Putting the kettle on the Sterling range, she looked around the tidy kitchen.

The fact that she hadn't come during the week hadn't meant the house went uncared for. It was a relief, she told herself, that the man could manage to take care of himself. She'd been needed enough in her life. What a luxury to think that her husband would require so little of her. A hot meal every day, a mended shirt here and there, clean sheets at night. . . .

Steam poured from the kettle spout and Annie reached for a dishrag with which to grasp the handle. As the hot mist rushed toward her she thought of Noah and Paulie, lost in the smoke of the schoolhouse fire, and shivered. As soon as she had Miller settled, she'd go check with Doc Woods and see if there was anything she could do for either of them. Yes, *either* of them, she thought, trying to be concerned for both victims equally.

Paulie, the more injured of the two, had his mother to

look after him. But who would see to Noah if he needed tending? Ethan would have to do the harvesting, so it appeared that taking care of their father would fall in with taking care of Hannah and Julia.

A soft knock at the back door broke her chain of thought, and she poured water over the loose tea and set the kettle down quickly. A second, slightly more forceful knock followed.

"Yes?" Annie said as she opened the door. It was rare that anyone other than a delivery boy came to Miller's back door.

But it wasn't a delivery boy who stood on his back steps that morning. It was Tessie Willis, her flyaway auburn locks tucked neatly into a bonnet, her navy mackintosh buttoned to the neck, her cheeks rosy from the cold. "Sissy," she said with a tremble in her voice. "I didn't expect to find you here."

"I might say the same," Annie returned. Tessie Willis didn't even attend church anymore. What was she doing at Miller's back door?

"Is the Reverend Winestock in?" She fidgeted with her gloves, pulling them tighter onto her hands as if making ready to do battle with the elements once again.

"Reverend Winestock?" It was a stupid question, but somehow Annie was having difficulty grasping the idea that Tessie Willis was here to see Miller.

"Well, he does live here," Tessie said dryly, losing some of her nervousness along with her patience. "And he did ask me to come this morning."

"Oh! Please, come in. I didn't mean to keep you waiting in the cold." She backed out of the way to give the woman room to enter. "I'll tell Miller you're here."

She found Miller where she had left him, still in his dressing gown and nightshirt. Chalky white ankles and feet emerged from beneath the robe and were lost in velvet slippers.

"Miller," she said tapping him gently on the shoulder. "Tessie Willis is in the kitchen. She says you told her to come here?" She tried not to make it sound as if she didn't believe the woman, but she wasn't sure she succeeded.

"It was because I loved her, you know," Miller replied.

Annie's heart stuck in her throat. "Tessie?" she asked.

Miller blinked a couple of times and then focused on Annie. "Tessie?" he repeated. "Tessie who?"

"Tessie Willis is here to see you," she repeated, watching him closely. On his face was that look he always got when he spoke about Elvira. Only this time she could swear it was mixed with pain and guilt.

"Oh." He looked down at his clothing and blanched. "I forgot she was coming." He looked at Annie helplessly.

"I could send her away," Annie whispered. "Why is she here?"

"I hired her to work for me," he said, as if everyone gave Tessie a job on Tuesday mornings. "She'll be doing the secretarial work for the church."

"But Miller," Annie began. She'd been learning so much this past week from Noah. She hardly ever, except under the strain of the fire, said *ain't* anymore. She was racing through the book Noah had loaned her and practicing with newspapers, as well. Her penmanship still looked like a grade schooler, but she was hoping to get Noah to help her with that too, after his hand was fully healed.

"I know," he said gently. "That should be your job. But she needed work, and your time could be so much better spent."

"I'm an embarrassment to you. I know it, but I could learn to be better at writin' and things. I'm gettin' better at them all the time."

"Don't," he said, rising and taking her face in his hands. "Don't try to change. It wouldn't do to have you perfect at everything."

"What?"

He dropped his hands and looked toward the kitchen door. "Tell Tessie I'll be down in a minute. I can't be meeting my new secretary in my nightclothes, now, can I?" He tried to smile but the attempt fell flat.

It wouldn't do to have you perfect at everything. Fighting to put one foot in front of the other she made her way back to the kitchen in a stupor. *It wouldn't do to have you perfect at everything.* Whatever did he mean by that?

Tessie was waiting, sweat forming on her upper lip as she stood in her heavy coat, gloves, and bonnet. Annie apologized and offered to take her things.

"Then he'll see me?" Tessie asked. Annie hadn't realized how much older Tessie had grown since she'd gotten a good look at her. A couple of years Annie's senior, Tessie had lines that joined her nose to her mouth and a sallowness to skin Annie remembered as pale and flawless.

Annie nodded. "He ran out to the fire in his nightclothes," she whispered conspiratorially. "He's gone up to change."

"The fire sure was something, wasn't it?" Tessie said. "That Mr. Eastman is one fine-looking man."

Annie bristled. "I suppose everyone has a right to an opinion."

"I suppose you haven't noticed those blue eyes of his, or the way the skin beside them crinkles when he smiles."

Annie felt her cheeks redden. There wasn't a thing she hadn't noticed about Noah Eastman, from the mole that the hair near his temple all but covered to the fact that the man's socks needed mending. "The girls have his eyes," she said, somewhat curtly.

"Cute as buttons, those two," Tessie said.

If they'd been there, Annie would have hidden them behind her skirts. As it was, she had an overwhelming desire to tell Tessie to stay away from them. "They're delicate children," she said. "What with losing their mama and movin' and such. I surely would hate to see them shook up any more than they have been."

"I had a nice talk with Ethan two weeks ago at the Harvest Social," Tessie said. "He sure has grown up."

"He's still a boy, Tessie," Annie said, a note of warning in her voice. "He's only just nineteen and he's still acting like he did when he was ten."

"He seemed very grown up and very nice."

"Well, that's 'cause he didn't show you his real self. The boy still wants to be a cowboy, just like when he was little. He's never lost that wanting to find adventure. Always looking for excitement, that one." She didn't know how to make it any clearer without being rude. Ethan's only interest in Tessie Willis would be the thrill of an older "ruined" woman. She was warning Tessie that she didn't want to see her brother involved.

"Well, looking for excitement can be the ruination of a person's reputation."

Annie didn't like standing around and talking to Tessie Willis, especially about the men in her life. She heard Miller's footfalls on the stairs with relief and directed Tessie to go on into the parlor.

"Is the tea for the minister?" Tessie asked. "I could take it to him."

First Ethan and now Miller. Was the woman shameless?

"I'll take it," Annie said authoritatively. "But then I've got to go."

"Oh, yes," Tessie said. "I guess you've got to get over to the Eastman girls. Watching them must be very hard. But then, it seems like you've been a mother for so long."

"I ain't their mother," she said, forgetting her grammar for the moment. "I'm just helping out for a short while. Until . . . well, just until."

"I see," Tessie said, and headed for the parlor with Miller's tea before Annie could stop her.

19

All anyone wanted to talk about was the fire at the school. Family after family stopped by at the Eastman farm afterward to thank Noah for saving Paulie and for trying to warn them all about their furnaces. It seemed as natural as could be for Annie to be there watching the children and helping out. No one seemed surprised or shocked to find her playing the mother hen in someone else's coop.

And no one except Risa made any assumptions that something might be going on between Annie and Noah. On the contrary, nearly everyone had a woman for Noah now that he seemed to be in need of one. Mrs. Wood had a distant cousin out in Montana who was a widow with two children of her own and would surely be interested in meeting Noah with the intention of matrimony. Jane Lutefoot had a dear niece with a pronounced overbite who would give the children all the love they needed and be a most passable wife to Noah as well.

And so it went, with each visitor. None of them seemed to notice, as Annie did, Noah's discomfort every time someone brought up the possibility of his marriage to their relatives.

None of them raised an eyebrow, nor batted an eyelash when he called her "Annie my sweet" or touched her gently in passing. Knowing she would never make a fuss in front of the neighbors, he seemed to get bolder and bolder.

A big sign with black lettering couldn't have been more obvious than he was about his feelings toward her.

"Annie is a godsend," he said to Peter Gibbs, when he and Della stopped by with the boys. "Taking care of the children, taking care of me. She walks in the door, and I feel better at the sight of her each morning."

"Oh, *Sissy*," Peter said when he realized who Noah meant. "Yes, well, you're a lucky man. I don't think anyone but Mr. Winestock would be so tolerant about their intended taking care of someone else's family."

"She's not Mr. Winestock's intended," Noah snapped back. "And sometimes there's a fine line between tolerance and pure stupidity."

Risa, who had been present throughout the conversation, nearly choked on her tea. "There's so much stupidity going around these days," she said, "it's a wonder anyone survives it."

Peter frowned, but he let the comment pass. "Della, don't you have a letter from Francie for Mr. Eastman?"

With one eye on the boys she fished in her purse and came up with a mutilated envelope, which she handed to Peter. Disgust crossed his face as he tried to flatten it before giving it to Noah.

"Well, what does she have to say?" Della asked. While everyone looked surprised at the question, no one looked as uncomfortable as Noah.

He cleared his throat, his voice still somewhat raspy from the fire. "I'm sure it's the same thing she usually writes. She asks after the children, tells me about her classes, and adds always that she misses the family." He put the letter in his shirt pocket without opening it.

"Does she write often?" Annie couldn't help but ask. She remembered well the look of disappointment on her baby sister's face when Noah hadn't shown up at the train to see her off. Not one of the letters that she wrote home failed to ask about him, as if she still carried a torch despite all that was happening in her life.

"Some."

"Mrs. McCormick says at least twice a week," Della corrected. "She was thrilled to hear we were coming out and could deliver it for her."

Twice a week! Now Annie couldn't help but wonder what was in the letter. While Noah was making eyes at her, was he receiving love notes from her sister?

"She hardly ever writes to me," Della complained. "After how close we were, and all. All the nights she cried on my shoulder when you wouldn't let her do one thing or another."

Annie sighed heavily. She had been as lenient as they allowed her to be, always. But being nearly a child herself, she knew the mischief, the lies, the tricks too well for her brothers and sisters to get away with very much. And they, especially the girls, resented her for it.

Noah looked tired. With his eyebrow half gone his face had a quirky look to it, as if he were always questioning everything around him. It made him look as if he wondered what everyone was doing in his parlor in the middle of the week. He closed his eyes for a moment. He'd complained that they burned still from the smoke, and resting them helped.

"Perhaps we should leave," Risa suggested, but Della wouldn't hear of it.

"Please just read us Francie's letter," she begged in that voice she used to get men to do as she asked. She batted her eyes at Noah and he grimaced in response. It was clear that he wanted to keep Francie's letter to himself, which only egged Della on. "Please? We'll go as soon as you're done."

Samuel and James were getting fidgety. Samuel had already tried to swallow the cap to the bottle of Munyon's Burn Remedy while Noah had been dabbing the area above his eye where his brow was gone. James had punched Hannah in the stomach and had only been allowed out of the corner because the girls had retreated to their room.

Annie hoped that either Noah would read the letter or Della would give in before the boys got into more trouble. The truth was, she hoped Noah would read the letter because she wanted to know how things stood between him and Francie, but at the same time something in her was fighting that knowledge, reminding her about what curiosity did to the cat.

"Mr. Eastman's tired, Della," Annie said. "It's time I got his supper on the table and headed for home. Lord knows what Willa's poisoning Bart with tonight." She bit her lip as her color undoubtedly rose. "I mean, she probably needs a little help gettin' his meal on."

Risa laughed. "They're alone and in love, Annie. Bart'll live on that for quite a while."

Love. It was all anybody seemed to talk about. Bart and Willa were losing sleep and meals over it. Risa and Ethan were shoving it down her throat like some kind of elixir that would cure ills she didn't even have. What ever happened to good old common sense?

"Get it out of your mouth," Annie said to Samuel more sharply than she intended. "Now." She stuck her hand beneath his chin and he spit the slimy centipede into it. It wriggled in her palm and she handed it to Peter to dispose of, wiping her hand on her apron and feeling a strong need for a long bath.

"Della, can't you do something about him?" Risa asked. "It's a dangerous habit he's gotten into."

Della gave her usual shrug and said something about the stages a boy goes through that the mother of a girl couldn't understand. Then she returned to the subject of Francie's letter and announced she wasn't leaving without hearing it.

Slowly, reluctantly, Noah withdrew the creased paper from his pocket and opened it. "My eyes are bothering me," he said, squeezing them closed. "Let's do this some other time."

But Della grabbed the letter from his hand and began.

"'Dear Noah',," she said, raising her eyebrows and making a big O with her lips. "Ooh, she calls you *Noah!*"

"What else would she call him?" Risa asked with disgust. "It *is* his name."

Della let it pass, but it stayed in Annie's mind just the same.

"'Your letter arrived yesterday. How slow the mail is! Especially to someone who is waiting so anxiously. I know that you will disapprove of what I've done, but I've written to my sister and begged her to let me come home.'"

Everyone's eyes turned to Annie. "It's just homesickness," Annie said, defending herself. "She'll get over it and be glad she stayed."

"'Every day I am here, I worry about you and the children more. Not that I am sorry I came, Noah. But now that we know where things stand, I want to come home and help you put Wylene's death behind you.'"

"I don't think you need to go on," Peter said, pulling the letter from Della's hands and returning it to Noah.

"An adolescent crush," Noah said. "She fancies me as some poor soul whose wretched life she can save."

"And how do you fancy yourself?" Risa asked.

Without a moment's hesitation he looked straight at Annie. "I am a one-woman man. To me Francie's just a little girl. She's like a sister to me, but she refuses to see that for now."

"How sad for both of you," Della said. She looped her

arm through Peter's possessively. "She loves you and you love a dead woman."

Noah's eyes widened and his jaw went slack. "No," he corrected, with just a hint of laughter. "Francie doesn't love me, she just thinks she does. And my wife is gone and life goes on. Don't feel sorry for me, Mrs. Gibbs. At least, not yet."

Risa's eyes went back and forth between Noah and Annie as though she were watching a lawn tennis match at the fairgrounds.

And between Annie and Noah ran a current that seemed every bit as visible to her as the arc of electricity the power company had exhibited at the start of all the wiring being done in town. It was as bright and hot and just as dangerous as any electricity. Wasn't it searing her very soul?

"Come, boys," Peter said rather abruptly, as though he sensed the change of mood. "Will you be coming back with us?" he asked Risa, who had come out with them while Charlie watched the store.

Looking at her nephews, Risa's face wrinkled in pain. She would have to share a seat with Samuel and James all the way back to town.

Annie usually went home via the back roads, but going through Van Wert on her way home wouldn't delay her more than a few minutes.

"I'll take you," she offered, much to Risa's delight. In fact, Risa looked a little too pleased, and the look she exchanged with Noah didn't escape Annie's notice, either.

Noah hurried them all out the door, barely giving Annie enough time to call out to the girls that she was leaving and would see them in the morning. Ethan had already hitched Blackie to the wagon, and Noah handed up first Risa, taking great care to make sure she had her footing, and then Annie. His hand clung to her elbow even after she had made her way into the wagon.

"Well, I hope you don't get so much company tomorrow,"

Annie said as she looked down at his crooked face, wondering when his hair would grow back in. "You hardly got
a lick of work done with everyone coming to praise you
about saving Paulie and ask you about their furnaces."

"Mm." He reached in the back of the wagon and pulled
out the lap robe, handing one end to Risa and tucking the
other around Annie. "I hope we don't get any company at
all." How was it, she wondered, that he could say the same
words as she and somehow make them sound so different,
so indecent?

"'Night, now, Noah," Risa said, as Annie picked up the
reins. "You sure are a hero in the eyes of this town."

"All depends who's looking, Mrs. Morrow," he said
with a laugh, as Annie pulled on the left rein and headed
Blackie for town.

Risa didn't give her time to get lost in her thoughts or
even fish around for something to talk about. She started
right in just as soon as they were out of Noah's earshot.

"He's a good man," Risa said.

Annie nodded but didn't say anything.

"Don't you think?" Risa continued.

Annie opened her mouth, but no words came out. Only
a sigh that sounded sad even to her.

"He'd make someone a real good husband." Risa pulled
her cloak closer around her neck.

"Cold?" Annie asked. "You can take more of the lap
robe. I'm plenty warm."

"Yes, I noticed your cheeks were kinda flushed all afternoon."

Annie felt them warm yet again.

"Are you at least considering him?" Risa asked.

"Who?"

Risa grimaced and a small breath escaped her lips. Now
that the ground had hardened with the cold, the road was
rutted and the ride was more jarring than usual. Still,

Annie knew the pained look on Risa's face had little to do with the bumpy ride.

"The way he looks at you. Oh, Sissy, he's in love."

There it was again, that awful word. If she knew anything, she knew that love had nothing to do with what was going on between her and Noah Eastman. Love was a warmth built on mutual respect and admiration, something that grew slowly and blossomed under the nurturing hands of God-fearing adults. What Mr. Eastman felt for her had no godliness associated with it. And what she felt for him . . . well, there was nothing she felt for him.

All right, maybe pity. She did feel sorry for him, alone, raising two little girls. But respect? Of course, the way he stood up to Miller and the whole town over the furnaces, even when it seemed like he was wrong, was pretty impressive, especially in light of the fire at the school. And saving Paulie: well, the whole town admired him for that.

All her life, Annie had been a reasonable, responsible person who was nothing if not sensible. She was cautious, careful, thoughtful. All those qualities led her to Miller Winestock and made her anxious to marry him.

And every time she so much as looked at Noah Eastman, each of those characteristics that she prided herself in, that she'd cultivated in herself since she was a child, seemed to simply walk out the door and leave her standing naked and alone and unprotected in his presence.

Risa's hand, nestled in a brown leather glove, gently tugged at Annie's sleeve. "Don't you like Noah, Sissy? Even a little?" Like him? Some days she wondered if she could breathe without the sight of him. Others, she found she couldn't breathe when he was around. But like him? "He's a nice enough man," she replied, trying to hold on to her common sense when just hearing his name made her heart flutter wildly in her chest. "He's fair with Ethan. And he's keeping his bargain with me."

"His bargain?"

Embarrassed, she said, "He's teaching me to read."

"Sissy Morrow! You know how to read." There was a quiet moment when all that could be heard was the wagon's wheels scraping the dirt and Blackie's hooves clopping slowly along. "Don't you?"

"Some. Lists, notes, and the like, but not good enough to help Miller." She turned and looked at Risa, unable to keep the excitement out of her voice or the smile from her lips. "Oh, Risa! I'm learning to read real books—I'm halfway through *Little Women,* and I've picked out a whole stack of others for when I'm done. Noah has a hundred books, maybe more, and he says I can read them all. And he's correcting my grammar so that I don't sound so ignorant, and he says he's got a book somewhere on penmanship, and he's going to—"

She caught herself and quieted down. A minister's wife shouldn't babble.

When she'd collected herself, she said, "By the time I marry Miller, I'm going to be the most perfect wife for him. And he won't need Tessie Willis to be his secretary, neither."

"Annie Patrice Morrow," Risa said sternly. "That man ought to be hitting you over the head with those books instead of loaning them to you. It might do you more good. You obviously need some sense knocked into you."

"What?"

Risa let her shoulders sag. "The man loves you. You love him, admit it or not. Why are you fighting it? You're perfect for each other. Anyone looking at the two of you can see that."

"No," Annie said, her head shaking like she had the palsy. "No. It ain't—Isn't so. I don't love him. I won't ever love him. He's got nothing. Nothing but a dirt farm same as ours, babies like I already raised, bills and debts and a privy to boot."

"And so much love, Sissy." Risa sighed, as if that counted for anything.

"Miller's got love. And he's got a fine house and a fine life to offer me. You know how long I've been dreaming of putting on a clean dress in the morning and having it still clean when I'm getting ready for bed?"

"Clean clothes and a bathroom." Risa huffed. "If those aren't the two lamest reasons I ever heard for marrying a man!"

Annie heard a harsh laugh and was surprised to realize it was her own. "Oh, Risa," she said. "You got one sweet little girl and another on the way. You been a mama for three whole years."

Blackie had begun to head for the farm on his own, and Annie had to pull the reins hard to the right to remind the horse they were going to town.

"I've been a mama nearly my whole life. I raised your husband. I raised all Cara's aunts and uncles. You think when your babies are all grown you're gonna want to start in all over again?"

"You know you already love Hannah and Julia. It's written all over your face every time you look at those girls."

Maybe she did, but that didn't mean she wanted to give up all her dreams to raise them. "He'd want more, don't you think?" she asked before she could stop herself.

"Maybe," Risa conceded. "But wouldn't it be wonderful to finally have one all your own?"

"Going back to bottles and diapers and wiping up spittle? Lord, Risa, what are you thinking of? I'm done with all that. Miller and me can live out our lives in comfort, him in that gent's chair reading the paper, me mending his shirts, one of those records on that gramophone he's got—"

"Sounds wonderful," Risa said dryly.

"You just don't see. You and me, Risa, we're at different stages. We want different things from life."

"Everybody wants love, Sissy."

Annie didn't respond. Van Wert was quiet, twilight falling early with the winter coming. Oil lamps glowed in windows, making the homes look inviting, especially to two women in an open wagon. Annie could have taken Summit Street to Main, could have gone right past Miller's door, but decided, with Risa huddled next to her, to take Walnut Street instead. Lining the elegant street were the houses of wealthy families, families like the Brothertons, the Cavetts, the Straddlers. Houses where the literary society met, where money was raised for the library, for the poor. Where the wife of the Reverend Miller Winestock would be invited to tea.

"Now's my time for *me*, Risa. The time for me to be raising children is behind me."

Risa nodded. "Of course," she said. "I suppose that when I'm as old as you, I probably won't want to have any more children either. All those diapers, the lifting, the bending—you just don't want to go back to that after all these years."

"No," Annie agreed. "I certainly don't."

"Not at your age. Why, when I'm that old—"

"Risa," Annie said with a laugh, "I'm only two years older than you are."

The words hung in the air, full of meaning. Darkness closed in on them as they sat in front of Hanson's Mercantile. Any minute now Charlie would come running out to help his wife down from the wagon—his wife and the infant that rested inside her, growing all the time like the love they felt for each other.

"Just two years?" Risa's breath made gray clouds between them in the cold air. "I thought you were so much older."

Maybe old was all a matter of how you felt, Annie thought, as Charlie's face broke into a warm smile at the sight of his wife and his sister.

"Thanks for bringing my girl home," he said, tucking

the lap robe around Annie's feet after setting Risa on the newly cemented sidewalk.

Annie pulled the wagon around and headed back toward Summit Street. She hadn't been anyone's girl since she was nine years old.

Tessie had offered to make Miller some supper before she left, but Miller had declined. She had done very well with the letters he dictated to her. In exquisite Spencerian hand she had taken down all that he said efficiently and professionally. If only her face hadn't worn a mask of melancholy he would have considered the day a good one, one of the very few he'd had lately.

The knock at the door took him by surprise. Calls at the dinner hour were rare. But he had learned to expect callers at any time: callers who came bearing donations to the Wylene Eastman Memorial Fund in honor of the way Mr. Eastman had risked his life for Paulie Mitchell. And what a Gordian knot that was turning out to be. A memorial for someone who wasn't even dead. A woman who walked out on two little girls and her wedding vows.

He peered out the window that sat squarely at eye level in his front door. The colored glass distorted his visitor, but there was no mistaking the woman who stood waiting patiently on the porch for him.

"Sissy!" he said, flinging open the door. "What a nice surprise!" Someone who wasn't coming with a donation for the fund. At least he hoped not.

"Miller, I hope I'm not coming at a bad time," she said.

She sounded different, formal. Her speech was clipped, more cultured. The *gs* were firmly in place at the end of her gerunds.

"Of course not." He swept his arm back, offering her the warmth of his house. "Come in, come in."

"It *is* getting cold out there," she said, heading for his furnace grate and standing by the register for a moment before loosening her bonnet ties.

Her coat belled slightly from the warm air forced up through the floor, bringing to his mind the furnace problems and Noah Eastman.

"Is something wrong?" Sissy asked him, her eyebrows coming together like seagull wings drawn with just a stroke. Her face was getting paler with the weather, making her look more fragile and fine-boned than she had in the heat of the summer.

He ignored the question, unable or unwilling to share what was bothering him. So she stood, questions written on that open, honest face, while he searched for something to say.

Finally, he offered to take her coat, and she accepted.

"How is Mr. Eastman recovering?" he asked when she moved away from the heater and tugged at her gloves until her work-worn hands were bare.

There was a shyness to her suddenly. An almost girlishness he'd never seen in her before. She stammered when she spoke. "He's fine." A hint of a smile brushed at the corner of her mouth. "He lost some of his eyebrow and looks kinda crooked."

Miller laughed, despite the way he felt toward Eastman. "But he's fully recovered?"

"Mm-hm." Her back was to him as she went to lay her gloves on the quarter-sawn oak hall tree's center box. Tessie had left the letters she had written there for mailing, and they fell to her feet as she turned back to him. He rushed to pick them up, but her hands beat his and he watched guiltily the sad look on her face as she traced the address on the top envelope.

"Tessie do these?" she asked.

He nodded, but could think of nothing to say.

"Writes real nicely, don't she?"

It was as though his chin were tied with some kind of string that kept his mouth closed and his head nodding. As though he had a kerchief tied around him for a toothache and someone was jerking on the knot. He thought the image quite suitable, since her unhappy face caused him a certain amount of pain.

"I'm learning, you know," she said, her light brown eyes steady against his own. In fact, he didn't know. "Mr. Eastman's got a Spencer book he's offered to loan me. So you won't ever have to be ashamed of me, Miller."

He felt petty and small and stupid standing there in his fine house with his fine ways and fine things around him. "If I made you feel that way, I'm sorry," he said softly. Sissy Morrow was a good hard-working woman. He doubted there were more than a handful of people who could make her feel unworthy. He didn't like being one of them.

She seemed to think before she spoke. "It doesn't matter," she said deliberately. "I'd rather know I was saying or writing or doing something wrong, so that I could fix it, than think that someone was laughing at me behind my back or thinking I wasn't smart just because I didn't have the same opportunities they did."

Miller Winestock had never placed a wager in his life, but he'd bet money that those words came out of Noah Eastman's mouth before they came out of Sissy's. Not that she wasn't smart. Not that what she said wasn't true. He just couldn't believe the thought had occurred to her, since it had never occurred to him.

"Anybody who could raise five sisters and brothers, run a farm, look after an ailing father, and still find time to be kind to an old man like me ought not to be ashamed of poor penmanship. Don't you agree?"

"You gonna tell that to everyone I need to write to? Please excuse my wife's pen—" She stopped, red-faced, and put her hand over her mouth.

He knew he should tell her it was all right. After all, she would be his wife sooner or later; what harm was there in saying it aloud? He should tell her it sounded surprisingly good to his ears. Better than he expected. What had started out of some sense of duty and an admission that every minister needed a wife had begun to take on a new dimension.

Sissy was cheerful, she was conscientious, she was compassionate. Her qualities were those a man could grow to love, as the years went by.

But for now his heart still belonged to Elvira, and his tongue stayed mute in his mouth while his eyes remained fixed on the floor.

"Well," Sissy said after a strained silence. Her chin was thrust up proudly and her eyes glistened just a little too brightly with the hurt he had managed to inflict. Time, he thought desperately. He just needed more time. If she would only give him more time.

"So he's teaching you things? I wasn't aware he was an educated man."

"Being a farmer, you mean?" Sissy asked. There was just a hint of anger in her voice. "According to Ethan, he doesn't come by the farming naturally. In fact, he's better at teaching than at farming, it seems."

"Is that so?" he said. He wondered what Noah Eastman had done before he came to Van Wert. It occurred to him that the man had never said. Farming now, everyone just assumed he'd been farming before. But then everyone assumed a great many things about Mr. Eastman which Miller knew only too well weren't necessarily true.

"His house is full of books, and there's a globe like the one at the schoolhouse in the girls' room."

At the mention of the school Miller was overwhelmed once more with guilt. "Paulie Mitchell's doing very well," he said. "I spoke with Dr. Woods this afternoon, and he

said his face is healing very well. His hands, though . . ."
His voice drifted off.

"It was lucky that Mr. Eastman came when he did."

"Yes," he had to agree. "Quite remarkable, really. The
man is somewhat of a mystery, don't you think?"

That look crossed Sissy's face again, the one that spoke
of shyness and youth. He wondered just what Sissy thought
of Mr. Eastman. Did she find him attractive? Interesting?
He was a good deal younger than Miller, though he
doubted that youth was something that would appeal to a
woman of Sissy's status. After all, she'd been an adult
almost as long as he had, even if she was younger in years.

"A mystery?" she said, as if she had been considering the
word he had chosen. Perhaps she didn't understand him. He
was always forgetting that her education left her lacking.

"Yes," he said. "It means—"

She cut him off, rather abruptly for the well-mannered
woman he knew her to be. "I know what it means, Miller.
He hardly seems mysterious to me. He's a poor dirt farmer
struggling to get by, not much different from the rest of us.
He hates the rain and the cold and loves his daughters and
a good peach pie. He works hard and does his best. What's
the mystery?"

It sounded like a defense and an indictment at the same
time. As though she liked him and yet she didn't. He'd
never seen anyone through Sissy Morrow's eyes. How, he
wondered, would she describe him?

He realized suddenly, with embarrassment, he hadn't
even offered her a seat. Now he led her to his gent's chair
and encouraged her to sit. He perched on the edge of
Elvira's chair and faced her. He took one of her hands in
his, an intimate gesture he wasn't entirely comfortable
with, but he wanted to impress upon her the seriousness
of what he had to say.

"How well do you know this man?" he asked.

"I know he's a good man, an honest man."

He shook his head, fighting with himself, wanting to warn her yet wondering what his motives were. Did he just want to see the man destroyed the way he had destroyed Elvira's father's memory? Was he, perhaps, jealous that Sissy spent her days at Mr. Eastman's farm and had abandoned him to fend for himself?

"You don't know, Sissy," he said, then bit his lip. "But you should. Ask him. Ask him about his life, the life he led in Johnstown. Ask him why he moved. Ask him about his wife."

Sissy looked confused. "But we know all that," she said cautiously. "He moved here because of the flood that took his wife and his family. When Stuart Eastman died and left the farm to him, it let him leave all the terrible memories behind and start over here. What more is there to know?"

"Perhaps a great deal," he said.

"You might be right," she admitted, as if just considering it. "I don't get the feeling that even though they work together all the time, Ethan knows that much about him. Francie fancies herself in love with him, you know. Do you think I ought to ask him about himself, or would that be prying?"

Innocent eyes stared at him. It felt good to be the one she turned to for answers, and it was a relief not to have to be the one to tell her.

"By all means," he said patting her hand. "Ask him."

"I will," she said with conviction. She rose and went toward the hall tree to don her coat. "And Miller, you will come to dinner on Sunday, won't you? We're having turkey."

"I look forward to it," he said honestly.

A smile lit her face and a twinkle touched her eyes. "Don't worry. Willa won't be cooking."

She was a dear woman. And he could do a lot worse.

20

She'd spent half the night going over the conversation with Miller in her mind. Countless times her thoughts were interrupted by Bart, who kept coming in to her room to ask her how to fix lemonade for Willa (in November, for goodness' sake!), or how to make coffee (naturally, she was cold after the lemonade!), or whether there were any pickled beets (luckily, there were), or a hundred other requests for an expectant mother. Certainly it was annoying, but to see her big oaf of a brother sheepishly asking for some kind of cream to stop the itching of Willa's stretching skin was touching, too.

Love had bitten Bart Morrow right on the heart, and after her evening with Miller, Annie was just a little jealous. Maybe more than a little. And a little angry, too. Miller had been polite, concerned, friendly. He'd been the perfect minister. But she hadn't come to him as a parishioner, and he had left her feeling embarrassed once again about bringing up their marriage.

It wasn't as if he had never asked her; he'd only said he

had to wait a year. But there was no bended knee. No flowers. No declarations of love.

"You're being a fool," she said to the reflection in the mirror as she looked at the woman in the blue wool dress who stared back at her. "You're not seventeen. You're not beautiful. You're not going to be swept off your feet."

She pulled the hair back for her bun so tightly it made her eyes slant.

"You're twenty-six. You're used up, old. And lucky enough to have the most respected man in town willing to marry you, take you into his house, and give you a life you've only dreamed about. And you're thinking about flowers."

It was Risa's fault. Risa's and Willa's and Bart's. All this talk about love and devotion. It was Ethan's fault. And Charlie's. Everybody claiming they wanted her to be happy.

It was Noah Eastman's fault.

The thought sobered her. It was no one's fault but her own. One foolish old maid who thought that because a man once said her hair was the color of spun sugar she was entitled to the dreams of a young girl.

She knew better than to change direction in the middle of a furrow. She'd been planting this field a good long time, and now that it was nearly ready for harvest she was letting the horse run loose. Miller Winestock was everything she ever wanted in a husband. He was a pillar of the community, respected, admired. He was as far from a farmer as you could be in Van Wert. He was kind, patient, giving.

And right. He was right about Noah Eastman. What did anyone know about the man? A memory hit her as she made her way down the staircase: Francie running in, the sun just low enough in the sky to come through the window and show the tears on her face. She'd run right past Annie on the stairs and up to the room they had shared as children.

Annie had gone after her like so many other times. Her

Francie was such an earnest child. Everything that happened to her was the best or the worst; there was no middle ground. That was where Annie lived, and Francie never wanted any part of it.

"He could have told me!" Francie had cried. "He could have trusted me, you know."

Annie had rubbed her back and handed her a hankie. "Mr. Eastman?" she'd asked.

Francie had turned over on the bed where she had flung herself and stared at Annie with red-rimmed eyes. "God, I love him so much," she'd said.

"But honey," Annie had reasoned. "Only a month ago it was Fred Hott you loved. And a month before that it was the Conn boy."

"You don't understand. They were just children. I was going to marry Noah. And now I can't."

"No," she had agreed, "you can't. You have Teachers College in New York and a whole wonderful life in front of you. Mr. Eastman is practically old enough to be your father."

"You don't understand," Francie had said again. "And I can't tell you. I couldn't even tell him that I know."

Annie had been thoroughly confused. Francie had only admitted that she had been snooping despite all of Annie's warnings, and now her heart was broken. Forever, as she put it.

Miller was right, as usual. They knew nothing about Noah Eastman.

With Blackie hitched up and ready to go, Annie lit out for the Eastman farm. And some answers.

He refused, flat out, to discuss his past with her. She had her rules, he said, and he had his. He left for the fields in a huff, the door slamming behind him. At lunchtime he returned with Ethan in tow, and she suspected it was to stop her from asking any more questions.

As always, when it came to Noah Eastman, she was wrong.

"Ethan will watch the girls," he said gruffly. "Get your coat." It was an order. She obeyed.

He led her to the barn. The cold stung her eyes and she was grateful when they got out of the wind.

"It'll be colder with the door open," he said. He looked at her and held up an open palm. "It's up to you. Close it or not?"

She looked around. Hay was stacked neatly near the door, just like her barn at home. The chickens were cooped on the left side, as hers were; the two cows were penned at the front right. Ethan had apparently copied the Morrow barn when he'd gotten Noah set up to run his place. It felt like home. It smelled like home. Even Blackie was there, hidden for the day from the wind.

"You can close it," she said softly.

He looked surprised but not really happy.

"What do you want to know?" he asked. They were still standing in the center of the barn, and she could only read his face as unfriendly.

"Why out here?" she asked.

"Hannah's old enough to understand what we're talking about," he explained.

The answer surprised her—and gave her a starting point, as well. "And what you have to say would upset her?"

"That's putting it mildly," he admitted.

"Was she very close to her mother?"

He laughed. It was a hard laugh, and then suddenly his whole face changed. It softened as though he remembered who it was he was talking to, and his body began to ease, his shoulders sagging just a little. He looked around and then led her to the bales of hay. He moved one so that if they sat they would be facing each other, and gestured for her to choose one.

After she was seated he lowered himself to the bale across from her. He was too tall to look comfortable on it, his knees coming way up, nearly to the height of his shoulders.

"Oh, my Annie," he said. It was a whisper that caressed her. "How can I explain to you? How could you possibly understand a woman like Wylene?"

An unexpected pang of jealousy stabbed her in the chest. "Was she so wonderful?"

His elbow rested on his knee and his hand made a resting spot for his head, which shook back and forth sadly. "She hated me. She hated Johnstown, and she hated being married to a teacher."

"A teacher?"

"Surely you guessed I wasn't cut out for farming."

"But why did you leave teaching? When you could do so much good? You know they need a teacher. Miss Orliss came to me about Francie."

He closed his eyes and shook his head. "It's behind me. All of it. And that's where I want it to stay. People leave a farmer alone. They don't point at him on the street and wonder how such a smart man is being fooled." He opened his eyes and gave her half a smile. Maybe it was a whole one, but with his eyebrow scorched it looked like only half. "Besides, this way I can take only the pupils I want. And I want only one."

She was very quiet. What could she say to a man whose wife didn't love him? Hadn't been faithful to him? Her heart ached for the humiliation he must have felt, must be feeling again as he admitted all this to her.

"It's none of my business," she said, putting her weight on her feet and starting to rise.

"She hated the girls too," he said, and she could hear the tears in his throat, smell the shame he felt as if it were his own and not that of the woman he'd married. "That was the worst part. It wasn't too bad after Hannah was born. At least she seemed glad that the pregnancy was over, and her mother helped with the baby. But when she found out she was carrying Julia, she ran off."

He swallowed so hard it was like thunder in the quiet of the barn. His eyes were filled with tears that refused to fall, and though she wanted to stop him, tell him not to go on, the words wouldn't come.

"There was a woman, a doctor of sorts. She . . . well, she agreed to help Wylene out of her trouble."

He nodded when the shocked look on her face said she knew what he meant.

"But she didn't," Annie said. "I mean, that beautiful little girl. She changed her mind?"

He shook his head. "I got there in time. I told the doctor if she ever saw my wife again, even on the street, I'd break every finger she had so she'd never operate again. I think I really meant it."

He looked up and reached his hand out to wipe her tears away. His calloused fingers felt warm against her cheeks.

"I promised Wylene there would be no more children after the baby was born. I was resigned to living a monk's existence. It was a hard delivery. Wylene was slow to recover. She was dependent on elixirs and remedies—anything that contained more alcohol than herbs. She refused to take care of the baby. I'd come home and Julia would be lying there, a day's worth of pee burning her bottom."

Annie rose and stood just inches from him. When he leaned his head forward she clutched him against her stomach. His sobs shook her body, and if his arms weren't so tightly wrapped around her waist she'd have fallen for sure.

"We will never *ever* talk about this again," she said, her hands running through his hair and caressing his head.

"I told the girls she loved them," he said, as though his lie was worse than the horrible things he had told her. "I couldn't let them think—"

"That was good," she told him, in the same voice she had used to praise her brothers and sisters when they'd done something they thought might have been wrong, but for the right reasons. "Oh, Noah. Hannah and Julia are two lucky little girls."

"Lucky?" he said, like she was crazy. "To have a mother like that?"

"Lucky," she said, and tilted his head back so that he could look into her eyes, "to have a father like you."

They left the barn together, but as Annie headed for the house, Noah walked toward his fields, his head down and his collar up against the wind. She wiped her face and tried to find a smile for the little girls who were waiting for her, babies who had known so much unhappiness in their short lives. She glanced once more at the fields and the solitary man who stood in them. Her heart ached for the whole Eastman family.

She and the children would bake a special cake. One with burnt sugar icing all around it like a nest, a sweet nest where they could all be safe. It wasn't much, but it was all she could do.

In a lot of ways Annie was sorry that she had found out about Wylene Eastman. Keeping a secret was not something she did with ease. And, after confiding in her, Noah kept his distance, making himself scarce and, when they were together, hardly talking to her at all.

By the end of the week she wondered if they would ever get over this new awkwardness. Friday had been a wonderful

day with the girls. Knowing they had been deprived of the
love that they deserved, she had begun to hold nothing back
from them. They hugged and kissed and played and sang
and baked, and Annie watched them blossom like flowers
in the sun. Even Julia's potty training was successful.

She had been so busy with the girls that she had paid
little attention to what Ethan and Noah were doing. There
was banging and clanking from behind the house much of
the day, but until she saw Noah and Ethan come in the
door Friday evening as she was getting ready to leave, she
hadn't even wondered what the two of them were up to.

"Do you think it'll work?" Ethan asked.

Noah shot him a look that piqued Annie's curiosity.
Besides, she was eager to make normal conversation with
him.

"What will work?" she asked.

"You'll know soon enough," Noah said. On his face
was the first genuine smile she had seen since their talk in
the barn.

"I see," she said, allowing them their secret if it brought
him such happiness.

"That's all?" Ethan demanded. "Not even curious?"

"Oh, I'll get it out of you at Sunday dinner," she said
with a smile. "Turkey. Care to come, Mr. Eastman?"

He shook his head, but she didn't see any regret there.
Instead, he exchanged a sly glance with Ethan, both of them
having difficulty keeping their surprise to themselves. "Can't.
Neither can Eth. We've got some work to do that can't wait."

"But, Noah," her brother whined. "Turkey!"

"I could bring you over some," she offered, hoping
she'd get an inkling of what they had up their sleeves.

Noah shook his head, his eyes twinkling merrily all the
while. "Best if you don't show your face before Monday."

"Apple-quince pie." She dangled the imaginary treat
before their eyes.

Ethan groaned.

"Maybe we'll be over for some pie toward evening," Noah said. "If that's all right."

Four pairs of eyes begged Annie's permission.

"Of course it's all right," she said. "Miller will be sorry he missed you."

Ethan snorted. She was going to have to talk to him about his conversational skills.

"Yes," Noah said, not looking at all sorry that he and the minister would not cross paths. "Right."

The smell of turkey roasting filled the Morrow house, overwhelming the earlier smells of quince pie and rutabaga relish. When she opened the oven door, a burst of mouthwatering steam billowed toward her. Splatterings of fat hit the walls of the oven and sizzled. Carefully, Annie pulled out the big roasting pan, the cover already removed to allow the bird's skin to turn brown and crisp, and basted the bird one last time.

As she worked, she listened to the sounds of her family filtering through the kitchen door. Della was showing off her new dress to Willa and promising to write down the address of the store in New York—Bloomingdale's—for her. As if Bart could afford to send for a new dress for Willa, especially in her condition! Charlie was complaining to Miller about the new Sabbath school teacher and how she had refused to allow Cara to attend classes because she was too young, despite her good behavior.

Peter was making a fuss over his wine, and the boys were playing cowboys and Indians. She counted her guests in her head: the Gibbses, four; Charlie's family, three; Willa and Bart and Miller, another three. Ten people in the house including her, nine of them family. So how could she be lonely?

She'd busied herself from the moment she returned from church, where Noah and Ethan, in fine spirits, had barely said hello and good-bye before hightailing it back to their farm. Well, they had given her enough time to kiss each girl, Noah lifting them to her face, his hands brushing her arm in one case, the edge of her breast in the other.

Her cheeks flamed again, just as they had in front of the church. "Sorry," he'd said, jostling Julia's squirming body to get a better hold on her.

But his eyes had been locked with hers, and though she knew he hadn't intended to touch her intimately, the contact had caused his breath to quicken as surely as it had made her blush. If he was sorry, she was Benjamin Harrison.

"Need any help?" Charlie asked, his head and shoulders peeking through the door. The look on his face said he had made as much conversation with Miller as he could and was hoping to be rescued.

"You could take this out of the oven for me," she said, pointing to the twenty pound turkey in the cast-iron pan.

From the main room they could hear the running of small feet and the effort of adults to be heard over the shouts of children.

"Peter," Della was saying, "check Samuel's mouth, dear."

Charlie and Annie exchanged a look of disgust. They had both long ago agreed that their sister had spent so much time on the line for good looks before she was born that she'd had to forgo the mothering skills department. To make matters worse, God had played the trick of blessing her with twins to handle.

"Spit it out!" Della's shrill voice sliced through the room with an urgency that made Annie and Charlie stop what they were doing and look toward the door.

"Smack him on the back," Bart said. "Turn him upside down and smack his back!"

Charlie set down the scalding pan and they both hurried out to the living room, to join the men who were in a close circle surrounding Samuel. Risa and Willa stood with their backs to the cluster around the boy, their faces pale and their thumbs tucked superstitiously into the waistbands of their skirts. Della was screaming and Miller was trying to pull her away from the crowd of men.

"Squeeze his chest," Bart suggested.

"Pound on it."

"Shake him."

"Can you reach it? Can you see it?"

"What did he swallow?" Annie mouthed at Risa. Tears fell down Risa's cheeks in rivers that stained the front of her shirtwaist. She clung to Willa, keeping the woman's back to the scene that was barreling toward a horrible conclusion.

"The wine cork." Risa whispered it.

How many times had Annie told Peter she didn't want alcohol in her house? How many times had he told her it was harmless and convinced her to give in?

"No," she said, as if she could take back her permission and change the drama that was playing out in her living room. "No."

Risa looked back over her shoulder and swallowed convulsively. She searched the room until she found Cara. The little girl stood pressed against the wall with wide eyes fixed on her mother's face. At a signal from her, Cara threw herself at Risa and pressed her little body into her mother's skirts. Risa's arm wrapped quickly around her and held the child tightly against her.

James! Where was James? Annie found him in the hallway. He lay curled in a ball, his eyes squeezed shut, his breathing irregular. She bent and took him in her arms, rocking him gently and crooning meaningless words.

She was far enough away from the others to watch

them like some actors on a stage in a great tragedy. They beat their breasts, they clenched their fists, they bit on the knuckles of their first fingers as though something awful were truly taking place. She just couldn't believe it was.

In her arms, James said nothing. He didn't cling, didn't nuzzle, didn't whimper. His body was tensed, his muscles taut as if in readiness.

Miller still held Della as she struggled to see Samuel over his shoulder. "Oh, my God, My baby! He's blue!" Della shrieked. "He's dead!"

There was silence in the room. No one corrected her. There were no words shouted in annoyance that she was just being dramatic. No comforting noises about how Samuel would be all right. There was just a heavy, stunned silence as the women waited for Peter Gibbs to deny the truth that crept its way into each of their hearts.

Samuel Gibbs, age three, lay motionless in his father's arms, his skin a ghastly blue, his eyes staring up at his father without seeing anything at all.

In her own arms, James Gibbs, twin brother of Samuel, went limp.

21

There was an unnatural quiet to the Morrow farmhouse when Noah and Ethan pulled up. Hannah and Julia slept soundly under a blanket in the back of the wagon, so the men decided to leave them there until they found out what the problem was. Undoubtedly there was a problem, for while lights glowed in the window and smoke billowed from the chimney, there were no sounds of laughter or conversation.

On the porch the quiet seemed to grow louder. Ethan shrugged at Noah and reached for the doorknob.

Noah stopped him. "Perhaps we should knock," he suggested.

Without asking why, without arguing that it was still his home, Ethan raised his fist and knocked gently on the door.

Miller Winestock opened it, the light from the house setting him in silhouette and making his gray hair look metallic. Beyond him, members of Ethan's family sat on the chairs, the sofa, stood leaning against walls. Annie had one of the twins in her arms. Noah didn't see the other boy, or Della and Peter.

"What's happened?" Noah asked. Ethan pushed past the minister without waiting for an answer and went straight to Annie. Even from this distance Noah could see the tears on her face as they caught the light from the fireplace. To push past Miller Winestock, to take her in his arms and soothe her—his own need was almost overwhelming.

Instead, he waited for the minister to ask him in and tell him what had happened.

Obviously shaken, Winestock took two breaths to steady himself. Then, rather than upset the family once again, he motioned for Noah to step back and joined him on the porch, where he told him about Samuel and the wine cork. To his credit, he seemed as much at a loss at God's mysterious ways as Noah himself felt.

"Mr. and Mrs. Gibbs took their son back to town. He wanted her to stay here, but she couldn't bear to think of the boy alone at the undertaker's." The breath he took rattled in his chest. He shook his head. "One minute he was a hellion, running around and making a nuisance of himself. And the next, gone."

"How are the others taking it?" Noah asked. His heart ached for all of them: Annie, who thought they all belonged to her; Bart, whose heart exceeded his size; Risa, who carried a new life within her. "Mrs. Morrow, is she all right?"

The minister nodded. "Yes, both Mrs. Morrows. They're a close family. We're a close community. They'll take care of each other, and we'll take care of them."

He'd encountered this wall before. It had come down some since the fire at the school, but it still existed. He wasn't one of them. "I'd like to help," he said. "Please." He gestured toward the door, knowing he wouldn't go in without Winestock's invitation. Annie was going through enough. He would do nothing to make it harder for her.

The minister nodded, and Noah removed his hat and entered the living room as quietly as he could. Annie raised her eyes to him, but before he could even respond, Ethan came barreling toward him and thrust himself into his chest, sobbing. He comforted him as a father would comfort a son, patting the rough wool of his jacket. Had Noah ever cried like Ethan was doing, his father probably would have cuffed his ear and told him that men didn't give in to sorrow.

Ethan had obviously had a much healthier upbringing. He looked over the boy's head toward the woman who had managed it when she was only a child herself. Next to her, Miller bent and whispered something into her ear, to which she shook her head and clutched the child in her arms more tightly. He asked her something else, to which she again shook her head.

Noah's stomach turned as Miller took Annie's chin in his hand and tilted her face up to his. Reluctantly she nodded and handed the child up to him.

As Winestock carried the sleeping child from the room, Noah extricated himself from Ethan's embrace. "I want to make sure your sister's all right," he said in the boy's ear. "I'll be right back."

The glow from the fireplace lit Annie's cheek and one side of her hair. She looked miserable and tired and confused as he came toward her. Her lip trembled as he watched her fight for control.

"You spend your whole life making sure they're safe," she said, so quietly that he had to bend to hear her at all, "and then in a moment, an instant, you turn your back for just a second—and all the years you watched don't matter. They don't count for anything."

The warmth of the fire burned his face. The hair that had been singed had not yet come back and the skin was sensitive to heat. Yet he wouldn't have moved one inch from her at that moment no matter what the pain. For she had reached out and taken his hand and seemed to draw strength from it.

She gave him a weak smile. "Where are the girls?"

"Asleep in the wagon," he said. Her hand was softer than when he had last held it. He supposed gardening was over for the season.

She went to rise. "They must be cold." She shivered and new tears fell. Samuel would be cold forever after they placed him in the ground.

"They have warm blankets," he assured her with a squeeze of his hand. "But I can't stay long. I'm afraid I've already intruded."

Miller returned and placed a proprietary hand on Annie's shoulder. "I'll get you some tea," he said, then turned to Noah. "Can I get you anything?"

Noah thanked him but declined. Eventually Miller went on to the others—Risa, Charlie, Willa, Bart.

"There must be something I can do," Noah said. "How can I help?"

"Francie," Annie said softly. "Could you let Francie know? She sent me a telephone number for emergencies. I've got it somewheres . . . I never thought I'd really use it. There's a telephone in Hanson's." She looked over at Risa and Charlie, who were huddled together with Cara between them. Risa's face was white and Charlie was consumed with calming her. "I can't ask them."

"I'll telephone her," Noah said. "I'll stop there on my way home."

"Mr. Hanson lives upstairs," Annie told him as she rose and went to her desk to find the number.

"I have it," Noah said, stilling her hand.

Her eyebrows came together in a question, but she didn't care enough at the moment to voice it. There would be plenty of time to tell her all that Francie had done for him. For now, he had to call her with the Morrow family's sad news. He wondered if telephones were the marvelous invention they were touted to be. So far, they seemed to reek of death and disaster. It was no wonder they looked like little wooden coffins, filled with black ribbons of wire.

Mr. Archie Hanson rang up the operator and gave her the telephone number Francie had sent to Noah. With one eye he guarded the stock of his store from what he perceived as Noah's sticky fingers, and with the other he pinned Noah to the counter and checked out his features.

"New York College for the Training of Teachers!" Hanson shouted into the mouthpiece. "It's a school there for girls that don't know their place!"

Noah reminded himself why he was there.

"Hello?" he shouted again. "This the college?"

He nodded and Noah took the phone from his unwilling hand. Hanson stayed where he was and Noah had to lean his body sideways to speak into the mouthpiece. "I need to get in touch with Francine Morrow of Van Wert, Ohio," he said loudly. "Can she come to the telephone?"

A voice crackled over the line. For all his sophistication and book learning, Noah still felt his insides bubble up as a woman in New York City, some thousand, or so miles away, told him that Miss Morrow was at an evening lecture along with the other girls.

"Can I leave a message for her?" he asked, pronouncing each word carefully and distinctly.

The voice assured him that a message would be delivered.

"Please tell her Noah Eastman called and she is to come home as soon as possible. Tell her to wire her arrival time, and I will meet her at the train."

The voice repeated roughly what he had said.

"Tell her, please, that it is an emergency."

The voice crackled again and then the line went dead.

He looked at the earpiece in his hand and knew he was holding the future. From now on the world would get smaller and smaller because of Bell's invention. The receiver was still warm from his touch and he pressed it to his chest before giving it back to Mr. Hanson, who rang up the operator and asked for the charges.

"Just put it on my bill," Noah said as he headed for the door. There was a mannequin on his way, and he stopped to admire the soft yellow dress she was clad in. The price tag read $4.85, a hefty sum for a man who was still paying off the wind wheel with which he hoped to win Annie. He touched the satiny fabric and imagined Annie in it. He could feel Hanson's eyes on his back and let the fabric drop.

He thought of poor Samuel, whom he never really liked, but who surely deserved a chance to grow up and taste what life had to offer. For the child, life had been much too short, but then how long did anyone have?

For some people yesterday was too late. He wasn't going to be one of them.

Miller checked again on the other twin. Which one had died and which one still lived?

He had removed himself from his community with Elvira's death, as if his grief relieved him of his duties. But watching the child on the bed before him reminded him that God's mysteries kept unfolding and it was his duty to help his parishioners cope.

The boy slept uneasily. A rigidity would come over him; then, just as abruptly, the stiffened arms and legs would soften and his breathing would ease. Wasn't that what life was like? The soul hardening with each hurt, only to soften once again and be open to yet another pain?

Life was God's greatest gift, and to squander it with

years of grief was to trivialize its worth. He would miss Elvira fervently until they were reunited in the kingdom, but he would live every day until then to the fullest of his ability. Samuel Gibbs—yes, that was his name—would not have died in vain.

He pushed the curly hair back from James's brow and made a promise to watch over him.

Then he tucked the covers under the child's chin and descended the stairs to the living room. Risa and Charlie had taken Cara and gone home. Willa was asleep, her breathing deep and even as she lay in the curve of Bart's arm, her head resting on his chest.

Sissy was putting away the dishes from the meal no one ate, her arms and legs moving through the quicksand of grief. Silently he fell in beside her and helped gather the silverware, the glasses, the pitcher of still cool water.

She made trip after trip between kitchen and living room on legs that were ready to buckle beneath the weight of her fatigue and her sorrow. He tried to carry the brunt of it, tried to make her job lighter, but nothing stopped her until he laid a hand on her shoulder and forced her into a chair.

"Enough," he told her. "Everything else can wait until morning."

It was a mistake to stop her. Keeping busy had been holding her together, as he should have remembered from his own grief. With hollow, empty eyes she looked at him.

"Why?" she asked. Her voice croaked and she tried to clear her throat. "Can you tell me why?"

"God has a plan," Miller offered, meager though the answer seemed even to him. "I can't tell you what it is, but He has a plan."

"Is James in my bed?" she asked.

He nodded. James could count on her to take care of him. Everyone could count on Annie. "You should get some sleep," he said softly. It would be nice, he thought, if *she* could count on *him*.

"You know I didn't want the wine here," she said.

He nodded. He knew there'd never be wine in the house again, but it was like locking the schoolhouse after the fire.

"I should have been out there, watching the children."

"Don't be silly," he said. "You were making supper. There were six adults in that room. If anyone is to blame, it's us."

She looked stricken. "Oh, no, I didn't mean to say that it was anyone's fault. You mustn't blame yourself. Children do things, stupid things, and no one can stop them."

"You managed to stop all those brothers and sisters," he said. "You protected all of them from harm."

She tried to smile, but her face cracked and the tears rolled down her cheeks. "Until tonight. All the years I kept Della safe, let her be carefree and irresponsible because she was so lovely and full of life. And look what I did. Della would cry over a broken iris stem. She's not ready for pain like this."

Miller wondered how she could look at Della and see such goodness and softness where everyone else saw self-centeredness and pride. "She'll be fine," he said. "She's stronger than you think."

She shrugged and rose. "There's a lot to do tomorrow. I wonder if Noah reached Francie."

"Will she be coming home?"

She nodded. "You know what they say, Miller. Be careful what you wish for, you might get it. Well, Francie's been begging me to let her come home."

From the top of the stairs came a small boy's shriek.

"That'll be James," she said and hurried toward the steps.

"I'll see myself out," Miller said, but he doubted Sissy even heard him. She was going up the stairs two at a time toward a child who needed her.

He wondered what the chances were of their having children of their own.

22

Condolences were being paid at Della and Peter Gibbses' house in town. Wagons lined the streets, reflecting both Peter's position at the bank and the warm feeling of the townsfolk for the Morrow family. Noah took Hannah's hand and, with Julia in one arm, made his way to the front door of the Gibbs home.

"I'm so sorry," he told Peter, letting go of Hannah's hand to take Peter's extended one. "Is there anything I can do?"

Peter was dry-eyed. He appeared composed in his business suit with his well-groomed hair. Only the trembling of the hand Noah held gave away his grief. He shook his head in response to Noah's question, then seemed to remember something.

"Francie. Were you able to contact Francie?" he asked.

Noah had stopped at the Western Union office, and a wire from Francie said she would be home early the next morning. He told Peter he would meet the train at 6:02 A.M.

"I'll just tell Della," Peter said and excused himself, leaving Noah to greet the next mourners and direct them inside.

He put Julia down and directed her sister to keep an eye on her as he shook hands with the Kelly family and pointed out to Brian and his wife where Peter and Della now stood.

"Hannah," the silky voice for which he was waiting said, "you and Julia are to stay right by your father or with me. You understand?"

"Yes, Miss Annie."

"No wandering around."

"No, Miss Annie."

He greeted Tessie Willis and her aunt and then turned to speak with Annie, but she was gone, as were his girls. He caught a glimpse of them, holding Annie's skirt and following her toward the back of the house where he supposed the kitchen must be. He tried to follow her, but Charlie stopped him to ask about Francie, and then Risa, looking rather tired, asked him for a glass of water, and it was one thing after another as the afternoon wore on and he had to settle for a glimpse of Annie here, a flicker of Annie there.

"Would you like to come back to the farm for supper?" Annie asked him when the gas jets were lit and the world turned as black outside as the dresses the women around him were wearing. "I'm afraid there's nothing for you to heat up at your place." Her sad eyes searched his for answers he didn't have.

"I'd like that," he said, about supper. "Very much."

"I'll be leaving soon," she said, looking around at her brothers and sisters. "Della ought to rest, and surely Risa and Willa need to get off their feet. One tragedy is about all I can handle."

She bit her lip and Noah snapped into action. "I'll get your coat," he said. "Just wait here with the girls. I'll tell Della and Peter I'm taking you home."

Surprisingly, since Annie didn't like to be told what to do, she nodded. "Tell Bart too. I don't want him searching for me after I'm gone and holding up poor Willa."

With a quick nod he took off, gathering coats and children and delivering messages and condolences. In a short time he had the girls and Annie out at the wagon, and after lifting in Hannah and Julia, he gave Annie his hand.

She steadied herself and raised her skirts to find her footing on the wheel hub. She leaned ever so slightly on his shoulder and then sat daintily on the wooden seat. He made a mental note to add some padding—either to the seat or her behind or both.

"Girls," she said over her shoulder, "you sit up close to the front now. No dangling those feet off the edge."

"They're fine," he assured her, knowing that her fear for his children stemmed from the knowledge that bad things did happen and that tragedy, unlike lightning, could strike twice in the same place. He turned to look at the girls and the same fear ran through him, despite his ability to rationalize it. "You heard Miss Annie," he barked at them. "Get your bottoms up by the seat or I'll come hammer them in place."

The girls scurried toward the front of the wagon and settled themselves under the blanket. When they were secure enough for Annie's liking, she nodded at Noah and he flicked the reins and headed the horse toward the Morrow farm.

"I don't understand you," Noah said, after they had finished their meal and the girls had settled down on the divan and fallen asleep. "I know you love those children. I can see it every time you look at them. Yet you stand there and tell me you're relieved that you're done raising children and you're looking forward to marrying some man old enough to be your father."

"Miller is not old enough to be my father, and you don't have to understand me," Anne answered. She didn't owe him any explanations. Her plans had been made long before she even met Mr. Noah Eastman.

"Can you look at me and tell me you don't love me?" he demanded, his one whole eyebrow raised in outrage.

"Love you?" she said. "I don't even know you, hardly."

"I don't make your pulse beat faster? Your palms don't sweat when I'm around? Your lips don't itch for me to touch them with my own?"

If she were naked, he couldn't have made her feel more exposed. She said nothing and looked at the floor while he closed the gap between them.

"I know all that," he said, as he lifted her chin and insisted that she look at him, "because it's how I feel. Only I'm not fighting it. I know I want to spend the rest of my life going to sleep with my arms around you and waking up with your hair sweeping across my face."

"Oh, yes," she said, as haughtily as she could manage. "When roses bloom in winter I'll be in your bed."

"If that's what it takes," he said with a smile.

Where were Bart and Willa? Shouldn't they have gotten home already? How could her brother leave her alone with a man who talked about taking her to his bed and lips that itched and who made her nipples harden and her insides knot?

"I'm marrying Miller Winestock," she said, with a conviction that didn't sound like pleasure, even to her. "I raised all the children I'm gonna raise and planted all the furrows I'm gonna plant. I milked enough cows and fed enough chickens and I don't want to be part of any of it anymore. Not the farm and not the family." Her chest was rising and falling as though she had run up and down the stairs a dozen times. "I don't want more children. I've got no more love for children. I'm out. Done. Used up."

"You want me to believe you don't love children anymore?" he asked. "The way you mother my girls? The way you watch after your nieces and nephews?"

"Well, I didn't do that so good, did I?" Her eyes were

flooding and it was hard to see Noah's face, but his body was clear enough. His hands were on his hips and his feet were spread in a fighting stance.

"Don't be a fool. Accidents happen. Tragedy was bound to reach out and grab that child by the throat. Hell, he tempted fate at every turn."

"He was a baby," she shouted, "and I loved him!"

The words rang throughout the kitchen, echoing off the cabinets filled with her mother's dishes, circling the paintings Cara did that were stuck to the wall.

"Marry me, Annie. Marry me and have my children and love me until the day we die. Didn't you learn anything from Samuel's death? We could be gone tomorrow, and all there'd be left is regret."

"If I married you all I'd know is regret. I know what I want. I've planned for it and prayed for it and now it's here just for the taking. You ask me if I didn't learn anything from Samuel's death. Isn't it there as plain as day for anyone to see? I learned what I already knew. That loving children hurts."

He moved in closer to her, so close it was hard to think. "No, Annie," he said quietly. How she would miss the sound of her name—*Annie*—as though it belonged only to him. "*Losing* children hurts, not loving them."

"You always lose them," she said, backing away from him until she was smack up against the wall. "You have to stop loving them because they leave. Sooner or later they're gone and you're alone."

"Is that what this is all about?" he asked. There was no place to go to get away from him. His face was inches from hers. Every word he spoke caressed her forehead, fluttered her hair. She bent her knees to put a greater distance between their faces, to be out of range of his lips. "Giving them up when it's time for them to move on?"

"They're all gone," she whimpered, her body sliding

down the wall as she opened up her heart to him. "Ethan keeps talking about moving west. Charlie and Risa have a life, Francie is half a continent away."

"What about Della? Don't you think she needs you, now more than ever?"

A sob escaped from Annie's chest as she hit the floor with her bottom. Della hadn't turned to her, hadn't wanted her comfort. She'd needed Peter. Annie wasn't her family anymore.

She simply shook her head at Noah hopelessly.

"Oh, Annie," he said, slipping down beside her and cradling her in his arms. "That's what life is all about, but nobody gave you the time to let it happen for you." He kissed her forehead and left his lips against her as he spoke. "Maybe there is a plan after all. Maybe God was saving you for me. Lord knows no one could love you more, need you more. You won't be alone, Annie, not as long as I'm alive."

"But . . . Miller," she said, struggling to keep her sanity. "Miller and I have an understanding."

"Your Reverend Miller Winestock is a fool. Diddling and dawdling and keeping you waiting as though you were some doll gathering dust on a shelf. If you agreed to marry me, I wouldn't waste one minute telling the whole world just who you belonged to. And I'd have you at the altar an hour before you even had a chance to change your mind."

"You're not being fair," she said. His tongue was tracing the edge of her ear and she could hardly think. "Miller has his congregation to consider. He is in the service of the Lord."

"Then let Miller revere the Lord," he said quietly, taking her face in his hands and studying it like some fancy sculpture in a museum, "and let me revere you."

She didn't fight him as he took her in his arms. He kissed the path of tears on one cheek and then the other while his hands rubbed her back the way her mother had when she was a little girl, a lifetime ago.

"Let me take care of you," he said, as if she were still that small girl. "Let me keep you safe and loved." His lips, which were dusting kisses on her eyelids and her cheeks, sought out her mouth.

Soft and warm they pressed against her own. And she found herself pressing back, leaning eagerly into the curve of his body, letting him gather her into his lap, his lips never leaving her own.

He tasted of apple cider, smelled of smoke. He must have worn this coat when he saved Paulie Mitchell and then never aired it out. A man like Noah Eastman needed a woman to tell him to do a thing like that.

"Hold me," he said, and she found her arms go around his neck as naturally as if they'd made the trip a hundred times before. But his sigh spoke of never before having felt her warmth.

He pulled his lips from hers and read her eyes, eyes that she knew shouldn't be saying what undoubtedly they said: *Touch me. Don't let me go. Never let me go.* He leaned his forehead against her lips and let her kiss him until kissing his face wasn't nearly enough.

She tipped her head back, trying to catch her breath, trying to control the warmth that was filling her chest to bursting, making her breasts strain against her blouse. If she thought she could calm herself that way, Noah's lips against her throat convinced her otherwise.

"I knew you would taste like this," he said, his breath dancing on the wet skin of her neck and making her shiver. "Like honey. Sweet and silky. So exciting and yet so familiar."

One of his hands was playing with her collar while the other rode up and down her side, getting closer and closer to the soft mounds that were aching for his touch. She felt her neckline loosen and gulped for air. As she drew the breath in, his palm found her breast and cupped it gently, one finger making contact with her nipple.

"Oh!" she said, her breathing rapid, her lips so dry she had to lick them.

"Oh!" he said, shifting her on his lap and making her aware that what was happening between them was not just exciting to her.

"Noah, we can't," she began, but his head dipped and his mouth closed around the very tip of her breast, wetting the fabric of her dress. He heated her with his breath, and though she told her body to pull away, shouted in her head to run from him as fast as she could, she thrust herself toward him and let him open the buttons of her shirtwaist in the middle of her kitchen floor.

"You are as beautiful as I imagined," he said.

Embarrassed, she tried to cover herself, but his hands stilled her. She looked away, unable to face him, but let him see what no man had ever seen before.

"Please," he begged, his voice ragged and his breathing uneven. "Let me look at you. I've dreamed of this, day and night, since the first time I saw you. It sounds awful, but I couldn't help it. I can't help it."

He buried his head against her chest, inhaling the smell of her, kissing and sucking and gently easing her down onto the hard wood floor, cradling her head in his palm.

Her body was limp in his hands, despite the tension she felt inside. It was as if she had no power over her movements, no ability to control so much as her tongue. She let his hands roam over her, let him find the flare of her hips, the smallness of her waist. God help her, she even let him trace over her belly and cup the mound that lay below.

He moaned against her, more pain than pleasure, it seemed. And then he grasped her skirts and gathered the fullness in his hand, raising the fabric higher and higher until she could feel the cold air crawl between the top of her boots and the bottom of her drawers.

"No," she said, finally coming to her senses when she felt Noah's hand edge its way beneath her skirts. "No, please."

He stopped at once. His hand stilled for a moment and then he withdrew it and carefully righted her skirts so that from the waist down she was a proper lady again. Breath after breath, each one calmer than the one before, he lay next to her without speaking, without touching, while she fastened the buttons on her blouse and tried to put herself together.

"I know I'm not what you wanted, Annie. I never set out to ruin your plans. But you must see, must know, that we belong together."

He tipped her chin so that she had no choice but to look into his eyes, eyes that begged her to tell him that she saw what he wanted her to see.

There were lights in town that would glow with the flip of a switch. There were telephones just doors away, and doctors and dentists and so many grocers she would have to choose where to buy her produce instead of needing to grow and can it. The ladies of Van Wert, the ones that mattered, would welcome her into their circle as the wife of the most respected man in town.

But her skin still tingled and she hadn't felt as safe in anyone's arms since her mother had died after giving birth to Francie. Francie, who was on her way home to help bury poor Samuel and do what she could for Della. Francie, the last of Annie's little chicks and the hardest to kick out of the nest. Harder even than Ethan, her special joy, who'd already begun to pull away from her as he became a man.

Noah rose and held out his hand. "I'm asking you to

give up a lot," he admitted. "But I'm promising I'll never let you regret it."

She could hear Bart and Willa come into the parlor, their low voices carrying into the kitchen and reminding Annie that yet another of her siblings now had a life of his own.

Noah plucked a shawl from the peg on the wall and wrapped it around her.

"Annie, I—"

She shook her head to silence him and called out to Willa and Bart, "We're in the kitchen." The kettle was next to the sink and she shook it, found it full of water, and placed it on the stove.

"I love you, Annie Morrow," Noah whispered as he stood too close behind her. "Will you think about that?"

She turned and nodded, then with difficulty she pulled her eyes from his and smiled at Willa as she pushed through the kitchen door. "Della all right when you left?" she asked.

Willa shook her head. "She's taking it real bad. I hope Francie can snap her out of it."

"I'd better go," Noah said quietly, sensing that he was intruding on family time as Bart came into the room and put his arm around his wife.

All her brothers and sisters seemed to have a shoulder to lean against, a strong arm to bolster them, a backbone to share when their own seemed too weak to support them. Oh, Ethan hadn't settled down yet, and Francie hadn't made her mind up either, but Annie was alone. And although she had stood beside Miller most of the day, she had been all alone until this evening.

"I'll think on it," she said, meeting Noah's even gaze and giving him a tremulous smile. It was worth thinking about, anyway.

23

In the dark and cold of early morning, Noah sat with hunched shoulders and listened for the train whistle that would announce Francie Morrow's return to Van Wert. She'd been gone one and a half months. He wondered if the time had changed her as much as it had changed him. He hoped not.

Oh, he would be more than happy if she'd given up her silly crush on him, but it would break his heart if she'd lost the skip in her step, the smile on her face, and the gleam in her eyes somewhere in New York City. She was a special girl, almost as special as the woman who'd raised her from birth, and he had to admit a certain thrill accompanied the thought of seeing her again, even under such tragic circumstances.

If it hadn't been for Francie there would be no chance of marrying Annie, no hope for the future, no mother for his girls. He had Francie to thank for everything, and he intended to let her know the depth of his gratitude just as soon as she descended the steps of the Chicago & Atlantic Railroad.

A long blast of a whistle broke the silence of the predawn

morning, followed by two shorter blows. The train was stopping in Van Wert. Though he'd checked it twice already, Noah pulled his watch from his pocket once more and looked at it. Six A.M. Just two more minutes and Francie would be back in their lives, even if only for a few days.

He wondered if Hannah and Julia would still feel so strongly about her.

She was the first one off the train, her pale hair catching the light of the old gas lamps.

He leaped from the wagon and hurried toward her, waving and calling her name in the empty station. "Francie," he yelled. "Over here!"

She turned at the sound of his voice, and the smile that lit her face unnerved him. He'd have to tell her why she was sent for. He couldn't bring her back to her family with that wonderful smile on her face and make them break the news to her themselves.

"Noah!" she shrieked and ran toward him, one hand holding on to her hat and the other lifting her skirts so she could get to him faster. "Oh, Noah!" She catapulted into his arms and nestled against him. She was half a head shorter than Annie and even more childlike than he remembered.

He lifted her and swung her around, not wanting to ruin the moment. He would tell her in the wagon. Bad news could always wait.

Her arms went around his neck, nearly choking him. When he put her feet back on the ground, she pulled his face to hers and kissed him, smack on the lips. And not a friendly nice-to-be-home kiss either.

"I knew you'd come to your senses," she said when she finally released him. "Every man needs a wife." She brushed some lint from his jacket and lifted his collar around him.

Shit.

That was all he could think. Especially when he saw the

trainman unload two cartons and a suitcase onto the platform. She'd brought home everything she owned. Annie wasn't going to like this, not at all.

"Francie," he began. "I think you've misunderstood."

"Hmm?" she said as she looped her arm into his and headed toward her luggage. "Why didn't you bring the girls? I can't wait to see them. And whatever happened to your eyebrow? It looks like you missed with your razor."

"It's nothing."

"Good. So it took you long enough. Wait until I tell you all about the men I had to fight off in New York while I waited for you to—"

"Francie honey, you're not listening to me." He tried to extricate himself from her arm, but instead of getting free she just let her hand slide down until her gloved hand rested in his. If he didn't know better he'd think she'd been learning a few things in the big city.

She shook her shoulders, a wiggle that reminded him of Della. "I always liked it when you called me honey. Are we going back to your farm?" She picked up her gladstone bag and left the larger suitcase and the cartons for him.

"Francie," he tried again. "You don't understand."

"Oh, don't tell me. Sissy wouldn't like it if I went back to your farm." She stuck out her lower lip. "But I miss my girls."

"Francie!" he said, trying to still the whirlwind around him. "Will you shut up?"

Her eyes widened and her mouth opened slightly. As soon as she became aware of it, she snapped it shut and folded her arms across her chest. "What did you say?"

She seemed every bit a grown woman to him now, with angry eyes glaring at him like a schoolteacher waiting for a naughty pupil's unacceptable excuse.

"I'm sorry," he said, "but I've got some bad news for you and you just refuse to let me speak."

Her face went pale. "Oh, my God," she mumbled and

looked for something to hold on to. Noah was the nearest thing, so she steadied herself on his arm. "It's the girls, isn't it? Hannah? Julia?"

He kept shaking his head. He didn't remember Francie being such a talker. Maybe after all the silence in the house once Wylene was gone, he had enjoyed Francie's chatter.

"What is it then?" she demanded.

"Annie asked me to send for you," he said. She seemed confused. "Your sister. Sissy." He hated that name. Somehow it seemed to take away her identity.

"I know who Annie is," Francie said. "Is she sick?" There was a kind of false bravado to her question, as if she was pretending not to care. "She must be if she let you send for me. I think she wanted to keep me in New York for good."

"For *your* good, maybe," he agreed.

"She isn't sick, is she?" she asked. This time her voice trembled with the concern that even her childish resentment couldn't erase. The hand that held his arm tightened into a death grip. "Noah? Is Sissy all right?"

He nodded and patted the hand that was now cutting off his circulation. "She's fine. It's Della's boy, Samuel."

A slight grimace touched her lips. He supposed there weren't too many people to whom the thought of Samuel would bring a smile. "What about him?" It seemed as though she was putting all the pieces together in her head, and he gave her a moment to come up with the answer. If Annie had sent for her surely it could only mean one thing. The look on her face showed she understood.

"Please don't say it," she said softly.

"I'll put your bags in the wagon and take you home."

"To your place?" she asked and then laughed at herself. "I thought—" she began, but he patted her shoulder gently and reached down for the luggage.

"Yes," he said. "I know. I'm sorry if my message misled you."

She waved away his words. "Well, I'm home now. Maybe I'll be able to change your mind."

"Very funny," he said, trying to brush off her comment as a joke.

"You haven't married anyone else," she said when they got to the wagon. "I'd have heard from Ethan."

"No," he said. "But—" Did he have the right to tell her about Annie? If she chose Miller—and just the thought set the hairs on his neck on end—she surely wouldn't want anyone to know that she had even considered marrying him.

"But nothing," she said, then changed the subject as he handed her up into the wagon. "How's Della taking it?"

"Not well." He was relieved to talk about Samuel. Though sad, it was a safer subject between the two of them.

He explained the accident as best he could, having gleaned the important facts from the talk at Peter and Della's home the day before.

He stayed away from the subject of marriage entirely. Surely she was just teasing him with her proposal. He just hoped Francie had the good sense to keep her childish fantasies to herself. He didn't want anything interfering with his plans, now that he was so close to convincing Annie she belonged with him.

They fell silent halfway to the Morrow farm. Noah kept his gaze straight ahead, but that didn't stop him from feeling Francie's eyes bore into him the whole way to Annie's front door.

The footsteps on the porch echoed in the living room where Annie waited for Noah and her sister to arrive. Francie would be devastated by Samuel's death. Della and Francie were two peas in a pod, and what hurt one would hurt the other just as deeply.

There was a hesitation at the door, then a knock. She

supposed Noah had suggested it because he was there with Francie and wouldn't want to just burst into her house. Not that he hadn't just burst into her life and turned it upside down.

Annie opened the door and drank in the beauty of her sister's face. It had been so long since she'd seen the pale blond hair, the light green eyes, the translucent skin. If it was possible, Francie was even more beautiful than when she'd left. And despite traveling all night, she was tidier and less rumpled than Annie herself.

"Oh, Francie!" The words poured from Annie's heart as she spread her arms for her sister. And Francie rushed into them and cuddled against the softness of Annie's breast and hugged her sister hard.

"It's good to be home," she said, the words muffled in Annie's shirtwaist. "Even though—"

"Della will be so happy to see you," Annie said. Over Francie's head she tried to read the look on Noah's face. Hopeful? Yes, but there was something more. If Annie hadn't known better, she'd swear it was fear.

"Mr. Eastman?" Before she could ask if everything was all right, Francie's head snapped back.

"Are you still calling him that? I thought by now he'd be just Noah." She turned and gave him a dazzling smile.

How beautiful she was! She had none of Della's brazenness, but all of her charm. Just standing there, her back erect, her head at just the slightest angle, she was Venus come to life; she was a portrait that breathed.

Noah saw it too. How could he help it? Her frailness brought out the protectiveness in him in a way that Annie never could. Just the way he looked at her showed his concern. He seemed to be awaiting her every word, her slightest move.

And when he moved his gaze to Annie it seemed to waver, as if he wasn't as sure this morning as he had been the night before.

"I'll get Francie's luggage," he said finally, and turned to leave.

When Francie thanked him there was a purr to her voice that struck Annie as odd, but no odder than the shrug that Noah gave her in return.

While Noah was out at the wagon, Francie pulled off her gloves and coat. She was wearing a new wool jersey, one that must have been purchased in New York. It nipped so tightly at the waist and spread so lushly above and below that it was evident Francie had taken to wearing a corset.

Annie knew better than to compare herself to either of her sisters. She could only be found wanting. It had never bothered her overly before. After all, she took pride in their appearance, just as her mother would have. And she'd heard enough sermons on envy and jealousy to know that the green-eyed monster had no place on the Morrow farm.

Still, standing next to Francie as Noah came back in with her luggage, Annie became again what she had always been: plain. Plain and passed over. It was all right if Noah had changed his mind after seeing Francie again. After all, Annie was good and kind and a hard worker, and she knew those were important qualities for the wife of a minister. She never shied away from the sick or the crippled, she could bake for a whole congregation on just a day's notice, and she could mend and clean as well as any woman in Van Wert County.

Francie asked Noah if he would bring her things up to her room, then preceded him on the stairs to show off her newly purchased figure. He shot a glance back at Annie as if pleading for her help. She didn't blame him for a second. What man wouldn't feel like things were out of his control around the new improved Francie Morrow?

*   *   *

Miller Winestock was preparing his eulogy for poor little Samuel Gibbs, trying to think of something pleasant to say about the boy. He was known throughout the county for his personal touch at weddings, funerals, and confirmations. While he worked he kept a watchful eye on Tessie Willis, who was taking care of his correspondence with a diligence and a competence that had quite frankly taken him by surprise.

He'd hired her to prevent any impropriety between her and Mr. Eastman, for whom he had a dubious regard. He hadn't been unaware of Tessie's reputation; there weren't many people who hadn't seen her in some degree of drunkenness, though he himself had never been a witness to it. Still, the most reliable sources had told him of her slurred speech, her uneven gait, her inability to remember conversations that had taken place and promises that had been made.

So when it turned out that she was actually a first-rate secretary with excellent penmanship, superb organizational skills, and a fine vocabulary, he was surprised and delighted. She also kept herself neat and appeared exceedingly refined for someone who had succumbed to the perils of alcohol.

"Can you think of a synonym for 'devilish' that has a brighter twist?" he asked her.

She looked up from her work, startled by his question. "Working on the eulogy?" she asked. "What a shame about that little boy. It makes you wonder. Well, not *you*, of course, but the rest of us."

"Some good will come of it," he said without thinking. It was what he always said, what he had been taught to say. He didn't know whether anyone was expected to believe it, whether he even believed it himself.

"I don't see how," she said with the pencil she was using poised in midair. "But of course, you would know better than I how the Lord works."

Did she really think that just because he was a man of God he understood His ways? More than anyone else he was mystified by the twists and turns of fate. There were mean old misers who seemed to last forever while good people were plucked from their midst every day. He knew the theories as well as the next preacher, all the right words to say. The Lord wanted this wonderful woman now, or that child now sits at the hand of God.

But the truth was that with every death his faith got shaken just a bit, made him unsure of what the master plan was, or even if there was one. And it frightened him. What if he made Sissy wait for what he considered a decent interval and the Lord took her away from him before he got the chance to marry her? Or what if he was the one to die? He was getting on in years, and no one lived forever. What a shame for a woman as warm and caring as Sissy to be a spinster for life.

And then it came to him, just like that. It was an inspiration, as divine as any he had ever felt. And he knew just what he would say at Samuel Gibbs's funeral service, convention be damned.

"Do you honestly believe good things can come out of bad?" Tessie asked him. Her voice sounded strange to him, and he looked up.

"What?" he said. She was slouched in her chair, her jaw hanging at a slight angle and her tongue protruding just slightly from her mouth. "Miss Willis?" he said.

She seemed to be trying unsuccessfully to focus on him, her brows knitted together, her eyes squinting.

"Tessie?"

Without answering, she rose and crossed the room on wobbly legs, using the backs of chairs for support.

"Are you all right?" he asked.

She looked at him and her knees gave way. Had he not been sitting with her all afternoon he would have sworn for all the world that she was falling-down drunk.

But Tessie Willis hadn't touched a drop.

24

The wind blew around them, whipping black skirts and black coats and the black ribbons that held black bonnets fast to every woman's head. There was a chair for Della, who sat without expression on her face, flanked by Peter on her right side and Francie on her left. Beside Francie, Annie stood stiffly, some imaginary rod holding her erect.

There wasn't a funeral she went to, a burial she witnessed, that didn't bring back the nine-year-old girl who stood with Francie in her arms and watched them lower into the ground the wooden box that contained her darling mother. The baby she had held then was now a grown woman, lending her strength to her sister. And this was no mother being buried, but a child.

Which was worse, she couldn't say. She wasn't Samuel's mother, but the waste of that short life cut her to the quick. And watching her sister in pain filled her heart with an overwhelming grief.

But not so full that there wasn't room for the pain put

there by Francie's announcement that she was back for
good and intended to marry Noah Eastman and raise his
children. He wasn't like the others, she had told Annie.
She hadn't gotten over him. She would love him, she
swore, until the day she died.

What a moment for her and Francie to finally have
something in common.

As Miller began the service, her eyes searched the
crowd that encircled the small hole in the cold earth and
the mound that bordered it. She could make out Noah's
forehead and eyes shaded by the same black derby as
nearly every other man wore. The stark pain she saw there
reminded her that he, too, had suffered a terrible loss.

"Samuel Gibbs was not an angel before his death,"
Miller said, "but surely he is one now. Life is brief and
cannot be taken for granted. Who of us would have
thought, a week ago, that a healthy-three-year-old would
be called to his maker so soon? And where, you ask, is the
purpose?

"The purpose I see in Samuel Gibbs's death is that we
must seize the life we have, each day, each hour. We must
love those around us with all our hearts because we can
never know which hour will be our last."

The wind died down, and Miller's voice carried over
the crowd like a warning bell that was ringing for each and
every one of them.

"In that spirit, and with the most sincere and profound
respect for my first wife, Elvira Wells Winestock, I
announce the betrothal of myself and Sissy Morrow.

"May Samuel Gibbs rest in peace, and may he not have
lived in vain if he hath opened up our eyes to the fragility
of life and the necessity of embracing it to the fullest."

Annie had no idea whether anyone thought it odd or
inappropriate for the minister to announce his nuptials at
the funeral of the future bride's nephew. There were sad

faces around her and happy ones, shocked ones and blank ones, but she couldn't tell which belonged to who. It was like one of those flip books where heads and torsos and feet could all be switched around.

"Too bad you can't be happier," Bart said from behind her. "With poor Sammy and all."

"Yes," Willa agreed. "This should be the happiest day of your life."

"Ashes to ashes," Miller said as he threw the first shovelful of dirt over the coffin that held her nephew.

Francie bent over and hugged Della, as she sat motionless in the chair. Then she turned to Annie and put her arms around her, squeezing hard through the layers of winter clothes. "Congratulations," she whispered. "I hope I'm next."

Over her head Annie's eyes met with Noah's questioning ones. "I'm sure you will be," she said to the girl in her arms.

It seemed as though everything had fallen into place. And who was Annie to challenge it? After all, it was what she had always wanted, wasn't it?

"You aren't trying to tell me this is what you really want, are you?" Risa demanded. She and Annie had gone back to the Morrow farm to pick up the pies and cakes Annie had baked for the condolences at Della and Peter's home.

"I don't know why you're so surprised," Annie said with a sigh. "I've told you and everyone that I was going to marry Miller. And now that I am, you act as though it's come out of the blue."

"You're saying you love Miller Winestock? Is that it?"

Annie nodded her head. She was placing the pies in baskets, covering them with overturned bowls and stacking a second layer of pies on top of them. After Noah left she hadn't been able to sleep and had made an even dozen pies before giving in to exhaustion and going up to bed.

"Put the pies down," Risa said quietly, and took Annie's hands when she complied. "Sit."

Annie sat. "It's done, Risa. And it's for the best."

"I see," Risa said. "For the best."

Annie knew Risa wouldn't let it go at that, and waited, lining up her arguments in her head. Miller was a good man. He owned a lovely home, *in town,* and would provide well for her. He had no children. And she saw the way Noah looked at Francie and, worse, the way Francie looked at him. Francie was young enough to raise his girls. Why should a man like Noah settle for Annie when he could be tasting Francie's lips?

"All right," Risa said at length. "So you're going to marry Reverend Winestock. As a married woman I think I'd better tell you what your mama would tell you if she were here."

Annie felt the color flee her cheeks.

"It's not so bad," Risa said, patting her hand gently. "Not when you love your husband. Then you'd be surprised how good it feels when he touches you."

"Risa!"

"You've got to know all this," Risa said sternly. "You don't want to be embarrassed on your wedding night, do you?"

Annie just looked at the table and fiddled with its edge.

"All this time he's kissing you to take your mind off it. Is Miller a good kisser?"

She thought of the kisses Noah and she had shared right in this very kitchen just the night before. Kisses so intoxicating she'd let him touch her breasts and run his hand down her thigh. "I don't know," she admitted with a stammer.

"Well, I'm sure if you love him it won't matter."

"Won't matter?"

"When he puts his tongue in your mouth, you know, and—"

But Annie didn't hear the end of Risa's sentence. The chair fell back and banged the floor as she jumped up and ran to the front door, threw it open, and began to heave. Breakfast came up, spilling onto the dirt beside the porch steps and landing on the toe of a man's boot.

Horrified, Annie looked up and saw Noah Eastman's face.

"Is that it? Are you done?" he asked, putting one hand on her back and rubbing her soothingly.

Sheepishly, she nodded. He produced a handkerchief from somewhere and handed it to her. After she'd wiped her face he put his arm around her.

"Ready to go inside?" he asked.

She nodded, and before she could stop him he swooped her up in his arms and carried her inside.

"Her room's at the top of the stairs," Risa said. "I'll make some tea."

He carried her gently up the steps and set her down on the bed. There was a spare blanket at the foot, and he tucked it around her. With his lips he felt her forehead. "You don't seem to have a fever," he said. "Do you have any other symptoms?"

"I'm all right," she insisted, trying to sit up while his strong arm pressed against her shoulder, keeping her right where she was. "I said I'm all right."

"Fine," he said testily. "Then what the hell do you think you're doing letting Winestock think you're going to marry him?"

"I *am* marrying Miller."

"No," he said simply. "You're not."

"You don't understand," she said, sitting up and mustering all the dignity she could. "Francie's back and she loves you. She'll make you a wonderful wife. She's beautiful and she loves your children and she's read lots of books and you can—"

"Francie is a little girl. I adore her, but as a sister. Or sister-in-law. She is not the woman I love. You are. And while you may be generous and kindhearted enough to toss away my love and give up what we have for someone else, I am not. And I am not going to let you do it, either."

He said he loved her. He loved her and wanted her more than Francie. And something about the way he said it made her believe him. "But what about Miller? I can't just—"

"Do you know what I felt like coming over here? Thinking about the possibility that you really meant to marry him? Thinking about him putting those pasty-white hands on your golden skin?" He cringed. "It made me want to pitch my breakfast right over the side of the wagon."

She raised her hands quickly to her face when she felt the small smile start, but it was too late. He had seen it. He gestured toward the porch and she nodded.

He threw his head back and laughed. "Well, I sure am glad we see things the same way. Now just say you're marrying me and maybe we'll be able to keep some supper down."

"But Francie—" Annie began.

Risa stepped into the room with Annie's tea. Behind her, Francie stood tentatively in the doorway.

"Francie wants to be the first to wish you all the happiness you deserve," Risa said and yanked the younger girl into the room. "Don't you, Francie?"

Annie reached out a hand for her sister. "I never meant—" she began.

Francie shook her head and sniffed. "No, I don't think you could."

"I wouldn't hurt you for the world," Annie said. "If you—"

"Don't say it," Noah warned her.

"There's no need," Francie said, her chin raised proudly. "There are men in New York who have been promising me the moon, and they have a lot more to offer."

"Don't settle for less than love, Francie," Noah said gently, his eyes on Annie. "And don't ask for more."

"Have your tea," Risa said, handing Annie a cup. "Francie and I will wait for you downstairs."

At least that was what Annie thought she said. She wasn't hearing anything too clearly, what with Noah's words of love ringing in her ears. She only knew that the women were gone, or at least she thought so. She didn't sense anyone else's presence, but her eyes were only on Noah, drinking him in, the tea in her hands forgotten.

"Are you ready to go to Della and Peter's now?" he asked. "They'll be wondering where we are."

"I'm ready," Annie said. "But I think I'd better make a stop at Miller's house."

"I'll go with you," he offered.

"No," she said. "It would be better if I went alone." It was a sobering thought, but she couldn't help the smile that tugged at the corner of her mouth as he put out his hand to help her from the bed.

"Being sick is nothing to be ashamed of," Miller told Tessie, as she sat teary-eyed across the table from him. "How could you let people make assumptions about you?"

"The first few times it happened I thought it was my imagination. That it only sounded funny to my ears. I was so dizzy I just didn't realize. The double vision is the worst part. It makes me fall down a lot. By the time I saw a doctor, the rumors had already started."

"What did you say it was called? Cirrhosis?"

"Sclerosis. Multiple sclerosis."

"It must be very hard for you," he said sympathetically. Living with embarrassment was something he was grateful he'd never had to do, though he had felt the pain of it for his wife and would willingly do it for another.

"So I suppose congratulations are in order," Tessie said, obviously hoping to change the subject. "I think Sissy Morrow is a wonderful woman. I remember when she was too little to get on the swing at the schoolhouse by herself and I had to lift her up."

"Everyone thinks of her as older than she is because she had to grow up awfully fast when Zena died."

Tessie smiled. "I remember Mrs. Morrow too, though only a little. She was such a happy woman. I imagine she wouldn't know how to feel today, happy for one daughter, sad for another."

"Life plays tricks on us all, doesn't it?" he said. There was no one he knew who hadn't lost someone or something precious to them. Tessie had lost her reputation, Sissy her mother, Della her son, and he had lost his wife. Well, life was hard. It was man's job to try to make it easier for someone else while he muddled through himself.

The knock at the door, as always, startled him. No doubt it was some parishioner on the way to the Gibbs home and stopping to ask for the right words to offer.

"I'll get it," Tessie said.

He nodded and sat in his gent's chair. It had been a hard few days, but he had come to grips with his life and was doing what he thought best.

"It's Miss Morrow," Tessie announced. "I'll be in the kitchen if you need me." Efficient and considerate. If he had to write a recommendation for Tessie Willis, those were the two words that would come to mind.

When Sissy didn't appear, he pushed himself up using the arms of the chair and went to find her in the front hall. She stood nervously waiting, her gloves and coat still in place.

"I had planned to come out to your place tonight," he said, reaching to take her coat and realizing it was still fastened. "Are you on your way to Della's then?"

"Mr. Winestock," she began.

He didn't like the sound of that. She had been calling him Miller for months. But the distance between them had been his fault, and he could rectify it. Really, Elvira had only been gone a short while. He couldn't have been expected to jump with both feet into a new relationship.

"Sissy, take your coat off and sit down with me awhile. Tessie can make us some tea. I'd like to get some things straight between us."

She seemed torn, as if she thought she should stay, but then again perhaps she shouldn't.

"Come now," he said by way of encouragement. "You look like you could use some tea."

She looked past him toward the parlor and licked her lips. "I need to speak with you alone," she said, almost under her breath.

"Certainly," he agreed. Her nervousness was contagious. "I'll send Tessie home."

She nodded but said nothing. The juices in his stomach rumbled, a sure sign that his nerves were acting up.

Tessie left quickly by the back door without raising an eyebrow. He added "discreet" to her list of attributes.

"How would New Year's Day suit you?" he asked when he returned and found Sissy seated, her coat off, fumbling with the gloves in her hand.

"What?" She nearly jumped out of her skin.

"I thought perhaps a new year, a new beginning, resolutions—" It was close to babbling. He felt himself floundering but couldn't understand why.

"Mr. Winestock," she began, but he interrupted her.

"That's twice now you've called me that. What happened to 'Miller'?" He wasn't sure he wanted to know.

She looked frantically around the room. Finally her eyes settled on his shoes. They needed polishing. He wished he were wearing his sermon shoes if she was going to stare so intently at his feet.

"I don't know how to say this," she began.

"Has something happened?"

"No," she said quickly. "That is, yes. Oh!"

"Did you hear about the lights? Did you know that it'll be any time now? The next day or two and *poof!*—electricity."

"What?"

"The lights. As soon as they get the power from some main station." He had no idea what he was talking about. Electricity, like so many new devices, was a mystery to him. But he knew he didn't want to hear whatever it was Sissy had come to tell him, knew deep in his stomach where he felt a burning, knew deep in his soul where he felt a chill.

"There is only one way to do this," she said sharply. "I've never beaten the devil around the stump before, and I don't think this is the time to start. I can't marry you, Mr. Winestock. I thank you for the offer. I'm flattered—honored, really. But I have to say no."

He had lost his tongue. Well, it was there, in his open mouth, but he couldn't use it.

She continued. "As you know, I've been working for Mr. Eastman."

He nodded. Eastman! The man managed to be at the bottom of everything.

"I didn't plan for this to happen. Really I didn't. In fact, I didn't want it to happen."

He gripped the arms of his chair until his knuckles turned white.

"I'm in love with him. And he says he loves me, hard as that is to believe. Only, I do believe him, because he had the chance to have Francie."

"Have Francie?"

"Marry her. But he wants me and, God help me, I want him. I want the girls and I even want the cows and the chickens, though you can keep the mud."

He couldn't be hearing her clearly. He put his fingers in his ears and wiggled them, trying to dislodge any wax that could account for the strange things she appeared to be saying.

"Again?" he asked as though he hadn't heard her right.

"I'm marrying Noah Eastman, Reverend Winestock. Just as soon as you can perform the ceremony."

He shook his head. It was impossible. It was as simple as that. Relief flooded through him. Noah Eastman couldn't marry her, couldn't marry anyone. Sissy was still his.

"You won't perform the ceremony?" she asked in response to the shaking of his head. "Really? I suppose the new minister at the First Presby—"

"My dear, sweet Sissy," he said, taking her hand and clutching it to his chest. Someone must have moved the chairs farther apart since Elvira's death. The movement pulled her clear out of her seat.

"Miller, I'm marrying Noah."

"But Sissy, Noah is already married."

"Well, yes, he was, but his wife died in the flood—" her voice drifted off as the shake of his head denied what she said.

"Wylene Eastman ran off to New York shortly after the younger girl—what's her name?"

"Julia." Her voice was flat. Dead.

"Julia was born. She abandoned the whole family, but that doesn't make him free to marry you."

She didn't move a muscle. As far as he could tell, she wasn't so much as breathing or blinking.

"It will be all right," he assured her. "I too have come to love you, in my way. We will go ahead with our plans as if this conversation never took place. There is no reason for us not to marry. Look around you, Sissy. You'll be very happy here."

She lifted her head, and as she did the room brightened. Shouts came from outside as people in the streets cheered.

"Look," he said, pointing toward the new electric fixture that hung above them. "They've done it!"

The three electric bulbs he had purchased all glistened in her damp eyes and shone on the tears that fell silently down her cheeks.

"Sissy?"

She shook her head as if she were incapable of speech. With a sniff and a hard swallow she walked toward the door, reaching for her coat but not putting it on.

"How soon will be soon enough?" he asked. "Thanksgiving? We can have your whole family here, under the lights. Would you like that?"

She shook her head again and turned to give him one last look. Tears streaked her face but there was no sound of her crying, no sobs, no heaving of her breast.

"No," she said, fighting to keep control of herself. "I guess I was meant to be a spinster after all."

She said it with a finality he couldn't broach.

"At least let me see you home safely," he said, hurrying to the door.

She shook her head yet again. "The worst has already happened to me," she said, with the saddest smile he had ever seen. "I'm very sorry, Miller," she added before she turned the knob.

"As am I," he said after the door had closed behind her.

Married. He was married. Somewhere out there in New York City, if that was where she was, Wylene Eastman still existed. Noah's wife.

The farm was empty when she returned home, all of her brothers and sisters were at Della and Peter's. Poor Della. Poor Peter. Poor little James, the twinless twin. And poor, poor Aunt Sissy, everybody's spinster aunt. Greedy Aunt Sissy, who wished for love. Well, if wishes were horses . . . she'd be trampled to death. She'd never expected love. Never counted on it. How had it come to mean everything in just two short months? She could have had everything she'd ever wanted. If only she hadn't met Noah Eastman and started wanting things she never knew existed. Like love.

She'd been born on this farm and she would die on this farm. Alone.

She was nearly out of self-pity when she heard voices from downstairs.

"Sissy? You upstairs?" It was Risa, and she wasn't alone. "I'll go check," she heard Risa say to someone, then heard the footfalls on the steps.

"What in the world?" Risa said when she saw her sister-in-law huddled on the bed in her chemise, covers wrapped around her, in the dark. "Sissy? What's wrong?"

"Nothing," she lied. "I was tired and came home to lie down."

"Safe to come up?" Noah yelled from the living room.

Her breath caught in her throat. She jumped from the bed and scurried around the room like a trapped animal. "No! Don't let him come up! I can't see him!"

Risa stared wide-eyed as if she were watching a madwoman.

"Make him go away!" Annie insisted.

"What in the—" Risa began.

Annie heard her voice quiver unnaturally. Her hands twitched and her breathing became so rapid she thought that for the first time in her life she might truly faint.

"All right," Risa said as calmly as she could. "It's all right. I'll tell him to leave. Is that what you want?"

"Yes!" she said rapidly. "Yes. Tell him to leave. Tell him never to come back."

Risa nodded her head slowly and put out her hands to calm Annie down. "All right," she kept repeating. "It's all right."

Risa went down and Annie could hear her arguing with Noah. The door slammed hard enough to make the windows rattle. He was mad? What right did he have to be mad? She was the one to whom the injury had been done.

Risa found Annie pacing the room when she returned.

"He's married," Annie said as soon as she saw her. "There's no dead Mrs. Eastman. She's alive and she lives in New York City or somewhere and he kissed me and I wanted him to do everything you said."

Embarrassed, she raised the neckline of her chemise and held it tighter. "Maybe not everything."

"He's married?" Risa said. "He can't be. Reverend Winestock collected all that money for his wife's memorial. She has to be dead. She died in the flood."

Annie shook her head. "No. Miller told me himself. After I told him I couldn't marry him because I was in love with Noah."

"This is all my fault. I pushed you into his arms. I let him have those shoes for wholesale." She rolled her eyes. "God, don't tell my father!"

Somehow that struck Annie as funny. So funny that tears popped into her eyes and she leaned against the wall and laughed until she cried. And cried. She cried so hard that Charlie and Bart and Willa and Francie all came running up the stairs and stood in the doorway.

"What's wrong?" they all asked, and Annie shook her head at them. But the shame of all of them standing there and watching her didn't stop her and she cried on, banging her fist on the wall and shouting about how much it hurt.

"Do something," Charlie said to Risa. "Make her stop."

"Cover her, for heaven's sake," Bart said. "She's half naked."

Willa waddled over. It was the first time she actually looked pregnant, and the thought that she would never know the miracle of carrying a new life inside her set Annie off on a new round of tears before the old one had ended.

"Jeez," Bart said. "I've never seen her this bad. Did something happen with Winestock?"

Her tears had turned to hiccups and made her seem even more pathetic. What a stupid, foolish woman. She couldn't even cry like a lady.

"Did you know about him?" Risa demanded of Francie. "Did you know he was a vile worthless despicable creeper? All that time you spent out there at his farm. Did you know he was playing on everyone's sympathies and setting us all up?"

"What are you talking about? Noah made her cry? *My* Noah?"

"*Your* Noah?" Bart howled. "How many Morrows is he trying to diddle?"

"He didn't try to diddle anyone," Francie shouted back, outraged.

"Well," Annie said, thinking about the way he'd raised her skirts on the kitchen floor and wishing Bart would go over and give him two black eyes.

"What?" Charlie and Bart yelled in unison.

Somehow, after all the crying, Annie was light-headed. Two on one didn't seem fair, and then of course Ethan would be there, and he'd no doubt take Noah's side and it would be the civil war all over again, brother against brother. And the girls would see. *Her* girls. But they weren't her girls. Wouldn't be her girls.

"Why are you so mad at Noah?" Francie asked. "I thought you two were in love." She pronounced love as if it was part of a song, raising her eyebrows to mock her oldest sister's foolishness.

And foolish she was to jump at the chance to marry the first man who tried to get up her skirts. Well, at twenty-six it wasn't likely there'd be any more attempts.

"That hypocrite came to me swooning with love for your sister, telling me he wanted to marry her, and all the time he was already married," Risa said. "I feel like this is all my fault."

Everyone looked at Francie, who was strangely silent.

"You knew?" Risa said. "You knew he was leading your sister on and he wasn't free to marry her?"

"He is not married," Francie shouted, her hands on her hips, her cheeks flaming. "Wylene's been dead over a year. They fished her body out of the East River in New York."

There was dead silence in the room.

"I can prove it. I sent her death certificate to Noah." She turned to Annie. "That was why I agreed to go to New York in the first place. I thought if I could find Wylene and convince her to give Noah a divorce he would want to marry me."

He'd tried to tell her about Wylene, tried to be honest with her, but she'd said they wouldn't speak of it. But he'd never listened to her about anything else, hadn't stopped courting her just because she'd told him not to do it.

"Then he told you she was alive?" Risa asked.

"Not at first. But I found letters to detectives he had hired. And then I found a letter from her saying she needed money and asking him to send it. The letter came from New York City."

At least he hadn't told Francie but not told her.

"So you went there?" Risa prompted.

"And the landlady said she left one day and never came back. Left her clothes, left no forwarding address."

"And she fell into the river?" Charlie asked. "In a city as big as New York? Didn't anybody hear her yell for help?"

Francie shrugged. "I don't know exactly what happened.

All I know is what they said at the coroner's office. That they thought she might have lost her balance, being pregnant and all, and fallen into the river."

"Pregnant?" Annie was sure now that the story was true. That everything he had ever told her, including how he felt about her, was all wonderfully, marvelously true.

The door slammed downstairs and a voice boomed throughout the house. "I'll be damned if I can't see the woman I'm going to marry. I'm coming up and I've got both fists ready, so don't think you're going to stop me."

Annie's smile must have said it all. For no one told him to stay where he was, though each brother was watching her carefully, ready to leap to her defense at just a word or gesture.

He took the steps two at a time, clunking loudly on each.

Willa pushed Bart away from the doorway with her hip so that Noah could make his way in.

"Hi, Noah," Charlie said casually, leaning against the wall with a smirk on his face. "How's things?"

"Well, I guess we'll be going," Risa said, winking at Annie. "See ya, Noah."

"Gosh all hemlock," Bart said to Annie. "Cover up! You're half naked!"

"I'm awful tired, Bart," Willa said. "Would you help me to our room?"

That left Francie, Annie, and a very confused Noah Eastman.

"I guess I could go make some tea," Francie said feebly.

"Good," Annie said distractedly. "That would be nice."

"Take your time," Noah added. He walked over to where Annie huddled on the bed and sat down next to her.

She touched his face gently, her fingers memorizing his features, and then she closed her eyes and leaned her head back against the wall. Her throat was raw from crying.

"Say it, Annie," he said as he gathered her against him. "Say it."

"I love you, Noah Eastman," she whispered against his chest. "With all my heart."

"I know that," he said impatiently. "Now tell me you'll marry me."

25

It was to be a small wedding. Miller was glad for that. Not that everyone in Van Wert didn't already know that Sissy Morrow had thrown him over for Noah Eastman. Only two days after he had stood beside the grave of Samuel Gibbs and told everyone that he and Sissy would marry, Eastman had stood up at Sunday services and announced that he and Annie Morrow would be exchanging vows the following Friday and that because of the short notice and the recent tragedy in the family there would be just a brief ceremony and a small reception hosted by the bride's brother and sister-in-law, Charlie and Risa Morrow.

As he changed into his best suit, he hoped the cooking wasn't left to Willa. Performing the ceremony would turn his stomach quite enough. And he couldn't even find anything in the man to dislike, now that the true story of Wylene Eastman had been confided to him. Eastman had even had the good taste to refuse the memorial in her honor.

"Umph!" he said when the button on his shirt came off in his hands. Being a minister of God and responsible for setting a good example, he never swore. But here and there he allowed himself a few choice groans, which he knew in his head substituted for words he longed to utter.

The past week had been full of such noises. If there had been one bright spot in it all, it was Tessie Willis. Even now she was downstairs finishing up the last of his correspondence while he readied himself for church. Tessie was a good woman who didn't deserve the reputation that her illness had foisted upon her. And he had determined to set the town straight. Why, she needed their help, their understanding, even their pity, not their condemnation and avoidance.

In the last week, the Morrow family, whom he would have expected to shy away from him now that he was not to join their circle, had embraced him warmly. He knew that if he asked them, they would accept Tessie for the wonderful woman that she was and convince others to do the same.

The idea of helping Tessie put a smile on his face, but it did nothing for the button in his hand. He wondered if Tessie would be so kind as to sew it on for him. He slipped off the shirt, put on the one he had been wearing, and went downstairs to ask.

Tessie sat at his desk, her back straight and her hair neatly pulled into a chestnut bun. When she heard his footsteps she turned and smiled.

"Do you realize there is almost three hundred dollars in that memorial fund?" she asked.

"That much?" he said and couldn't hide the grimace. "That's a lot of money to return."

"Whatever do you mean?"

Miller had agreed not to reveal the true circumstances of Wylene Eastman's death, for it would hurt two innocent little girls. It was yet another instance of wanting to fault Noah Eastman and being unable to. "Mr. Eastman has declined the memorial. He feels the people of Van Wert never knew Mrs. Eastman and shouldn't be obligated to give their good money on her behalf." Just because he condoned the lie, it didn't mean he would tell one himself.

"Oh, but that's wonderful!" she said and turned her bright smile once again to him.

"It is?"

"The schoolhouse, Mr. Winestock," she explained. "If the money was used to repair it, it would benefit the town and even Mrs. Eastman's little girls."

Miller returned Tessie's smile with one of his own. "You remind me of my dear Elvira, just a bit," he said, pleased beyond measure with her suggestion.

"Really?" she said. "I always thought she was a lovely woman."

Annie was nervous.

Noah was worse.

She'd never been a married woman before.

He'd already been a married man.

All three of her brothers wanted to walk her down the aisle.

He was all alone.

The plan had been to have a small ceremony, just family and a few close friends. Of course, when you started counting up the whole Morrow clan and those who were their close friends, they packed the church.

Noah picked up bits of one conversation after another as he made his way down the aisle *Not surprised in the least,* someone said. *I knew it all along,* was someone else's comment. *It surely took them long enough to realize. Such a perfect match!*

At the front of the church Ethan stood waiting. "Risa says I'm to be the best man," he explained.

Noah took his hand and shook it. "Risa's taken care of everything, it seems. She's got Hannah and Julia all dolled up and sitting with Cara in the front row."

Ethan pinned a white rose and a sprig of something green to Noah's lapel. "You were right," he said. "Mrs. Lutefoot had plenty in her greenhouse. And she said to remind you that if it hadn't been for her, none of this would be happening."

Noah remembered the picnic where Annie had lost her button all too well. It was then, in the far meadow, after having received Francie's letter about Wylene, that he knew in his heart Annie would be his wife for as long as they both lived and forever after.

A commotion started in the back of the church, and Noah and Ethan looked behind them. Annie, flanked by Bart and Charlie, was coming into the church. She had on a cloak he had never seen before. He guessed it might be Della's, with its fancy braid. Charlie took it gallantly off her shoulders and she stood in the doorway in the same rust-colored sateen dress she had worn to the Harvest Social. That was the night he had first kissed her, had tasted the honey he had until then only dreamed about and which had haunted him ever since.

Lord but she was beautiful! She gave him a tremulous smile, and he felt it reach in and warm his heart.

She stood waiting at the back of the room, an arm held by Charlie, an arm held by Bart, as if she'd turn and run if they weren't there to guard her.

"Are you ready?" Willa whispered, handing her a small bouquet from Jane Lutefoot's greenhouse. "Should I tell Mrs. Webb to start?"

She stared down at the roses in her hand and knew that miracles did come true after all.

"Sissy? You ready?"

She wanted to savor every moment, yet she didn't want to waste a single second. She wanted to hold this moment in time and still move ahead to the rest of her life. When she turned and left this church she would be tied to Noah for life. His children would be hers, his farm, his bed. And everything she was and could be would be his. "Yes," she told Willa. "I'm ready."

The first strands of "Here Comes the Bride" pealed from the organ. Charlie covered her hand with his own and squeezed it gently.

"Go," Willa said to Bart and gave him a slight shove, setting the three off unevenly.

"Good luck, Sissy," someone said as they started up the aisle.

"Congratulations, honey," Jane Lutefoot whispered.

Brian Kelly said something that sounded like "He's a good man."

And so it went as she made her way up the aisle toward the man who would teach her that life on a farm with someone you love is far, far better than life in town with someone you respect.

Her brothers stopped two thirds of the way down the aisle and waited as Noah stepped forward to claim his bride. Charlie gave her a kiss and a hug, then shook Noah's hand.

"You're getting a wonderful girl," he said, his voice choked with emotion.

"Yes," Noah agreed, unable to take his eyes from her own, "I know."

Bart kissed the top of her head and held out his hand to the man she was about to marry.

"I'll take good care of her," Noah promised solemnly.

"You better," Bart barked back. His voice, too, seemed choked.

Miller stepped forward from the side of the podium and raised his hands to the couple to join him at the altar. A hush descended on the church as Annie looked at Miller. She bit her lip slightly and felt Noah's hand take hers and raise it to his lips. Then he took her arm and they walked slowly to where the man Annie had for so long planned to marry stood waiting for them.

"Dearly beloved," Miller began. His familiar voice sent chills down Annie's back, and she was grateful when Noah threaded his fingers through hers and squeezed her hand gently. She looked up into his loving face and read his lips. *I love you,* he mouthed.

Yes, she thought. I know.

She had heard the vows a hundred times before, daydreamed through them, told them to a mirror when she was young enough to pretend, whispered them into a pillow when she was too old to even hope.

"I do," Noah boomed, so loudly that a chuckle went up behind them.

"We believe you!" someone called out.

And now she was promising to have and to hold, from this day forth, in sickness and in health, for richer or poorer.

"I do," she said softly when it was her turn.

"Can't hear you," a woman shouted. Annie thought it might have been Risa.

She turned and looked at the congregation, loving friends and family, each and every one of them.

"I do!" she said with a smile. Noah raised their joined hands in a sign of victory, which prompted several people to cheer, her three brothers included.

"This is very unorthodox," Miller said when the crowd had settled down. "But I suppose I should have expected nothing less from Sissy Morrow, for everything she touches is sparked with joy. Let each and every one among you look upon this couple and wish them well. And let us all remember that he who hesitates is lost."

His meaning was squandered on no one. He shook the groom's hand, kissed the bride's cheek, and turned them to face the crowd of well-wishers.

"Cara says I'm her cousin now, Papa. Is that right?" Hannah asked as he lifted her into the back of the wagon.

"I guess it is," Noah said. He turned to take Julia from Annie's waiting arms and she gave him a slight nod, as if to say *You tell them.* "You've got lots of family now. Cousins and aunts and uncles."

"And?" Annie prompted him.

"And a mama." The two of them stood staring into the back of the wagon, waiting for a response. Annie's heart was beating as desperately as a moth's wings against the porch light.

"That boy said I didn't have a mama. Wait till I tell him my mama's Miss Annie! He'll be sorry." Hannah balled her little mittened fist and shook it in the air.

"What boy?" Annie asked.

Noah whispered to her that it had been Samuel, and Annie nodded understandingly. Before he could chastise Hannah, who couldn't really understand that Samuel was gone forever, Annie lifted Hannah's little chin in her hand and said, "Let's just be happy about what we have and not worry about anyone else for tonight, all right?"

"It's a special night," Hannah told her sister. "It's the first night we have a mama again."

Noah cleared his throat and offered his hand to his new wife. "Ready?" he asked.

She hoped her smile seemed less tentative than she felt. She'd waited since she was a little girl to be someone's wife, but from the moment she'd agreed to marry Noah, everything had been a blur. She'd packed up all her belongings in just three days, said good-bye to the house she'd lived in all her life, left the cows she'd milked, the chickens she'd fed, and donned Della's dress to say "I do."

And now her husband, wonder of wonders, was waiting to help her into his wagon and take her to a whole new life. Oh, there would be cows and chickens and dirt, same as on the Morrow farm, but Annie had the feeling nothing would ever be the same once she stepped up on the hub of the wagon and settled into a new seat for life.

"Annie?" he asked, his hand still outstretched. His Adam's apple bobbed furiously. A slight twitch she'd never noticed before touched the corner of his mouth, making him look as nervous as she felt. His one eyebrow was raised in question.

"I'm ready," she said, with what she hoped passed for a smile. She had time for one deep breath, then her boot was on the wheel and she was up in the front of the wagon, Noah's hand steadying her as if he had helped her into a wagon a hundred times before.

In a second he was seated beside her. They spread a blanket across the girls' laps, asked if they were ready, and then waved at the well-wishers who stood on Risa and Charlie's porch shouting words of encouragement.

"I could get used to having a large family," Noah said as they headed out toward the farm.

"I guess you'd better." Annie laughed. "You're stuck with them now." *And with me.*

He switched Bess's reins into his left hand and took hold of Annie's hand with his right. "Good," was all he said.

They fell silent, a companionable silence that promised years of quiet times spent side by side.

"Are you nervous?" Noah asked after a while.

Risa had spoken with Annie again, and while she contended that everything she had told her was true, she promised it would be better than she had made it sound. Still, Annie answered honestly. "Maybe a little." ·

"Yes," he agreed. "Me too."

Annie was surprised, but before she could ask him what he meant, the farm came into view. In the dusk, something about it looked different. At first she wasn't sure what. Then she realized what she was seeing.

"A wind wheel! Noah, there's a wind wheel behind your farm!"

"*Our* farm," he corrected.

"But how . . . where . . . Noah, why do we have a wind wheel?"

He laughed and pulled her closer to his side. "For madam's bathroom, of course!"

"Whose what?"

"Papa isn't building you a bathroom," Hannah piped up from behind them, "and Ethan isn't helping him!"

"What?" she asked.

He stopped the horse by the front of the house. "It's all right to tell her now, Hannah. You kept the secret real good."

"What secret?" Annie demanded. She was afraid to hope it was really what it seemed.

"I thought if I could offer you a bathroom—I knew that the minister's house had electricity and plumbing, and I couldn't give you all of that, but I *could* give you a room with a bath."

Noah, his children, and a bathroom, too? And she had been sure just moments ago that things couldn't get any better! "There's a bathroom in there? Where?"

"Ethan and I are putting it in over the winter." He shook his head and tipped his hat back. "I never thought I'd get you to say yes so soon."

"Or you wouldn't have built it?"

"Or I would've started sooner."

He kissed her forehead, then the tip of her nose, and sighed.

"You girls tired?" he asked hopefully over his shoulder. "Ready for your new mama to put you to bed?"

"I'm not tired at all," Hannah said rather convincingly.

"Me too," chimed in Julia with her favorite phrase.

"Great," Noah said, but Annie didn't think he sounded like he meant it.

He jumped down from the wagon himself, then came around to her side and offered her his hand. When she was close enough, he put his hands on her waist, as if he'd always been permitted the liberty, and swung her to the ground. He didn't release her right away but kept her pressed against him.

"Feels good, doesn't it?" he asked.

"Yes," she admitted shyly. As good as she'd always expected it would.

He lifted the girls out of the wagon and swatted their bottoms gently, herding them toward the house.

"You unhitch the horse," Annie offered. "I'll take the girls in and get their coats off."

He stood staring at her as if he hadn't heard what she'd said. His mouth opened slightly and his eyes narrowed in on her lips. Self-consciously she licked them and waited for him to tell her to go inside. He said nothing at all, just watched her as if he wondered what she was doing there.

"Papa?" Julia said softly, pulling lightly on his trouser leg.

He let his gaze linger just a moment longer on Annie and then looked down at his daughter. "Hannah," he said. "Show Miss Annie where your nighties are. It's time for bed."

"But Noah, it's not even dark," Annie argued. She didn't like being referred to as Miss Annie, but it wasn't nearly as important as keeping the children up at least until it was dark outside. She wasn't ready to be alone with her husband at all, let alone in the light of day.

"They can at least get ready for bed," Noah replied. "I'll see to the horse."

By the time he returned to the house the girls were in their nightgowns and in the kitchen with Annie, where they were busily making cookies.

"What's this?" he asked. He did not seem at all pleased, and Annie cringed slightly when she admitted that the girls hadn't wanted to go to bed so she'd suggested some cookies and warm milk to help them sleep.

"But there weren't any cookies," she explained.

"I guess it was lucky they didn't want turkey or you'd have gone out with a rifle and tried to find one in the dark."

"Are you angry with me?" she asked. It was an unfamiliar feeling, one she didn't like at all.

His face softened and he ruffled Hannah's hair and pretended to gobble the mess Julia was mixing. "I just wanted tonight to be special," he said quietly.

"This *is* special," Hannah insisted. "And Miss Annie said—"

Noah interrupted her. "She's not Miss Annie anymore," he corrected. "She's your mama now." He looked at Annie. "If that's how you want it."

She'd raised five children, washed them, fed them, nursed them through sickness, and seen most of them married. In all that time, no one had ever called her Mama. Only in her most private thoughts and dreams, and those she had given up so long ago, had anyone called her Mama. And now the two most precious girls in the world were staring at her intently, waiting for her permission to do just that.

She bit her lip to keep from crying. "I'd like that a lot."

"OK," Hannah said, as if it was nothing at all. "Mama said we could have honey in our milk to make our dreams sweet."

"By all means, then," he said. There was a slight quiver in his voice. His eyes caught hers and held them tenderly.

When they were ready, Annie placed all the goodies on a tray and Noah carried it into the living room and placed it on the table by the sofa. "Now it really is late," he told the girls. "One cookie each, drink up, and it's time for bed."

"But Noah," Annie started, "it's only—" She looked at the clock. All the baking had taken longer than she thought and she was surprised that it was so late. Noah had been so patient and good-natured that she had lost track of the time.

"This is delicious," he said as he sipped the warm milk. "Come sit by me and have some."

He patted the sofa and she settled next to him, careful that their bodies didn't touch.

"Comfortable?" he asked.

She nodded.

"Good," he said, then shifted so that he was smack up against her and she was trapped between him and the arm of the couch. "Drink this," he said, handing her his cup. "It'll calm your nerves."

"Oh, I'm not nervous," she lied.

"And you can't grow roses in winter," he mocked.

"Why is Miss Annie nervous?" Hannah asked, glaring at her father as if somehow it was his fault.

"Mama," he corrected. "Not Miss Annie. And Mama is not nervous, she's just had a big day, like you, and she's tired, like you."

"But I'm not—" Hannah began. She stopped when she saw the stern look on her father's face that demanded she be truthful. "Well, not very tired."

"Tired enough," Noah said. "Would you like Mama to tuck you in?"

The girls nodded eagerly and Annie reluctantly put them to bed with kisses and hugs and a bedtime story that she would have continued if only the girls hadn't fallen asleep and Noah hadn't come in to check on what was taking so long.

"Come," he said. "You must be tired."

"Oh, not really," she said, then faced that same look he had given Hannah and laughed. "Well, not very."

In his bedroom he had cleaned and straightened and placed some evergreen boughs in a jar by his bed. Their bed. Ethan had brought her boxes over and they stood by the chest of drawers. She had marked one with a heart. It stood on top of the others and contained her nightclothes, her hairbrush, and the other essentials she would need for her first night as Mrs. Noah Eastman.

She stood in the bedroom doorway staring at the bed and he came up behind her.

"You looked beautiful today, in church. I could hardly breathe when I saw you."

He ran his hands down the arms of her dress, and gooseflesh danced along his fingers' path.

"It was Della's dress," she explained, turning and modeling it for him. "She has lovely things."

"That may be," he agreed. "But it isn't the dress I find so exquisite."

"Oh, but it's a very special dress," she said. "It's what I call a married woman's dress."

"Because?"

She turned and showed him the buttons that ran down her back. "A woman can't get in this dress alone."

"Or out of it."

"Or out of it," she agreed.

"Would you like me to unfasten it?" he asked.

"Now?" It was a foolish thing to ask. What did she think he meant? Next week?

"There's no rush, Annie. We have the rest of our lives."

She stared at the face she would see each night before

she closed her eyes in sleep, each morning as she woke to a new day. "I've waited my whole life for this day and this night. And now I don't even know what to do."

He dragged her against him and pressed her tighter and tighter, as if he couldn't get her close enough. "I'll teach you," he said. "Didn't I tell you that you were the only pupil I wanted?" His fingers tangled in her hair and she reached up, found the pins that held it, and let it down.

"Spun sugar," he said, lifting the strands and kissing them. "Lips of honey," he said and dipped to taste them. "So sweet. So sweet."

Her arms went around his neck and her fingers gripped his hair. "Now," she said softly by his ear. "What do I do now?"

Circling around to her back, he gathered her long hair in his hand and set it over her left shoulder so that he could work the buttons on her neck. "I'm sorry," he apologized when it took longer than either of them expected. "Nervousness."

"You too? But you've done this before. I mean, you've been married, you know how . . ." her voice trailed off. She was too embarrassed to finish the thought.

"Oh, Annie," he said, looping his arms around her middle and pulling her back against him. "I love you so. I want it to be perfect. All of it. As perfect as you are."

"But I'm not—" she started. He spun her around in his arms and kissed her words away. His lips barely touched hers, just grazing them again and again until all she knew was she wanted more.

While he kissed her he worked at the cuffs of her dress and managed to work her arms free of the sleeves. And all the while his lips kept moving against hers, making it hard for her to breathe and kiss and think at the same time.

He began to press his mouth harder against hers and his tongue traced the seam of her lips. It was soft and smooth and it seemed like the most natural thing in the world for her to open her mouth and let his tongue seek out hers. He invaded her mouth and she steeled herself to stand it for his sake. His tongue danced in and out, tracing her lips, teasing her own tongue, and instead of hating it she found it not at all unpleasant. In fact, when she could manage to think at all, she thought it was the loveliest sensation she had ever felt.

But that was before he lifted her out of her sister's dress and brought her to his bed and laid her down on the coverlet. He was still fully dressed, and she reached over shyly and tried to cover herself with the edge of the blanket.

"Oh, don't," he pleaded. "You're so lovely, and I've waited so long to see you like this."

"You can't have been waiting so long. We've only known each other a couple of months." The thought that she lay in his bed, undressed, and hardly knew him only served to embarrass her further. She worked harder at covering herself, rolling in the blanket like a caterpillar in a cocoon.

"You're wrong," he said, slipping his suspenders down over his shoulders and opening the buttons on his shirt. "I've waited my whole life for this night. Just the way you have. I've dreamed of it and longed for it and I'm as scared as you that it won't be all you hope."

How was it that before she even thought it he knew her mind?

He shimmied out of his trousers and stood beside the bed in his Derby ribbed underwear. She could see plain as day his arousal, and everything Risa had told her about her wedding night closed in on her, making her shiver within the confines of her quilted nest.

"Are you coming out of there?" he asked. "Or am I coming in?" He stood patiently waiting for her answer.

Slowly, almost painfully, she pulled the covers away and lay still and motionless, waiting for him to mount her. Instead, he turned the edge of the covers back for her and

ordered her to scoot under. After he turned out the lamp
by the side of the bed, he joined her beneath the quilt and
put one arm loosely around her.

"Did you like the kissing?" he asked her in the dark-
ened room.

She nodded against his shoulder.

"Then turn around so I can kiss you again."

She turned and felt the heat of his body against her
breasts, her belly, her thighs. Loosely his fingers threaded
through her hair, brushing it away from her face and tracing its length down her back. When he reached her bottom
he cupped it and pulled her closer to him.

He smelled faintly of sweat mixed with bay rum. It was
a masculine smell and she found it altogether pleasant,
especially combined with the warmth of his body against
hers. He lifted his head a little and kissed her.

"You taste like honey," he said, and she could feel the
curve of his lips as he smiled against her face in the dark.

"The milk," she explained.

He moved his kissing to her cheek, her closed eye, her
temple. "Nope. Unless you took a bath in it."

One more kiss, full on the mouth, and then he began to
move his kisses lower, over her chin, down her throat. Just
as Risa had said. Involuntarily she stiffened, and he
stopped immediately.

"Ssh," he soothed. "I'm not going to hurt you. I just
want to see if you taste like honey everywhere." His kisses
continued down her throat, and she felt him untying her
chemise and fiddling with the buttons. One hand lightly
grazed her breast before his head bent to the task of test-
ing it. "Sweet," he murmured. "So sweet."

She had been prepared to see her duty through, to bear
what a woman must bear. But she hadn't been prepared to
enjoy it. That was a surprise that made her gasp. And her
gasp made Noah chuckle, and somehow the ice seemed to

melt around the two of them. Her fear lessened enough to place her hand against his chest, and before she realized it she was playing with the buttons to his underwear and they were unfastening beneath her hand.

The hair on his chest was soft and curly and twined around her fingers like a vine, unwilling to let her go. And while her hands explored his chest he continued his own wanderings, taking her chemise straps with him, over her shoulders, down her torso, taking her underthings as he went, lower onto her belly, the chemise no longer covering anything vital to her privacy.

His hand found her darker, curly hair and she thought for the last time about what Risa had warned her to expect. Risa had told her *what* he would do. She hadn't told her how it would feel. She hadn't told her about the liquid fire that built in her belly, the need that fanned it higher and higher until suddenly all the soft touching wasn't enough. She pulled on his sleeves to free his body so that she could feel his skin against hers and wrapped her arms and legs around him, kissing his neck, his shoulder, anywhere her lips could reach.

And he readied her and brought her to the peak and warned her about the pain. In a moment it was gone and then the indescribable pleasure took over and still it got better and better until she screamed out and he had to put his hand over her mouth and remind her that there were two little girls just beyond the wall.

They lay close and still, their breathing beginning to return to normal. A breeze from the slightly open window felt cold against their damp bodies, and Noah covered them with the quilt and turned Annie on her side, scooping her against him like two spoons in a drawer.

"What are you thinking?" he asked in the darkness.

"I was trying to decide which felt better," she said honestly. "Being called Mama or that."

"That?"

"You know," she said shyly.

"Oh, *that*. Well, it wasn't a fair test. I mean, I didn't know you were making comparisons."

"I wasn't," she said. "I just didn't think things could get any better, and then they did."

"Do you think you're up to a second attempt?" His hand slid down her hip and insinuated itself between her thighs. "I want you to be sure which one feels better."

"And if I'm still not sure?" she teased.

"I guess I'll have to try harder."

The door opened with a creak and a small voice called out to them in the dark. "I can't sleep," it said.

"Hannah?" Annie asked. "Is that you?"

"Miss Annie? What are you doing in Papa's bed?" Her voice was full of surprise.

Annie was silent for a moment, so Noah said, "Mama's right where she belongs, Hannah. She's where she's always belonged."

He kissed her cheek and wiped away the wetness there. "Oh, boy," he said. "I guess I'm gonna have to try real, real hard."

She nodded her head against him.

"Go back to bed, Hannah," he told his daughter softly.

"Will you still be here in the morning?"

"Mm-hm," she said, feeling herself drifting off to sleep. "And the morning after that, and the morning after that."

"Good night, Hannah," he said firmly.

"Good night, Papa. Good night, Mama," she said before she shut the door.

"Doesn't it sound wonderful?" she asked him when they were alone again.

"How 'bout I try to convince you again that *that* was better?"

She pushed her bottom against his privates and snuggled herself in against him. With a yawn she said, "How about tomorrow night? And the night after that, and the night after that."

She had it all. For the first time in her life, Annie Morrow Eastman fell asleep with a smile on her face.

Noah listened to her even breathing and said a short prayer of thanks. He and his daughters had paid an awful price, but he no longer doubted for a moment that it had been worth it. In the morning he and Ethan would begin work on the bathroom.

He wondered what Annie would make them all for breakfast. Pancakes with maple syrup and kisses, he thought idly as he drifted off to sleep.

Epilogue

Noah had set her up on the living room sofa, pillows propping her up, two coverlets keeping her warm. Dr. Emma Randall had proclaimed it one of the easiest deliveries she'd ever seen for a first-time mother, surprising no one.

The baby, Grace, slept soundly in a cradle by the fire, Ethan rocking it gently with his toe every now and then. On her hip, Willa balanced Rory, now a strapping seven-month-old who would obviously grow to his father's size. He already seemed nearly twice as big as his cousin Lucia, Charlie and Risa's newest daughter.

The cookies Hannah had managed to bake herself, with Annie giving directions from her perch on the couch, smelled ready, and Noah and the children ran to the kitchen to remove them from the oven before they burned.

"Don't you want to help them?" she asked James. It worried her that he appeared to still be grieving for his brother. And it didn't help that Della was so preoccupied with her own misery she hardly paid attention to the child. Nor did Peter, who had buried himself in his work and was rising quickly at the bank.

James refused to leave his place over the furnace register, as if he couldn't get warm enough no matter what he tried.

Cara, newly enrolled in school and anxious to show off her numbers, asked for a show of hands for coffee, tea, or milk and skipped back to the kitchen to report her findings to Noah.

"This one's Mama's," Julia said, as she came back into the room with a steaming mug of milk laced with honey. Noah always served it to her that way, claiming he loved the taste of honey on her lips. "I'm being real careful with the cup," she explained to her audience. "It's her mama's mama's mama's, right?"

"Yes, sweetheart, that's right," Noah said, his eyes full of pride as he looked over his whole family.

"And she'll be mad if I break it," Julia added.

"I could never be mad at you," Annie said, surprised that Julia would even think so.

"Oh, not you, Mama," she said as she handed her the cup. "Her!" She jerked her head in Hannah's direction, and Annie had to agree, silently, with Julia's assessment. Her great grandmother's dishes would be in good hands for another generation.

Annie put the cup down on the table with exaggerated care and opened her arms for Julia to clamber up for a hug, which she did just as regularly as everything else wonderful that seemed to take place in the Eastman house.

"Oh, look! Here come Reverend and Tessie Winestock," Risa said, looking out the window. "They must want to see the new baby."

As if on cue, Grace began to cry and Ethan, looking somewhat overwhelmed, picked her up and carried her to Annie, who cradled her and cooed until the infant quieted down. She knew she only had a few minutes before Grace demanded the sweet milk that was all her own.

Tessie and Miller kissed the girls and made their way to the couch.

"Oh, but she's beautiful!" Tessie exclaimed. "And Grace. What a perfect name."

"Well," Annie admitted, "it falls between Francie and Hannah in the alphabet."

"I guess you'll have to have another one to name with an I," Charlie said, nudging Noah gently in the ribs.

"I plan to start work on that just as soon as Annie is up to it," he said with a smile, looking so intently at his wife and his newest daughter that Annie could feel the love from across the room.

Grace balked in her arms, opened her tiny bow mouth, and let out a loud bawl that demanded attention. Discreetly Annie tucked her under a little blanket and let the baby latch on to her breast.

"So," Risa said when she deduced what Grace was doing beneath the cover of the cloth, "how does it feel to finally have one of your own?"

Annie looked around the room. Bart, gruff and quarrelsome as ever, was there with his wife and baby. Charlie was there with Risa, as much a sister now as he was a brother. Lucia was on his hip, Cara by her mother's side. Della was there, much the worse for wear, along with Peter and James. Ethan was staring at the picture they had just received from Francie, who stood with a man she had pointedly remarked was not a beau, in front of a tall building in New York City. The man, well dressed and bespectacled, had his hand on Francie's shoulder.

Hannah and Julia were on the couch with Annie and Grace, huddled up tight as ever a family could be.

Tears slipped down her cheeks, which the relatives attributed to the emotions of a new mother. But she and Noah knew better.

"They're all my own," Annie answered Risa. "They've always been my own."

Author's Note

Van Wert still sits peacefully in the western part of Ohio, still having an annual county fair that is one of the best in the state.

According to a History of Van Wert County published in 1906, "Dr. Miss Emma Pearson [Randall] had a large practice here, but gave it up for a man and moved to Michigan." Much later it was reported that she was living on North Jefferson Street, so at some point she returned to her practice in Van Wert. Both Dr. R. J. Morgan and Dr. John K. Woods had their practices there.

And while it was true that George H. Marsh, Esq., did own one of the town's many saloons, he also was a great philanthropist who was responsible for the first County Hospital and the YWCA, among other gifts to the city, and following his death the Marsh Foundation was set up with funds provided for in his will. Peter Gibbs was hardly alone in his admiration for Mr. Marsh's good deeds, and even Annie would have had to admit that the attorney was a wonderful man who gave a great deal back to his community.

In 1890, electricity did indeed come to Van Wert, though whether its timing was as meaningful to anyone as it was to Annie and Miller is questionable. It was found in about two hundred homes that first year.

As to the Library Association, Hattie Brotherton and Clara Cavett were only two of many women who saw the need for a public library and canvassed the town for subscriptions, and by the end of 1890, the first year of the Association, they had a collection of 600 books and had to hire a librarian and rent a room. Readers might like to know that in 1897, J. S. Brumback left to the people of Van Wert the funds to build a public library, which was dedicated in 1901. By then Annie must have been reading well enough to make use of the library for herself as well as her children.

And while I can't be certain it was *Romeo and Juliet* that Annie was able to see in Van Wert, Waverly Hall played host as early as 1876 to outside companies that performed *Hamlet, Rip Van Winkle, Lucrezia Borgia,* and *The Gilded Lady.* In 1879, when Annie would have been eleven, there was an exhibition of Edison's phonograph, followed a week later by a production of *H.M.S. Pinafore.*

The town could boast at the time an Ahern steam engine, kept in City Hall on Central Avenue and used to fight fires. Jake Fronfield, the actual fire chief at the time, had good reason to be as proud of his men as he was of his equipment.

One other note: Multiple sclerosis, a disease for which there is still no cure, was discovered in 1885. Until recently its diagnosis was difficult, and on occasion its sufferers are still mistaken for people who have had too much to drink. Tessie was one of the lucky ones who went into remission and was able to live a somewhat normal life.

Let HarperMonogram Sweep You Away!

Touched by Angels by Debbie Macomber

From the bestselling author of *A Season of Angels* and *The Trouble with Angels*. The much-loved angelic trio—Shirley, Goodness, and Mercy—are spending this Christmas in New York City. And three deserving souls are about to have their wishes granted by this dizzy, though divinely inspired, crew.

Till the End of Time by Suzanne Elizabeth

The latest sizzling time-travel romance from the award-winning author of *Destiny's Embrace*. Scott Ramsey has a taste for adventure and a way with the ladies. When his time-travel experiment transports him back to Civil War Georgia, he meets his match in Rachel Ann Warren, a beautiful Union spy posing as a Southern belle.

A Taste of Honey by Stephanie Mittman

After raising her five siblings, marrying the local minister is a chance for Annie Morrow to get away from the farm. When she loses her heart to widower Noah Eastman, however, Annie must choose between a life of ease and a love no money can buy.

A Delicate Condition by Angie Ray

Golden Heart Winner. A marriage of convenience weds innocent Miranda Rembert to the icy Lord Huntsley. But beneath his lordship's stern exterior, fires of passion linger—along with a burning desire for the marital pleasures only Miranda can provide.

Reckless Destiny by Teresa Southwick

Believing that Arizona Territory is no place for a lady, Captain Kane Carrington sent proper easterner Cady Tanner packing. Now the winsome schoolteacher is back, and ready to teach Captain Carrington a lesson in love.

And in case you missed last month's selections . . .

Liberty Blue by Robin Lee Hatcher

Libby headed west, running from her ruthless father and her privileged life. Remington Walker will do anything to locate her, as long as her father keeps paying him. But when Remington does he realizes she's worth more than money can buy.

Shadows in the Mirror by Roslynn Griffith

Iphigenia Wentworth is determined to find her missing baby in West Texas. She never expected to find love with a local rancher along the way.

Yesterday's Tomorrows by Margaret Lane

Montana rancher Abby De Coux is magically transported back to the year 1875 in order to save her family's ranch. There she meets ruggedly handsome Elan, who will gamble his future to make her his forever.

The Covenant by Modean Moon

From the author of the acclaimed *Evermore*, a spellbinding present-day romance expertly interwoven with a nineteenth-century love story.

Brimstone by Sonia Simone

After being cheated at the gaming tables by seasoned sharper Katie Starr, the Earl of Brynston decides to teach the silly American girl a lesson. But soon the two are caught in a high stakes game in which they both risk losing their hearts.